P9-DHP-773

ALL HE WANTS FOR CHRISTMAS

"Listen to me, Mr. Roxbury. I do not wish for you to call on me again. In fact, I do not wish to be in your presence again while I'm in Brighton. I am engaged to be married and in no position to be out walking with you alone. No matter what my mother thinks!"

She looked unbearably lovely with her fair skin colored pink from the wind, her wild green eyes filled with ire, and tendrils of her rich auburn hair escaping from her fur-lined hood. He stepped closer to her as if magnetized, staring at her full lips.

She stood her ground, placing her hands on her hips. "Your visit today was inappropriate in every respect, especially when I told you quite clearly on the train that I did not wish to see you. People will get the wrong idea and think that we have feelings for each other—oh!"

Quinton, unable to control himself any longer, pulled Lisette into his arms and covered her mouth with his. Instantly he knew he had made a dreadful, irrevocable mistake, but by then it was too late. Too late to stop. He could do nothing but lose himself in the honeyed sweetness of her mouth . . .

Books by Kaitlin O'Riley

SECRETS OF A DUCHESS

ONE SINFUL NIGHT

WHEN HIS KISS IS WICKED

DESIRE IN HIS EYES

IT HAPPENED ONE CHRISTMAS

YOURS FOR ETERNITY
(with Hannah Howell and Alexandra Ivy)

AN INVITATION TO SIN
(with Jo Beverley, Vanessa Kelly, and Sally MacKenzie)

Published by Kensington Publishing Corporation

It Happened One Christmas

KAITLIN O'RILEY

ZEBRA BOOKS
KENSINGTON PUBLISHING CORP.
http://www.kensingtonbooks.com

ZEBRA BOOKS are published by

Kensington Publishing Corp.
119 West 40th Street
New York, NY 10018

Copyright © 2011 by Kathleen M. Milmore

All rights reserved. No part of this book may be reproduced in any form or by any means without the prior written consent of the Publisher, excepting brief quotes used in reviews.

If you purchased this book without a cover you should be aware that this book is stolen property. It was reported as "unsold and destroyed" to the Publisher and neither the Author nor the Publisher has received any payment for this "stripped book."

All Kensington titles, imprints and distributed lines are available at special quantity discounts for bulk purchases for sales promotion, premiums, fund-raising, educational or institutional use.

Special book excerpts or customized printings can also be created to fit specific needs. For details, write or phone the office of the Kensington Special Sales Manager: Attn. Special Sales Department. Kensington Publishing Corp., 119 West 40th Street, New York, NY 10018. Phone: 1-800-221-2647.

Zebra and the Z logo Reg. U.S. Pat. & TM Off.

ISBN-13: 978-1-4201-1239-9
ISBN-10: 1-4201-1239-2

First Printing: October 2011

10 9 8 7 6 5 4 3 2 1

Printed in the United States of America

*To Janet Milmore Wheeler
for being so fine, always making me laugh,
and for those first sixty pages.
Thanks, Bud!*

ACKNOWLEDGMENTS

Although writing is pretty much a solitary pursuit, I am lucky enough to have people who assist me along my literary journey. I must first give thanks to my amazing agent, Jane Dystel, and my wonderful editor, John Scognamiglio, for all their support and encouragement. I also continue to thank my lovely cousin, Laurence Maurin Cogger, for giving the character of Genevieve Hamilton a French accent. For maintaining my website and putting up with my many technologically challenged questions, I extend an immensely grateful thank-you to my very talented brother-in-law, Scott Wheeler. Because of her excellent assistance with editing and for providing me with a beautiful place to spend my summers and holidays, I have to especially thank my sister, Jane Milmore. Many thanks also go to my friends and family: Yvonne Deane, Adrienne Barbeau, Billy Van Zandt, Kim McCafferty, Gretchen Kempf, Cela Lim, Melanie Carlisle, Greg Malins, and Jeff Babey for all of their help, good humor, and wonderful friendship.

And as always, a special thank-you to my four incredible sisters: Jane, Maureen, Janet, and Jennifer. I love you, girls. And Merry Christmas!

Note to Riley
You are better than the bestest best.
I love you more than you know.

1

All Is Calm, All Is Bright

Lisette Hamilton never saw him coming.

Later on she supposed that because she was rushing, it was her own fault. But still he was just as much to blame. A man should always be mindful of where he is going and should take more care when rounding a corner and not throw himself about like a cannon out of a barrel. None of it would have happened at all if she had simply stayed in the carriage. But no, she had to stop for a moment to visit with Mrs. Brooks. Since Lisette was planning to marry the woman's son, of course she should take time to speak with her. It was Henry's mother, after all, and she would eventually be her mother-in-law. Then Yvette had complained of a headache, so Lisette had instructed their carriage driver to take her younger sister home while she remained. She chatted with Mrs. Brooks longer than she'd intended before realizing how late she was. Lisette detested being late. Hated to think that anyone was waiting for her or inconvenienced in any way by her tardiness. To Lisette it was the height of rudeness.

Consequently she was walking as fast as she could, her little black boots clicking along the cobblestones of the neat lane behind Devon House. As usual, her long auburn hair was pinned neatly under her fur-trimmed hood and her hands pocketed deep inside her matching fur muff. She didn't typically walk through the back lane, but she now needed to hurry. The narrow lane was empty of people except for Lisette that chilly December afternoon, and the sky was heavy with dark clouds. She pulled her muff closer to her body for warmth and increased her pace. Just as she reached the corner, which was bordered by a high brick wall covered in a thick blanket of ivy—*bam*—she ran smack into a wall of another kind.

Knocked flat on her back with an impossibly tall man lying on top of her, she could not even breathe.

When Lisette opened her eyes, she found herself drowning. Drowning in a pair of the bluest eyes she had ever seen. Not just a regular, ordinary blue, but the clearest, purest sky blue. The word "cerulean" came to mind. The color of the sky on a clear spring morning. At first, those eyes were wide with surprise, but then they narrowed their focus on her. His eyes gleamed with an inner fire, and her heart seemed to stop and the world faded around her. The fall must have knocked the sense out of both of them, for neither she nor the man spoke or moved for a full minute.

They simply stared in mute fascination with each other.

Oh, but the rest of him was fine also, Lisette thought. His face was arresting in its perfection. A strong jaw, which was clean-shaven and smooth. An aquiline nose with just the slightest tilt at the end. A mouth that looked as if it smiled easily. He was not smiling now, though. No, but his lips were close enough for her to feel his breath on her cheek. A lock of his light golden hair fell across his forehead in a charmingly rakish way.

She wondered if she knew this gentleman. The familiarity of him called to her, but she could not place him. Had she met him recently? At the bookshop perhaps? No. No, Lisette had never met this man. For she certainly would have remembered him. And how wonderful he smelled, like spices and bayberry.

As she lay with this handsome stranger, Lisette completely forgot where she was going and why she was in such a hurry to get there. She lost herself in the feel and the weight of the length of his muscular body pressed against hers, barely noticing the cold cobblestones beneath her. His long legs nestled intimately between hers. The heat and strength emanating from him kept her quite warm. A strange lethargy crept over her as her body seemed to melt with his.

The gentleman lightly touched his gloved hand to her face in a soft caress.

"Are you all right?" His voice fell in a silky whisper around her as he traced the side of her cheek.

The hypnotic sound of his voice contributed to the strange spell she had helplessly fallen under. Lisette only nodded her head in response to him while her heart pounded in a wild rhythm.

He slowly leaned even closer to her, placing the lightest of kisses on her cheek. The brush of his warm lips on her skin sent a shaft of pleasure coursing through her entire being. Lisette thought she would faint. This was mad! She did not even know this man, yet here he was . . . Oh, my . . . His lips moved closer to her own, and she held her breath, suddenly hoping against hope that he *would* kiss her. Heaven help her, for she desperately wanted this man to kiss her. It was madness, but she wanted to feel his lips pressed against hers. She inexplicably yearned to kiss him.

The unexpected and loud barking of a dog in a nearby yard pierced the air around them, breaking their intimate reverie.

Suddenly aware of their awkward position, they both roused themselves in a fluster. The gentleman made a move to stand up. Lisette, her cheeks burning, took a shaky breath as she removed her hands from her muff and rose on her elbows. Taking her gloved hand in his, he helped her to her feet. As she stood, he did not release her hand. Nor did she pull away from him. Something about him holding her hand felt natural and she did not want to let go.

"Are you quite sure you are all right?"

"Yes," Lisette murmured in a whisper, but she was not all right. Far from it. She had never felt less like herself.

"I am terribly sorry," he began again. "Forgive me. I did not see you."

She had to tilt her head back to look up at him. Again she became lost in those blue eyes. Was it a figment of her imagination that he had kissed her cheek? Had she merely dreamed that he almost kissed her lips a moment ago? "I . . . ah . . . I did not see you either."

He still held her hand, and he pulled her slightly closer. "Oh, but we have seen each other now."

"Yes," she breathed. The sound of his voice, low and husky, made her shiver with delight. "Now what?"

A slow, magnetic smile spread across his handsome face. It was as if the sun had suddenly burst through the clouds. Lisette could do nothing but smile back helplessly in response.

"Now I believe we ought to introduce ourselves. I am Quinton Roxbury."

Quinton Roxbury. His name repeated over and over in

her mind. Who was he? And why should this man have such a magical effect on her? *Quinton Roxbury.* She suddenly had butterflies in her stomach. "I . . ." She paused a moment to recall her own name. "I am Lisette Hamilton."

"Well, Miss Hamilton, please forgive my clumsiness. In my haste I seemed to have knocked us both off our feet. Are you sure you are not hurt?"

Lisette shook her head. No, *hurt* would not be the word to describe how she felt. Mesmerized. Enchanted. Awestruck. Those were much better words.

"May I escort you home?"

Again, she shook her head. A strange sense of loss surged through her, realizing that their astonishing encounter was coming to an end. She did not want him to leave. She glanced across at her hand, still clasped firmly in his. That reassured her somewhat.

He looked disappointed by her refusal. "No?"

"I am already home." Lisette gestured to the tall white house just beyond the brick wall.

"Devon House?" he questioned, his dark blond brows raised. "You live here?"

"Yes."

He smiled and then explained, "I was just there, meeting with Lord Waverly."

"He is my brother-in-law." Lucien knew Quinton Roxbury. This changed everything and she relaxed a bit. He did not seem like such a stranger to Lisette now. But then he hadn't right from the start. There was a strong familiarity about him that drew her to him.

"Well, I can at least escort you to the door. I owe you that much courtesy."

He released her hand and took her arm. As long as he was touching her, Lisette did not care what he did. At this moment she would have followed him across London if he wanted. Instead she walked with him to the front of Devon House. Her heart fluttered against her chest at the feel of his strong hand on her arm. Good heavens! What on earth was wrong with her?

"Once again, I offer my sincerest apologies for knocking you down, Miss Hamilton."

"It's quite all right," she murmured as they stood in front of the gate, noting with some satisfaction that he did not apologize for kissing her cheek. She stared into his eyes, mesmerized by what she saw within them.

"I should be on my way," he said.

"Yes, of course."

"It was a pleasure running into you." He laughed, deep and throaty, and her heart skipped a beat at the sound. "I hope I have the pleasure of meeting you under more usual circumstances sometime."

"That would be lovely."

With what seemed like some reluctance, he released her arm. "Good afternoon, Miss Hamilton."

"Good afternoon, Mr. Roxbury," she whispered softly. Her eyes followed him as he walked away, his long black cloak swirling behind him. The assurance and grace with which he moved was surprising for a man of his height. She stood outside the gate to Devon House, completely incapable of taking a step forward. Flooded with emotions she did not know existed before, she didn't even hear the footsteps coming up behind her.

"Lisette!"

She turned around at the sound of her name. Henry Brooks stood beside her. *Henry.* "Henry!"

"Good afternoon, Lisette. Who was that gentleman you were talking to?" His kind, bearded face was drawn in obvious concern. His gray eyes stared at her intently.

Lisette blinked. "I don't really know. I just met him. What are you doing here, Henry?"

"I was coming from the home of Lord Grisham, my new client, and his house is across the street. I was planning to stop by Devon House to say hello when I saw you with that gentleman. You were speaking to him as if you knew him."

She placed her hands inside her muff and clenched them together tightly. "He . . . He was just leaving. He was here to meet with Lord Waverly," Lisette explained. "His name is Quinton Roxbury."

She thought it best to leave out the part about the gentleman lying on top of her and almost kissing her. There was no need to upset Henry. Still, the memory of it sent a delicious shiver through her. She pulled the fur muff closer to her body.

"Quinton Roxbury?" Henry asked with sudden interest. "The Earl of Kingston's brother?"

"He did not say."

"Well, if that's who he is, he's quite a bright and ambitious man. I just read an article about him in *The Times* last week. Something about him designing a new museum building and some special houses, if I recall."

She gave Henry a blank look.

"Anyway, it's a happy surprise to see you, Lisette."

"It's good to see you as well." She smiled, feeling slightly calmer, talking about ordinary things. And she was glad to see Henry. If not a little surprised. "It's a funny coincidence meeting you here, because I just ran into your mother. She invited me to have tea with her and your aunt next week."

"That was thoughtful of her." He removed his gold pocket watch and checked the time. He snapped the case shut and returned it to the pocket of his navy broadcloth coat. "My dear, I'm afraid I do have to rush off. I must get these papers to the bank."

"Very well. I shall see you tomorrow evening. You'll be joining us for supper at Devon House, remember?"

"How could I forget? Of course I will be there tomorrow. Good-bye, my dear." He squeezed the top of her muff with his gloved hand and walked away with sure and steady steps. She watched him go, trying not to compare him to the mysterious Mr. Quinton Roxbury.

Almost forgetting what she had been rushing home for, Lisette gave a little gasp and hurried to the house.

2

Their Old Familiar Carols Play

Granger, the Devon House butler, opened the door for Lisette. She thanked the man as she removed her fur muff and matching coat and hat. He took her things with a good-natured smile.

"Good afternoon, Miss Lisette. You seem to be in a hurry," Granger said in his usual unflappable style.

"I am!" She nodded quickly, for she was now late and Colette would be sure to be put out with her.

Lisette made her way to the staircase of Devon House, the rather majestic house she had called home for the past few years. But it did not truly feel like her home. Oh, it was grand to be sure, but in her heart the stately and elegant town house belonged to Lucien Sinclair and his family, not to her. After living above the bookshop for her entire life, Devon House felt entirely too large for her taste. Besides, she wanted a home of her very own. A place she could love, care for, and do with as she pleased.

And that would happen as soon as she and Henry married.

Henry. He was a wonderful man, steady and reliable. He

would take good care of her, and she would be happy married to him. Yes, she would. Yes.

Almost stumbling on the steps, she steadied herself as the image of a handsome, blond gentleman with penetrating blue eyes sprang unbidden into her mind when she should have been imagining Henry. She shook herself with determination and grasped the handrail firmly. Such foolishness! Quinton Roxbury. He was just an accident. She didn't even know the man!

Lisette moved her feet quickly but carefully up the grand, marble staircase in a hurry to reach her own bedroom. She was rushing down the corridor when a voice stopped her.

"There you are!"

Colette had called to her. Lisette turned to face her eldest sister. "I'm sorry I am so late. I will change my clothes and be ready in just a few minutes."

"Oh, never mind about that. Aunt Cecilia sent a note around that she is ill, so she is not coming to tea this afternoon."

Lisette relaxed with a heavy sigh. She did not have to spend an interminable afternoon with her critical and demanding aunt after all. What an unexpected relief!

"But I need your help," Colette began in a harried tone, while beckoning her into her own suite of rooms. "I just received a letter from Mother."

Lisette knew where this conversation was headed. Reluctantly she entered Colette's private sitting room and took a seat on a lovely lavender and white striped damask chair. Her nephew, Phillip, toddled over to her, his round cheeks pink and his fingers sticky as he held his chubby arms out to her in eagerness.

"'Sette, 'Sette." He babbled the name everyone understood meant his Auntie Lisette.

Smiling, she reached down and scooped the boy up in

her arms, settling him on her lap and breathing in the sweetness of him. Phillip rested his tousled head on her chest and gave a contented sigh. Instinctively she rocked the child with a gentle swaying of her body, holding him close. She would love a baby of her own when she married.

Suddenly the image of Quinton Roxbury's face flooded her mind. He stood beside her while she held a baby. How odd! His face replaced the usual image of Henry. Lisette shook her head in amazement and not a little guilt.

"Although he's been fighting me all afternoon, Phillip's more than ready for a nap," Colette explained. She moved with practiced slowness to her own chair and lowered herself down gingerly. "And I am as well," she added with a light laugh. Colette's hand moved over the rounded form of her once slim waist.

"Your new baby brother or sister is making your mother very tired," Lisette whispered to the little boy in her lap. He smiled at her and closed his eyes. She brushed her hand over his soft dark curls in a calming motion.

"Thank goodness," said Colette in relief, watching her son fall asleep in her sister's arms. "It's funny how you have that soothing effect on him."

Lisette glanced up at her with a helpless smile. "I don't do anything differently with him than you do."

"No, but you're a natural," Colette grinned. "You'll make a very good mother someday."

"I hope so."

"You will. Now, about *our* mother," Colette began, her voice weary.

Lisette nodded, knowing exactly what was expected of her. Unaccountably irritated, she longed for the solitude of her room, wished she could lie down on her bed and close her eyes. A sudden vision of Quinton Roxbury lying atop her in the lane flashed before her. Unable to breathe for a moment, she blinked in rapid succession, trying to erase him from her memory.

"Mother is not feeling well and wants us to visit her. Obviously"—Colette patted her stomach for emphasis—"I cannot go to her right now. With Christmas coming up, Paulette needs to stay and oversee the bookshop, and Yvette—"

"Of course I'll go to her," Lisette interrupted without hesitation. Her mother needed her and she was the only one who could be spared. It was always this way. Her nature was such that Lisette would never not do what was expected of her, never not help when she was needed. Hit by a sudden urge to flee the room, she remained seated, not wishing to disturb the sleeping child she held so sweetly in her arms.

"I would go, truly," Colette began, but Lisette shook her head.

"You are in no condition to travel anywhere. It's fine. I shall go tend to Mother."

"Thank you, Lisette." Her sister sighed in relief. "Even if I could go, you know how things are between Mother and me. And I'm so very short-tempered right now, I'm sure to say something terrible to her."

Lisette nodded in understanding. "It's quite all right. I don't mind."

Her sister's relationship with their illness-prone mother had always been fraught with tension, ever since they were young. When Genevieve Hamilton first retreated from the everyday world of responsibilities and took to her bed, declaring herself not well enough to care for the family any longer, it was Colette who had assumed the daunting task of raising her four younger sisters, along with helping in the bookshop. After their father died, Colette had completely taken over the management of their finances, their bookshop, and the daily life of their family.

For this, Lisette and her sisters were all grateful, but this apparent usurpation of power caused untold friction between Genevieve and Colette, making Lisette's relationship with Genevieve seem placid by comparison. Which was why her sisters had looked to Lisette to calm their mother's frayed nerves when they could not. It wasn't that Lisette found their mother's dramatics any less irritating than her sisters did, it was just that she did not usually allow them to bother her. It was easier simply to agree with her mother than argue with her, and because of that, Genevieve took comfort in Lisette's serenity. This would not be the first time that Lisette had made the journey to Brighton alone to placate their demanding mother.

"I'll have Lucien handle all the travel arrangements right away. Do you want to go by train or in one of our carriages? I always feel better if you take the carriage, although I know the train is faster and you enjoy it more. If you leave tomorrow, you could be home by next week. Unless of course"—Colette rolled her eyes heavenward—"something serious is wrong with her."

Both sisters laughed as softly as they could so as not to wake Phillip. Their mother's numerous ailments were never as severe as she declared them to be, and they had grown accustomed to her theatrical illnesses over the years and learned to dismiss them. Laughing, they knew this time would be no different.

Lisette said, "I am sure she's just lonely and longs for some company."

"It was her choice to move so far away," Colette responded, her attitude a bit defensive.

"Yes, but she still gets lonesome for us." Lisette kissed the top of Phillip's hair and thought for a moment. "I think I shall take the train this time. Perhaps I can bring her back with me early and she can stay here through the holidays and the birth of the baby."

Colette made a face and Lisette knew her sister was unhappy with the thought of their mother visiting for such a long period of time. "Why don't we let her arrive when we originally planned? I don't think I could bear her to be here an entire month. Not in my condition."

"All right then." Lisette shrugged and changed the subject. It was all the same to her. "Do you think Juliette will be home in time for Christmas?"

"Her last letter said she would," Colette said. "But then again, it's now the first of December and the last letter we received from her was back in early September."

Lisette continued to rock the little boy and gave a rueful shake of her head. "Well, we never really expected her to be a good correspondent, now did we?"

"Now that's quite true, but it would be nice to know if our sister is alive or not."

Who could even be sure where Juliette was? It had been a year since they saw her last. Juliette and her American husband were sailing around the world together on their clipper ship, the *Sea Minx*. Juliette was living the adventurous life she had always wanted. A pang of envy shot through Lisette's heart, startling her. She was not jealous of Juliette, not really, for she had no desire to travel the world. And yet . . . Something about how her older sister lived the life she wanted called to her, too. Made her want to do the same. Juliette always did what she wanted to do and didn't give a care for what anyone else thought of her because of it.

What would it be like for Lisette to do exactly what she wished? To live her life as Juliette lived hers? This thought gave her pause. For what was it that Lisette truly wanted? Nothing as exotic as an around-the-world adventure! Heavens, that was not Lisette's style at all. No, Lisette merely longed to be married and have a husband. She wanted a home of her own. And children, of course. She had the usual aspirations that the majority of women her age had. There was nothing uncommon about Lisette, nothing extraordinary. Her desires were simple enough.

The startling encounter she had just had with Quinton Roxbury flashed through her mind once again. Golden hair. Blue eyes. Velvet voice. Tall. Broad shoulders. Heart-melting smile. The memory of the feel and weight of his body on hers caused her to shiver. Now that had been something extraordinary . . .

A deep sigh escaped her.

It was silly really, the way she continued to think about meeting that man. Why did he keep intruding into her thoughts? Especially when she would most likely never see him again.

Besides, she had Henry Brooks.

Dear, sweet Henry. She had been waiting patiently for him to be settled enough to marry her for years now. They would be wed soon enough, she hoped, and then Lisette would have her husband, a home of her own, and eventually children. Everything would be fine and she would be contented.

The alluring image of Quinton Roxbury's blue eyes caused her to shake her head once again.

"Thank you for getting my little man to sleep for me," Colette whispered.

Lisette noted her sister's eyes were heavy. "You should nap, too," she suggested.

"I think I shall."

"Colette?"

"Yes?"

She hesitated a moment. "Do you know the gentleman who was just here to see Lucien a little while ago?"

"Was someone here to see him?" Colette yawned a little. "I had no idea. I've been up here with Phillip all day. Why do you ask?"

Lisette paused, feeling a trifle awkward. "No particular reason."

"Lisette?"

Her eyes met Colette's. "I met him outside as he was leaving. I just wondered who he was."

Colette struggled to suppress a larger yawn, covering her mouth with her hand. "You shall have to ask Lucien about him."

Lisette was not sure if she would do that. Perhaps it was best not to know more about the handsome man who had quite literally swept her off her feet. Yes, perhaps that was best.

With great care, Lisette stood and shifted the weight of the sleeping child to her hip. She carried him into the adjoining nursery. Decorated in pastels and soft fabrics, the room was warm and sweet-smelling and a cheery fire burned in the hearth. After placing Phillip in his ornate cast iron and brass crib draped with swaths of silk, Lisette placed a kiss on his chubby cheek and tiptoed from the room.

As she passed by, she caught her reflection in the mirror and paused. Her green eyes looked overly bright, and her usually fair complexion was flushed with color. Still reeling from her encounter with Quinton Roxbury, she gave herself a helpless smile. With a sweep of her hand, she smoothed her auburn hair, which was pinned loosely on her head, and took a calming breath before rejoining Colette.

"I can't get up."

Lisette giggled at the sight of her pregnant sister trying to hoist herself from the chair. Reaching out her hands, she helped to pull Colette to her feet.

"You shouldn't sit in that chair anymore! It's too low. Come, let me help you to the bed."

Colette accepted her assistance readily and followed

her into the master suite. "I hope I have this baby before Christmas."

"I do, too. Now slip off your shoes and lie on your side."

After Colette had managed to situate her petite body on the bed as comfortably as her growing shape would allow, Lisette covered her with a soft woolen blanket.

"Thank you," her sister murmured.

"You're very welcome, but you need to let Rose help you with Phillip more often. You're exhausted."

Lisette noted that her sister's delicate facial features, which were so like her own, were drawn and tired. Colette's blue eyes had circles around them, and her dark hair hung loose and thick about her shoulders. The pregnancy had given her tresses a lovely shine, but her usually beautiful and vibrant sister appeared wan and weary.

Colette insisted upon taking care of her son without the assistance of a nurse or nanny, leaving the perfectly capable Scottish woman that Lucien hired in spite of Colette's protests with very little to do. Even after Phillip was born, Colette had spent at least two afternoons a week at the bookshop working with Paulette. Her sister's independence and determination to do everything herself was wearing her ragged.

"Let Rose help you," Lisette suggested again. "She passes most of her day in the kitchen gossiping with the cook when she should be here helping you with Phillip."

"Maybe you're right," Colette murmured, unable to keep her eyes open any longer.

"No maybes," Lisette declared firmly. "I shall send Rose up later with Phillip's supper and a tray for you. Now get some rest."

Once again, Lisette tiptoed from the room, leaving her sister and nephew in peaceful slumber. Out in the hallway she made her way to her own bedroom in the opposite wing of the house. A nap sounded like a good idea to her, too. Now that she knew she would be traveling to visit their mother in Brighton in the morning, she would need all the rest she could get.

"Lisette!"

She turned at her name. Paulette, her younger sister, came rushing toward her, her blond curls flying around her anguished little face.

"What is it?" Lisette asked.

"Did Colette speak with you? Are you going to visit Mother? I cannot—"

"Yes, I know," Lisette interrupted what she knew would be a list of reasons Paulette could not be spared. "I'm going to Brighton by train tomorrow. Don't worry."

Paulette's expression lit up with a radiant smile. "Oh, thank you! I would go to her, but with preparing the bookshop for Christmas and everything, I just can't leave. And you know how Mother can be. You are so good with her. I don't know what we would do without you—"

"It's fine. Truly. I don't mind going at all." She turned and continued to walk to her room, simply wanting to be by herself to think about . . . things.

Paulette called after her, "You are an angel, Lisette."

3

What Child Is This?

Oh, sometimes stealing was just too easy.

Tom didn't like stealing from people. He really tried not to, but sometimes it was simply far too easy.

Some fancy toff would walk by with a big fat purse acting as if he owned the world, and Tom just couldn't resist taking something from him. Besides he needed that money. And so did Mama. He always told her he earned whatever money he stole because Mama thought he was still working for the old shoemaker. But Tom promised himself he would go to hell before he ever went back to work for that old blighter again. Not after what he tried to do. No sir! Tom was no fool.

It pained him to know that Mama would worry if she knew that he was stealing, but what she really feared was that he would get caught. Tom feared that, too, to be sure, but he knew he wouldn't get caught. He was too quick on his feet, his touch so light, he was long gone before anyone realized that they'd been pinched. Besides he knew he would not always be forced to steal to survive. So he let

Mama believe he was still working for the shoemaker. That giant arse! How he hated that man.

Tom had a plan. Yes sir. He had a fine plan to help him and Mama.

Because he certainly didn't squander all the money he stole. No sir. In fact, he saved more than he spent, and he'd saved up quite an impressive bit so far. Someday he and Mama would live in a proper house and she wouldn't have to work her fingers to the bone for a few measly shillings.

Now, eyeing the fancy gent with the long navy coat as he stood and bartered with the young lass selling matches, Tom watched with calculated carefulness as the man removed the purse from his pocket and gave her a coin. With practiced skill Tom observed which pocket and slid off the barrel on which he had been perched in a casual pose, pretending to bite his fingernails. Pulling his tattered tweed cap low over his head, Tom slowly moved toward his intended target.

As the gentleman ambled through the busy lane, he did not notice the small boy who followed him, nor did he feel the quick little hand that slipped inside his coat pocket and removed his purse in the blink of an eye. Jostled by the bustling crowd, the man walked on his way, oblivious of the boy who raced in the opposite direction with all of his money stashed inside his threadbare shirt.

His heart pounding with excitement and exultation, Tom did not stop running through the crowd until he reached the grimy alley he knew like the back of his hand. Only then did he stop and catch his breath for a moment. It wouldn't do for the big lads to see him all rushed and breathless. Tall Jerry Gray and his little gang would be all over him in an instant and take his money as they had a time or two before. The purse was safe enough inside his shirt for now. Ignoring the guilt that threaded through him, he would count it all later, in the safety and privacy of his home.

Instead he walked casually along the grimy Saint Giles alleyway toward the rundown building in which his mother rented a tiny garret room. Stepping over scattered refuse and dipping under tattered clothing hung on lines to dry in the freezing cold December air, he kept his eyes peeled for any sign of trouble from the gang boys.

One thing Tom had learned to stay clear of was trouble.

"Hullo, Mrs. Framingham." Tom nodded his head at the practically toothless old woman who stood in the doorway of the wooden building, her filthy apron covering her even filthier skirt. She always stood guard at the door on rent day, making sure each of her tenants was accounted for and no one slipped by her.

"Got the rent money?"

Tom had the rent money all right. It was right there in his shirt. It just wouldn't do to tell old Mrs. Framingham that just yet. He flashed her a wide smile. Ladies always liked when he smiled at them. "Ma will bring it home today."

"She'd better." The woman reached out to smack Tom's head affectionately as he passed by.

Tom ducked, missing her hand. "She will. I'll bring it to you myself."

"You do that, little Tom," she cackled at him as he ran inside.

He climbed the four flights to the garret, taking the warped steps two at a time. The sound of Mrs. Greenway's two little babies screaming and the Johnsons' mangy hounds barking, as well as the drunken voice of old Mr. Hollister yelling and cursing obscenities at his cheating wife, followed him up the staircase. But these were usual sounds and he paid them no mind. Only quiet would make him worry. Silence in this place would signal that something was terribly wrong.

He fiddled with the key in his pocket and unlocked the door to half the garret. It was a tiny space, even considering it was just for the two of them. The Greenway family on the other side of the wall had eight people crammed in the same-sized space, so he and his mother felt lucky to have so much room. The little garret was neat as could be, sparsely furnished with a few sticks of used furniture. A small table stood before the fireplace with two spindly chairs. A large old trunk was crammed into the corner under the lone round window. The thin pallet he shared with his mother occupied the corner farthest from the one little window, which was broken and stuffed with rags. The garret was brutally cold and damp in winter and sweltering in the heat of summer. In the summer they moved their pallet close to the window and pulled the rags out to catch a bit of a breeze when one would come.

But now it was bitter cold. It was just as cold inside as the December afternoon outside and filled with dark shadows in the late afternoon gloom. Tom lit a stubby tallow candle and pulled the purse from inside his shirt. Turning it upside down, he poured the money onto the cracked wooden table. He loved the noise the coins made as they clattered. In the flickering candlelight, he counted the money three times, just to be sure, because he couldn't believe his good luck. It had to be a dream. Two whole pounds. He stared at the fortune on the table before him. Two whole pounds!

A smile spread across his freckled face and he gave a little whoop of joy.

He had guessed the toff was loaded, but this was the largest amount he'd ever pinched! He knew just what he would do. First, he would go out and buy some meat pies for supper to surprise his mother. He would set aside some of the money to pay his part of the rent. Then he would save the rest, adding it to his little treasure hidden beneath the floorboard behind the trunk. And perhaps he would take a little extra and buy his mother some new thick gloves for Christmas, to keep her hands warm. She would like that.

As usual, he slid the battered trunk by sitting on the floor and pressing against it with his back and pushing hard with his feet. With the trunk out of the way, he then lifted the warped wooden plank and removed the leather pouch that had once belonged to his father and where he stashed his ill-gotten gains. The bag was becoming heavier and heavier, and a wave of pride swelled within him at the sight. He had accumulated a lot of coins in the last few months.

Picking pockets was a trade he'd begun just last spring, after he quit working for Mr. Rutledge, the shoemaker. It seemed Tom had a good eye for the perfect pocket and always managed to pinch a loaded one. He never stole from people he didn't think could afford the loss. He had to have standards, after all. He was not a common thief. Not like the gangs that terrorized the neighborhood and robbed from everyone, even the poor, like Mama and him. That's why Tom kept his money well hidden and never let on that they had any more than anyone else.

If Jerry Gray and the rest of those blighters had any idea how much money Tom had stored under the floorboard, they would tear the house down to get it. He had no doubt of that. They were always trying to recruit Tom to be part of their gang, but Tom just steered clear of them as much as possible.

He patted the bag of money, knowing he now had close to three pounds, a bloody fortune, and fitted the board back in place. He moved to the other side of the trunk and pushed it back on top of the loose board.

When he finally told her about the money he'd saved, his mother would be surprised and so happy she wouldn't care that he had stolen it. At least he hoped so. He took the remaining amount of money and ran out to the street by going down to the cellar and climbing out the cellar window to avoid old Mrs. Framingham. From the vendor on the corner he bought two hot meat pasties, a loaf of crusty bread, and a small fruit tart. He returned to the garret in the same roundabout manner and set the table for their little dinner feast. His mother would be tired when she came in, and this would cheer her. He grinned just thinking about it. He put some coals on the fire as well, to help take some of the chill out of the attic.

Mama didn't want him to steal and would be heart-broken to know that Tom had. But he wouldn't ever tell her. He would say he found a shilling on the street, as he had done before. She always said, "My Tom has the keen-est eyes and can spot a coin on the ground a yard away!"

She had warned him to stay away from the gang lads, and he had kept that promise. He had been so good. The first time he stole, it really had been an accident. But he couldn't help stealing when he knew the money would help them. Mama wouldn't let him be a chimney sweep's chummie because she said it was too dangerous, even though Tom was small and spry enough, even at the great age of ten. She wouldn't let him go to the factories either. There wasn't much else a small boy could do to earn a decent living. He needed to help his mother.

He was the man of the house now, and he had been for as long as he could remember.

Papa had died when Tom was just a little boy. He had been only five years old at the time. If he closed his eyes real tight, he could almost see Papa's smiling face. His wide green eyes, with crinkles in the corners. His long brown mustache that he let Tom tug on once in a while. He could almost hear his deep voice. But those memories were getting more difficult to recall, becoming hazier and cloudier. He tried hard not to forget Papa. Or Ellie. Back then it had been the four of them. Mama. Papa. Tom and Baby Ellie. Then Papa got sick, real sick with the cholera, and they took him off to hospital and he never came back. Mama had cried for days. Weeks. Months. She cried late at night when she didn't think Tom was awake. But he was.

Then a year ago Christmas, Ellie had died, too. His little sister caught a fever and died right there in the garret. She was only four years old. He missed Ellie. He hadn't forgotten her, as he had Papa. Her memory was still fresh and painful. He could still see her sweet freckled face, so like his own, and her long red braids. Ellie had the best laugh in the world, and he could make her laugh so easily. He missed his little sister.

Now it was only the two of them when it had once been four. He and Mama.

Tom had just finished arranging the meat pasties on the chipped china plates with the tiny blue flowers that had once belonged to his grandmother, when he heard the latch on the door and Mama came in. The weary look in her eyes filled him with sadness, and he wished she would smile and laugh as she used to. It had been a long time since he had seen Mama smile a real smile with her eyes.

"I found a shilling on the way home, so I got us some hot supper tonight."

"Bless you." Anna Alcott sighed, sitting at the wobbly table and eyeing the little feast he had set for them. "You do have a talent for finding money, my sweet Tom." She patted his arm.

Relieved she didn't question him further, he sat beside her and dug into the tasty meat pie. It was a minute or two before he realized that Mama hadn't touched the food in front of her. "Aren't you going to eat?"

"I'm not hungry right now. Perhaps I'll save it for later."

She rubbed her hands together, warming them and massaging her aching joints.

Tom knew her fingers hurt from sewing all day at Madame La Fleur's dress shop. She had been working there for years now, but the physical toll such labor required had begun to show its effects upon her body. Ten to twelve hours a day hunched over expensive fabric and lace, sewing ball gowns, dresses, and undergarments was taxing. Her eyesight had weakened and her muscles ached. She suffered terrible headaches as well.

"Have a bite," he encouraged her. "It's good."

She nodded, stabbing at the pie with her fork. She nibbled on a small piece and placed the fork on her plate. "It's delicious. Thank you."

"There's bread, too."

"I'll have some in the morning."

"And a fruit tart."

She shook her head and frowned. "You shouldn't have spent so much."

"We have to eat, Mama."

Her expression softened. "You are a good boy, Tom. And you work too hard for a nine-year-old."

"I'm ten now. Remember?" He squared his shoulders with pride.

"Yes, that's right. You are, but you still take on too much for a boy your age." Her blue eyes filled with regret and sadness.

"I'm almost a man."

"You may think so, but you've got a ways to go." Mama rose from the table and moved to the thin pallet of blankets that served as their bed. With a heavy sigh she laid her body down, tucking her hands under her head, and closed her eyes in abject weariness.

Filled with an unspeakable helplessness, Tom watched his mother, exhausted from working her fingers to the bone, and wished fervently that he could ease her burdens somehow. He longed to make her smile as she used to. His eyes moved across the room to where the little sack of money lay hidden under the floorboard beneath the trunk. He needed to fill that sack, fill it to overflowing. There had to be a way. Once he overheard some of the lads talk about the trains. Tom thought about Victoria Station and all the fancy people that traveled and how much money they might carry with them on a trip. He might just have to visit Victoria Station.

4

Follow Me
in Merry Measure

Tuesday, December 2, 1873

"I promise I will meet your train on Tuesday when you return," Henry Brooks said as he held Lisette's gloved hand in his. They stood among the crowd of travelers at Victoria Station waiting to board the train.

"Why, Henry, that would be lovely! Thank you," Lisette said with a smile of appreciation. Henry's sandy brown hair was covered by a tall black top hat, and his gray eyes looked into hers. He had never escorted her to the station before, and Lisette had been touched by this show of caring on his part.

"I shall miss having you with me at the dinner party this evening, Lisette, but duty toward your mother and your family comes first. You are a good daughter."

She gave him a bright grin. "The week shall fly by before we know it!"

He returned the smile and nodded in agreement. "As will this year. You have been so patient with me, Lisette. Next year at this time, we shall be a married couple." He paused a moment for a bit of a dramatic effect. "We can have our wedding in June."

"Oh, Henry, do you mean that?" she exclaimed in delight. Lisette had been waiting for this for three long years. At times it had seemed as if Henry would never settle on a date for their wedding.

"Yes. My uncle has decided to retire for good and will let me take over his practice completely. He told me the news just last evening. With what I have saved now, I can afford to buy us a little house. We can start planning our wedding in earnest when you get back, my dear. Something modest, of course." He squeezed her hand tightly.

"Oh my!" A little thrill raced through her, and she couldn't stop giggling. "That is wonderful news! I cannot wait to tell my mother and sisters! They will be so pleased."

They had waited so long to marry, delaying until he had enough money to support her. It seemed he had finally amassed enough to satisfy himself that he could properly take care of a wife. She had never seen Henry's sweet face so alight with happiness. His eyes twinkled at her, and he smiled broadly beneath his neatly trimmed sandy mustache and beard.

The train whistle blew with a pronounced shrillness and steam billowed around them. In an impulsive gesture, Henry leaned down and brushed her cheek with the lightest of kisses.

"Henry!" she squealed, pleased by his sudden display of affection. Henry had never kissed her in public before. In fact, he was so proper, he had rarely kissed her at all.

"Now, hurry before the train leaves without you. The porter has already taken your bag inside and your seat is in the first-class compartment in this car right here," he instructed her as if she had not been there when the porter took her portmanteau. As if she had not taken the train to visit her mother a dozen times before without his help. Yet she knew it made Henry happy to take care of her, so she nodded obediently.

"Thank you," she said as she ascended the steps of the car. "Good-bye!"

He waved to her as he watched her board the train. Lisette entered the car and found her seat in the elegant first-class compartment. There were no other passengers but herself, which she was pleased to notice.

"Is there anything else I can do for you, miss?" the barrel-chested porter inquired, popping his head in the compartment to check on her.

"No, thank you. I'm just fine."

"Let me know if you need anything then. Good afternoon, miss." He nodded politely and left, closing the door behind him.

Just as she'd settled herself on a dark green velvet seat, the train emitted another ear-splitting whistle and jolted into motion. She pulled back the dark velvet curtains and peered out the window, but Henry had already gone from the platform. He would never waste time standing there when he had work to do. Pretending her fiancé was watching her departure, she gave a little wave with her fingers anyway as the engine chugged with slow determination away from the station.

Lisette relaxed and loosened the ties around the neck of her black velvet, white fur-trimmed cloak, setting aside her matching fur muff. Still brimming with surprise over Henry's announcement, she kept her eyes on the window. It was her favorite part of traveling. Watching the landscape change as the massive train sped through the countryside, seeing all the buildings and the houses and the roads and the people, and wondering about all the different lives and what was happening with them fascinated her.

She especially wondered about the people and what

their stories were. Were they happy or sad? Was there a life-and-death emergency happening somewhere? Was it another routine day in their lives? Endless stories abounded while she watched from the train window.

Now there was a nicely dressed woman standing on the platform, holding the hand of a little girl with long dark curls. The little girl was crying. Were they just saying good-bye to someone on the train, her father perhaps? The woman stood stoically, no expression on her hardened face.

Then she caught the eyes of a small boy with a tattered tweed cap covering most of his red hair. The ill-fitting jacket he wore was too thin to keep him warm during the winter. He had an angelic face with a serious, world-weary expression, and his large blue eyes locked with hers. He stood there by himself, watching the train. Who was with him? Was he lost? Where did he live? She could tell by his clothing he was a street urchin. But what worried her more was that he seemed to be alone and this pulled at her heart-strings. She offered a smile through the train window but he did not smile in return. Fascinated, Lisette could not take her eyes off the child as possibilities of his circumstances flitted through her head.

It was then that the door to the compartment flew open and a man entered. A bit disappointed that she would have to share the compartment but lost in her musings, Lisette barely glanced away from the compelling scene outside the train window as the man continued to stand at the doorway.

"Miss Hamilton?"

Her heart raced as soon as she heard his voice. The little boy forgotten, with slow anticipation she faced the gentleman who had just entered the compartment.

"It is you." He stared at her, a wide grin on his incredulous face.

"Mr. Roxbury!"

Surprised she found her voice so swiftly, Lisette wondered what in the world had happened to allow this man of all men to be on the same train with her. He stood above her, his face clean-shaven and his warm smile melting her into a million pieces. He wore a black top hat, but the golden edges of his blond hair were visible beneath. His tall and very masculine presence seemed to take over the entire compartment and she found it difficult to breathe. Especially when he turned the force of his blue eyes on her.

"What a wonderful surprise to see you," he continued with carefree ease. "You aren't traveling all the way to Brighton, are you, Miss Hamilton?"

"Yes, I am."

"Well, this is a most pleasant coincidence, for I am as well. It seems we are sharing this compartment and will be traveling together today." He sat upon the seat across from her and let out a sigh of relief. "That was a close one. I almost missed the train!"

"Well, I am very glad that you did not miss it."

"Now that I see you, I am even more thankful I did not miss it. It's lovely to see you again, Miss Hamilton."

For a moment Lisette thought she might very well faint from a combination of panic and delight. Quinton Roxbury was so very male. His tall muscular form filled the space, his long legs almost touching hers. There was a magnetic energy about him and it made her giddy. The man sent shivers down her spine simply by looking at her. And now he was sitting with her in a confined space for the entire duration of the journey to Brighton.

They were on a train heading to the seaside on an overcast day. Together. Alone. How wonderful that she had decided not to travel by carriage after all! That wild thought made her sit up straighter.

"What a surprise to see you again so soon!" he exclaimed. "I would not have expected this."

"Neither would I." Although she had not stopped thinking

about him since yesterday, she hadn't expected to see him ever again. Now here he was, sitting across from her. "It is quite a coincidence after yesterday."

"Yes, but it is much more pleasant to be seated with you on a train than being tripped over in a back lane." The warmth and intelligence in his eyes, as well as a definite twinkle of humor, drew her to him.

"Our meeting *was* most unusual," she admitted with a little laugh. "I've never met anyone before simply because they knocked me down."

"Nor have I ever knocked anyone down before. At least not by accident. And never anyone as lovely as you."

"Thank you," she murmured softly, and a little shiver of excitement raced through her at his words. Was it only yesterday that his body covered hers? His lips had brushed against her cheek the day before, and she had wished that he would kiss her. Had he wanted to kiss her? Did he remember that part of their encounter? His full lips fascinated her, and she could not stop her eyes from focusing on his mouth.

"I apologize once again for running into you the way I did, Miss Hamilton. I still feel terrible about hurting you. You are not experiencing any ill effects from your fall, are you?"

The genuine concern in his voice touched her. "No, none at all. I assure you, I am quite well. I believe I forgave you yesterday."

"That you did and most charmingly. So please tell me, what brings you on this journey today?" he asked.

Lisette relaxed somewhat as the conversation turned to a more ordinary subject and she could put aside the memory of this gorgeous man lying on top of her and almost kissing her. At least for the moment. "I am going to see my mother. She's not feeling well and wishes for me to visit with her for a bit."

His brows drew together in concern. "Nothing serious, I hope?"

Lisette smiled and shook her head. "No, I do not believe so. My mother . . ." She paused a moment, searching for the most polite way to phrase it. "My mother tends to overemphasize quite minor ailments."

Quinton Roxbury tilted his head in sympathetic understanding, a knowing smile playing around the corners of his luscious mouth. "Ah . . . I understand. I have an aunt with a similar type of nature."

"Yes, I am most certain that my mother will be quite recovered by the time I arrive."

He laughed and the rich sound wrapped around her like a warm, velvet gown. "Well, that is good news."

Curious, she ventured to ask, "What takes you to Brighton today, Mr. Roxbury? This is not the usual time of year to visit the seaside."

"No, it's not, is it? The month of December is a little cold and dreary for most people in general, but I actually enjoy the sea air no matter what the season. However, in answer to your question, I'm going to Brighton on business, not pleasure."

"I wish you the best of luck with your business then," Lisette said.

"Thank you very much." He settled back in his seat.

In the silence, Lisette could not take her eyes off him, and it felt like there were a thousand butterflies in her stomach. Well, she certainly had not overemphasized how handsome he was in her recollections from yesterday. The man was like a golden god from a mythology story come to life and plopped down in front of her. It was most disconcerting. She forced her gaze away from him and out the window

They sat in companionable silence as the train continued its journey, leaving behind the bustling thoroughfares and crowds of London and moving into the placid English countryside.

"I gather you are traveling alone, Miss Hamilton?"

She blinked in rapid succession, realizing he was staring at her. "Yes."

"I'm a little surprised Lord Waverly would not provide you with an escort or a companion of some sort."

"My brother-in-law always offers and at times I do travel with one. But I prefer to be on my own," she explained with a matter-of-fact air. "We Hamilton women are notoriously independent."

"I'm just beginning to notice that." He raised a brow at her, his expression one of appreciation.

Flushing a little under his blatant regard, she continued, "I have traveled to Brighton many times before on my own. I'm quite capable."

"That's a pity."

"I beg your pardon?"

Grinning, he attempted to clarify. "I did not mean that it's a pity that you are a capable woman, for certainly that is a good quality. What I meant to say was that it's a pity that you are alone."

She sighed in exasperation, becoming slightly irritated by his attitude. "That statement did not improve upon your last comment in the least, Mr. Roxbury."

His eyes sparkled with good humor. "I see I am digging myself into a hole and I apologize. What I meant to say, but did so rather clumsily, was that the unfortunate consequence of your being alone deprives someone of the pleasure of your company."

The ravenous look he gave her made her stomach flip over.

"Oh." Her cheeks warmed at his compliment and she could not stop the grin that spread across her face. "Well then, Mr. Roxbury, you are forgiven."

Mr. Roxbury nodded his head in her direction. "Thank you."

A brief silence descended over the compartment as the train made its way south, the rhythmic swaying of the carriage rather soothing and hypnotic.

"A moment ago when you said 'we Hamilton women,' to whom were you referring?" he asked.

"My sisters and myself."

"I know you have a sister who is married to Lord Waverly. There are more?"

"Three more."

That gave him pause. "You mean to say that there are five of you Hamilton girls?"

"That is correct."

"No brothers in the lot?"

"No, just us girls."

"That is fascinating." He chuckled a little, as if imagining the prospect of so many sisters. "How does your father stand it?"

"He passed away a few years ago." From his shocked expression she quickly amended her statement. "Oh, but not from anything we did!"

He laughed and then she did, too, realizing how ridiculous her comment sounded.

With a smile Lisette explained, "I can assure you that we were exemplary daughters in every way. We even assisted him in running the family bookshop."

"Well, I am relieved to learn that you and your sisters did not bring about your father's early demise." He said this in a dry tone, but then began more earnestly, "I am sorry about your father's passing. My father passed away a few years ago as well, so I understand your loss."

"Thank you. It is quite difficult to lose a parent . . ."

He quickly changed the subject from the depressing topic of death. "Yet you have a bookshop?"

"Yes, Hamilton's Book Shoppe," Lisette explained, proud of her family's business. "It's just off Bond Street. Perhaps you have heard of it?"

"The name rings a bell, but I don't believe I've ever been there. However, I shall now make a point of visiting there without delay."

"Oh, you should! You won't be disappointed, I assure you. It's quite a lovely shop and well known for its innovative design and large selection of books. It has become so busy, in fact, that we are thinking of opening another bookshop. My two sisters, Colette and Paulette, manage everything now, but we've all helped there throughout our lives and still do."

"Women running a shop on their own! That's quite extraordinary. Did your mother work there as well?"

Lisette shook her head. "Oh, no. Mother detested the shop and fled to Brighton at the first opportunity after Father passed away. But we girls love it still."

"Now I am more curious than ever to visit your shop. It sounds wonderful."

"Then I extend an invitation for you to stop by anytime you wish."

He gave her a pointed look. "I shall take you up on that offer, Miss Hamilton."

A little shiver of pleasure raced through her at his words and she lowered her eyes, wondering what it would be like if he visited the bookshop one day while she was there. She was curious to know more about the handsome man across from her.

After a moment she dared another glance at him and asked, "May I ask what kind of business brings you to Brighton this time of year?"

"I am an architect and I have been requested to design a house for a family there."

"An architect!" she exclaimed in wonderment. She

vaguely recalled Henry mentioning yesterday that Quinton had designed something. What was it? She had been so flustered by their meeting she could not remember what Henry had told her. "How fascinating! I don't believe I have ever met an architect before in my life. What else do you design? Cathedrals? Office buildings? Or strictly houses?"

His face lit up, becoming even more handsome if such a thing were possible, and he seemed genuinely pleased at her interest. "I've designed a number of different types of buildings, although nothing as grand as a cathedral. I did design the new art museum that just opened in London. Private homes are my main focus at the moment. Designing houses will just afford me the money to create what I truly wish to build."

"And what would that be?" she asked. This man surprised her. She had assumed he was a typical London gentleman who spent his life in idle pursuits and being waited upon by others and here he was an industrious soul. And a creative one at that.

He gazed at her steadily, a hint of wonder in his blue eyes. "You are truly interested to know what I want to build?"

Lisette nodded with genuine enthusiasm. "Yes, of course I am interested. I have never had the opportunity to question an architect before."

He seemed thrilled to confide in her. "Well, I am working on a project now to hopefully create new housing for those in the tenement areas of London."

"What kind of housing do you mean?"

"Real houses. Not those dilapidated buildings that perpetuate the squalor and filthy conditions the poor live with now. How can anyone improve themselves in such dire circumstances? How can one get clean while living in a place covered in grime and refuse without access to decent water? I am quite sure you have never visited such areas,

Miss Hamilton, nor would I expect you to have. But I can tell you from my experience that these places are over-crowded without basic sanitation or clean water, which only perpetuates diseases and death. We need to tear down these tenement flats and build real homes for these families outside London, where there is more room, fresh air, gardens, and trees. Functional, sturdy, and beautiful houses with proper light and ventilation. A place anyone would *want* to live in. And not just houses, but an entire neighborhood, a real community."

Although surprised by the passion of his words, Lisette was captivated by the magnitude of Quinton Roxbury's ideas. "I think that is the most wonderful thing I have ever heard."

He looked at her with an expression of awe. "Do you really?"

"Yes," she admitted readily, filled with excitement at the prospect of his venture.

"More often than not, people tell me I'm mad to take on such a project."

"They must be the closed-minded type."

"I admit that I'm pleasantly surprised by your appreciation of my venture. It's a rare quality in a woman. I've found that most women I know have very little interest in building projects."

She slanted a look at him. "I am not most women, Mr. Roxbury."

"I can see that, Miss Hamilton," he said with a look of admiration on his face.

"What you are doing is most worthwhile. I don't believe you are mad at all."

Lisette thought of the terrible places she passed while on the train and the desperately hard lives of the people she saw outside the window. "I've often imagined how dread-ful it would be to live in such dire circumstances, through no fault of your own except an accident of birth. I admit to you that my own family came very close to being in such terrible straits after our father died, and we learned how he had left us in debt. We almost lost the shop, and things could have gone quickly down from there. I shudder to think what could have happened to all of us if Colette had not met Lucien Sinclair when she did. He took all of us in when he married her."

"I had no idea that you and your family had been through such struggles." His golden-brown brows drawn into a line of concern against his expressive forehead, he reached out and patted her hand in comfort.

"I'm so sorry." Lisette withdrew her hand, suddenly embarrassed to have confided in him such intimate family details. She had never even discussed those events with Henry! "Please forgive me. I did not mean to go on so about myself."

"There is no reason for you to apologize. I understand completely."

"I have great admiration for what you are trying to accomplish, Mr. Roxbury." Lisette could not seem to stop from talking. "Most people have a terribly callous attitude toward the poor, blaming them for being in such a state. As if they wanted to live like that or as if it were an easy matter to get out of such circumstances! If the poor worked harder, if they saved more, if they went to church more often, then they would not be in such a terrible situation. But that is not always true, as you obviously know. I agree with you that proper housing would make a world of difference. But aside from a clean living environment, I believe that education is the key to helping people."

Lisette had never given voice to her opinion on such matters before and surprised herself to find them so well formed.

Quinton Roxbury gave her a look of utter satisfaction. "I'm pleased to know you see it that way, Miss Hamilton."

"In our own small way, my sisters and I have helped by teaching the young boys who run errands and make deliveries at the bookshop for us how to read. We insist upon it. They cannot collect their wages until they have attended our reading sessions."

"That is amazing!" he exclaimed with enthusiasm. "I was unaware that your family was doing such a remarkable service. That is most impressive."

"It's not much," Lisette amended, "but it pains me to see a person who cannot read. Perhaps because I spent my life surrounded by books and learned to read at a very young age."

He nodded in understanding. "Yes, I can see where that would shape your beliefs on reading."

"We also continue to educate the young women who assist us in the shop. Women and girls are terribly neglected when it comes to education."

"I can see that you are obviously not one of their number."

"That pleases you?"

Again, he smiled appreciatively at her. "More than you know."

Flustered by his approval, she paused a moment before asking, "Have you considered having schools in your community?"

"Yes, I have, but that is all tied up in the government and politics and the new reform act. Schooling is not compulsory and these children will choose earning a living to sitting in a schoolroom any day. I'd like to have schooling in this neighborhood because it is of the utmost importance. This undertaking requires a great deal of influence and money. However, I hope to make some changes in that arena someday as well. That is the second stage of my plan, to take on a role in the government. But first we have to get the houses financed before we can move forward."

"Are you having any success with your venture?" she asked.

"Well, that's taking some time. Most people feel that the poor don't deserve new houses. As you so eloquently said, most people believe being poor is their own fault. At the moment I'm looking for investors to help finance the actual building of the houses. Which is why I was visiting your brother-in-law when I ran into you yesterday."

This was most interesting. Lisette had not had an opportunity to ask Lucien about Mr. Roxbury before she left for the station that day. She would make a point to inquire about him as soon as she returned. "What did Lord Waverly say about your idea? Did he agree to contribute?"

"You know your brother-in-law better than I do," Quinton countered with a charming grin that sent another wild thrill through her. "What do you think he said?"

Lisette pondered for a moment, thinking of the man who was now more or less the head of her family. When Lucien Sinclair married Colette, he had welcomed all four of her sisters into his home without a moment's hesitation. Lisette had grown to love him as her true brother. "Lucien is a fair man, a good man, but he is not one to rush into matters. Did he tell you he would have to think it over for a few days?"

"That was exactly what he said!" Quinton exclaimed with a laugh. "You do know him well."

A crazy feeling of delight that she had pleased him washed over her.

"So, Miss Hamilton, when I see Lord Waverly again next week, what do you think his answer will be?"

She did not hesitate. "I think he will want to help your cause, Mr. Roxbury."

"That reassures me greatly." He leaned closer to her.

"Could I also presume to count on your sweet nature to whisper a good word in his ear for me and my cause?"

Her heart raced at his proximity. The masculinity that emanated from him threatened to overwhelm her. She fought against a strong desire to reach out and touch his face, to run her fingertips along the edge of his clean-shaven jaw, wondering what it would feel like. "Well, since it is for a good cause, and not simply for your personal gain"—she paused for dramatic effect—"I might be persuaded to assist you."

He raised his brows, and a smile tugged at the corner of his mouth. "Might?"

"Yes, I might. I shall have to think about it." She was flirting with the man. Lisette was not a flirt! Yet she could not help herself. Indeed, she did not feel like herself at all.

"Ah . . ." Quinton tilted his head toward her. "So you leave me to wonder . . . How might I best persuade the lovely Miss Hamilton to do my bidding?"

He was flirting back and her heart leapt to her mouth. "Well, Mr. Roxbury, you should know that I am not a woman who is easily persuaded."

"Is that a challenge?" He leaned even closer to her, his blue eyes gleaming.

"Perhaps," she whispered, slightly breathless.

He inched a bit closer to her. "Then I suppose I have no recourse but to wait upon your good favor then."

Close enough to touch him now, she could not help smiling at his response. "Yes, you shall."

He regarded her with a steady gaze as if considering whether to continue their flirtatious conversation. "How long will you be staying in Brighton, Miss Hamilton?"

"I'll be there for a week. I shall return to London next Tuesday. And yourself?" Lisette could not deny the intense undercurrent in their exchange.

"I'm not entirely sure as of yet." His eyes met hers,

lingering, and a meaningful look passed between them. "It depends."

"Depends on what?" she asked, losing herself in the blue of his eyes. There seemed to be so much more to what they were saying than the actual words. She had never had such a conversation before, and the pleasure of it excited her.

His eyes gleamed. "On how things go . . ."

She held her breath for a moment. "With your business?"

"Yes." He tilted his head in her direction. "Among other things."

"Other things?" The very nearness of him made her head spin. The urge to reach out and touch him became unbearable. He'd almost kissed her in the lane yesterday. Would he kiss her now? Did she wish him to? Yes. This desire to be close to him was unfathomable. She wondered what it would be like to reach out and run her fingers along the line of his jaw, and over the sensitive curve of his lips. Wondered what it would be like to press her lips against his. A kiss. Yes, she wanted to kiss him.

"Yes," he said.

"And what might those other things be?"

"Might I call upon you tomorrow?"

Lisette took a deep breath as cold reality settled over her and her little fantasy of kissing him evaporated. He wanted to call upon her! Thrilled and terrified by his intent, she trembled. How she wished she could answer yes . . . But she might as well let it be known from the start, before he got any more ideas into his head about her. "Mr. Roxbury, I . . . You should know that . . . I . . . Well, I am engaged to be married."

His eyes widened slightly in surprise, but his expression remained guardedly neutral. Slowly he sat back in his seat away from her. "And you should know that I am engaged as well, Miss Hamilton."

"I see," Lisette murmured, unable to squelch the sudden and bitter disappointment that surged within her. She turned to face the window, afraid her disenchanted expression would betray her. He was betrothed! The fact stunned her, yet why should it matter to her if this man was engaged to someone else? She was marrying Henry Brooks in June, and it was nothing to her that Quinton Roxbury had a fiancée. Her fiancé had just escorted her to the train, for heaven's sake.

Yet she felt terribly hurt and saddened by this unexpected development.

"When are you to be wed?" he asked, his voice very soft and low.

She faced him. "June." She had to know, had to ask. "And you?"

"The third of January."

So soon! She bit her lip just in time to prevent herself from crying out in protest. Today was the second of December. In a few short weeks he would be married to another woman! An indescribable sensation of loss overwhelmed her. It was completely irrational, she knew, but she could not shake the feeling that she had just lost an opportunity for something wonderful and magical. It was ridiculous. She should not care that this man was engaged. She squared her shoulders and stared back out the window, watching the hills speed by her.

As the train rolled along, they both sat in silence for the remainder of the journey. Ignoring the undeniable feelings of attraction that hovered in the air between them like a living thing, lost in their own thoughts, they said no more. For what was there to say now? Once she dared a glance at him, and he, too, stared out the window, looking rather pensive.

At last the train chugged slowly into the station with a shrill whistle. It stopped with a harsh squealing of brakes as it jerked to a halt with a long shudder. Lisette began to gather her things together and rose from her seat.

Quinton Roxbury also stood, taking a step toward her. "You haven't yet answered me, Miss Hamilton."

She glanced at him in surprise. "I'm not quite sure I know the question."

He pinned her with his intense blue-eyed gaze. "I asked if I could call upon you tomorrow afternoon."

Her heart now stopped. Really! What on earth was the man thinking? He still wished to call upon her knowing full well that she was an affianced lady! "Mr. Roxbury, I believe I gave you my answer when I told you I have a fiancé."

"No. You merely told me that you are to be wed. You did not give me an answer about visiting you."

She had to stop herself from reaching out and touching him. He was so close to her. Again. "That fact that I am engaged precludes my accepting your calls, Mr. Roxbury."

"Not necessarily."

A small gasp escaped her lips, and her heart pounded wildly in her chest. "What does that mean?"

"It means that if I were unattached, it would be somewhat untoward of me to ask to call upon a woman who is engaged, but since I, too, am affianced, there is no problem."

"Isn't there?" Her voice squeaked, a little stunned by the path of the conversation. Had she misread all that had happened between them? She felt certain that he had wanted to kiss her. And she . . . Well . . . She had wanted him to kiss her! And now, now once again she wished he would kiss her.

The uniformed porter opened the door to the compartment.

"Miss Hamilton, we have arrived." He lifted her embroidered tapestry portmanteau.

"Yes, thank you." She nodded as he carried her bag from the compartment.

Quinton continued to press her. "Can we not be two acquaintances, Miss Hamilton? Can we not be friends?"

His request sounded so easy, so simple. Being friends with him would be wonderful and she wanted to be his friend in an almost desperate way, yet her conscience pricked her madly for she desired him as more than a friend. But it was not so easy or so simple. It was far more complicated than that. Being friends with Quinton Roxbury would be considered improper. In fact, it was most scandalous. Lisette detested scandal.

"No." She shook her head lightly. "I am afraid that we cannot."

"Good. Then it's settled." A wide grin spread across his face. "I shall call upon you tomorrow to tell you more about my project, for there is much I wish to share with you about it. You can then pass that information on to your brother-in-law for me."

"Mr. Roxbury, you will do no such thing! Good day to you."

Lisette hurriedly followed the porter from the train, anxious to have their unusual encounter at an end before he could say another word to her.

However tempted she was to be with him, not seeing Quinton Roxbury again was the safest course of action and the only proper thing to do.

And Lisette Hamilton was nothing if not proper.

5

How Still We
See Thee Lie

Wednesday, December 3, 1873

"Lisette, bring my tea to me here by the fire," Genevieve La Brecque Hamilton demanded in an irritable tone from her place on the divan. "I have a dreadful headache again. *J'ai un terrible mal de tête.*"

As Lisette walked from the kitchen balancing a tray laden with teacups and saucers in her hands, she was happy to have something to occupy her mind from the maddening Mr. Roxbury.

When she arrived the night before, her mother had been thrilled to see her and, miraculously, had seemed cured of her mystery illness. However, this afternoon she had become quite fractious. Her serving woman, Fannie, had rolled her eyes and warned Lisette as soon as she had come downstairs after luncheon.

"Oh, but Miss Genevieve's in a state, I tell you. Thought her good humor might last a spell since you got here, but she's as cranky as a cat with no tail. Don't know what's got into her. I fixed her favorite lunch, but she wouldn't touch a bite of them chicken pasties. Now she's just wanting mint tea and calling for you."

"Thank you, Fannie. I'll bring it to her." Lisette also brought the new lavender-scented eye pillow she had made for her mother last week.

She set the tray on the table beside her mother and handed her the teacup.

"Merci, ma petite," Genevieve whispered.

Lisette took a soft woolen blanket from the sofa and covered her mother's legs. It was chilly in the room, in spite of the fire burning in the hearth. The day had dawned with a heavy downpour, and the damp and cold seemed to permeate the little house.

When their mother had left London and Hamilton's Book Shoppe to live in a cottage by the sea, she had indeed moved to the shore. However, "cottage" was a relative term. Through Lucien Sinclair's generosity, Genevieve had purchased a rather small but elegant house for herself. Situated outside the main part of town on a small hill with a lovely view of the sea, the pretty white house was surrounded by a garden, which in warmer months bloomed and blossomed with a profusion of colorful flowers and vines. But now the cold December wind whipped around like a fury and made the gables shudder.

"Sit back after your tea, *Maman*. See, I have a new eye pillow for you. The lavender will help ease your headache."

As she made her mother more comfortable, Lisette wondered if she would ever see Quinton Roxbury again. Their encounter on the train yesterday made her feel giddy, like a young schoolgirl. And here she was almost one and twenty. Such ridiculous nonsense! She must put the idea of him out of her head immediately.

"Ah, my sweet Lisette, it is so good to have you here with me. *Ta place est içi avec moi.* You belong here with me. You girls are too far from me, all the way up there in London."

Lisette was careful not to fall into that trap. It was their mother's decision to leave them living at Devon House, when they had begged her not to go, and she was content to have her cottage by the sea. Yet she expected them to be in Brighton all the time.

"There, is that better?" she asked, placing the scented pillow over her mother's eyes. She smoothed her gray hair from her face as she did so. Her mother had been a beauty once, and Lisette could see the shadows of past heartaches in the fine lines that wrinkled Genevieve's care-worn face. Her unhappy marriage to her father, Thomas Hamilton, and her disappointments in her life had etched their sad stories across her countenance.

"*Oui, ma petite chérie.* Yes, my dear. Thank you. I always feel better when you are here and taking care of me. *Tu es la plus douce de mes filles.*" With a wave of her hand, she motioned to the sofa. "Sit down, Lisette, and tell me everything that is happening with your sisters in London."

Lisette sat upon the chair and began, "Well, Uncle Randall and Aunt Cecilia are still at their wits' end with Nigel. Aunt Cecilia canceled having tea with us the other day, claiming she was ill, but Lucien discovered that Nigel had been gambling and is in debt over his head again."

"That family is terrible," Genevieve muttered in disgust. "*Ils sont effroyables.* Your father's brother always hated me."

Lisette's opinion was that Uncle Randall disliked all the Hamilton girls, but ever since Colette married Lord Waverly, he had kept his disdain well hidden. So had Aunt Cecilia.

"How is Phillip? My precious grandson. *Le plus merveilleux au monde des petits garçons!*"

"He is simply adorable and getting so big already, *Maman*. I am afraid we are all spoiling him."

"That is as it should be. With so many people to love him, how could it be any other way?" She sighed. "I hope Colette has a daughter this time. *J'aimerais tant avoir une petite-fille.*"

"I think we are all hoping for a little girl."

"Yes, another pretty little girl in the family again would be lovely." Her mother turned her attention to Lisette. "And what of your Henry Brooks? *Il est devenu si lent.* He has been so slow. Has he made up his mind yet?"

"It just so happens that I have some news regarding him," Lisette said, not without a bit of pride. "He told me yesterday that his uncle has decided to retire at last and is giving Henry his law practice. Henry and I can finally be married in June!"

Genevieve remained silent, a definitive frown on her lined but still attractive face.

"Mother?" Lisette asked in concern. "Isn't that good news?"

"It is if you think so, *ma chérie*," her mother said with a simple gesture of helpless resignation. "If it is what you want, so be it."

"It's what I have been waiting for all these years," Lisette said, feeling more than a little defensive. She hated when her mother pretended to act as if nothing were bothering her when it was quite obvious that she was perturbed. "I thought you would be happy about it. Or at least happy for me . . ."

Genevieve sat up in a quick motion, as if she were not suffering from a debilitating headache at all, and removed the lavender pillow from her eyes. She looked directly at Lisette, her eyes glittering with intensity. "Are you happy about it, Lisette? *Est-ce que tu es heureuse avec lui? Es-tu amoureuse de lui?* Are you happy with this man? Are you in love? Are you truly happy to marry Henry Brooks?"

"Of course I am!" What a ridiculous question for her mother to ask. "I would not be marrying him otherwise."

"Are you convincing me or are you convincing yourself?" her mother responded, her eyes staring with quiet speculation at Lisette. "*Qu'est-ce que ce serait, hein? Quelle est ta réponse?* What would it be, eh? Which is it?"

"I don't need to convince anyone of anything. Honestly, Mother, you are acting as if you don't care for Henry or that you do not wish for me to marry him."

"It is true. I do not."

"Mother!" Lisette gasped, horrified at her mother's words. "You cannot mean that!"

"I do," Genevieve said in a calm and cool manner. "I do not wish for you to marry him. I never did wish it. You deserve better. You deserve a man you love. *Tu mérites d'aimer un homme.*"

"Henry is a good man!" she protested heatedly. "He loves me. We have known each other for years."

"I am aware of that, Lisette. I have watched you waiting for him. I have also watched your two sisters follow their hearts where you have bided your time and accepted what came along. I had hoped you might meet someone special while you waited so patiently for your Mr. Brooks and changed your mind. He is a nice man, my dear, I do not argue that point. He is just not for you. Do not marry him if you do not love him. *Rien de bien n'en ressortira.* Nothing good will come of it, *ma petite.* Do not settle for him as I did with your father. That would be a terrible mistake you will regret for the rest of your life. *Ce serait l'erreur que tu regretterais pour le restant de tes jours.*"

With no words for her mother's outburst, Lisette blinked back stinging tears. Never had her mother spoken so bluntly to her.

"I am being honest with you, Lisette. I do not wish for you to marry this man. *C'est l'entière vérité.* I had not said a word about it before because I did not believe this wedding would ever come to pass."

Lisette sat motionless, a bit stunned by this development.

Genevieve continued to speak plainly. "You should have allowed Lucien to give you a Season. With all the advantages you have now! Such a waste! *Quel dommage que tu ais perdu une pareille opportunité.* You have been handed opportunities your father could never give you. But no, you spurned making your debut for this simple solicitor. This Henry Brooks. You never gave yourself a chance to meet someone special, and you settled on the first man who came along."

Her stomach formed a tight knot, and still Lisette blinked back the tears. She did not wish to cry in front of her. "That is not true, Mother, and you know it."

Her mother sighed heavily. "You still have not said that you love him. That you are happy to marry him."

"Of course I am." Wasn't she? She thought of her aching desire to kiss Quinton Roxbury on the train yesterday and the cold disappointment that flooded her at the news of his upcoming nuptials. A confused pang of guilt washed over her.

"You do not seem happy, *ma chérie.* Do not marry him if you do not love him enough. Life is too short to waste by marrying the wrong man, my darling. I know the truth of that all too well. *S'il y a une chose à retenir . . . tire une leçon de mes erreurs!* Learn from my mistakes if nothing else."

A sudden knock at the front door drew their attention.

"Who could be calling on such a blustery afternoon?" Lisette asked, grateful for the timely interruption. She had had all she could take of this conversation. A deep breath helped to calm her, but still her mother's words spun around her like a spider's web and she could not brush them off.

"Mrs. Wheeler said she would stop by to see you and say hello. I told her you were coming," her mother explained, settling back into the divan, and placing the lavender pillow back over her eyes. "Fannie will get the door."

Lisette remained rooted to her chair, relieved that, for the time being, her mother seemed to have dropped the subject of her marriage to Henry.

What her mother thought about her feelings for Henry bothered her more than she cared to admit. It surprised her to realize that.

In spite of what anyone thought, she did love Henry. She had always loved Henry, for they knew each other as children and had been friends. His father used to bring him into the bookshop from time to time and he would play with her and her sisters. They started out as playmates but things between them changed as they grew older.

When she was sixteen, she had been helping in the bookshop with her father one afternoon. Henry had come in looking for law books and Lisette had been sent to fetch them. When she returned with the books, Henry was waiting for her, his warm smile melting her heart. She was drawn in by his good looks and quiet manner. He visited the store regularly when he knew Lisette would be there, and they spoke of their families and his interest in the law. Her sisters teased her relentlessly before Henry eventually gathered enough courage to ask her to a local dance, which was about the same time that Colette met Lucien.

It had all happened naturally and easily between Lisette and Henry. Very proper and calm. They just began spending time together. Henry's mother approved of her and encouraged the match. Henry had just always been there, a fixture in her life. With sandy hair and gray eyes. No, there had been nothing extraordinary about their courtship, unlike Colette and Lucien's tumultuous path to marriage. And there had been nothing outrageous to attribute to it like her sister Juliette's shipboard romance with the American, Captain Fleming.

She and Henry had simply met and knew they would get along well together.

And that was exactly how Lisette liked it. She didn't want all the attention and the fuss and heartache.

Still, it stung to suddenly discover that her mother did not approve of her choice of Henry as her husband after all these years.

Fannie entered the parlor, her round face beaming with excitement. "Miss Lisette, there's a gentleman here to see you. A very handsome gentleman by the name of Mr. Roxbury."

6

Heedless of the Wind and Weather

Quinton held his breath in anticipation. Would she see him? He half hoped she would turn him away and then he would be done with it. It was the height of foolishness for him to be at her door in the first place. He was marrying Emmeline Tarleton in a month. He had no business calling on the lovely Lisette Hamilton, especially when she had specifically dissuaded him from doing so.

Yet here he was. Standing in the front hall of her mother's house, after he spent half the morning tracking down her mother's address from the locals.

He simply could not help himself.

Lisette appeared in the hallway, her eyes glowing a dark green. Dressed in a fetching gown of deep burgundy that complemented her creamy complexion, she was even lovelier than he remembered. The urge to touch her was so strong he had to stop himself from reaching out and drawing her into his embrace.

"Why, Mr. Roxbury, I wasn't expecting to see you!" She looked a bit frantic, and there was a distinct edge to her voice. For his ears only, she whispered furiously, "What on earth are you doing here?"

He answered with deliberate loudness, so anyone could hear, "I was in the neighborhood and thought I would stop by and pay my respects to you and your family."

"Lisette!" an accented female voice called from the parlor. "You must invite your guest inside! *C'est le summum de l'impolitesse que de laisser un invité à la porte!*"

"What a nice surprise!" Lisette said with false enthusiasm through clenched teeth. "Won't you please come in and sit down? My mother and I were just having some tea."

Lisette's good manners required her to greet a guest, however unwanted, with grace and charm. There was a smile on her pretty face, but he could see the panic in her eyes. Her cheeks were flushed slightly, yet he sensed that she was excited to see him nonetheless. Happiness surged through him just at being near her.

He knew he should not have come, and it would be best simply to turn around and leave now, before things became more involved. Seeing her would only cause complications for himself. And most likely problems for her as well. But there was something about her that he could not resist and was what drew him to show up at her door this afternoon.

"It would be my pleasure to join you and your mother for tea." He returned a smile and followed her into the parlor.

It was a pleasant house, decorated tastefully and not overly stuffed with the fashionable knickknacks and trifles that filled the most stylish homes of the day. There was something simple and elegant about the little house that appealed to him. A cleanness of lines, an accentuation of empty space.

A woman with long gray hair reclined on a divan with a blanket covering her. She might have been a beauty once, but now that look was faded. She did not appear ill, just as

Lisette had predicted on the train yesterday. The woman was quite alert and eyed him with avid interest.

Lisette made the introductions. "Mother, may I present Mr. Quinton Roxbury. Mr. Roxbury, this is my mother, Mrs. Genevieve Hamilton."

"Good afternoon, Mrs. Hamilton," he began. "I hope I have not intruded on your visit with your daughter."

"Good afternoon, *monsieur*. You have not intruded at all. *Quel plaisir de partager la compagnie d'un bel homme.* It is an honor to have such a handsome gentleman visit us. Please be seated and join us. We shall have Fannie bring you some tea. I must admit I am most anxious to learn how you know my daughter."

Again, Quinton wondered what the hell he was doing there, about to be questioned by Lisette Hamilton's obviously not ailing mother. He took a seat on the sofa, and Lisette sat beside him. Just the nearness of her made him want to hold her in his arms and kiss her for hours. Her sweet scent wafted around him. This was the third time in three days he had seen her, and his desire for her had only increased. She gave him a nervous glance and then lowered her gaze to her lap.

"So, *Monsieur* Roxbury, tell me," Mrs. Hamilton began with excitement in her voice. "Do you live here in Brighton?"

"No, madam, I reside in London. I am here for a few days on business only. I'm staying at the Grand Hotel."

"*Oui, c'est un endroit magnifique.* Such a lovely hotel! Of course you would stay there, for it is the only place to be. Now, *monsieur*, to what do we owe the pleasure of your visit today?"

She spoke with a charming mixture of English and French, with an almost flirtatious quality. Although his first impression of her was one of fragility, he suddenly sensed a will of iron beneath the delicate surface of Mrs.

Hamilton. He imagined she must have led men on a merry chase when she was younger.

He cleared his throat before he began, thinking of an explanation for coming to their house that sounded more reasonable than his true motive.

"Your daughter and I met on the train to Brighton yesterday. Actually we first met by accident the day before that, as I was leaving Devon House. I had been there speaking to Lord Waverly about a special project I am involved in. While on the train, I explained my project to Miss Hamilton and she agreed to help persuade your son-in-law to aid my cause. I thought I would stop by to discuss a few more of the details with her."

Mrs. Hamilton's keen eyes darted from him to Lisette and back to him. She seemed quite amused about something. "Yes, I see."

"I also wished to inquire as to your health, Mrs. Hamilton, for your daughter mentioned that you were not well."

"That is most thoughtful and considerate of you. *Quel charmant gentilhomme!* Such a charming man! I am much recovered. Thank you very much. *Merci beaucoup.*" She favored him with a bright smile, full of health and vigor.

Quinton blinked. The woman unsettled him not a little.

"And you think Lisette can convince Lord Waverly to help you?" Mrs. Hamilton asked. "What is this project?"

"I am designing new houses outside the city to replace an area of tenement buildings in London, and I'm seeking contributors to raise the capital to begin. Lord Waverly was kind enough to express more than a polite interest in my plan."

"Why do you think my daughter would help you?"

"Because she agrees with what I am doing, and when I suggested speaking to Lord Waverly about it, Lisette said she would do so."

Mrs. Hamilton arched one elegant but faded eyebrow. "Did she now?"

Lisette looked up and nodded. "Yes, *Maman*. It's quite an extraordinary cause. Mr. Roxbury wants to build better housing for the poor. Think how it could change people's lives. You know as well as I that Lucien would want to be a part of such a noble endeavor."

"Yes, I imagine he would at that. *Mon gendre est un homme très généreux*. My son-in-law is a very generous man."

"Lord Waverly said he would consider my project and I thought Miss Hamilton could put in a good word for me in the meantime," Quinton added.

The older woman's eyes gleamed as if she knew a secret. "*Dites-moi la vérité, monsieur!* Now tell me the truth. So you are calling upon my daughter now for a purely selfish purpose?"

"Mother!" Lisette cried out.

"Not at all, Mrs. Hamilton!" Quinton protested politely. "The benefit is not for me. These houses will benefit dozens of poor families, allowing them to live better and more productive lives. It improves the community for all of us in turn."

Genevieve Hamilton's light laughter surprised him. "*Oui!* Yes, of course they will. That is not what I meant. *Je vois à travers toute ce*. I see through your subtle pretense. I think you are here not for your little houses at all, *Monsieur* Roxbury, but because you needed an excuse to see my daughter again."

Once more Lisette released a cry of embarrassment. "Mother! Please!"

Stunned by the turn of the conversation, Quinton paused before responding, afraid of digging himself in deeper. Although he had to admit the old woman was correct in her assessment of him and he had to give her credit. The only reason he was there was to see Lisette. "Yes, that is an added benefit. Your daughter is quite lovely."

"I do appreciate when a man is honest. *Ma fille est très belle, n'est-ce pas?* My daughter is beautiful, is she not?" Mrs. Hamilton smiled in satisfaction. "Well, then, you have no desire to sit here chatting with me, do you, when you came to see Lisette? *Je suis aujourd'hui une vieille femme, et vous avez besoin d'être ensemble, seuls. Allez-y.* I am an old woman. You two young people need time to be alone together. Go! Go take my daughter for a walk. The fresh sea air will do you both good after being in the city."

It was windy and cloudy with the threat of snow, not at all a day conducive to being out-of-doors. No one in his right mind would venture out on a day like today for a leisurely stroll. He had almost not come on the visit in the first place, since the weather was so forbidding, but he had decided to risk it anyway.

Incredulous at Mrs. Hamilton's startling suggestion, Quinton turned to Lisette, whose mouth was wide open with shock, mirroring his own. "Would you care to walk on the beach with me, Miss Hamilton?"

"I would love to," Lisette said in rapid response and rose to her feet, desperate to be away from her mother. "It will just be a moment for me to get my things."

As Lisette hurried from the room, Mrs. Hamilton watched her leave with a satisfied expression on her face. Like the cat that ate the canary, she grinned at Quinton. "It has been a pleasure to meet you, *Monsieur* Roxbury. Please do join us for supper this evening?"

Quinton and Lisette walked together from the house and instinctively headed away from the more populated area of the shore. The wind whipped around them and gray clouds hung heavy and low in the sky. Gulls screeched over the deserted beach and the sound of rough surf crashed around them. They said not a word to each other until they reached the damp sand.

"Are you angry with me, Miss Hamilton?" he finally asked her.

"Why would I be angry with you?" Lisette asked a bit caustically. "Because you called upon me when I expressly asked you not to?"

He gave a rueful smile. "Yes."

"Yes, I am quite angry," she blurted out. "I do not think this is a good idea."

"Yet you came out with me anyway." He had noted that fact, much to his delight.

"Yes," she admitted with reluctance. "But I did not want to."

Quinton had his doubts about that. He asked the question that had been puzzling him. "Why was your mother so determined to send us off alone together?"

Lisette grimaced. "She does not know that you are to be married shortly. An important fact that you neglected to mention to her, by the way."

He had not mentioned his wedding because he had not thought of Emmeline at all. In fact, he didn't wish to be thinking of her now. "But surely she knows that *you* are engaged?"

"Of course she does!"

It seemed odd to Quinton that Mrs. Hamilton should conspire to have her daughter spend time alone with another man when she was already engaged. Unless . . .

He paused and placed his hand on Lisette's arm, causing her to stop walking as well. She looked up at him, her pretty face surrounded by the white ermine that trimmed the hood of her black cape. The sweetness in the curve of her cheeks and the honesty in her green eyes, which were clearly upset with him now, made his heart constrict in a way it never had before.

"Your mother does not wish for you to marry him, does she?"

She pulled her arm from his grip and turned away from him.

It was true! It had to be, for she did not deny it. This was a very interesting development. Lisette's mother did not wish for her daughter to marry her fiancé. And in fact, preferred Quinton over the other man, or so it seemed from her actions this afternoon. His male vanity could not help being flattered, and he experienced a surge of happiness. Still, the situation called for caution.

Lisette suddenly spun back around to face him, her expression one of outrage.

"Listen to me, Mr. Roxbury. I do not wish for you to call on me again. In fact, I do not wish to be in your presence again while I'm in Brighton. I am engaged to be married and in no position to be out walking with you alone. No matter what my mother thinks!"

She looked unbearably lovely with her fair skin colored pink from the wind, her wild green eyes filled with ire, and tendrils of her rich auburn hair escaping from her fur-lined hood. He stepped closer to her as if magnetized, staring at her full lips.

She stood her ground, placing her hands on her hips. "Your visit today was inappropriate in every respect, especially when I told you quite clearly on the train that I did not wish to see you. People will get the wrong idea and think that we have feelings for each other—oh!"

Quinton, unable to control himself any longer, pulled Lisette into his arms and covered her mouth with his. Instantly he knew he had made a dreadful, irrevocable mistake but by then it was too late. Too late to stop. He could do nothing but lose himself in the honeyed sweetness of her mouth. Damn, but no woman had ever had this effect on him. He knew Lisette felt it, too, for she did not resist him in the least. She did not pull away. She did not slap him in outrage as she very well should. No, this incredible and beautiful woman kissed him right back, her arms reaching up around his neck, standing on her tiptoes to reach him, her mouth opening to him in willing eagerness. His heart pounding like thunder in his chest, he slipped his tongue into the heated warmth of her mouth and drew her tightly against him.

Quinton had kissed his share of women over the years. He was a well-to-do gentleman from a prominent family, and it was within his rights to do so. Yet none of the experienced beauties he had bedded had ever affected him quite the way Lisette Hamilton did at this very moment.

He wanted her more than he had ever wanted anything in his whole life.

It made no sense whatsoever. And scared the wits out of him.

He barely knew her. He had met her only the day before yesterday and here he was kissing her on a windswept beach. It was wrong. So terribly wrong for them to be acting this way when they were both promised to others. He did not think of Emmeline Tarleton. He did not think of the man who had already asked for Lisette's hand.

He knew with every fiber of his being that kissing Lisette this way was unconscionable and could only lead to dire consequences for one or both of them.

Yet he could not resist the feeling of rightness, of perfection, with her. He could not resist the feel of her body pressed intimately against his. He could not resist her soft lips and daring little tongue, which swirled within his own mouth. He could easily drown in the intoxicating fragrance of her being and not care if he ever saw the light of day again. He did not feel the chilly sea wind blowing around him, for he held in his arms all the warmth of a summer day in the heavenly form of Lisette Hamilton.

Her passionate response pleased him, and he held her tightly against his chest as she clung to him in wild abandon. They kissed as if they were not out in full view of anyone who happened to pass by. And if someone did happen to venture out on such an uninviting day and spied their scandalous embrace, they did not care. So lost in the sensations of their kiss, they did not even notice the increased darkening of the leaden sky.

Ignoring the cold wind that buffeted them, Quinton instinctively sought the heat between them, his arms wrapped firmly around her small body. He shielded her from the brunt of the wind. She was so small and slender, he could scoop her up in his arms without the slightest effort. And the thought of doing just that and carrying her to his warm bed consumed him. Making love to this woman would be sheer pleasure and nothing less.

He could not get enough of kissing her. And it scared him not to know if he ever would.

7

A Thrill of Hope

Swirling snowflakes scattered on the wind around them, covering the sand in a dusting of white.

Lisette could not have cared less about the snow. With Quinton Roxbury's strong arms wrapped around her, she had the oddest sensation that nothing could harm her. And nothing else mattered except this wild, extraordinary kiss. She was lost in the feel of his mouth on hers, the all-consuming heat. The driving need to feel him left her breathless.

This kiss made her forget that she was engaged. Made her forget Henry Brooks. Made her forget that she was standing on a beach in full public view. Made her forget that Quinton had a fiancée. His mouth on hers was her entire focus.

They finally broke free of each other's embrace and stared into each other's eyes, trying to regain their breath. Quinton held her hands in his, the wind and snow swirling about them.

It was then that Lisette remembered all that she had

forgotten just a moment ago. Henry. Her engagement. Quinton's upcoming wedding.

"What are we doing?" she whispered breathlessly.

He shook his head. "I don't know." He pressed his forehead against hers. "I don't know."

Good heavens but she wanted him to kiss her again. Wanted him to kiss her all night long. The intensity of this newfound desire terrified her. "You need to stay away from me."

"I know." He brushed his lips against her cheek. "You're right."

The warmth of his breath sent shivers of delight through her entire body. Lisette swayed and closed her eyes, unable to bear the look of longing in his eyes for she was sure it mirrored her own. Quinton held her closer, supporting her weakened state, and for that she was most grateful. She didn't trust her own legs to hold her. She leaned her head against his broad chest. He was so warm and strong and solid and smelled of bayberry. She could stay in his arms this way forever and not mind in the least. He sheltered her from the worst of the cold wind and the snow that sprinkled down on them but did nothing to cool their passion for each other.

His mouth came down over hers yet again. She did not resist in the least. No. Lisette leaned into him, eager for the feel of his mouth upon hers, longing to meet his tongue with her own. Giddy with the hot, swirling emotions that swept through her entire body, she was helpless to do anything else in the face of his desire for her. His kiss destroyed her resolve, her will to say no. His kiss gave her everything she ever wanted.

They clung to each other, embracing tightly, seeking the heat that burned between them. The passion only increased with each passing minute. They might have been there for hours, for time had lost all meaning. She forgot that she was on a cold and deserted beach. Forgot that she was promised to another. All that mattered was her uncontrollable hunger for this man. The wild desire to be with him in any way she could. Never had she felt this reckless, urgent need to be kissed, to be touched by another human being. And heaven help her, but she wanted more, needed more, from this man. From him. Only him.

Quinton.

He broke away from her and she almost cried out from the loss.

"Lisette." He breathed her name against her ear and she thought she would faint from the pleasure of it.

She tilted her face up to look at him. His blue eyes were filled with a mixture of passion and pain, and she suddenly felt the urge to cry. Her kiss-swollen lips trembled. He caressed them with his gloved fingers, touching her so delicately. Surprising herself, she pressed a kiss onto his leather-covered hand, wishing she could take his bare fingers into her mouth.

Good God! Had she truly thought of doing something so scandalous?

Of course she had allowed Henry to kiss her over the years. They had been sweet, chaste kisses, so brief she could hardly recall them now. But never had she felt this way. Reckless. Hot. Wild. Never. Not once. Never had she been awash with desire for Henry to kiss her as she was with Quinton Roxbury this very minute. Never had she wanted Henry to hold her and never let her go.

She suppressed the sob that tore at her throat.

"Let me go." Her words were barely above a whisper, because deep down she did not mean them. Not with any force anyway.

He did not release her, but held her tightly against him, and she was glad of it. Once again she rested her head upon his broad chest, soaking up his warmth. They stood for some time just holding each other, unwilling to move and break the spell they were under.

What had just happened between them? For it was more than merely a kiss. Kissing Quinton had changed her, awakened something within her she didn't even know existed. Lisette had never felt so uncertain of herself or was so unsure of her own emotions. Confusion about her very life welled within her. Quinton had done something to her.

Leaning down, Quinton pressed a soft kiss to her cheek before withdrawing from their embrace. His arms fell to his sides as he took a step back. "Forgive me, Miss Hamilton."

The chill that raced through her body caused her teeth to chatter. She breathed in deeply and the icy air filled her lungs, saturating her with a chilling dose of reality. She nodded wordlessly at him for there was too much to say.

Finally Lisette and Quinton moved with reluctant steps from the shore, neither of them in a hurry to face the consequences and obligations that awaited them once they returned to the house. He reached out and took her hand in his, and she almost wept at the sweetness of the gesture. The silence weighed heavily between them.

The sun had set behind the steel gray clouds, and darkness began to obscure their pathway home. The snow flurries turned to a sleety rain, and they reached the gate to her mother's house just as the worst of the storm that had threatened all day finally let loose. Quinton pulled her by the hand and they began to run, but they were soaked by the time they arrived at the doorstep.

"My goodness! Just look at the two of you!" Fannie exclaimed in dismay as they stood dripping in the hallway. "A couple of drowned rats you are! Miss Lisette, you get yourself upstairs and out of those wet clothes this instant. And no, don't think to argue with me, miss. Upstairs with you now. And Mr. Roxbury, you come and dry yourself by the fire."

Quinton saw Lisette freeze in place.

"Thank you, but I really must be on my way," Quinton protested affably. "A little water won't hurt me."

"Nonsense! Mrs. Hamilton already told me you are staying for supper. I've a delicious roast beef and some potatoes that will warm you right up. It's just about ready. You'd be a blamed fool to go back out in that nasty storm anyhow. Now give me your coat, sir, and leave those wet shoes of yours by the door." She held out her hand for his coat.

Quinton knew he should leave, and more important, he knew that Lisette wished for him to leave. But he could not refuse without being unforgivably rude. He *had* already agreed to stay for supper. Wouldn't leaving abruptly cause more suspicion than his staying? And the roast beef smelled delicious. His rumbling stomach attested to the fact that he was more than a little hungry. And there *was* a storm outside. He would simply have a fortifying meal and be on his way after the worst of the weather subsided.

He would not see Lisette again after tonight. Besides, he felt like a cad for the way he just acted, and he could not leave her without making amends of some sort. He could not let this be the end of things. Not after that extraordinary kiss . . .

He slowly removed his coat and hat, glancing at Lisette. She shook her head ever so slightly to discourage him. He gave his coat to Fannie. "Thank you."

"That's it," Fannie praised him for agreeing to stay, the expression on her round face one of triumph. "Now, Miss Lisette, get yourself upstairs and change like I told you. I'll take care of your gentleman right proper, don't you worry."

There was nothing for Lisette to do. "I shall be back down shortly," she mumbled before fleeing up the stairs.

Meanwhile, Quinton followed Fannie into the parlor. He raised his brows at the pretty table set for two in front of the blazing fire. It was quite the romantic setting and more than a bit odd given the circumstances. However, he stood gratefully before the mantel, absorbing the blessed warmth emanating from the fire, and accepted the thick towel Fannie handed him to dry off.

"Mrs. Hamilton isn't feeling so well this evening, so it will just be you and Miss Lisette for supper."

After seeing the table set for two, he was not surprised by this news. Nor did he imagine that Fannie just gave him a sly little wink.

"I'll bring in the food soon enough. Now you just make yourself at home, Mr. Roxbury," she instructed as she bustled about the room. "There's some nice red wine in the decanter there on the table."

"Thank you." He watched the wide-girthed woman waddle from the room and wondered at the matchmaking effort that was most definitely being executed this evening. What *was* Mrs. Hamilton thinking? She was practically throwing her engaged daughter at him! It made no sense. Was the man betrothed to Lisette such a poor choice for a husband that her mother saw fit to try to sabotage their engagement? For surely he had not misinterpreted the intimate overtones of the dinner table.

Intrigued by the play of events, he remained by the fire as his clothing began to dry out and warm up. Now he must face the beautiful Lisette, whom he had clearly wronged earlier with their kiss on the beach.

But Christ above, it was an amazing kiss!

Lisette had excited him like no woman had ever had. She was passionate and sensual and willing. Oh, so willing. He had had to use all his strength and resolve to end their embrace, reminding himself that Lisette was not the type of woman a man trifled with. Tonight he would make his apologies to her and then bid her farewell, for no good could come of their relationship at this point. It was too dangerous. For both of them.

He needed to stay away, far away, from Lisette Hamilton.

He was marrying Emmeline just after New Year's. He could not be kissing a woman like Lisette. It would only ruin his carefully laid plans for the future. He needed to marry Lady Emmeline Tarleton, even if she did not make his blood race the way Lisette had that afternoon.

Quinton glanced up as he heard Lisette coming down the stairs. She paused in the doorway and seemed hesitant to enter the parlor, her green eyes wide at the intimate scene. She had changed into a simple gown of midnight blue that hugged her figure perfectly, and she'd combed her windswept hair into a neat knot atop her head. In the glow of the firelight she looked stunning. His heart pounded at the sight of her.

Sensing her unease, he moved to her side, taking her small hand in his. The feel of her warm skin against his sent a jolt of desire through him. With a great force of will, he guided her to the table.

"I am so embarrassed," she confessed in an anguished whisper. "I don't know what is going on here."

He squeezed her hand reassuringly and gave her an encouraging smile. "It seems your mother wishes for us to dine alone together."

Lisette cringed and shook her head in disbelief. "I could just die of mortification."

"Please don't die on me," he said, attempting to lighten her mood with a bit of humor. He gave her hand another comforting squeeze. "It will be fine. We need to talk in any case. Now sit down and take a breath." He urged her to the chair and then took his own seat.

She glanced across the table at him, almost shyly. "Thank you, Mr. Roxbury, for being so understanding about all this."

"The funny thing is, I don't mind, Miss Hamilton." He could not help smiling at her as he realized he spoke the complete truth. "I don't mind at all."

Fannie bustled in carrying a tray and began serving them a hearty feast. The scent of fresh biscuits and succulent roast beef made Quinton's mouth water.

"If either of you need anything else, just let me know." She gave them an elaborate wink.

"That will be all, Fannie." Lisette's voice had a distinct edge to it. "Thank you."

Fannie shuffled from the room with a giggle.

Without a word, Quinton poured them each a glass of red wine. He raised his glass to her and she did so as well. "To good friends," he said pointedly, taking a sip.

She shot him a rueful glance before drinking her wine.

He picked up his fork. "You know, Miss Hamilton, I'm beginning to think you are not betrothed at all. That you just said so to me on the train to discourage me."

Lisette set her glass upon the table with such force wine sloshed over the rim, staining the delicate white lace a dark red. "I am getting married!"

He gave a skeptical chuckle. "Your family doesn't seem to think so."

"My mother . . ." Lisette began to explain and then stopped abruptly, closing her mouth. She sighed and began again. "Let me be clear with you, Mr. Roxbury. Henry Brooks is a wonderful man, a good man, and he loves me. He and I have known each other since we were children, and we have been planning to marry for years. We are quite devoted to each other. My entire family knows this and has known of our intentions to wed. For some reason I cannot fathom, my mother has suddenly taken it into her head that I do not love Henry and should not marry him, which explains but does not excuse her behavior with you and me this evening"—she waved her hand helplessly to indicate the intimate supper—"and all of this."

"I see," Quinton said. So his name was Henry Brooks. He wondered if the man was good enough for Lisette and found himself irrationally siding with Mrs. Hamilton. He ignored the sudden flash of jealousy at the thought of this "Henry" kissing Lisette the way he had just kissed her. Had she ever kissed Henry the way she had kissed Quinton with such passion? He cleared his throat. "If you and your fiancé both wish it, why the long delay in marrying?"

"Henry . . ." She paused as if considering her words with great care. "Henry is not a wealthy man, and he wanted to make sure that he could support me properly before we married. He's been working very hard at his uncle's law practice, but now he will take over the business completely. He told me yesterday before I left that we can plan for a June wedding."

Quinton stabbed the roast beef with his fork. "Perhaps it's best if we talk about something else."

She lowered her eyes. "Fine."

"Fine," he echoed. The last thing he wanted to hear about was her fiancé.

An awkward silence descended upon them. Lisette took a rather large sip of wine, and Quinton followed suit. In fact, he poured himself another glass.

"I know next to nothing about you, Mr. Roxbury," Lisette began, "except that you are an architect who is getting married in January."

He refrained from adding that she knew how he kissed and how it felt to be in his arms. And that he wanted to kiss her for days and days on end. She knew that much about him but he thought it wiser to keep that to himself.

Instead he gave her an agreeable smile. "There is nothing

unusual to report. I'm the youngest son of an earl. I had a traditional upbringing and a happy enough childhood—nannies and tutors, roughhousing with my three brothers and driving our mother crazy. When my father died, my brother John inherited the title of the Earl of Kingston and the estate. My brother George is now a good reverend, and Edward joined up with a regiment and is off in India. There's not much left for a fourth son, so I had to make my own place in the world. I took my love of playing with blocks as a child and learned how to design and construct houses and buildings."

"And a younger son must marry well, must he not?" she asked so softly he barely heard her.

"Yes." The awkwardness he felt at discussing his fiancée with Lisette astounded him. At the moment he had no desire even to think of Emmeline Tarleton or his reasons for marrying her, the least of which was financial. His motives for marriage with the daughter of the Duke of Wentworth had nothing to do with Lisette. In fact, nothing in his life had anything to do with Lisette Hamilton. Which brought him back to the reason why he was here in the first place, and just what the hell did he feel for Lisette Hamilton exactly?

Desire, of course. She was a very beautiful woman. Any red-blooded male would be crazy not to desire her. But it was more than that. She was intelligent and independent, yet there was an innate sweetness in her nature, an innocence, that called to him. No woman, and he'd had many, had ever had this effect on him before, and it was most disconcerting.

Lisette said, "I see."

"What do you see?" He hoped she hadn't seen through to his thoughts.

She rephrased her comment, her luscious mouth a tight line. "I think I understand you a bit more now."

Quinton gazed at her intently. He doubted she understood how much he wanted her. How much he longed to hold her again. Or how much he needed to stay away from her or all his plans for the future would be ruined. Lisette Hamilton was the most dangerous woman he had ever met.

"Good." He cleared his throat and picked up his fork once more, making an effort to eat again. "Yes, I will be married just after New Year's." He said that more for his benefit than for hers.

"That is only a few weeks away."

If he was not mistaken, there was a hint of panic in her voice. He was oddly touched by that. "Yes, it is," he agreed.

"And you are quite happy to marry her?"

"In spite of the way I acted with you earlier, yes, I am. She will make a suitable wife."

Her voice lowered to a fierce whisper. "And despite appearances to the contrary on the beach with you today, I am quite content with my decision to marry Henry."

"Fair enough." He put down his fork and looked directly into her eyes. "Speaking of our behavior on the beach, I don't know that I can apologize profusely enough for taking such liberties with you, Miss Hamilton. It was unforgivable."

"I forgive you, Mr. Roxbury. It is my own actions that I find utterly unforgivable." Her lips trembled and the look on her face caused his gut to clench in remorse. The urge to take her in his arms and comfort her overwhelmed him.

He felt awful about what happened. But did he regret kissing her? No. How could he regret the most passionate encounter of his life? "No, it was all my fault. I was responsible. You did nothing untoward. Please do not blame yourself."

"It can never happen again," she murmured.

"Of course not," he agreed readily.

She nodded and stared at her plate. He noted she had not eaten a bite all evening.

He added for emphasis, "So it is agreed that we shall not kiss again."

Her head jerked up. "Shh!" she hissed through clenched teeth.

He smiled indulgently at her. If her mother or the impertinent Fannie had been eavesdropping on them at all that evening, they would have correctly surmised by the conversation that a kiss had happened between them, but Lisette did not want him to say the word aloud!

"I apologize, Miss Hamilton," he whispered for her benefit.

"Please do not make light of this. It is not a laughing matter to me."

The pained expression on her sweet face chastened his play at humor. "You are right. Forgive me."

They finished the remainder of their meal in strained silence, neither of them referencing their passionate kiss on the beach or their upcoming weddings or daring to speak at all. For there was nothing more to say. Finally, Quinton rose from his seat.

"Thank you for a lovely evening, Miss Hamilton, but I should be getting back to the hotel now. The worst of the storm seems to have passed. Please give my kind regards to your mother for me."

"I will and you are most welcome." She remained in her chair. "Good night, Mr. Roxbury."

It suddenly occurred to him that he would not see her again, nor could he think of an instance when he would have an occasion to see her again. Disappointment washed over him at the prospect. More than likely it was for the best that they would not see each other. He should not have even come to visit her today as it was. That was quite clear.

Still he spoke his wish aloud to her. "I hope to have the pleasure of your company again sometime."

"I wish you much happiness in your marriage."

He startled a bit at her words. "I wish you the best in yours as well."

"Good night."

He wanted to kiss her good-bye. He wanted to touch her hand. Something. Anything. He looked at her as she sat with her head bent, the graceful curve of her neck appearing so fragile and delicate in the firelight. He wished he knew what she was thinking, what she wanted. "Good night, Miss Hamilton."

Her eyes would not meet his when he glanced at her before heading toward the front door, and for that he was grateful because he did not think he could bear the look of longing he was sure he would see within them.

8

Here We Come A-Wandering

Thursday, December 4, 1873

Lisette could barely contain her outrage the next morning. "How could you do such a thing, Mother?"

"*Mon dieu! Je n'ai rien fait de mal!* I did nothing wrong!" Genevieve protested her innocence with wide eyes, her hands pressed upon her chest. "You are making a fuss over nothing! I did nothing but suggest a little walk and invite a handsome young man to supper in my own home. Such a fuss you are making! It is not my fault I was too ill to join you both."

"There was nothing wrong with you! You are not ill! You deliberately left us alone!"

"He is a very nice gentleman, that Quinton Roxbury. Very handsome. *Un homme très beau.* Do you not agree?"

"That is beside the point. You know exactly what you were doing. You were encouraging him, *Maman*. But I should inform you that he is to be married next month."

Her mother gave a careless little shrug. "*Qu'est-ce qu'il en ressort?* What of it?"

"What of it? What of it?" Lisette echoed in disbelief.

"He is not married yet, is he?" Her mother eyed her knowingly. *"Tout est juste en amour comme à la guerre, n'est-ce pas?* All is fair in love and war, eh?"

"For all intents and purposes he is a married man! We are both betrothed to others and for you to be scheming to have us alone together . . . Oh, I cannot discuss this with you another moment!" Lisette's blood boiled at the notion of her mother's blatant interference.

"You are blind. *Ne sois pas idiote.* Do not be a stupid little fool. You feel something for him and he feels something for you, Lisette. *C'est la vérité.* It is the truth. Do not deny it. I felt it. I saw it with my own eyes here in this very room."

"You saw no such thing!" Lisette cried out in protest, shame washing over her. Her mother could see how she and Quinton felt about each other? It was unthinkable. "And I have had quite enough of this discussion." Lisette hurried from the room, unable to bear listening to her mother's outrageous words another minute.

"Lisette!" her mother called to her. *"Come back! Ne t'échappe pas comme cela! Reviens içi!* Do not run off like that! Come back here!"

Ignoring the pleas coming from the other room, Lisette pulled her cape and muff from the tall coatrack standing in the hallway. She grabbed her reticule, too.

"Where are you off to in such a hurry?" Fannie questioned as Lisette opened the front door and a rush of cold air blew in.

"I'm going into town," Lisette answered through clenched teeth.

"To meet that nice Mr. Roxbury?" Fannie said with a hopeful gleam in her eyes.

"No. I am not! I am going alone! And I might just go back to London!" Lisette fled from the house, anger surging within her veins. Her own mother was conspiring against her. And it seemed as if even Fannie was, too.

As she marched with angry steps along the path to town, she wondered what was so wrong with her marrying Henry Brooks all of a sudden? Why did no one believe that she loved him? It made no sense. There had been an understanding between them for years. Why should her mother be against her on this? It wasn't that she disliked Henry, she insisted, it was simply that she didn't believe he was the proper person for her. And how would her mother know who was right for her? Her mother, who barely thought of anyone but herself! How would she even know what was in Lisette's heart? Honestly! The thought of it all made her quite irate. She knew her mother loved her and only wanted the best for her, but still . . .

How could she not understand? Henry was a good man.

A good man who would be crushed to learn that she had been kissing another man.

Especially when Henry had never kissed her that way.

Oh, such kisses! Lisette had barely slept last night for reliving them. Over and over again. The pure excitement of it raced through her. The feel of Quinton's hot mouth on hers, his strong arms tight around her body, his warm breath on her cheek. Never had she felt such sensations. Hot, surging passions . . .

She should be mortified by her actions. She knew how wrong they were. Yet the strange part was that being with Quinton did not feel the slightest bit wrong. In fact, it felt very right. She seemed made to fit perfectly in his arms. And she had wanted to stay there more than anything in the world.

Enough! She had thought enough about the man's extraordinary kisses. They'd said good-bye last night and it was over. They would not see each other again. It was for the best. She simply had to put him out of her mind. And out of her mother's!

The fresh sea air and brisk December sunshine did much to calm her down. Yesterday's storm had left the sky crystal clear, and the sun had melted any remaining snow and ice. It was a gorgeous, if cold, day, and by the time she reached the main part of town, her spirits had lifted a little and her pace had slowed.

As she walked by the shop windows of the popular resort town, she glanced idly at the pretty things arranged within. As she passed a charming toy shop, she decided to begin buying a few Christmas gifts. Inside, she found the most adorable toy train for Phillip, carved out of wood with wheels that spun and a bright red caboose. He would love it!

Feeling a bit more cheerful after her impulsive purchase for her nephew, she next entered an interesting curio shop. The interior was overly crowded with every object imaginable, from old furniture to ornate vases to jewelry and feathered hats. There was an endless supply of books, dishes, toys, and even an ancient suit of armor in the corner.

The elderly shopkeeper gave her a lopsided grin, his left eye covered by a patch. "Good day, miss. How can I help you?"

"May I please look around the shop for a bit?" she asked. The craggy-faced man had to be eighty if he were a day.

"Look to your heart's content, my dear." He waved his gnarled hand in a gesture of welcome. "If you need any help, just whistle."

She smiled at his odd suggestion and said, "Thank you."

As Lisette wandered her way through the maze of merchandise, she realized the store was much larger than she'd first thought. She must have spent a good half hour gazing at the shelves and tables crammed with all kinds of objects, old and new. A lovely writing set caught her eye. Made from mahogany with brass fixtures, the lid opened to reveal a writing slope and black felt-lined compartments to hold papers and ink and writing implements. It would be perfect for Paulette. Her sister loved anything to do with writing. She next saw a pretty jewelry box delicately carved out of wood. Looking inside, she was surprised to see a silver locket. Not one usually drawn to jewelry, she could not help picking it up.

There was an elaborate *L* inscribed on the front of the oval-shaped locket. Funny that it should have her first initial on it. It was a bit tarnished, but a little polishing would brighten it right up. Carefully she popped the locket open and to her delight found it was not a typical locket. This one was designed in such a way as to unfold four distinct sections to hold miniature portraits. She immediately thought of buying it for herself to keep images of her four sisters close to her heart. Lisette never bought herself anything frivolous but this piece pulled at her heartstrings. It seemed made just for her, and even engraved with an *L*. She held it in her hand and carefully opened and closed the four minipanels, which were so cleverly designed. She loved it!

"Have you found something special you like, Miss Hamilton?"

Startled, Lisette spun around at the sound of the familiar voice behind her. "Mr. Roxbury!"

"I did not mean to catch you unaware," he apologized. "I was merely browsing and here you are!"

She smiled in spite of herself. He was so handsome and looked pleased to see her. After last night she had not expected to meet him again. "This is a surprise."

"We do have a tendency to run into each other unexpectedly, do we not?"

"Yes, we do." Lisette laughed in spite of herself, thinking this was the third time they'd met by chance in the last four days. It was quite extraordinary really.

He gestured to her package that contained the toy train for Phillip. "I see you've been doing some shopping."

"Yes. I just bought a Christmas gift for my nephew."

"And this?" He indicated the locket she held in her hand. "Who is this for?"

"I think it is for me," she explained as she showed him how it worked, relieved to have something safe to talk about. "I can put miniatures of my four sisters inside. It is even inscribed with an *L*."

He grinned and nodded in agreement. "It's perfect for you."

"Yes, that's what I thought. What are you shopping for?"

"I'm not shopping at all, I must confess. I have an appointment with Lord Eaton at his office across the street, but he has been delayed. I'm merely passing time. The shop looked interesting so I came in out of the cold to wait. I left word with his secretary that I'd be here."

Oh, he looked so incredibly fine. His handsomely sculpted face, aquiline nose, and strong jaw. A hint of a teasing smile around his mouth. His lips, so full and firm, had kissed her so passionately yesterday she thought she would faint. The air was strangely charged between them. It was true. They felt something for each other, just as her mother said. Lisette should flee from him before she did something she would regret again. Instead she made an attempt at conversation. Anything to keep from entertaining thoughts of kissing him! "Is this appointment regarding your business? Building houses?"

"Yes, I'm designing a new house for Lord Eaton here in Brighton. Perhaps someday I can design a house for you."

At first the idea pleased her, but then she realized it would be a house that she would be living in with Henry

Brooks. Her husband. Somehow she did not wish to live with another man in a house that Quinton had designed for her. Lisette shook herself at the thought. The conversation had gone far enough. It was not wise to tarry any longer with him. Nothing at all good could come of it. Yesterday on the beach was proof enough of that.

"Yes, well, I must be on my way now. It was lovely seeing you again. Good day, Mr. Roxbury." She moved to step past him.

"Wait."

She paused at his command and glanced up at him in expectation. He looked straight into her eyes and her mouth went dry. Heaven help her.

"I was not expecting to meet you today," he said, "but I cannot deny the pleasure I feel at seeing you again."

"Please do not say such things to me." She lowered her glance.

"I know I haven't the right, yet I cannot seem to help myself when I am in your presence."

"What do you expect me to say?" she whispered in a soft tone, afraid to meet his eyes again for fear of losing herself in their endless blue depths.

"I don't know. I don't know what to say either."

"I must go."

Once again she moved to pass him but Quinton reached out and took her hand in his and she dropped the locket on the cluttered table. He pulled her close against his body. The male scent of him washed over her, causing her to tremble.

"We should say good-bye . . ." she began.

Quinton whispered in her ear, "Lisette, after yesterday I . . . You are very special to me. I know you have no reason to trust me, but if you ever need anything, please know that I would do anything in my power to help you."

She looked up at him in confusion. His words made no

sense. She was special to him? He would do anything to help her? Help her do what?

With a deliberate slowness he leaned in closer and she had the wild sensation that he was about to kiss her.

And, God help her, she was going to let him. She wanted one more kiss from this man. And then never again. She would return to London and Henry and never think of him again. But for right now, for just this moment, she would have one last kiss from this man who made her heart race so wildly with an unknown need.

"Lisette," he murmured low, his lips so close to hers she could almost taste them.

The sound of her name on his lips thrilled her, and she trembled in anticipation, waiting for him to kiss her. Resisting the urge to lean up on her tiptoes to further the kiss, she stood perfectly still and held her breath. She waited for his warm lips to cover hers, as she knew they would. Slowly she closed her eyes in dreamy expectation.

"Mr. Roxbury, there you are!"

As if struck by red-hot pokers, Quinton and Lisette jumped apart from each other in startled surprise.

Quinton turned to face the female who called to him. He cleared his throat. "Miss Eaton."

A young woman with pale blond hair and a very fashionable hat with a long peacock feather eyed them most suspiciously. Beside her was another young lady, who looked even more disdainful than the first.

"Mr. Roxbury, our father sent us to find you and bring you to his office now," Miss Eaton stated, her sharp eyes darting between Lisette and Quinton, assessing the situation with a calculated glance.

Lisette felt her cheeks burn and wished the ground would swallow her up whole. Oh, to be caught at such a moment! It was humiliating. The woman must have known they were about to kiss each other.

"Thank you," Quinton said with an even calmness that impressed Lisette. "May I present Miss Lisette Hamilton, a dear friend of mine who is visiting Brighton this week. Miss Hamilton, this is Miss Penelope Eaton and her sister, Miss Priscilla Eaton. I am designing their father's new house here in Brighton."

"Miss Hamilton," Penelope Eaton said through tight lips.

"Miss Hamilton," Priscilla echoed with a definite frown on her face.

Lisette did not imagine that the two women looked at her with a touch of scorn and disapproval. "It is a pleasure to meet you both," Lisette murmured in wooden response.

The awkwardness could not be denied as they stood staring at each other.

Unable to bear the tension another minute, Lisette clutched her package with the toy train. The locket and writing set, everything else she had intended to buy, could wait. "I am so sorry to rush off, but I was just on my way out. Good afternoon, Mr. Roxbury. I wish you the best of luck with your venture and I promise to speak to my brother-in-law on your behalf. Misses Eaton, good day to you both."

She avoided his eyes as she hurried past the two scowling sisters and left the shop as quickly as she could, grateful for the cold blast of air that stung her flushed cheeks when she stepped outside. With her boots clicking furiously on the cobblestones, she made her way home without looking back at the curio shop. All the joy was gone from her little Christmas shopping spree, replaced by humiliation and shame at being found in such a compromising position with a man she barely knew. She was almost a married woman and he was as good as married! *Never again*, she vowed to herself as she stared at the waves crashing on the shore, never again would she let herself be seduced by Quinton Roxbury's sky blue eyes and charming smile.

She would not think of him ever again.

She finally reached her mother's home with a great sense of relief, forgetting that just hours earlier she had fled from her mother for throwing her into Quinton Roxbury's path. Now she sought sanctuary inside the cottage. She had no idea if he intended to seek her out again, but for the remainder of her stay in Brighton, Lisette dared not venture from her mother's house.

She could not risk running into Quinton Roxbury one more time.

9

When We Were Gone Astray

Friday, December 5, 1873

Quinton Roxbury tossed his coat and hat upon the rose-patterned sofa and poured himself a drink from the well-stocked bar on the sideboard.

"Whatever is the matter, darling?"

"Nothing at all," he responded, taking a gulp and letting the whiskey burn his throat. Thinking it was best to leave Brighton as soon as possible, Quinton had returned to London by train earlier that evening, stopped by his town house for his mail, and then had come directly as planned to see Lady Olivia Trahern.

"Something is wrong," Olivia said rather pointedly. "You didn't even kiss me hello and we haven't seen each other for an entire week."

Quinton turned around and faced Olivia. Approaching him, she gave him a practiced smile, her pale blue eyes glittering in amusement. Covering his hand with hers, she guided him to place the glass of whiskey down on the sideboard. Then she wrapped her arms around his neck, pressing her lithe body against his. He kissed her, for she expected it, but for some reason the desire to do so was simply not there.

Slowly Olivia withdrew from the kiss, tilting her head back and eyeing him with careful consideration. "What is it?"

"Nothing."

She released him and stepped back. She walked with elegant grace across the lovely sitting room, the showpiece of her expensive and stylish town house, and on which she prided herself. "Come sit with me, Quinton."

He followed her to a small table where they sometimes played cards together, and they both sat. The glass of red wine that she had been drinking before he arrived was already on the table, and the cards were laid out in a game of patience. Artfully resting her manicured hand under her chin, Olivia brushed a blond curl from her pretty face and stared at him.

"What happened in Brighton?" she asked.

"Why do you assume that something happened to me?"

She laughed, deep and throaty. "Because I know you, Quinton. I know you quite well, and I can tell when something is bothering you. But if you don't wish to discuss it, that is perfectly fine with me." She picked up the deck of cards and continued her game of patience as if he were not there.

It wasn't that he didn't wish to discuss it with her, for there wasn't much that he and Olivia Trahern hadn't discussed over the past year or so. No, it was more that he didn't know what to say. He had no idea how to put into words what he was thinking. And he hated that Olivia was so damned perceptive.

She barely looked up from the cards. "So you don't want to tell me?"

Olivia's persistence could be draining at times. Quinton said simply, "Not now."

With quiet deliberation, she set down the cards and picked up her crystal wineglass. She sipped the wine slowly before speaking. Gazing at him, she raised a delicately arched brow. "Then this is serious."

He rose to his feet and moved back to the sideboard to retrieve his drink, knowing she was watching him. "I don't know what it is," he muttered while he refilled his tumbler with whiskey and then returned to sit with her at the table.

Another knowing laugh escaped her, and she grinned in utter delight. "Oh, then this must be about a woman. And I'm guessing it isn't your blushing bride."

"Why do you always have to be right?" he asked ruefully.

"Because I am, darling." She gave an elegant shrug of her shoulders. "It's part of my charm."

It was the truth, for Lady Olivia Trahern was nothing if not charming, and she was more than well aware of that fact. With her silky blond hair, sparkling eyes, and pretty face, she made a most alluring and a most sought after widow. Never lacking for invitations, her life was filled with lively parties, gorgeously expensive dresses, and a waiting list of ardent suitors. But her life was not always so splendid, as Quinton well knew.

At the tender age of seventeen her parents married their pretty daughter off against her will to the obese but vastly wealthy Lord Trahern, a brute of a man over thirty years her senior. Nine months later Olivia dutifully produced the all-important and necessary male heir and spent the next ten years of her life in a hellish marriage, enduring untold indignities and abuses. To Olivia's way of thinking, Lord Trahern finally had the decency to have a heart attack one evening after consuming one too many of the rich meals he craved continuously and obliged his young wife by dying while seated at the dining room table during an elaborate supper party for twenty people before a doctor could be summoned. The only benefit and joy she derived from the hellacious union was her son, Drake, whom she loved to distraction and had managed to raise to be a wonderful young man, in spite of his beast of a father.

Finally free of her odious husband, Olivia vowed never to marry again and enjoyed her wealthy widowhood to the fullest extent possible. She moved effortlessly through society while scorning some of its strictest rules, discreetly taking lovers to her bed, Quinton Roxbury being one of them.

They met at one of Lord Hathaway's extravagant house parties in Sussex. While seated next to her at supper that first evening, Quinton had been instantly captivated by her casual wit and seductive beauty. By the end of the night, Olivia had invited him to visit her bedroom and they had been together ever since.

Quinton and Olivia had been a well-known society secret for the last year.

He enjoyed her company in bed and the fact that she did not wish to marry him, and she enjoyed . . . him.

"So?" she pressed him for more information. "Who is she?"

He groaned into his glass. "Must we do this?"

"Yes."

"It's no one you know, Olivia."

"Even better."

"It's nothing."

"It's something or we wouldn't be having this conversation."

"What conversation?"

"Quinton."

"What?"

"Listen, my darling, you and I have always been honest and frank with each other. When we began this affair, we both knew what we were doing. We have no illusions about each other and we knew it wouldn't last forever. I'm not a fool."

"No. You're not." No one could accuse Olivia of foolishness.

She continued, "I have no secret wish for you to marry me, Quinton, if that's what you are thinking or are afraid of. Or that I'm in love with you, because I am not. I do love you, of course."

"And who wouldn't?" he asked with a rakish half smile.

"My point exactly." She laughed, but her voice then grew somber and her gaze steady. "And I won't break down in hysterics if you are ready to end our little affair either."

"I know that," Quinton whispered. "And that is what I love about you." He did love Olivia. She had been a good friend to him since he first took her to his bed. Witty and accomplished, she was still a beautiful woman at thirty-eight with a lush and eager body.

"Are you?"

He drew his brows together in question. "Am I what?"

"Ready to end this?" she prompted. She stared at him intently, her warm eyes regarding him with curious interest. "To end our arrangement?"

He sighed heavily and thought for a moment. He and Olivia had been lovers for over a year now. They enjoyed an easy relationship and were more than compatible in the bedroom. They had both shown great discretion in public and took pains not to be seen together at social events. Theirs was a mutually amicable and satisfying arrangement that had suited them both quite well. He had not severed their relationship when he became engaged to Lady Emmeline last summer, and he had given no thought to ending things with Olivia once he was married. Nor had it been his intent to do so when he came to her house this evening either. But now . . . Somehow now it seemed the wiser course of action.

He answered softly, "Perhaps I should."

"It's all right, Quinton," she reassured him with a sly wink. "We've had a good run of it."

He smiled at her in agreement. "Yes we have."

"The change will be good for me." She slowly traced her finger around the rim of her wineglass. "And as I said earlier, this has nothing to do with Lady Emmeline, does it?"

"It has everything to do with her actually."

"Really?" She seemed astonished by his words. "In what way?"

"I cannot believe this"—he shook his head—"but I find myself questioning if my marriage to her would be a mistake."

Olivia's rich laughter rippled about them. "Why, Quinton! You're in love!"

"Don't be ridiculous," he scoffed at her words. "I'm not in love with Emmeline."

"Who said anything about Emmeline?"

He protested, "But you said—"

"No. I said you were in love, but you are not in love with Lady Emmeline and you won't ever be. While your marriage to her won't be quite the travesty that mine was to Walter, you will not be happy with her. Do you forget that I've met her? She will wear you down, Quinton. Mark my words, that woman will drain all the joy out of your life eventually." Olivia picked up her glass and sipped her wine.

A headache blossomed within Quinton's skull as Olivia spoke of her prediction. He rubbed his forehead with the pads of his fingers. Although he had a sinking feeling that Olivia was most likely right, he also knew that Lady Emmeline was the most logical choice for a bride. He was almost thirty and had to marry at some point, and having the Duke of Wentworth for a father-in-

law would open untold doors for Quinton in the future.
When the opportunity to wed Lady Emmeline fell into
his lap, he could not refuse. As a fourth son with no title,
he would be a fool not to.

Olivia reached across the table and placed her hand
gently on top of his. "You're suddenly questioning your
upcoming marriage to Emmeline and your relationship
with me because you've fallen in love with whoever this
woman is you won't tell me about. The one you obviously
met while in Brighton this week."

"I didn't meet her in Brighton."

"Don't be obtuse." She smacked his hand lightly. "But
at least you have admitted to me now that she exists."

Quinton had no idea if he was in love with Lisette
Hamilton or not because he had never been in love before.
How did one know? He had only ever known when he was
not in love. He was definitely not in love with Lady Emmeline Tarleton. He was not in love with Lady Olivia Trahern. He had never been in love with any of the gorgeous
ladies he had bedded over the years either. But Lisette
Hamilton . . . She was something entirely different from
anything he had encountered before.

Now he did not know what to think about anything
anymore.

Quinton wasn't sure why he was so reluctant to tell
Olivia about Lisette Hamilton. He had had no secrets from
her before. Although she did not agree with him, Olivia
knew how his engagement to Lady Emmeline had come
about and his reasons for marrying the girl. She was easy
enough to talk to and she had certainly confided her
secrets to him. But somehow speaking of all that had
happened with Lisette seemed wrong. He couldn't even
describe to himself what had happened over the last few
days, let alone explain it to Olivia. Frankly, he wished

Olivia would drop the subject. He didn't want to talk about Lisette Hamilton anymore. Or see her. Or think about her.

It was over and there was nothing he could do about it.

"Is this woman in love with you?"

Now that was a hell of a question. He would like to think Lisette was in love with him. But she was engaged to another man. A man she had known her whole life, whereas she had known Quinton only a few short days. They could not possibly be in love with each other when they barely knew each other, could they?

There was no point to any of it. Yet still he could not stop thinking of her. How she had appeared so suddenly, so unexpectedly, in his life. How he had literally collided with her that first day.

Nor did that seem to be the end of it. What were the odds of meeting her on the train the very next day? Or again in the curio shop in Brighton. He admitted that calling on Lisette at her mother's home he'd done of his own free will, but how did one account for the other *three* chance meetings? Was it fate? Destiny?

Quinton had never believed in any of that sort of thing. As far as he was concerned, each man created his own destiny, his own fate and fortune. He believed in hard work and careful planning, which he demonstrated in the painstaking designs he created. He had meticulously planned his future as well. For by marrying the daughter of the influential and powerful Duke of Wentworth, he was assured political backing when the time was right for him to run for Parliament. Once his political career began, he could make real changes, substantial improvements in the lives of the poor. His life was carefully mapped out with no room for a messy entanglement with the beautiful Lisette Hamilton.

But Lisette was so much more than simply beautiful.

Her bright intelligence and kind heart, her warm spirit and something in her sweet nature called to him like nothing he had even known before. She cared about the same things that mattered to him—the houses, the people, the lives of those around her. She had an interest in the world outside of her own. In her own small way, Lisette put forth an effort to make the world a better place by helping those who worked in her family's bookshop learn how to read. She cared for her mother enough to travel by train merely to keep the woman company. And there she was, independent enough to travel on her own. And from what she told him, she had also known personal hardship in her own family and yet she still had an optimistic approach to life. He admired her for that. Lisette was a curious mixture of sweetness and independence. He found that infinitely appealing.

And oh yes, her kisses . . . She kissed with a sweet abandon that was full of the enticing promise of even more. Her kisses left him reeling. There had been a strong undercurrent from the very first instant he met her. So tempting was she, he almost kissed her in the lane that day, for Christ's sake.

He had to stop thinking about her! Lisette Hamilton was a beautiful temptation but not one that he could afford to indulge in.

He was marrying Lady Emmeline Tarleton in a few weeks. Soon he would forget about the lovely woman with her sultry green eyes and auburn tresses and get on with his life.

He finished his drink in a long swallow. Then he shook his head with deliberate slowness in answer to Olivia's question. "No. She's not in love with me any more than I am with her. It's nothing and it can never be anything more than that."

Her eyes focused on him with skepticism. "If you say so."

"I do."

At this point, Olivia simply gave him a nod of acknowledgment and let the subject go. She was wiser than he gave her credit for. He lifted her hand and placed a kiss on her palm. She smiled at him.

"I think I'm going to go home now."

The words came out of his mouth before he realized he'd said them out loud. But it was what he wanted. If he stayed there any longer, he would end up in Olivia's enormous four-poster bed upstairs and spend the night with her. For the first time in over a year, that prospect held no appeal for him.

A shadow of disappointment flickered across her pretty face at his words. Still she flashed him her most brilliant smile. "My darling, you know I only wish you the best. And I shall still be here, if you ever have need of me. Even if it's just to talk."

He stood and stepped toward her. Leaning down, he placed a soft kiss on her cheek. "Thank you."

Olivia rose from her seat and took his hand in hers as she walked him to the front hall. "Good luck with your girl."

Quinton shook his head.

She laughed in amusement. "Do you realize that when word gets out that we've broken off, Lord Babey will be beating down my door?"

"Is that who you're thinking of next?"

"Not really. He has too much of a reputation, but he has made his interest clear on more than one occasion." She paused, her eyes alight. "I was actually thinking of Lord Eddington."

Quinton scoffed. "Eddington? His reputation is not much better than Babey's."

"Well, they can't all be you, now can they, darling?" She kissed his cheek and tousled his hair affectionately before she handed him his hat and coat.

10

On a Cold Winter's Night That Was So Deep

"Madame La Fleur let me go today."

Tom Alcott slowly put his fork down, his cold supper forgotten. No longer hungry, his mother's words chilled him to the bone. "Why?"

"She said I was too slow, making too many mistakes. It seems that I'm too old to be a seamstress anymore."

He stared across the little table at her, looking at her critically. Tom's mother had just turned thirty years old. Anna Alcott had been very pretty once, with long glossy red hair and fair skin. Now she looked pale and thin, with dark circles around her sad gray eyes. Still, he didn't think of her as old. She wasn't gray and wrinkly and toothless like Old Framingham. Now *she* was old!

"I just can't seem to get my fingers to work as well as they used to." Anna Alcott's voice was filled with despair. "I can't get them warm enough." She frowned as she rubbed her chapped and raw hands together, her delicate brow creased with worry.

Ignoring the knot forming in the pit of his stomach, Tom thought of the money hidden beneath the floorboard. If

Mama didn't get another job soon, they would have to use his hidden stockpile of coins. He hoped it didn't come to that. That money was to buy a house and he had saved so much already. He didn't know how much a house cost, but he knew he didn't have nearly enough yet. Mama losing her job put a hitch in his plans.

They lived off her income and the money he stole, but supposedly earned from the shoemaker. Without Mama's weekly wages it would be tough to pay Mrs. Framingham her seven shillings in rent. He hated the thought of spending his secret savings on food and rent money when it was meant for more important things, but at least they had that to fall back on. He wouldn't tell Mama about the money now. He'd just take out a little at a time as they needed it.

"Don't worry, Mama." He attempted to comfort her, but the worry in her eyes scared him more than he wanted to admit. "We'll get by. You'll get work in another shop soon enough."

"I don't think so, dear," she murmured in a voice low and full of humiliation. "Madame La Fleur will not give me a recommendation."

Silence descended upon them as the seriousness of their situation hit home. Tom wished he had something to offer, something to say to make everything well again. Being the man of the house was harder than anyone thought.

"Perhaps you could ask Mr. Rutledge for a raise," Mama suggested gently. "You've been working there a while now and you tell me that you are doing a fine job."

Guilt swamped him. He could never ask Mr. Rutledge for a raise, because he hadn't worked for the fat old shoemaker in months and months. And he never would again. He hated that old blighter. Tom hadn't lasted a week at his place. Rutledge had beaten him with a leather strap the first day for accidentally dropping a shoe in the fire. It was a terrible mistake to be sure and Tom most likely deserved the beating for being so clumsy. He bore it like a man, though, and never told his mother about that beating. But two days later, when Rutledge pushed Tom into the back room of the shop and tried to make him take his trousers off, Tom lit out of there like lightning and never went back.

Not wishing to burden his mother, he fell into the relatively easy world of picking pockets to earn his keep. It was certainly better than fighting off Rutledge's filthy advances. Out of his pickings, he brought home his paltry shoemaker's assistant salary and saved the difference, his mother never the wiser. He left the same time each morning as if he were going to the shoemaker's and returned in the evening before his mother did.

Stealing was much more satisfying than working for Rutledge.

With picking pockets, Tom was his own boss. He decided who to pinch from and where he would look for fancy toffs. And he liked having his days free to himself to do what he wanted. He could wander about the city, taking in the sights and sounds, observing everyone. He enjoyed walking along the nice neighborhoods, like Mayfair, looking in all the fine homes where the rich folk lived. When evening fell, he could see the warm glow of candlelight in the tall windows and families gathered around the table, and he wished so desperately that it were his family there. He and Ellie and Mama and Papa, all together again. He knew that could never be, but still he would pick out one house he liked especially and imagine he and Mama lived there now. She would be well cared for and happy then. And she would finally smile again. Living in one of those swanky town houses, Mama wouldn't have to work and could wear pretty dresses of her own, instead of sewing them for others.

He wanted that for her. He wanted his mother to be

happy again more than anything in the world. But he just didn't know what to do to make that happen.

Mama released a heavy sigh. "Yes, that's it. Maybe Mr. Rutledge can give you a little raise."

"Maybe I should look for a different job that pays more," Tom suggested.

"No!" Mama's eyes grew wide and panicked. "You stay there, where you are safe. I won't have you off in one of those horrid factories. Or working for a chimney sweep, God forbid. Your father would never forgive me if I let it come to that, if I let anything happen to you. And I can't lose you, Tom. I've lost enough already."

Yes. They both had lost enough. Tom's heart constricted at the thought of Papa and Ellie.

His mother rose slowly to her feet and walked to him. She ran her cramped hand through his tousled red hair. "You stay at Rutledge's, Tom. You've been doing so well there."

"But I don't like it there . . ." Tom's voice trembled as he began to confess.

"But we need your wages."

"Yes, ma'am." He felt a little sick inside at his deception. The charade would continue then, for he had not the heart to tell her that he'd been lying to her and stealing. Not tonight anyway, when Madame La Fleur had just let her go and she was so worried about finding another job. He didn't want her worrying more than she already did.

"I'm so sorry, Tom." Her voice quavered as she went to lie upon the thin pallet on the floor. "You're just a little boy and shouldn't be worried about these adult things. I wish I could send you to school, like your papa wanted. I wish I knew enough to teach you myself. Your father and I wanted so much more for you than this."

Tom had known that. From the stories his mother told him, his father had been a learned man, an educated man.

The only child of an impoverished pastor and his wife, James Alcott had been taught how to read and write and speak other languages. After his parents died, he had taken a position as a tutor for a wealthy family in a fine manor house in Wales. At that house, James met Anna Powell, a pretty parlor maid. His mother never talked about her own family, just that her parents died when she was a baby.

James and Anna fell in love and married each other. Tom knew something bad happened at the manor house, but his mother wouldn't go into specifics, just that they had had to leave in a hurry. The two of them came to London with the little bit of money that James had saved. They were able to rent some decent rooms and James managed to obtain a position teaching at a little parish school. Baby Tom arrived without delay and Anna stayed home and took care of him and did some sewing for extra money. She always said that Tom was the best surprise she ever had and how much she loved him. Things were going well for a while even though money was scarce. Papa and Mama were happy together and along came Ellie. Papa had big plans for the family, according to Mama's telling of it. He was teaching Mama to read better and he wanted both his children to go to school someday, too.

Then came that terrible day when Tom's whole world changed forever and Papa got sick, vomiting uncontrollably. Somehow he had caught the cholera and they took him away before he died. The landlord told Mama that they had to leave, because he didn't want a diseased family living in his building. Tom didn't remember much of those years, except for Mama's crying. They eventually came to live in the garret at Framingham's because it was all Mama could afford. It was not easy for a woman with two little children clinging to her to find enough work to support them, but somehow Mama survived by securing a position at Madame La Fleur's dress shop.

So the three of them lived in the garret room and Tom looked after Ellie while Mama went to work at the dress shop. But Mama never gave up on Papa's wish for Tom to learn to read.

Then they lost Ellie last Christmas.

Mama wanted Tom to go to school then. But school was not mandatory. And eating was. So he had gone to work instead of learning to read and write.

Tom stood above his mother as she lay on the pallet. "I don't need school. I'm doing all right, Mama. I'm as smart as they come already. And don't worry because I'll earn enough for both of us."

His mother cried then. Tom had meant to comfort her with his words, not make her cry. He curled up beside her on the pallet, feeling the sobs that wracked her thin body. Slipping his hand in hers, he squeezed her hand tightly. He wished with all his might that she wouldn't cry. But on that cold December night Mama cried and cried and he could not get her to stop.

11

Good Tidings We Bring

Saturday, December 6, 1873

"He was with whom?" Lady Emmeline Tarleton asked two days later, incredulous at what Penelope Eaton had just told her. Emmeline had been working on some details of her upcoming wedding with her mother, when her friend Penelope had unexpectedly called on her that afternoon. They now sat in the exquisitely decorated parlor of the Duke of Wentworth, who was Emmeline's father, at their grand home in Mayfair.

"A very pretty young woman," Penelope explained for the second time. "He said she was a friend who was visiting Brighton. He introduced her to me as Miss Lisette Hamilton."

Emmeline's eyes narrowed at the blond girl, who had been her friend since childhood. What had Quinton been up to while he was in Brighton?

"The only reason I am mentioning this to you, Emmeline, is that they looked rather intimate with each other, as if they were about to . . . about to . . ."

"As if they were about to what?" Emmeline demanded, her heart pounding in her chest.

Penelope paused, unsure whether to divulge this piece of information or not. "As if they were about to"—her voice dropped to a hushed whisper—"about to kiss."

Kiss! Images of Quinton and this faceless woman swirled in Emmeline's mind. It was impossible. Quinton loved *her*. They were about to be married, for heaven's sake! Penelope must be mistaken. The scenario was impossibly absurd. Emmeline laughed aloud, if somewhat forcefully. "Why, that is the most ridiculous thing I have ever heard in my life!"

"I am only telling you what I saw with my own eyes," Penelope responded defensively, a bit hurt that her scandalous news was being so easily dismissed. "He held her hand and was leaning very close to her. Their lips were almost touching. They looked quite intimate with each other. If I had not come along when I did and interrupted them, who knows what might have happened between them!"

Incredulous, Emmeline questioned in disbelief, "They were about to kiss in public? In the middle of a shop? In full view of whoever might be walking by? It does not sound at all like something my Quinton would do." Still, she could not ignore the twinge of panic that nipped at her heart. Quinton loved her and would never behave in such a manner with another woman. They were to be husband and wife in a matter of weeks!

Yet . . . there was no reason on earth for Penelope, her dearest friend, to concoct such an outrageous tale either.

"Believe what you will, Emmeline." Penelope sniffed, taking on an injured air. "I simply thought you should know."

"Yes, I understand, and I thank you for thinking of my well-being. But I believe you must be mistaken, Penelope.

However, if it eases your mind, I shall speak to Quinton about it."

Penelope harrumphed with a superior attitude. "I should think you'd want to talk to him to ease your own mind, not mine."

Emmeline wished wholeheartedly that Penelope had kept her mouth closed and her salacious tales to herself. But perhaps it was better to know what was going on. Who was this woman who threatened her happiness? Emmeline would find out the truth. First she would confront Quinton, although he would naturally deny it. Then she would learn who this Miss Lisette Hamilton was and just what her designs were on Emmeline's fiancé.

"Have you mentioned this to anyone else?" Emmeline questioned, trying to sound more casual about it than she felt.

"Of course not!" Penelope responded, clearly offended that Emmeline would suspect her of spreading scandal. "But Priscilla was with me and saw exactly what I saw."

Emmeline's heart sank a little at that disclosure from her friend. Penelope's sister was the worst kind of gossip. It would be a wonder if all of London hadn't heard that Quinton was kissing a mystery woman at a shop in Brighton! Her heart pounded in her chest and her face grew warm. She would be humiliated. If her father found out, he would probably shoot Quinton. Emmeline wouldn't mind if the story were true, but she simply did not believe it.

Or was it simply that she did not want to believe it?

Penelope made a point of adding, "But I made Priscilla promise not to utter a word about this to anyone!"

"Lady Emmeline, I beg your pardon for interrupting," a uniformed housemaid said, "but Mr. Roxbury is here."

Emmeline stared at the young housemaid who had just entered the parlor. *Quinton was here?* She was not ready to confront him just yet. She glanced nervously at Penelope, whose eyes had gone wide. "Please show him in, Minnie."

"Oh, he is in the study with your father now. I just thought you would want to know that he was here, in case you wished to fix yourself up a little and all." Minnie grinned broadly, happy to be delivering news to her mistress that her handsome fiancé was in the house.

"That was kind of you to inform me, Minnie. Will you please let me know when he is finished speaking with my father?" Emmeline pasted a bright smile on her face. Of course, Quinton would visit with her father before seeing his future wife. Why would she even entertain the idea that he would do otherwise?

"Yes, miss." Minnie nodded her head and left the room.

Penelope rose from her seat, gathering her reticule and gloves. "Perhaps it's best if I leave. I would think you would want to speak to him in private."

Emmeline stood and went to her friend. "Yes, thank you, Penelope. I shall call upon you tomorrow."

"Good luck, Emmeline," Penelope whispered before exiting the parlor.

Emmeline's heart sank at the pitiful, worried look she had seen in Penelope's eyes. She soothed herself with the thought of how foolish her friend would feel next month when watching Quinton and Emmeline wed at Saint Paul's!

Alone in the parlor, she walked to the mantel and glanced in the gilt-framed mirror hanging above. She stared at her own reflection. Dark brown hair and brown eyes fringed with long black lashes. Ivory skin. A heart-shaped face. There was nothing amiss about her personage. No blemishes. No scars. She had been told how pretty she was, and she was aware that she was attractive to gentlemen. But now she gave herself a keen inventory.

Perhaps she was not attractive enough? Not attractive enough to hold a man. Were her eyes too cold? Her lips too thin? Her chin too pointed? What if Quinton desired a more traditional-looking wife? The blond-haired blue-eyed type. Was it her figure? Was she too thin and shapeless? Perhaps too lacking in the bosom? Gentlemen tended to prefer females with a more hourglass shape, and she was taller than most girls and rather angular. At least she was young and healthy. But was she too young? Not sophisticated or worldly enough? What if she was not the right woman for Quinton?

Emmeline found herself blinking at her anguished reflection. These novel thoughts of inadequacy caused her unexpected apprehension. It was such a new sensation she did not know how to deal with it.

As the cherished and pampered daughter of a wealthy duke, Emmeline had never had a doubt about her importance and position in life. She grew up adored and indulged by her parents and brothers. Dressed fashionably and educated well, she had enjoyed a life of quiet privilege and pleasure, assured of her future happiness as well. Surrounded by family and friends who doted upon her, she knew only comfort and acceptance wherever she went. During her Season she had had many admirers and countless offers, from men far wealthier and titled than Mr. Roxbury.

But she had eyes only for Quinton from the moment she saw him in her father's grand ballroom.

His masculine handsomeness took her breath away. The golden warmth of his hair and his sky blue eyes were so very different from her own coloring that she was instantly drawn to his fairness. Classic features, an aquiline nose, and a strong chin combined with the charm of his smile made him irresistible. Tall, muscular, and broad shouldered, he carried himself like a prince and could probably pass for one if they put a crown on his head. Quinton Roxbury looked like he stepped right out of the pages of a fairy-tale book. Emmeline had been nervous and giddy in his presence, and as soon as he spoke to her, she had fallen in love with him. She could not recall now what he even said to her, but she knew right then and there that she wanted to marry him.

Since Emmeline had always gotten everything she had ever wanted, it did not enter her mind that she would not get Quinton Roxbury.

That same evening she informed her parents that she had found the man she wanted to wed. And of course, just as they always had her entire life, they set about arranging it for her. They did not question her desire, for her father knew Mr. Roxbury and his family and approved the match. Within the week, Quinton had appeared on her doorstep and their courtship began.

Quinton was charming and solicitous of her, escorting her to various dances and parties. They made a stunning pair, a study in contrasts, light and dark. Emmeline thrilled to the envious looks other girls cast in her direction when she was on Quinton's arm. By month's end they were betrothed and the planning for their grand society wedding was under way. Because her birthday was in January, Emmeline thought it a wonderful birthday present to herself to be married on the very day of her birth. So it was settled and she had been blissfully happy with the way it all turned out.

As the wedding day approached, it did not dawn on her that her future husband spent little time with her, so consumed was she with choosing the most beautiful gown, selecting the most extravagant cake, and creating the perfect guest list. All her friends told her how lucky she was to have such a dashing and handsome fiancé. The fact that Quinton had not kissed her only reinforced her opinion of him as a proper gentleman and demonstrated his great respect and regard for her person.

But now . . . Now she wondered.

Should not Quinton have tried to kiss his fiancée? At

least once? Should he not be a little more interested in the planning of their wedding instead of caring only about his little houses for the poor? Should not her intended come to see her before seeing her father?

Now as Emmeline Elizabeth Tarleton stood in front of the mantel mirror, doubts began to plague her. She bit her too thin lip.

Lisette Hamilton. She repeated the name to herself softly. Lisette Hamilton. She wished she had asked Penelope what the woman looked like. This woman Quinton wanted to kiss. Was about to kiss. May have already kissed!

That thought almost knocked her off her feet. He had probably done more than kiss this woman. What if Lisette Hamilton was Quinton's mistress!

In spite of her sheltered upbringing, she had heard about unsavory women that men consorted with before they were married. Then she gave a little sigh of relief. Of course! Quinton had a mistress. Only a woman of that type would be seen kissing in public. A dancer or a stage actress. That's who it had to be. A common, low, coarse sort of woman. It surprised her to think of him with that type of female, but she assumed it was the way of men and took it as a matter of course. Quinton would not keep this mistress after they were married; of that she was certain.

Now, should she mention to him that she not only knew of this creature's existence but also knew her name? No. She could not even bear the thought of discussing something so repulsive with Quinton. It might be better to keep the information to herself for a bit longer and see what came of it.

Before her wedding, though, Emmeline vowed to find out more about this woman who behaved with her future husband so scandalously in public. To be safe, she would discover just who this Lisette Hamilton was.

"Hello, my dear. Has Penelope left already?" Emmeline's mother, the Duchess of Wentworth, asked as she entered the parlor.

Startled, Emmeline turned away from the mirror, embarrassed to be caught staring at herself. She smoothed her dress with her hands. "Oh, yes, she had to go home."

"It's a shame I didn't have a chance to say good-bye. I wanted her to give a message to her mother for me, but I suppose it can wait." Victoria Tarleton was an elegantly tall woman who possessed the same coloring as her daughter. She picked up her needlework and sat upon a large chair by the fire. "It's very chilly out today," she murmured more to herself than to her daughter. "The fire feels nice."

Emmeline glanced nervously at her mother. "Is Mr. Roxbury still here?"

Victoria barely looked up from her embroidery, carefully stitching the leaves of a cascading floral bouquet. "Why no, he just left. He and your father went somewhere together. Something about looking at property for houses."

"Oh, he's gone already?" Emmeline could barely conceal her disappointment. Quinton had left without speaking to her, without even saying good afternoon. Had he no desire to be with her at all?

At her despondent tone, her mother glanced up. "What is the matter, Emmeline?"

"I just thought . . ." She paused, unsure about what was happening. "I just thought it would have been nice if my fiancé had seen fit to call upon me."

Victoria set down her embroidery. "Now, now. You mustn't be put out, my dear," her mother said in an attempt to soothe her. "Quinton is a very ambitious and busy man. You should be pleased that your future husband gets on so well with your father. Not many men get along with their father-in-law."

"Yes, I am pleased by that, of course. But just whom is

Quinton marrying? Me or Papa?" Emmeline folded her arms across her chest in a fit of pique.

"Your father is helping Quinton with his project, which would lead to a political career," her mother said matter-of-factly. "Do you not want your husband to be successful?"

"Yes," she admitted reluctantly. Perhaps her mother was correct and she was overreacting, Emmeline reasoned. But still, she would have liked to have had Quinton show her some regard. Some interest, at least. Was that too much for a girl to ask of her fiancé?

12

Oh, Tidings of Comfort and Joy

Tuesday, December 9, 1873

Henry was not waiting for Lisette at Victoria Station when she finally arrived back in London a week later. He had said he would meet her train, but he wasn't there. Feeling a bit put out, Lisette forced a smile at Davies, the young footman from Devon House who usually picked her up from the station. He carried her bag and helped her into the waiting carriage.

Davies had given her no explanation as to why Henry had not been there to meet her, so Lisette was left to wonder. Guilt immediately consumed her. Had Henry somehow learned about her kissing Quinton Roxbury? The chances for that were practically nonexistent, she knew, for who could have possibly informed him of such a thing? No one could know what had happened between them, aside from the two Eaton sisters, and they only had their suspicions. Logic had no place in her mind, however, and her guilty conscience ran rampant with worry. Did Henry sense on some intuitive level that she had been untrue to him and that was why he had not wanted to meet her as promised at the station?

On the other hand, she was a bit relieved not to have to face him so soon. What if he recognized the look of betrayal on her face? Could one tell by looking at her that she had been kissed so passionately by a man other than her fiancé? Oh heavens! Her stomach rolled at the very thought.

Worrying, she twisted her gloves in her lap as the Waverly carriage rolled through the crowded London streets. When they arrived at Devon House, Davies helped her out of the carriage. As always, she trod quickly up the front steps. The door was opened by Granger, and Lisette greeted him with a smile.

"Good evening, Miss Lisette," he said in his usual even tone. He helped her remove her cloak and handed it to a waiting footman. "Lady Waverly would like to see you in the dining room on a matter of the utmost importance."

Her heart pounded at the unusual request. "Is there anything wrong? The baby?"

"It is not for me to say, miss."

If something were truly amiss, she doubted Granger would be so calm. But whatever could be so urgent that she barely had a moment to remove her cloak?

She hurried after Granger and stood aside as he flung open the doors to the formal dining room.

A loud chorus of "Surprise!" almost knocked her backward.

Covering her mouth in shock, she stared at the people gathered in the formal dining room, which was festooned with decorations and bedecked with flowers. It was some sort of a party. For her. *What in heaven's name?*

She began to recognize faces in the room. Colette and Lucien grinned at her. Lucien's parents, Simon and Lenora Sinclair, looked on in delight. Her younger sisters, Paulette and Yvette, smiled like a pair of little cats that ate the canaries. Lord Jeffrey Eddington was there, too, an amused expression on his handsome face. Her Aunt Cecilia, Uncle Randall, and her cousin Nigel stood in the room also. She registered that Mrs. Brooks and Henry were standing there, as well as a number of their friends.

Henry!

Henry was there! Beaming with pride and excitement, he moved quickly to her side, placing his arm around her shoulder and drawing her into the room.

"Welcome home, my sweet Lisette. We decided to surprise you with a little engagement party. I told your sisters about our June wedding plans and they insisted we celebrate." He confessed sheepishly, "It was my idea to surprise you."

"That's why you were not at the station," was all she could think of to say to him before she faced the room full of beaming friends and relatives. Relief washed through her. Henry did not know about her and Quinton. And he never would as far as she was concerned.

"Congratulations! We're so happy for you!" Everyone called out to her as she was hugged and kissed by her family members. Henry was shuffled aside as one by one they gathered around her.

Mrs. Brooks squeezed her hand tightly, her face glowing with joy. Her white hair was pinned sedately upon her head, and her gray eyes, so like those of her son, gazed at her fondly. "My dear, I couldn't be happier for you and my boy. I have hoped for this for a long time, and I am proud to call you my daughter-in-law."

"Thank you," Lisette said, too choked up with emotion to say more.

Mrs. Brooks was a kind woman, and Lisette genuinely cared for her. Thinking of how she'd almost ruined everything and hurt all these people who loved her and expected her to marry Henry by acting so recklessly with Quinton Roxbury, she grew a little nauseous.

She was then overtaken by her Aunt Cecilia. The woman's pinched face was accentuated by her tightly pulled back blond hair, making her look even more sour than she was.

"Well, it seems as if your young man has finally come around, Lisette. We were beginning to have our doubts about him. He dillydallied long enough about proposing to you. However, I still think it was foolish of you to forgo the opportunity of a Season. Your mother should have insisted on your having a Season, but Genevieve always did let you girls run a bit wild and never took pains to assure you a proper upbringing." She sighed and shook her head in disappointment. "With Lucien's connections and your pretty face and sweet disposition, there is no telling what kind of match you could have made. But you seem determined to defy convention, much as Juliette did."

"I hardly think that my betrothal to Henry Brooks defies convention, Aunt Cecilia."

"Perhaps," she murmured with definitive regret. "But it does seem such a tragic waste of a perfectly good opportunity to meet a more eligible type of gentleman, Lisette. And Colette has been too occupied having children to properly introduce you to society. Why, she has hardly entertained at all since becoming Countess Waverly, and you have not attended a single social event of any note!"

"Truly, Aunt Cecilia, I have no interest in such pursuits." She nodded her head with forced politeness. "It's been lovely talking to you."

With as much haste as she could muster without appearing obvious, Lisette moved away from her aunt, eager to be free of her negative commentary. Before she could find a moment to herself, her youngest sister demanded her attention.

"Oh, Lisette, it's so exciting!" Yvette squealed, her eyes

sparkling with delight. Her sixteen-year-old heart was thrilled by the romance and glamour of an upcoming wedding. "I am so happy for you and Henry! I shall be a bridesmaid, shan't I?"

"Of course you will," Lisette responded automatically. "It wouldn't be a happy wedding without my sisters beside me."

"I think I already know the perfect material for our dresses! I saw the most heavenly shade of rose silk at Madame La Fleur's shop only yesterday. It would make such an elegant gown. And June is the best time of year, too. A June bride! We should have the wedding at Lucien's country estate, down on the lawn overlooking the river. The roses will be in bloom then, too. Don't you think that would be lovely?"

Lisette was in no frame of mind to discuss wedding details at the moment. "We shall talk all about the dresses another time, all right, Yvette?"

Overwhelmed with Yvette's enthusiasm, she once again stepped aside to have a minute to herself, to catch her breath from all that had happened. Still weary from her train journey and the surprise of facing an unexpected party, she simply needed to be alone for a moment to stop her head from spinning. She had just reached the doorway unnoticed when a voice stopped her.

"Well, well, well. Running away so soon, are we?"

She turned to see Lord Jeffrey Eddington, a longtime friend of Lucien's and therefore a close friend of hers and her sisters. He gave her one of his infamous smiles, the one that charmed everyone in an instant and had melted many a female heart in London. With his masculine good looks, dark hair, and piercing blue eyes, Jeffrey was almost irresistible. Lisette had grown to adore him and his teasing ways over the past few years.

Feeling instantly lighter, she could not stop the genuine

smile that crept over her at the sound of his voice. "Hello, Jeffrey!"

"Sweet little Lisette. You're finally going to do it, are you?"

"I'm still getting married before you, Jeffrey," she pointed out to him.

He shook his head, a devilish gleam in his eyes. "But you forget, I'm not getting married. Ever."

"You only say that now because you haven't met the perfect lady for you yet. But you will, mark my words."

He offered her a mischievous grin and winked at her. "There's no such perfect lady now that you are marrying Henry Brooks."

Helpless to do anything but laugh at his outrageous flirtation, she teased him back. "I'm too good for the likes of you, Jeffrey."

"That is the truth. You're the sweetest one of all your sisters and I must admit I have great affection for you, Lisette. You hold a special place in my heart." Jeffrey handed her a glass of champagne.

She accepted the crystal glass filled with sparkling wine. "Thank you, kind sir."

"You look as if you could do with a little champagne. You seem completely overwhelmed."

She sipped the cool liquid most gratefully. "Is it so obvious?"

"Only to me. And the fact that I caught you trying to sneak away from your own party."

Lisette began to explain. "Jeffrey, I'm just tired from the trip—"

"Is it the surprise party or the idea of marriage to Henry that has you in such a state?" he asked pointedly.

"Honestly!" She forced herself to laugh a little. Lord Eddington could be most impertinent at times, even with the best intentions.

"Call it off whenever you wish. There's plenty of time." He took her free hand in his, his expression becoming unusually serious. "You are not Mrs. Henry Brooks yet, you know. You can run away from all of this if you want."

It was not the first time someone had mentioned this to her, that she should not marry Henry, and again the words disconcerted her. The image of Quinton Roxbury came to her. In an attempt to keep the conversation with Jeffrey from becoming too much closer to the truth, she answered him sarcastically, "I'll keep that option in mind as the day draws nearer."

"Good. If you need an escape route, just send me the word." He gave her a knowing look, his blue eyes saying more than he voiced aloud. He squeezed her hand gently before releasing it.

Lisette had the oddest sensation that Jeffrey was more aware of her uncertain feelings about marrying Henry Brooks than anyone in that room. Then again she never knew whether Jeffrey was teasing or telling the truth. He had that way about him. Before she could respond to his comment, however, Henry approached them.

"Do you mind if I steal my fiancée away for a moment?" Henry asked with a proud grin on his face.

"Not in the least!" Jeffrey exclaimed, gallantly stepping aside.

Lisette handed Jeffrey her glass of champagne with a smile. He nodded in understanding.

Henry took Lisette's arm and led her from the room into the adjoining study. They sat beside each other upon a leather sofa.

"You were surprised by the party, weren't you?" Henry asked.

"Oh, yes!" she exclaimed. "I was most surprised. Thank you."

"No, there's no need to thank me. I wanted to do something special for you. To thank you."

"Thank me?" she asked. "Whatever for?"

He took her hand in his and pulled her close to him. "Oh, my sweet Lisette, you have been so patient, waiting for me all these years, when you could have accepted any number of offers from other men. Gentlemen from aristocratic families who are far wealthier and better prepared to provide for you than I."

"Henry, what are you talking about?"

His steady gray eyes held her gaze intently. He seemed almost shy with her when they had always enjoyed a rather easygoing friendship. She studied his attractive face. He had a straight nose, an intelligent brow, and a wide mouth covered with a neatly trimmed beard. Sandy brown hair was combed back from his earnest and eager face.

She tried, she really tried, not to compare him with the golden beauty of Quinton Roxbury, but it was suddenly impossible not to.

"I know you could have had a Season and you didn't. If you had, you would have been deluged with marriage proposals from the most eligible bachelors in town. I know your family didn't approve of your decision to refuse a debut. You gave all that up to marry me instead. And who am I? Merely a struggling solicitor. Lisette, you have been nothing but constant and loyal to me since the day I first met you."

Lisette's cheeks flamed in sudden embarrassment. And overwhelming guilt. She had not been constant and loyal to him while she had been in Brighton. She cringed at the memory of kissing Quinton Roxbury on the beach. She did not deserve someone as good and kind as Henry Brooks.

Making her feel even worse, he continued to compliment her. "You are so lovely and special. I don't know what I would have done without your support while I was working for my uncle. Knowing that you would be mine kept me going. I am the luckiest man in the world to have you as my wife."

Hot tears stung her eyes and she blinked rapidly to keep from weeping in front of him. "No, I am lucky to have you," she cried, "and I promise to be a good wife to you."

"I know you will." He leaned close to her and placed a kiss upon her cheek.

On impulse Lisette placed her hands on either side of his face to draw him into a kiss. A real kiss. Although surprised by her overture, he willingly obliged her and she kissed him almost feverishly, pressing her lips against his. His mustache tickled her face, but she persisted, waiting for that all-consuming desire to overtake her as it did when she kissed Quinton Roxbury. Henry pulled her closer to him, his arms wrapping around her in a firm grip and easing her against the back of the sofa. Now that was more like it. Lisette leaned her head back and opened her mouth to him, something she had never done before. Without hesitating, he accepted her unspoken invitation and slipped his tongue inside her warm mouth. They kissed for a minute and she knew instinctively that Henry was thrilled by it.

When he quickly broke away from their embrace, she stared at him. Red-faced and breathing heavily, he had a smile from ear to ear. Pleased beyond recognition, he shook his head in disbelief at their unexpected intimacy.

"I am luckier than I have a right to be," he uttered hoarsely. "But as wonderful as that was, my dear, we should stop now."

"Yes," she choked out. This time she could not stop the tears spilling from her eyes.

Henry immediately froze at the sight of her crying. "Forgive me, darling. I should not have kissed you that

way." He reached into his pocket and retrieved a mono-
grammed linen handkerchief, which he used to dab at her
cheeks. "Lisette, please don't cry. We are engaged. It's not
wrong for us to kiss. I only said for us to stop before things
went any further."

She nodded and sat up straight, taking the handkerchief
from him. She wiped her eyes and took a deep breath. Her
tears were not because they had kissed but because of how
that kiss made her feel. Or more precisely, how it did not
make her feel. "I'm sorry. I don't know what came over
me." She mustered a smile for him.

"I think you are overwhelmed with excitement and exhausted from traveling all day on the train. I bet you
haven't eaten anything since breakfast. Let's get you something to eat, shall we?"

"Yes, that would be wonderful." Her stomach was in
such a knot she did not think she would be able to eat anything, but she wanted him to feel that he was helping her.

In a tender gesture, he brushed a stray tendril of hair
from her face. "You are so lovely, Lisette."

"Thank you," she whispered, almost unable to bear another kindness from him.

"I have something for you first. It's the reason I wanted
to see you alone for a moment. Although that kiss almost
made me forget completely." He reached into his other
pocket and withdrew a small box. He handed it to her with
an expression of nervous excitement on his face.

With a trembling hand, she took the box from him and
opened it. Inside was an elegant gold ring set with a single
pearl.

"It's an engagement ring. I thought you should have one."

"Oh, Henry, it's beautiful. Thank you." She had never
possessed a ring before.

"Put it on."

She slipped the delicate ring over her trembling finger.

It was entirely too large and slid around her finger in a ridiculous manner.

"I told the jeweler I thought it too large. You have such slender fingers." He shook his head in disappointment. "We shall go back and have him size it properly for you," he said, attempting to be positive.

"Yes, just as soon as we can," she agreed, placing the pretty ring back in the box. While she had been away in Brighton kissing a veritable stranger, Henry had planned a party for her and bought her a lovely ring. Feeling perfectly wretched, she handed the ring box to Henry and he placed it in his pocket.

The door to the study swung open and her younger sister Paulette stuck her blond head in, staring at them. "There you are! We've been looking for you two! Everyone is wondering where you had gone off to."

Henry rose from the sofa and helped Lisette to her feet. "We were just coming to rejoin the party."

Paulette eyed them with skepticism. "Of course you were."

Lisette smoothed her hair nervously. "We shall be there in a moment, Paulette."

After her sister closed the door, Lisette faced Henry. "Thank you for everything, Henry, for the party, for the ring. I am most happy to be home again and with you."

He placed a light kiss on her cheek. "You make me very happy, Lisette." He took her arm and led her back to the party.

13

And So It Continued Both Day and Night

Wednesday, December 10, 1873

Lisette sat at the breakfast table early the next morning, anxiously waiting for her brother-in-law to enter the dining room. She hoped Lucien would come to breakfast before her sisters arrived so she had an opportunity to talk to him in private. She and Lucien often breakfasted together, for they were both early risers. That morning she made sure she was in the dining room first.

She had barely slept the night before. Wracked with guilt over her behavior with Quinton Roxbury and overwhelmed by Henry's sudden demonstrations of love, she lay awake most of the night.

"Good morning, Lisette," Lucien said as he went to the buffet and piled his china plate high with scrambled eggs, ham, and toast.

Lisette smiled broadly, relieved to see her brother-in-law alone. "Good morning."

"Did you enjoy your engagement celebration last night?"

he asked, taking a seat across the table from her. A footman poured him some coffee.

"Yes, thank you again for everything." She stalled for a bit of time. "How is Colette feeling this morning?"

"She is still sleeping. I didn't have the heart to wake her after such a late night. This baby is making her more tired than I recall her being with Phillip."

"That is because she didn't have an active little boy to care for when she was carrying the first time," Lisette pointed out as gently as she could. Honestly, could the man not figure that out for himself? Lucien was a good husband and an unfailingly kind brother-in-law. She genuinely liked him and had grown to love him over the years, but sometimes she had her doubts about the common sense of men in general.

"Ah, yes." He nodded in agreement, his handsome face a bit sheepish in expression. "That makes sense."

"I spoke to Colette before I left for Brighton. Lucien, she needs to let Rose help her more often. She's exhausting herself."

"You know I agree with you, but your sister is very stubborn. However, I think once the baby arrives, she will have no choice but to let Rose help her."

"I hope so," Lisette murmured.

Lucien continued to eat his breakfast and she bided her time. Paulette would be down before long. She had promised to help Paulette at the bookshop later that day. Because Colette was so far along in her pregnancy and unable to work in the shop and Yvette was no help whatsoever, Lisette had agreed to assist Paulette during the Christmas season instead of only teaching the errand boys and shop girls as she usually did a few days a week. She had to talk to Lucien before Paulette came in.

"Lucien," she began, feeling nervous, "I was wondering if I could ask you something."

"Of course," he said, scooping up eggs with his fork.

"Last week, a gentleman called upon you to discuss a building project," she stated in as casual a voice as she could manage. "Mr. Quinton Roxbury."

Lucien nodded. "Yes, he came to see me to ask if I would invest in his venture. Are you acquainted with him, Lisette?"

"Yes and no," she responded hesitantly, unsure just how much information to divulge. What if Lucien became suspicious about her association with Quinton Roxbury? She would be mortified if her brother-in-law found out that she had been kissing the man in Brighton. "That is . . . We met accidentally as he left Devon House that afternoon he was here to see you and then by chance again the next day we happened to be in the same compartment on the train to Brighton. He then explained to me about his project to build houses for the poor and how he had approached you to be a contributor to his endeavor."

Lucien sipped his coffee and eyed her with keen interest. "And what did you think of his idea?"

"Oh, I think it's wonderful!" she said with more enthusiasm than she had intended. "I agreed with him wholeheartedly. No one can be a productive member of society living amidst the filth and squalor of a tenement with no way to stay clean or healthy. People need to live in real homes in order to have hope of a better life. He spoke so eloquently about it, he quite convinced me."

"I can see that," Lucien uttered dryly, raising an eyebrow.

"Mr. Roxbury and I spoke at great length about it on the train." She paused before asking, "What did you think of his plan, Lucien?"

"It certainly has its merits."

"Are you going to help him then?"

"I'm seriously considering it. Why do you ask?"

"I promised him I would put in a good word for him with you."

"Consider your word taken," he said with a smile. "What is your interest in Mr. Roxbury, Lisette?"

"I've no interest in Mr. Roxbury!" she protested, perhaps a little too vigorously. "I merely wished to help a good cause."

"That is very commendable of you."

She thought she detected a slight note of sarcasm in his voice. "Thank you." Lisette hesitated but could not help asking, "How well do you know Mr. Roxbury?"

"I know of him well enough, I just don't know him personally, if that's what you are asking. His brother John is the Earl of Kingston and I believe there are other brothers as well. Roxbury is a talented designer. I've seen some of his work and it is very impressive for a man not yet thirty. The new town house that Lord Hartwell built in Saint James's Square was designed by Roxbury and it has caused a high demand for his services. There was an article in *The Times* a week or two ago about the new museum he crafted. He's making quite a name for himself."

"Then you are going to help him?" she asked with excitement. She had no idea that Quinton was so well respected and could not help a sudden burst of pride in learning of his success. And more than anything, she wanted his new project to succeed.

"Most likely, but there are a few points I need clarified first. He is coming by to see me later this afternoon to discuss some terms."

Lisette's heart thudded and almost stopped at the news. She hadn't expected to see Quinton again and had quite resigned herself to that fact. Now he was coming to her home that very day.

"Here? He's coming here?" Her voice squeaked.

Lucien regarded her with an odd expression, but before he could respond, Paulette entered the dining room. Paulette, who never missed a word anyone ever said.

"Who is coming here?" Paulette questioned eagerly as she took a plate from the buffet.

"No one you know," Lisette said at the exact same moment Lucien said, "Just a business associate."

With her long blond hair braided tightly behind her head, eighteen-year-old Paulette sniffed with an injured air, a bit put off by their dismissal of her. "Well, if you don't want me to know, then fine."

Lisette silently blessed her brother-in-law for not saying Quinton Roxbury's name aloud and instantly forgave him for his obtuseness in understanding his wife's exhausted state earlier. Lucien was more insightful than she gave him credit for.

"Not everything concerns you, Miss Nosy," Lucien teased her younger sister.

Paulette stuck her tongue out at him and turned away to fill her plate. He and Paulette had always enjoyed a playful and teasing camaraderie from the day they met in the shop.

"So you are helping out at the bookshop today, Lisette?" Lucien asked, skillfully changing the subject to one that would prompt Paulette to lose interest in the mysterious business associate.

"Yes, she is," Paulette said, taking a seat beside her sister and answering for her. "We have so much to do today! We are expecting a large delivery of Christmas cards this morning and I expect we will be quite busy."

"Christmas cards?" Lucien asked, his brows rose in question. "This is something new?"

"Yes, they are becoming very popular and I predict we are going to sell out rather quickly," Paulette answered with great confidence. "Oh, and wait until you see them! They are quite beautiful. Anyone would be happy to receive such a Christmas greeting."

Paulette was very proud of the fact that she had added a rather extensive line of fine stationery and writing instruments to their inventory at the shop. It had proven to be a very successful business venture that Colette had begun two years before and Paulette had taken over and expanded upon. For someone so young, Paulette showed a remarkable talent and business sense that, in conjunction with a little guidance from Lucien, had tripled the sales at Hamilton's Book Shoppe.

Even though they no longer needed the bookshop to support them financially as they once did, because of Colette's marriage to Lucien, Lisette's sisters loved the shop too much to sell it to someone else. Colette and Paulette still oversaw the general day-to-day operation of the business and made all the major decisions, but they had also hired help to assist them. While Lisette had never had quite the passion for the bookshop that Colette and Paulette did, she did not detest working there as Juliette had. Lisette actually enjoyed being in the shop from time to time, and she especially liked working there during Christmastime. Helping people choose Christmas gifts made her happy.

Lisette had also taken over the education of their workers. Anyone employed by Hamilton's, from the young errand boys to the shop girls, had to read and have a sound literature background. Since they tended to hire those needing assistance in that area, they provided the lessons. This tradition had sprung from Colette's idea of exchanging employment for lessons in reading when she had no money for wages. The first errand boy she hired was illiterate and so she taught him his letters and in return he delivered books for her. Now that the shop was doing so well, they could afford to pay their employees a more than fair wage and they gave them an education. Lisette had loved teaching the younger ones how to read, and that had become her area of expertise at Hamilton's Book Shoppe.

"The Christmas cards are a wonderful idea," Paulette, filled with pride, stated again.

"I cannot wait to see them," Lisette said, although her pulse was still racing at the possibility of seeing Quinton Roxbury later that day.

14

Let Nothing You Dismay

Later that day the little bells above the door of Hamilton's Book Shoppe jingled cheerily as Lady Emmeline Tarleton entered with careful steps. She took a deep breath and looked around the store with observant eyes.

"Good afternoon and welcome to Hamilton's. May I help you?" The voice of a pretty blond-haired woman asked from behind a neat counter.

Good Heavens! Was that her?

But no. This couldn't possibly be Quinton's mistress! She was entirely too young. Why, she was still a girl! She'd probably not even had her coming-out yet. As pretty as she was, she couldn't imagine Quinton involved with someone barely out of the schoolroom. Emmeline sighed in relief.

"I'm not quite sure what I'm looking for," Emmeline stated in all honesty. She still was not certain she was doing the right thing by coming to the shop in the first place. When she had made discreet inquiries about Lisette Hamilton, all she had learned was that a Hamilton sister had married the Earl of Waverly and done exceedingly well for a girl of little consequence and that her family owned a bookshop. So while out shopping this afternoon, she had decided to stop by and see for herself. "Do you mind if I look around for bit?"

"Not at all," the girl said graciously. "If you have any questions, please let me know."

"Thank you." Surprised to see a female in business, and one so young, for she couldn't be more than seventeen, Emmeline didn't know what kind of conclusion to draw.

She looked around the store and found it to be quite charming. Although not one for reading books in general, Emmeline had visited bookshops on occasion and had to admit that this one was the nicest she had ever seen. It was light and airy and very welcoming. Shoppers milled about, browsing through books that were attractively arranged on organized shelves and tables while elegant and tasteful signs hanging from ribbons indicated each subject area. Comfortable leather armchairs were situated in secluded nooks for quiet reading and perusing. There was even an area designated especially for children's books, and a colorful rug covered the floor with small tables and chairs at just the perfect size for small readers. Another area was devoted to stationery, which was much more to Emmeline's liking. There was a vast array of writing paper, calling cards, pens, and the like.

Emmeline wandered through the aisles, impressed by the high quality and gracious atmosphere, and she wondered why she had not happened to shop there before. If she searched her memory, perhaps she had heard a friend or two mention a lovely shop off Bond Street but she'd most likely dismissed it owing to her lack of interest in books.

Now she was enchanted, for she hadn't seen anything like it. It was almost as if she had stepped into someone's tastefully decorated home. The store was also decorated for

Christmas with bright red ribbons and festoons of green garlands. She almost forgot the reason she had come.

She made her way back to the front of the shop to the young woman. The girl was just wrapping up a book for a woman with a fur hat. Emmeline watched as the girl tied the package with dark green ribbon with startling efficiency.

"I'm sure your son will enjoy this book, Mrs. Deane," she said.

"Thank you, Miss Hamilton," the woman said. "I will return to pick up my calling cards next week."

Miss Hamilton. Emmeline's heart quickened. The lady left the shop and Emmeline was face-to-face with the girl.

"Is there anything in particular I can help you with?" she asked.

Are you kissing my future husband? Emmeline wanted to ask but dared not. No, she knew that this was not the woman who had been seen with Quinton.

"I'm . . . I'm not sure," Emmeline began.

"We have a lovely selection of Christmas cards that just arrived this morning. Would you care to see them?" she suggested brightly.

Emmeline nodded in agreement as two shoppers came to the counter to pay for their purchases.

The girl looked just beyond where Emmeline was standing. "Oh, Lisette, there you are! Would you please show this lady our new Christmas card selection?"

Emmeline froze.

"Yes, of course," a lovely voice uttered from behind. "Won't you follow me?"

Slowly Emmeline turned to face her. Lisette Hamilton. Her heart plummeted to her feet. Oh God. This, *this* was the woman Quinton had been kissing in Brighton. There was not a doubt in Emmeline's mind that a man would want to kiss this woman.

She was incredibly beautiful. Although eerily similar in looks to the younger girl behind the counter, who was obviously her sister, Lisette appeared much more womanly. She stood shorter than herself, was more petite, and wore a well-cut gown of pale violet with darker velvet trim. She had rich auburn-, almost russet-, colored hair arranged fashionably atop her head with a few loose tendrils around her face and deep green eyes fringed with long dark lashes. She possessed a small, straight nose and a mouth that looked as if smiling came very easily. Her skin was creamy and undoubtedly soft. There was intelligence and humor in her expression and an unmistakable sweetness.

Emmeline was stunned. She had not been entirely sure what she would discover on her little outing today, but she had expected to find an entirely different sort of woman. A woman far worldlier and far less innocent-looking . . .

Lisette Hamilton gave her a pleasant smile. "Would you care to see the cards?"

"Yes, of course," Emmeline answered woodenly and followed behind as she was led to another counter with an attractive display of prettily designed Christmas cards.

Any other time she would have been delighted to see such a collection of adorable and cheerful greeting cards of glowing, chubby-cheeked children and pastoral snow-covered scenes. But not now. Now she simply stood there with a false smile plastered on her face while Lisette Hamilton explained the different sizes, types, and prices of the cards that were available for purchase. Emmeline heard none of it.

It suddenly occurred to her that this woman was not Quinton's mistress. She was just not mistress material. Call it female intuition, but Emmeline did not believe that Lisette Hamilton was anyone's mistress. There was too much of an air of morality or goodness or old-fashioned sweetness about her to think of her as a party to anything so sordid.

And this revelation terrified Emmeline.

She could excuse a mistress as merely a meaningless dalliance with a low-class woman as some men were wont to do. But if Quinton had been kissing *this* particular woman in a shop in Brighton, their entanglement together was far more serious than a mistress. Emmeline was certain of that.

"Now this is a charming one . . ." Lisette held up a pretty card embossed with gilt featuring a bright bouquet of poinsettia and edged with garlands of flowers.

"You are Miss Lisette Hamilton?" Emmeline asked abruptly.

The woman gave a brief nod. "Yes."

"And this is your family's shop?"

"Yes, my father first opened it before I was born, but since he passed away, my sisters and I now manage it."

Emmeline's eyes darted around. "It's a lovely shop."

"Thank you," she smiled with pride. "We like to think so."

"Do you work here every day?"

"No, not always. I'm simply helping more during the Christmas season because I enjoy it."

"It's most unusual for women to manage a store."

"It's unusual, yes, but becoming more common," Lisette explained matter-of-factly. "Women are just as capable as men when it comes to business. In fact, in some ways we are far superior."

Struck by Lisette's warm and personable demeanor, Emmeline grew braver in her questioning. "Do you find it is difficult to acquire a husband with such thinking?"

"Not at all." She shook her head and seemed to blush. "I'm already engaged to be married."

As if struck by a thunderbolt, Emmeline cried in disbelief, "You are?"

"Yes. I'm to be married in June. Is that so shocking?"

Yes! Emmeline thought. "No . . . No. I was just a bit surprised. From what I've found, most men prefer women who are less . . . independent, shall we say?"

"Yes, that is true," Lisette agreed with her. "But I am lucky in that Henry approves of my being independent."

"Henry?" Emmeline questioned, stunned by this turn of events. Surely Penelope had to be mistaken. It simply was not possible that this sweet woman, who was betrothed to another, had been kissing Quinton a few days ago in Brighton. But there was a way to find out.

"He is my fiancé."

"Well, I wish you much happiness in your marriage, Miss Hamilton. I'm going to be married, too. Next month, as a matter of fact." It was on the tip of her tongue to say Quinton's name to gauge Lisette's reaction, but she thought the better of it.

"Oh, how wonderful!" she exclaimed. "I wish you happiness in your marriage as well."

"Thank you," Emmeline said, turning her attention to the display on the counter. "Now, about those Christmas cards. I think I like the ones with the horse and sleigh. They would be perfect to send to my dear friends in Brighton." She paused deliberately, tilting her head. "Have you ever been to Brighton, Miss Hamilton?"

"Yes, as a matter of fact, I was just there last week visiting my mother. It's such a lovely town."

Emmeline's heart sank and her head spun. Oh, something was terribly, terribly wrong and she had not the first idea how to remedy the situation. This woman *had* been in Brighton with Quinton. Penelope was right. What was Quinton thinking? And worst of all, Emmeline realized that she did not know her fiancé at all. Feeling sick to her stomach, Emmeline needed to leave the store immediately. She had to get out of there, away from this woman.

"I think I shall bring a friend of mine by first to ask her opinion of the cards. Perhaps I shall come back tomorrow," Emmeline said hurriedly, hoping she did not burst into tears.

Maybe it was all a horrible misunderstanding and Penelope mistook the woman for someone else. Maybe Emmeline was speaking with the wrong Lisette Hamilton. Or maybe, or maybe . . . Emmeline found it difficult to catch her breath.

"Of course you can return anytime you like." Lisette eyed her with a concerned expression. "Are you sure you are quite well, Miss . . . Miss?"

"Miss Tarleton. I'm fine, truly. I just need to get some air. Thank you for your time, Miss Hamilton." With that, Emmeline fled from the pretty bookshop, the bells above the door jingling merrily as she left.

15

Goodwill to Men

That evening Quinton Roxbury stood overlooking the carefully crafted plans that were spread across the wide oak desk belonging to Lucien Sinclair, the Earl of Waverly. As he explained the details of the houses he wished to have constructed just outside the main part of London, he could see the well-built, attractive homes perfectly in his mind.

"Now what are these?" Lucien asked, pointing to the elongated rectangles depicted in the plans.

"Those are the gardens separating the houses. Each house will have its own. Not only can the families grow their own food but the gardens provide space and add beauty to the surroundings as well. I've also taken into consideration the mature trees that are already there and we shall build around them, allowing the trees to stay in place."

"Well, I see you have considered all the possibilities and it certainly seems feasible and is a worthy cause," Lucien began slowly, nodding his head.

"So what do you think?" he asked, holding his breath. Having Lord Waverly's backing would persuade other investors and Quinton genuinely liked the man. Waverly was intelligent and understood what Quinton was trying to accomplish.

Lucien grinned. "I can't in good conscience refuse your request to help finance the venture."

Quinton could hardly contain his elation. "Thank you, Lord Waverly! It's an honor to have you join this project. With your help, we can now move forward and begin construction right away."

They shook hands heartily.

"You have no idea how long I have wanted to do this," Quinton explained.

"I congratulate you. It's admirable to see someone so sincere in helping those less fortunate and I am happy to be a part of it," Lucien said. "Would you care to stay and join my family for supper this evening?"

Quinton immediately thought of Lisette and wondered if she would be present. It was risky to visit Devon House, knowing the probability of seeing her was rather high. He knew it was wrong, but God, how he wanted to see her! He had not been able to stop thinking of her since the afternoon in the little curio shop in Brighton. She had rushed out so quickly that he had not been able to say what he wanted to tell her. And he had acted foolishly that day, he knew. Penelope Eaton had almost caught him kissing Lisette. It would have been disastrous had she arrived a moment later and found them doing just that.

For as much as he wanted to, seeing Lisette again was not the wisest of decisions. When he accepted Lord Waverly's invitation to discuss the housing project at Devon House, Quinton decided he would not seek out Lisette as he had so recklessly done at her mother's house in Brighton. Now it would be best if he left the house before he encountered her, but he also had no wish to offend Lord Waverly by refusing his hospitality. Not when Lucien had just agreed to donate a very large sum of money to his cause.

"Yes, thank you. I'd love to stay," he answered. "Without your financial backing and the Duke of Wentworth's, these houses would never have a chance to be built."

"Has the duke agreed as well?" Lucien asked.

"Yes, as my future father-in-law, he has given me his full support. We finalized the purchase of a large tract of land just outside the city a few days ago."

"Your future father-in-law?"

"I'm marrying the duke's daughter, Lady Emmeline, after New Year's."

"Well, congratulations once again, Mr. Roxbury!" Lucien exclaimed.

"Thank you."

Lady Emmeline Tarleton would be his wife in a few short weeks. Although it should be a joyous event, the thought of it weighed upon him heavily. Oddly enough, the prospect of marrying Emmeline had not bothered him until he met Lisette Hamilton. Now a lot of things about Lady Emmeline bothered him.

He was filled with conflicting emotions.

"I seem to recall hearing about your engagement last summer. Perhaps my wife mentioned it. Forgive me for not being aware of your good fortune. This calls for a celebratory drink," Lucien suggested.

Quinton rolled up the plans and carefully set them aside, while Lucien opened a decanter of bourbon and poured them each a glass. He handed a crystal tumbler to Quinton.

"Have you given any thought about taking this passion of yours for making social changes and beginning a political career, Roxbury?"

"As a matter of fact, I have. It's too early to say just yet, but I have some wonderful plans to make reforms."

"I would be interested to hear them because I like what I see so far." Lucien lifted his glass in a toast.

Quinton raised his glass as well. "To good fortune."

Just as he sipped the amber liquid, the door to Lord Waverly's study flew open and a dark-haired toddler came racing into the room.

"Papa! Papa!"

"Phillip!" Lucien's expression changed to delight and pride as he placed his glass on the desk and reached out his arms to the little boy. Lifting him up, he said to Quinton, "This is my son."

Quinton smiled at the boy, more than a little moved by the obvious affection between the father and son. He supposed he would be a father himself soon enough, probably by next Christmas. Yet suddenly the idea of fathering a child with Emmeline did not inspire him. The image of Lisette Hamilton kept intruding into his thoughts. Perhaps he should not stay for supper after all.

"I'm sorry if we interrupted you and your guest, Lucien. He ran too fast for me to catch him!"

Without a doubt the beautiful woman who entered the study was Lady Waverly, and she was clearly expecting another child. Quinton was struck by how much alike she was to Lisette. Her hair was darker than Lisette's and her eyes blue, not green, but the resemblance was uncanny. Their voices even sounded the same.

"Mr. Roxbury, may I present my wife, Lady Waverly, and my son, Phillip. Colette, this is Mr. Quinton Roxbury. I've just agreed to help him build new housing in the city, and he has agreed to join us for supper this evening."

Lady Waverly greeted him warmly and extended her hand. "It's a pleasure to meet you, Mr. Roxbury. How lovely that you will be joining us."

He stared at her, almost transfixed, taking her hand in his. For the briefest instant he had the sensation that it was

Lisette who stood before him, carrying *his* child. The image caused his heart to thud in his chest and a wave of happiness surged through him. He shook himself back to reality before he made a fool out of himself. "It is a pleasure to meet you as well. Thank you for having me." He hesitated. "Forgive me, Lady Waverly, but you look remarkably like your sister."

She laughed lightly, her blue eyes sparkling. "Yes, I have heard that once or twice before. Might I ask which sister you are referring to?"

Quinton then recalled Lisette saying that she had four sisters so he could understand Lady Waverly's need for clarification. "I met Miss Lisette Hamilton on the train to Brighton last week."

"What an extraordinary coincidence!" she said.

"Yes, it was." There had been more than one extraordinary coincidences where he and Lisette were concerned, and Quinton still had not gotten over them.

"Mr. Roxbury, I'm sorry to say that my husband and I had to decline the invitation to your wedding in January, due to my condition." Her hand moved instinctively to the large curve of her belly, which was concealed as discreetly as could be beneath the cut of her rich blue velvet gown.

"I quite understand." He smiled at her, but in truth he had no idea that Lord and Lady Waverly had been invited to his wedding, since he had taken little to no interest in the preparations of the event, but he supposed they would be on the Duke of Wentworth's guest list.

Lady Waverly turned her attention to her husband and son. "Lucien, why don't you take Phillip upstairs and read him a story before supper, and I shall take care of our guest."

"Papa, read me a story!" the dark-haired little boy cried in delight.

"If you'll excuse me." Lucien nodded to Quinton with

a smile. "It seems I am in demand at the moment. I shall return shortly." He left the room, carrying the boy.

Lady Waverly placed her hand gently on Quinton's arm. "Now, Mr. Roxbury, you can escort me to the parlor, where I can take a much needed rest and we can have a nice little chat before supper."

"It would be my pleasure to join you," he said, setting down his drink.

As he escorted Lady Waverly into the grand entryway of Devon House, their butler opened the front door. Quinton stopped short when Lisette and what had to be another sister entered the house. Absolute joy surged through him at the sight of her. Lisette was more beautiful than he remembered. Auburn hair framed her face. Her cheeks were tinged a rosy hue from the cold December evening, and her sultry green eyes were bright. They widened considerably upon seeing him and she, too, stopped in her tracks.

"Oh, hello," she whispered, her eyes on him alone.

He grinned at her like a silly schoolboy. He couldn't help himself. If truth were told, he wanted to scoop her up in his arms and carry her away to a private room and kiss her until they were both senseless. He had the good grace not to do so. "Good evening, Miss Hamilton."

They simply stood there, staring, while the butler closed the door and her two sisters eyed them both with blatant curiosity.

"Mr. Roxbury," Lady Waverly said in an attempt to gain his attention, "may I present my sisters. This is Miss Paulette Hamilton, and I believe you are already acquainted with my sister, Lisette. Girls, this is Lucien's business associate, Mr. Quinton Roxbury. He is joining us for supper this evening."

He forced himself to look away from Lisette's magnetic eyes and instead focused on her younger sister. She, too, looked unbelievably like Lisette, yet different. Paulette was

IT HAPPENED ONE CHRISTMAS 151

a blonder version of the other two sisters, with a keen intelligence about her.

"Miss Hamilton, it is a pleasure to meet you." He bowed politely.

"Mr. Roxbury." Paulette nodded in acknowledgment, her eyes darting suspiciously between the two of them.

He added, "You Hamilton sisters all look startlingly alike."

"Yes, and there are two more you haven't met yet," Colette said, her tone one of amusement. "Now, girls, go change for supper and then please join Mr. Roxbury and me in the parlor."

An hour later Quinton was seated beside Lisette in the formal dining room of Devon House, surrounded by three of her pretty sisters. Yvette, the youngest and blondest of the five, had joined them as well. Lucien's parents were there, too, Simon and Lenora Sinclair, the Marquis and Marchioness of Stancliff.

Quinton found himself the object of the intense scrutiny of the sisters, but they were so charming, he did not mind in the least as he explained to them his building project and Lucien's involvement in it all. They made him feel quite welcome and almost a part of the family. Having been raised in a family with only brothers, being in the midst of all these sisters was a novelty to him. Yet he felt right at home and comfortable with them.

He discovered that Lisette helped in the bookshop. In fact, through the chattering of Paulette and Yvette, he learned a good deal about the Hamilton family. He now knew about Juliette, the second oldest, who'd married an American and was expected home for Christmas any day. He also learned that they had surprised Lisette with an engagement party last night when she returned from Brighton.

Although Lisette barely said a word throughout the

meal, he was keenly aware of her presence beside him. He had to restrain himself from reaching out and touching her. Once their hands brushed accidentally and the shock of desire he felt at the slightest touch of her skin left him light-headed.

When the questions arose about his upcoming nuptials, he could feel Lisette almost freeze beside him, and he longed to take her in his arms and comfort her.

"How exciting!" the young and vivacious Yvette exclaimed at the news. "You shall be married in less than a month! The Duke of Wentworth's daughter is a lucky girl, indeed."

Lady Waverly nodded with a smile. "I believe I met your fiancée at a party last summer, Mr. Roxbury. You are quite fortunate to have such a kind personage as Lady Emmeline Tarleton as well."

Lisette dropped her silver fork on her gilt-edged china plate with a loud clatter.

"Excuse me," she murmured distractedly. Quinton noticed the increased heat in her cheeks when she gave him a rather frantic look.

The conversation continued without incident, but Quinton could feel the change in Lisette and wondered what had happened to upset her. She had known he was about to be married so surely that was not a surprise.

As the meal drew to a close, Lucien invited him to share some brandy. "We never did get to enjoy our drink before supper."

Quinton knew he should take his leave, for being this close to Lisette and not being able to talk to her as he wanted or touch her as he longed to was putting his nerves more than a little on edge. He knew he should go home, yet he followed Lucien into the study, knowing full well that the ladies would eventually join them.

They smoked cigars and sipped their brandy, talking

all the while, and Quinton found he truly liked Lucien's company. He was a good man and would be an asset to his future political career.

"So how do you manage all these sisters under your roof?" Quinton asked.

Lucien gave him a rueful glance. "Now there's a question! It's been an education, I can tell you." He paused and nodded his head with a smile. "But I knew when I married Colette that the girls came with her. It's been quite wonderful actually. I grew up alone, with just my father, and being a part of a large family has been one of the greatest benefits of my marriage. I love those girls as my own sisters."

"There is much to love about them," Quinton said quietly, although his mind was fixed upon Lisette.

Lucien rolled his eyes skyward. "You haven't met Juliette."

Quinton laughed, for he had gathered from the dinner conversation that the second eldest Hamilton sister was something of a firebrand, but he thought he would like to meet her someday. "Their mother is a bit of a character as well, isn't she?"

His eyes narrowed. "You've met Mrs. Hamilton?" Lucien asked, clearly surprised.

"When I was in Brighton, I stopped by Mrs. Hamilton's for a visit," Quinton explained, feeling a little uncomfortable. Earlier he'd led Lucien to believe that he had only met Lisette on the train.

"You and Lisette seemed to have spent a great deal of time together in Brighton."

"Yes," Quinton admitted, not meeting Lucien's eyes. There was no reason to say more.

At that very moment Lisette entered the parlor. "Excuse me, Lucien," she began in a soft voice, "but Colette would like to see you upstairs for a moment. Something about Phillip crying for you."

Lucien rose to his feet, as did Quinton. "Pardon me,"

Lucien apologized. "It seems I am being summoned by a two-year-old. I shall return shortly." He hurried from the room, leaving Quinton alone with Lisette.

They stood looking at each other, not saying a word. For a moment it felt as if they were the only two people in the house.

"It's wonderful to see you again, Miss Hamilton," Quinton finally said. In fact, he was ridiculously happy to see her. When she smiled at him, his heart raced at the sight.

"Lucien mentioned that you would be stopping by today, but I didn't know if I would get to see you."

"We were fortunate that we did, weren't we?"

She nodded and her cheeks colored prettily. Again he fought the desire to draw her into his arms and kiss her. She was the most kissable woman he had ever met.

"Mr. Roxbury . . ." she began with hesitation. "There is something I feel I must tell you."

Concerned by the worried expression in her face, he took a step toward her. Now he could smell the sweet scent of her. Lavender. He asked, "What is it you wish to say to me?"

"A lady came into the bookshop this afternoon to look at Christmas cards."

Lisette was acting nervous, wringing her hands together. He could not imagine what had caused her to be so distressed.

She continued, "This lady was very pretty and charming and we spoke for a little while. She asked me my name and asked about my fiancé."

Quinton refrained from scowling at her reference to being betrothed. The idea of Lisette belonging to another man made him feel more than a little jealous. He wondered if Olivia Trahern was right. Did his possessiveness of Lisette indicate that he was in love with her?

"She told me she was to be married just after the New Year."

He listened patiently to her speak, not understanding what she was saying or what any of it had to do with him. All he wanted to do was kiss her.

"She asked me if I had ever been to Brighton."

His eyes narrowed at the mention of Brighton, and suddenly he had a very bad feeling. He stepped closer to her.

Lisette looked almost distraught. "When I told her I had just returned from Brighton, she became noticeably upset. Before she left the store, she told me her name was Miss Tarleton."

He expelled a long breath. "I see." But he didn't. Emmeline in a bookshop? Quinton doubted if the girl had ever read an entire book from start to finish in her life.

"I did not realize it at the time, but I now know that she was your fiancée. When I heard her name at supper, I put it together and realized she was Lady Emmeline Tarleton. Those two sisters who saw us in the curio shop when we . . . when we were about to . . . about to—" Lisette broke off, unable to say it aloud.

"Kiss?" he finished for her.

She nodded, unable to look at him. "I believe they must have said something to Lady Emmeline about us."

"That's possible, but nothing for you to worry about." No doubt Penelope or Priscilla Eaton had made up some gossip about them. He wondered why Emmeline had said nothing to him about it. Then it occurred to him that he had not seen her since he returned.

Lisette continued, "Your fiancée did not say anything to me specifically about it. However, I had the distinct impression that she was not there to buy Christmas cards at all but to seek more information on . . . the situation."

"It would be the only reason that Emmeline would ever visit a bookshop willingly."

"I feel terrible to think that she suspects us of kissing." She paused, her cheeks flushed in embarrassment. "Especially because all her suspicions would be well founded."

The anguished look on Lisette's face was more than he could bear. He moved another step toward her. He was so close now. Close enough to kiss her. It was ridiculous, this effect she had upon his senses.

"We shall forget what happened in Brighton," he said with a more forceful tone than he intended, wishing that he could follow his own advice. "We need never mention it again."

"Yes," she nodded woodenly.

He ached to touch her, to embrace her and hold her against his chest. He wanted to soothe the worry from her brow with a soft kiss. Yet he dared not.

"Thank you for telling me. Do not worry yourself about any of this. I shall tend to Lady Emmeline."

"Thank you." She nodded and turned to leave the room, whispering, "Good evening, Mr. Roxbury," before she left.

Quinton stood staring after her for some time, lost in thoughts he never expected to have.

16

Brightly Shone the Moon That Night

Lisette just finished changing into her nightclothes later that same evening when there was a soft knocking on her bedroom door. She tied the ribbons of her embroidered dressing gown together and opened the door to allow Colette to enter.

"Do you mind if I come in?" Colette asked. Her sister walked directly to the divan in front of the mantel and sat herself down, wrapping a thick woolen shawl around her shoulders for warmth. "With the party last night and you being at the bookshop all day, we haven't had a moment to speak privately since you returned."

Lisette joined her on the divan near the fire. "What is it you wished to speak to me about?"

Colette gave her an innocent look. "Tell me about your trip. How was Brighton? How was Mother?"

"Fine. Mother is fine, just as we knew she would be." Lisette sighed. She had not left her mother on the best of terms since they had continued to argue over her engagement to Henry. "She will be here Saturday to stay until Christmas and until the baby arrives."

"I've no doubt of that," Colette responded with weariness. "What else happened in Brighton?"

"What do you mean?"

"You know what I mean. Lucien just told me that Mr. Roxbury mentioned visiting you at Mother's house. Why on earth would he come to Mother's?"

Lisette felt the sting of tears and blinked rapidly. "Oh, Colette. It is the most dreadful mess."

Her older sister took her hand in hers and squeezed. "I had a feeling something was going on. Tell me."

"We met by accident the day before I went to Brighton." She laughed a little at the memory. "He knocked me down in the back lane. I had no idea who he was, yet he had the strangest effect upon me. But I believed I would never see him again. Then the next day we were on the same train, sharing a compartment. The coincidence was remarkable. We spent the trip talking about everything and he told me of his houses for the poor. He is the most amazing man I've ever met and we talked easily the whole way. But I let him know from the start that I was betrothed and he told me he was to be married within the month." Lisette paused. "I thought that was the end of it. Until he showed up at Mother's the next day. And Mother was the worst. She practically threw the two of us together!"

Colette gasped in astonishment. "She did what?"

"Oh, Colette, Mother was horrid. She told me that I should not marry Henry, that I would be making a terrible mistake."

"Lisette, no!"

"Yes. And she encouraged me to pursue Mr. Roxbury, even though he is to be married."

"She didn't!"

"She even arranged for Mr. Roxbury and me to have an intimate supper alone together."

Stunned, Colette remained speechless for a moment. "I

had no idea something like this happened! And what of Mr. Roxbury? What did he think of it?"

"He seemed almost amused by it all . . . But, Colette, he . . . we . . ." She swallowed. "We kissed each other."

"Oh, my." Colette bit her lip in worry.

"Yes. And that's not all."

Her sister squeezed her hand tightly.

"We were seen kissing, or practically kissing, by Quinton's friends in Brighton, and I believe they told Lady Emmeline about it. She came into the bookshop today."

"Good heavens!"

"I don't know what to do about it," Lisette whispered.

Colette put her arm around Lisette and rubbed her back in a soothing gesture. Her sister's voice was calmer than Lisette would have expected as she asked, "What do you wish to do, Lisette? Have you feelings for Mr. Roxbury?"

"No!" she cried in desperation. "Yes," she then admitted miserably. "I'm not sure."

"Has he feelings for you?"

"I don't know. Perhaps. At times it feels as though he does . . ."

"Has he said so?"

She gave Colette a knowing look. "Not with words exactly."

"This is far more serious than I thought," Colette whispered. "Does Henry suspect anything?"

Lisette shook her head and sniffled a little. "No. Not a thing. He's so sweet and loyal and would never expect me to behave in such a manner. I do not deserve his love. Oh, Colette, what if I have caused a scandal? I would die if Lady Emmeline thought I was trying to steal her husband."

"Well, he is not her husband yet."

"Colette!" Lisette cried out. "That is just what Mother said!"

"Well, it's true. It's scandalous, but better for it to happen before the wedding than after, I would think."

"For what to happen?"

"For Lady Emmeline to learn that her betrothed has feelings for another woman."

"But he doesn't have feelings for me!" Lisette protested.

"He had feelings enough to kiss you when he is promised to another. That alone says something," Colette stated in a quiet tone. She paused a moment before adding, "I seem to recall hearing a snippet or two of gossip about him before."

Lisette's heart raced at the thought. What had Colette heard about Quinton? "What is it? Is it something awful?"

"Not terribly, no. He is rumored to be quite the rake, but I believe he is now involved with a widow."

Lisette let this bit of news sink in. Quinton was so handsome, of course he would have lots of women in love with him. She wondered about the widow, though. "Who is she?"

"I don't remember her name. You know, I'm not overly involved in society gossip, but I do pick up information from Jeffrey now and then. The man knows everything about everyone."

"He knows Mr. Roxbury?"

"I believe they are acquainted but not good friends. Would you like me to ask him?"

"Heavens no!" Lisette protested vehemently. She would be mortified if Jeffrey Eddington knew about her and Quinton. "That would only make Jeffrey question why you were asking, and I don't want anyone to know what a terrible mess I'm involved in!"

"All right. I won't say a word."

Lisette squared her shoulders. "Besides, it doesn't matter about the widow. He is going to marry Lady Emmeline. Tonight he said we should forget everything that happened."

"And just what happened?" Colette asked softly.

"I told you. He kissed me."

"Lisette?" Her sister prompted.

"We kissed so much it was indecent." Lisette felt her cheeks burn.

Colette leaned her head to one side and eyed her carefully. "You liked it, though."

"It was beautiful." Lisette could not deny it. Kissing Quinton was the most extraordinary thing that had ever happened to her.

"And Henry?"

"Henry has never kissed me the way Quinton did. I've never felt such things for Henry as I did with—" She broke off. "I'm wicked."

"Don't be ridiculous," Colette laughed off Lisette's worry. "Don't think that I didn't kiss Lucien like that before we married!"

"But I'm not marrying Quinton," Lisette said soberly.

"That's true," Colette amended quickly. "But perhaps you should marry him."

"He's marrying Lady Emmeline in a little over three weeks. Oh, how is it that I'm involved in such scandalous goings-on? I'm terrible—"

"No you're not!" Colette cried. "You are the most thoughtful, giving, and loving of girls. You think of everyone else first, always putting yourself last."

"I didn't this time, though, did I?"

"No," Colette paused for a moment, deep in thought. "Perhaps Mother is right. Maybe Henry isn't the right man for you."

"You, too?" Lisette wailed in exasperation. "You think I'm making a mistake in marrying him?"

"Yes," Colette said with a bluntness that startled them both.

Lisette whispered, "Truly?"

"We have all thought so from the start. Henry is a wonderful man, kind and thoughtful. But I don't believe you love him. It just seems as if you are settling, as if you are afraid to find someone to love with your whole heart."

"That's what Mother said."

"Well, for once I think Mother and I agree on something together. We've discussed it before in private. I'm just surprised she said it to you."

"I am, too."

"It's nothing against Henry. It just seems as though you let him choose you and instead of you choosing him. He asked and you agreed. You denied yourself a chance to meet any other prospects by refusing a Season. Henry was safe, a sure thing, and you didn't have to risk anything. If we honestly believed you loved him, everyone would be thrilled to pieces for you, Lisette."

Lisette remained quiet, absorbing her sister's blunt words. "Why does no one believe I love Henry?"

"Do you?" Colette asked, looking her directly in the eyes. She sighed heavily. "I thought I did once."

"I'm not an expert in love, by any means, but I just don't see that there is anything between the two of you. Don't you remember when Juliette first came back from New York? I knew by looking at her and Captain Fleming together that they were in love with each other. There was a magical air about them. I've never seen that with you and Henry. But then again some marriages are happy enough without love. I just don't know if you would be."

There was some merit to what Colette said. *Had* she accepted Henry only because he was the first one to want her? What if she did not even know what love was? What if she was making a dreadful mistake in marrying him?

Henry was all she'd known and she had been content enough with him, but now Quinton stirred so many wild emotions within her that it seemed there was no room left for her feelings for Henry.

"Maybe you need to be sure."

"How do I do that?" Lisette asked. "How did you know you loved Lucien?"

Colette's expression turned soft and a bit dreamy. "I just knew. I couldn't stop thinking about him. I wanted to be with him every minute and I could not foresee a future without him with me."

"Oh." She had not been able to think of anything or anyone but Quinton since he swept her off her feet in the lane, even though she struggled not to think of him. She tried to remain constant in her regard for Henry, as a true fiancée should. But Quinton Roxbury, with his golden looks and caring heart, invaded her thoughts, her dreams, her very being.

Yet he was not hers. He could not be hers.

He belonged to another and so did she. Wanting him defied every single moral fiber she possessed, every belief she was raised with. Imagining a future with him, desiring his kisses, and wishing to help him in all his endeavors were wrong. Yet the images and thoughts sprang unbidden into her mind all through the day and night. Especially the night.

She could excuse her dreams for she could not control what happened when she slept. While she was awake, however, that was another matter altogether. During the day she fought to subdue the illicit thoughts of Quinton Roxbury that tempted her.

"Lisette, I should tell you that I noticed something between you and Mr. Roxbury tonight. It was obvious when you walked in the front door, you both stood there staring at each other like a great pair of fools."

Mortified, Lisette covered her face with her hands.

Colette continued, "Whether you love Mr. Roxbury or he loves you is not the real question, for he is not yours to love nor is he free to love you at the moment. It seems to me that the question you must answer first in your heart is whether you love Henry enough to marry him and spend your life with him."

Colette's wise words made sense to her. Now Lisette had to figure out if she truly loved the man she'd already promised to marry.

17

Long Lay the World in Sin

Thursday, December 11, 1873

Quinton Roxbury climbed the steps of the Duke of Wentworth's massive town house the next afternoon. Although the house was impressive by any standard, he thought the place a bit too large and believed the architect should have scaled the size to be more proportional. Mentally comparing and redesigning buildings was a habit Quinton indulged in whenever he saw them. He learned something new from every structure he studied and filed it away for future reference.

After the Wentworth butler showed him in, he walked with more than a little reluctance to the blue drawing room to see Lady Emmeline Tarleton. This was not a visit he looked forward to, but one that was a necessity. Of late he had been rather neglectful of his future bride and he needed to make some reparations.

"Why, Quinton! This is a surprise!" Emmeline exclaimed upon seeing him.

She was seated at an elegant writing desk and immersed

in penning a letter when he entered, but she rose to her feet and came to meet him. A rare smile lit Emmeline's heart-shaped face, and she seemed genuinely pleased to see him.

He took her hands in his and gave them a light squeeze.

"I was not expecting you," she said with a bit of nervousness in her voice. "Will you have some tea with me? I had just sent for some."

"That would be fine," he said, escorting her to the chair near the tea service and taking a seat nearby. He had never been particularly at ease with Emmeline before, but now he felt terribly uncomfortable with her.

She poured a cup of hot tea and handed it to him.

"Thank you, Emmeline." He placed the full teacup on the side table, having no wish to drink it. "It's good to see you."

"Is it?" she questioned. Her dark eyes narrowed at him and she studied his expression carefully, causing him to feel even more ill at ease.

"Yes, of course," he insisted, making an attempt to smile in her direction. Shouldn't smiling at his future wife be effortless and not something he reminded himself to do? He did not have to force himself to smile when he was with Lisette Hamilton.

"I haven't seen you since before your business took you to Brighton," she said, her voice calm as she stirred her tea. "Did you have an enjoyable trip?"

"Yes. Everything went well. I met with Lord Eaton and drew up a rough sketch for his new house, but the final plans won't be finished for another week or so. I'm still working on them, but he is quite pleased with my design ideas so far."

"Yes, Penelope Eaton said her father was thrilled with your new plans, and I thought how amusing it is to have a fiancé who dabbles in construction."

"I do not 'dabble' in construction, Emmeline. I'm an

architect," he corrected her, concealing his irritation. Now he regretted coming to visit her. He gave her a hard look. "And you were well aware of that fact when we first met."

"Oh, yes," she said, not meeting his eyes. "Forgive me for overlooking that little detail."

He had forgotten how difficult Emmeline could be sometimes and how disinterested she was in most things other than herself. She would be happy enough to see him rise to the top politically and would be more than a willing partner to him socially, but she made no pretense that she would prefer not to hear about his buildings and his cause to help the poor. She usually was polite enough to feign interest in his doings, yet today he detected a biting edge to her words that was not normally present.

"Penelope also mentioned that she saw you while out shopping one afternoon in Brighton," Emmeline uttered in a cool tone before taking a sip of her tea. "Did you see her?"

In that instant he knew without a doubt that Emmeline had been told, and he experienced more than a twinge of guilt over his inexcusable behavior. He wanted to regret kissing Lisette Hamilton, but no matter how hard he tried, he simply could not. He regretted only that they were seen together.

"I am sure Penelope Eaton told you all you needed to know and then some," he said dryly. Emmeline could suspect the worst, but Penelope saw nothing definite. He had not kissed Lisette in the curio shop that afternoon, although he had wanted to and had come achingly close. Still they had done nothing but stand too near each other. Emmeline had only rumor and suspicions, and they could be easily dismissed.

"Whatever do you mean, Quinton?" Emmeline asked, her lashes fluttering in mock innocence.

"I take it you believed Penelope's story?"

"Should I not have?"

"I'm quite certain it has been embellished."

"Why don't you tell me what happened then?"

He shrugged. "There is nothing to tell."

Emmeline's teacup rattled in her shaking hand. She set it down. "Well, then answer me this, Quinton. How would you feel if one of your closest friends said he saw me in an intimate embrace with another man in a public place?"

He sighed in weariness. Emmeline had a point, but still, nothing happened in the curio shop. "I don't know what Penelope thinks she saw that day, but I assure you it was misinterpreted."

She cleared her throat. "So you were not kissing Miss Hamilton?"

"No. I was not." Not in the shop that day anyway. He could at least answer that question truthfully.

Emmeline became very quiet, and neither of them spoke for a minute before she said softly, "She is very beautiful, your Miss Hamilton."

"She is not *my* Miss Hamilton. She merely agreed to ask her brother-in-law, Lord Waverly, to donate to my building project," Quinton said, his conscience pricking him like the devil. He had hurt Emmeline and her anger was justified no matter how he tried to trivialize it. "I apologize if my behavior caused you any worry or concern."

"Should I be worried?" Her eyes locked on him, almost pleaded with him.

He paused before answering, so tempted to say something he should not. To say what was in his heart. Instead he told his future wife exactly what she wanted to hear. "No. There is no need for you to worry."

Her expression softened in relief. "Then I shall believe you."

"Thank you."

They sat in silence again, neither drinking the cups of tea that had grown cold. Quinton felt terrible, because he had wronged her and she now believed that he had not. For all her indifference to his passions and interests and lack of concern about anything in the world outside her own pampered existence, she deserved his respect if only as his betrothed. She would be his wife just after the New Year and she should not be distressed that he had been seen with another woman. Having a mistress in private was one thing. He and Olivia Trahern had always been circumspect in their dealings with each other, and no breath of scandal had touched them, especially after he became engaged. But to publicly embarrass Emmeline was not well done of him. His behavior was reprehensible. He was about to confess the truth to her and beg her forgiveness.

Emmeline's whisper of a voice finally broke the strained silence between them. "Do you still wish to marry me, Quinton?"

He held his breath at her question. Did he still want to marry Lady Emmeline? Was it even a matter of what he wanted anymore?

Quinton observed his fiancée's face carefully. She was not smiling. It suddenly occurred to him that he rarely saw Emmeline smile. Her dark hair fell around her attractive heart-shaped face, her nose upturned ever so slightly, her soft brown eyes watchful. She was dressed fashionably and attractively this afternoon, as she usually did, in a gown of expensive silk in a striking jewel tone. But her mouth was drawn into a thin, hard line, as it was so often. When he had first agreed to marry her, he had not noticed this about her.

In fact, he had found that Lady Emmeline Tarleton had quite suited his needs.

Choosing her as a bride had been a stroke of good luck. She would be an asset to him socially, possessed an extremely generous dowry from her father that would allow him a life of privilege, and would be a suitable mother to their children one day. That she did not inspire romance or love sonnets from him did not matter. Having the Duke of Wentworth as a father-in-law would open doors for him that he'd never imagined.

Quinton's building plans would finally become a reality and his political aspirations could take shape. As he saw it, their union benefited him more so than it did her, for as the only daughter of the Duke of Wentworth, Emmeline Tarleton could have had her pick from many wealthy and titled men. But Quinton knew why Emmeline had set her cap for him, a mere younger son of an earl.

She fancied herself in love with him. Which was only natural for a fiancée to feel for her future husband. But Quinton held no such illusions about her.

Quinton had not even been in the market for a bride when he'd agreed to wed Emmeline. The duke approached him with the idea of marrying his daughter last summer. The enticement to make her his wife was the promise of the duke's financing of Quinton's building projects and his support of his political career. Quinton had not grown to love Emmeline since the engagement either, but most marriages were not based on love anyway. More often than not, marriages were a business arrangement and a financial transaction, an exchange of property. Quinton had to marry at some point, and Emmeline was good wife material. She would be a gracious hostess, manage his household smoothly, and help promote his projects. Love had never entered his thoughts, for he had not given marriage itself any thought beyond the ceremony of it and how a well-connected wife could facilitate his political career.

However, things had changed somehow. Now the beautiful visage of Lisette Hamilton haunted his every waking moment and tortured him through sleepless nights.

Now when he thought of marriage, a real marriage, he saw himself with Lisette and not Emmeline. When he thought of a woman he wanted to build a life with, create a home with, raise a family with, and share a bed with, he pictured Lisette Hamilton.

Did he *want* to marry Emmeline? His wants were not a priority. Even if he wanted to, it was far too late to call off the wedding at this point. The ridiculously lavish reception that her parents had spent more than a small fortune on planning was only three weeks away. There was no decent way out of it without causing untold grief for her and her family and an unforgettable scandal that neither of them would ever live down.

To his mind a better question was, "Do you still wish to marry me, Emmeline?"

She took her time before answering him, and her response was not at all what he expected.

"There are hundreds of guests coming to our wedding, Quinton. The invitations went out weeks ago. We cannot disappoint them."

"No. I don't suppose that we can." And that, he supposed, was that. He rose to his feet, anxious to be on his way.

"Remember that we are to attend the Duke of Rathmore's Christmas Ball next week. Everyone will see us there together and any rumors will be laid to rest by then."

"Yes, of course." He made a move toward the door.

"If you wish any chance of a successful future in Parliament, a scandal with another woman and renouncing your bride just before your wedding would not be the wisest way to begin a political career, Quinton."

Her icy words sent a chill through him and he paused, slowly turning back to face her. "I am well aware of that, Emmeline."

She gave him a pointed look. "Are you?"

There was an implied threat in her words. It did not sit well with him to be threatened, although she did nothing but speak the complete truth. If his behavior with Lisette Hamilton were to be known publicly and Lady Emmeline were to call off their wedding, the disgrace would be such that his ambitious dreams would be ruined before they even began and all his hard work and careful planning would have been for naught. Emmeline knew this quite well. For all her disinterest in anything other than herself, she possessed a keen social acumen that would be a necessary asset to him in the political world he wished to enter.

He said in a low voice, "I understand completely what you are saying."

Yes, he understood all too well. Emmeline Tarleton had the power to destroy all that he had worked for and dreamed of.

18

Strike the Harp
and Join the Chorus

Friday, December 12, 1873

Devon House was in a state of joyous upheaval. At long last, Juliette had returned home, bringing with her a trunk full of exotic and extravagant gifts, her handsome American husband, and the surprise of all surprises, her infant daughter.

Lisette cradled her tiny niece in her lap as she swayed gently back and forth in the rocking chair. The feel of a baby in her arms almost made her cry, she wanted one of her own so very much. "Oh, Juliette, how could you not even have told us you were expecting?"

"I was afraid something bad would happen, so until my child arrived in this world safely, I wasn't risking anything," Juliette, her blue eyes gleaming, explained with her usual breeziness. Her long dark hair hung loose around her, giving her the appearance of a gypsy.

The Hamilton sisters were all gathered in Colette's sitting room late that afternoon, happy to be reunited.

Not hiding her sarcasm in the least, Paulette demanded, "When did you become so superstitious?"

"Since I began spending time with sailors." Juliette smiled cryptically at her four sisters. "And they are a very superstitious lot, I can assure you. They may seem brave and hearty, but they will quake in their boots at the slightest sign of bad luck."

They nodded in understanding then, for Juliette's husband was a sea captain and she'd spent the last two years sailing around the world on his ship, the *Sea Minx*.

"Harrison thought I was a little overzealous in my wariness," Juliette continued, "but my daughter was born without a bit of trouble. You'll never guess where!"

"Where?" Colette asked.

"At home! After all our traveling, I thought for sure my first child would be born in China or on an island in the Pacific somewhere, but no. She was born at our home in New Jersey. Can you believe it?"

The girls chuckled at the irony of their world traveler of a sister.

"Well, we are very glad to have you all here in time for Christmas," Lisette said, still holding the sweet baby girl in her arms. "Especially this little angel," she cooed to the sleeping infant.

Yvette, always impatient, asked, "Must we wait for Christmas to open your gifts, Juliette?"

"Yes, I am afraid we must!" Juliette declared emphatically, happy to torture her youngest sister. "It's why we call them *Christmas* presents."

"Do you know that this is the first time all five of us have been together since Juliette's wedding?" Paulette mused as she lay sprawled on the divan, her delicate chin resting on her hands.

"It's nice, isn't it?" Lisette asked with a smile.

Colette, her hand on her burgeoning belly, agreed. "It's wonderful."

"We've come such a long way since the days we lived above the bookshop," Juliette reflected, watching her daughter sleeping in Lisette's arms, while she cuddled her nephew Phillip in her lap. Phillip had been delighted to see his Aunt Juliette, for she had brought him a miniature ship.

"And now we have darling little Sara to join us," Lisette whispered. The baby was beautiful and looked like a more peaceful version of her mother. Lisette placed a soft kiss on her niece's delicate forehead.

"And another one on the way," Colette added with a little laugh.

"Mother will be arriving tomorrow, won't she?" Juliette asked.

"Yes, and won't she be surprised that you are here already! We didn't know when to expect you and Harrison," Lisette said. "And she will be thrilled to learn that she has a granddaughter!"

"Oh, Juliette!" Yvette exclaimed, twirling her blond tresses with her finger. "Lisette has some exciting news, too!"

Juliette noted Lisette's blushing cheeks. "Wait, don't tell me. Let me guess. Old Henry finally got around to setting a date!"

The girls' bright laughter floated around the room, but Lisette did not join in their levity. She had been the object of her sisters' teasing on the subject of her courtship with Henry Brooks for years. Long enough to know that their gentle mockery was good-natured and they meant no harm by it. She usually laughed with them, because she knew Henry loved her and would come around when he was ready.

Yet this time their laughter struck an emotional chord deep within her and she was not quite sure what triggered the change in her feelings, but she did not feel like laughing.

She responded in a quiet tone. "Yes, we've set a date for June."

Juliette gave her a quizzical glance. For all her apparent thoughtlessness, Juliette was surprisingly astute in noticing the feelings of those she loved. "That is happy news, Lisette." She congratulated her. "I shall make sure that Harrison and I return to England in time for your wedding."

Still stretched out on the divan, Paulette piped in, "Henry even gave her an engagement ring."

"Oh, let me see!" Juliette exclaimed in excitement.

Lisette cringed. She and Henry were supposed to visit the jeweler to have the ring adjusted to fit her finger. They had both forgotten. She must make a point to remind Henry. She was determined that they would go together tomorrow. "I don't have it with me at the moment," she explained. "Henry has it. It's too big so we need to have it sized to fit me."

"Oh, well, I suppose you will show it to me later then," Juliette said.

"Yes, of course."

Their conversation turned to plans for Christmas but Lisette was lost in her own thoughts. She suddenly felt uncomfortable with her sisters for the only time she could ever recall. She had not met Colette's eyes when they talked of her engagement ring. She couldn't. Not after everything she had told her about kissing Quinton Roxbury.

"Do you think we shall be able to attend the ice-skating party the Fontaines are hosting next week?" Yvette asked. "Their pond is completely frozen, so it should be nice. Besides I have a new fur-lined cloak I would love to wear."

"Yes, that sounds like fun," Juliette added. "Let's all go skating together."

"Well, I certainly shan't be ice skating!" Colette declared, causing them all to laugh again.

This time Lisette laughed with her sisters.

19

Love and Joy Come to You

Saturday, December 13, 1873

Jubilant and full of excitement, Quinton left a special meeting of the board of directors of the housing commission, who had deemed his plans satisfactory and had just given him their approval. Everything was coming together perfectly and he couldn't be more pleased with the fact that his houses would finally be built for the people who needed them the most. Oh, he designed houses for the wealthy, of course, because they paid well, but these other houses meant more to him. These were homes that would make a real impact in the lives of people. He would be creating a whole neighborhood, an entire new way of life for dozens of poor families who would otherwise be spending their lives in miserable squalor.

And this was just the start. Eventually he could get more homes built, and when he could get elected to Parliament he could make a real difference. He would be able to make sweeping changes and reforms then.

Walking along the crowded street toward his waiting

carriage, he noted the heavy gray sky threatening to snow once again. There was a definite chill in the air and he increased his pace. Pulling his scarf up around his neck to ward off the cold, he rounded the corner of the street. Distracted, he did not watch where he was walking. He crashed into someone, a woman. He grabbed her delicate shoulders to keep her from falling down.

"Lisette!" he cried in surprise when he realized it was she. "Miss Hamilton." He amended as an afterthought. "Forgive me. Are you all right?"

Her sweet laughter warmed his heart as he held her by her arms, her hands tucked into a white ermine muff. She gazed up at him with wide eyes full of amusement.

"Mr. Roxbury," she continued to laugh. "We really *must* stop meeting this way!"

"We do tend to run into each other unexpectedly, don't we?" He smiled at her, joy surging through him at the sight of her. Her face was so beautiful it almost took his breath away. Her green eyes sparkled with an inner light, as if she were brimming with a most delicious secret. The hood of her black cloak trimmed with white fur framed her face prettily.

"It's beginning to feel ridiculous how we meet like this." She laughed again.

"Yes, I suppose it is." It was now the fourth time they had met by utter chance. He wondered at the odds of such coincidence. Or good fortune. Or fate. Whatever it was called, he was grateful for their crossing paths. He was simply happy to see her.

People brushed by them as they stood immobile in the middle of the walkway. He realized he still held her. With great reluctance, Quinton released her shoulders from his grasp, his gloved hands sliding slowly down the length of her arms. They stared at each other.

"It is good to see you, Miss Hamilton."

"It is good to see you, too, Mr. Roxbury."

"May I ask where you are headed this afternoon?"

A cloud crossed her face and she seemed flustered and a little embarrassed. "Oh . . . I . . . that is," she stammered awkwardly, her eyelids fluttering. "I am meeting Henry."

Quinton forced a smile he did not feel. "That's wonderful. Where are you meeting him?"

Surprised by his response, she answered slowly, "I was on my way there just now. It's Bradbury's Jewelry Shop, just around the corner."

"I would be honored to meet your fiancé." He added with a sly smile, "And to be fair, you met my fiancée." Honestly he was interested in finally seeing the solicitor who had claimed Lisette's heart to the dismay of her mother. "May I walk with you?"

Lisette seemed to answer without thinking. "Yes, of course, if you wish."

He extended his arm to her. "Then shall we?"

She took his arm. A sudden gust of wind swooshed by, causing her black velvet cloak to swirl around her. Neither shivered from the wintry blast, so busy were they basking in the warm glow of each other's company. They walked the brief distance in the direction of the jeweler's shop. When they reached the storefront, Lisette hesitated.

"Shall we go in?" she whispered.

Her nervousness at his intention to meet her fiancé intrigued him. What had she to be so anxious about? Was the man disfigured in some way? Was he old and decrepit? Quinton had no idea what to expect as he opened the door to the jewelry shop and held it for her.

"Miss Hamilton! Miss Hamilton!"

They both turned at the sound of her name. A young boy hurried along the pavement toward them. Lisette seemed to recognize him and moved in his direction. Pausing to watch, Quinton closed the door to the shop.

"What is it, Jeremy?" she asked, her face concerned.

The youth took a big gulp of air to catch his breath. "I have a message for you from Mr. Brooks." Reaching into his pocket, he produced a folded paper and handed it to Lisette.

Lisette read the note quickly, her expression revealing nothing. She shoved the paper into her reticule and pulled out a coin. Giving it to the boy, she said, "Thank you, Jeremy."

He grinned happily at the tip he received. "No message in return?"

"Please tell Mr. Brooks that everything is fine."

The boy tipped his cap to her. "Thank you. Good afternoon, miss." He raced off in the direction he'd come from.

Quinton gave her a quizzical look but had a feeling he already knew what the message contained. "Not bad news, I hope?"

She sighed and answered in a matter-of-fact tone, "It seems Henry has been unexpectedly detained by an emergency with a client and must travel to Portsmouth this evening."

"And he will not be able to meet you here," Quinton stated the obvious.

"Apparently not." She squared her petite shoulders. "Well, then. I suppose I shall return home."

"I will take you in my carriage."

She protested politely, her nervousness returning again. "Oh, that won't be necessary, Mr. Roxbury."

"I insist. It has grown colder and the wind is picking up. I won't take no for an answer, Miss Hamilton. Besides . . ." He offered her a cryptic smile. "I have an ulterior motive for wanting you to accompany me."

He watched her green eyes widen.

"I have some news to share about my building project

and would also like your opinion of some of the new plans I have in mind."

She relaxed visibly at his words and nodded in agreement. "Then it would be my pleasure."

Another strong gust of wind whipped around them, almost knocking Lisette's slight frame over and blowing her fur-trimmed hood off her head. Instinctively he reached out to steady her and she grabbed hold of him. The weather was becoming decidedly worse. He drew her near him in protection.

"We should hurry," he said.

He held on to her hand and guided her quickly back up the street toward his waiting carriage. Once they were safely ensconced within the well-appointed vehicle, he instructed his coachman to take them to the planned site for his houses, just outside the city. In spite of the dreary weather, Quinton was not quite ready to take Lisette home now that he had her to himself.

"How would you like to see where we're going to build the houses before I take you home?" he asked her.

"Oh, that would be wonderful!" she exclaimed.

"Good, because that is where we are headed." He settled back in the opposing seat, facing Lisette. "Are you disappointed that your fiancé could not meet you?"

Lisette inclined her head slightly. "A little." She paused before adding, "We were to have my engagement ring fitted properly this afternoon."

He did not like to think of Lisette wearing this Henry Brooks's ring and was oddly satisfied that even now she still could not wear it. "Although I am pleased by this unexpected chance to see you, I am sorry that you have been let down."

She did not meet his eyes. "Thank you."

"I have good news that I think you shall be glad to hear," he began in an attempt to brighten her mood. "I have raised enough capital for construction to begin on the new housing development. Building will definitely start in the spring."

Her entire expression transformed into one of absolute delight. "Oh, how wonderful! That is exciting news!" She clapped her hands together.

"Isn't it?" Thrilled by her response to his news, he had known instinctively that she would share in his enthusiasm. It was the reason he had wanted to tell her. Now having told her, he fought the impulse to embrace her. Instead he described to her the details of his meeting with the housing commission that afternoon. "And I took to heart your ideas about education. I've designed a schoolhouse for the neighborhood as well."

"You are going to vastly change people's lives for the better, Mr. Roxbury. Do you realize that?" Her voice was incredulous and tinged with awe.

"That is the point. The poor need to have their lives changed in a dramatic way; otherwise nothing would ever change. A real house gives a person a sense of dignity and comfort and makes for a better community overall and benefits everyone in the long run. But the change needs to occur. It doesn't matter who does it as long as it gets done. The credit does not belong to me."

"But it was your idea to build these houses in the first place," she insisted. "I think what you are doing is quite inspirational. I would be proud to help you in any way I could."

Quinton remained quiet. Lisette's reaction to his work pleased him. In such a short time Lisette had taken an interest in what he did and found his work commendable, even laudable. It was one of the reasons he found her so attractive. Whereas Emmeline . . . Emmeline had no interest in anyone other than herself.

"I would love to have your assistance. We are about to

form a committee to help with finalizing the details and selecting the families that will be the first inhabitants of this neighborhood. I think you would be an asset to such a cause, Miss Hamilton."

She shook her head and a soft color suffused her cheeks. "Oh, no. Not me. I've never done anything like that. I couldn't possibly."

"You would be the perfect person for such an endeavor," he insisted. "You are intelligent and caring and you have common sense. Besides, you are already part of a committee."

"What are you talking about?" She gazed at him quizzically.

"Your family. Do you or do you not decide things together with your sisters about what you will do as a group or what you will do at the bookshop?"

"Well . . . yes we do," she admitted with a bit of reluctance. "But that is completely different."

"No, it isn't really. It's the same principle, only more official. On the housing committee there would be other people working with you, coming up with ideas, solving problems, and making decisions. That's how it works. You have well-formed ideas and would be a wonderful addition. You inspired me with the idea of creating a neighborhood, not just homes. Adding a school and a church. Besides, you do such remarkable service already by teaching those boys in the shop how to read. I think you should consider it."

A look of intrigue came over her pretty face, and he knew he was winning her over.

"Do you truly think so?"

"Absolutely."

"I shall give the matter some thought," she promised with a smile.

He admitted, "I've already submitted your name."

"You have?" her voice squeaked a bit in surprise.

"Yes."

The carriage came to a stop, and Quinton glanced out the curtained window. "We're here." He extended his hand to her. "Come with me."

Lisette took his hand and he helped her down from the carriage. Being a gentleman had its advantages because he loved that he had such a good excuse to touch her. Braving the cold, together they walked hand in hand across the hard ground. The sky above was heavy with thick gray clouds, and the wind continued to whip around them in unexpected bursts. This area of undeveloped land on the western edge of the city was covered with many large trees and encompassed empty fields and meadows.

"It's so pretty here," she said, taking in the expansive view from atop a small rise they climbed.

"Isn't it?" A feeling of contentment filled him being there with her, simply holding her hand on a cold afternoon.

"Is all of this land yours?"

"Well, it's not mine exactly, but yes. There are about twenty or so acres that we will use to construct the houses and other buildings on." He could easily picture the houses there already and it filled him with satisfaction.

"How good it will be to move some of those families out of the city, to live here, in their own homes."

"In my view, poverty only begets more poverty. There has to be a way to break the cycle. Hopefully this will do it. Most important, the families we select to live here will have access to clean water, which they don't get in the city and what causes much of the diseases that run so rampant through the slums. Each home will have its own garden so they can grow their own food. And they will have a beautiful space to move and breathe in. There will be a church over there and the main street of the village will run along here, with shops and a school." He pointed with his free hand. His other hand still grasped Lisette's. He noted with pleasure that she had not pulled away from him.

"What about employment?" she asked, her face alight with interest. "How will they earn a living and support themselves?"

Impressed with her intelligent questions, he answered, "That will be the goal of the selection committee to choose families with some sort of trade skills to start with. We will also train some of them to work in the stores and shops. We are only a short train ride into the city, and they can seek employment there as well. They will live in the houses free to start and eventually begin to pay rent, with a possibility to owning the home at some point. All the rent money we collect will go back into improvements on the houses and the community in general."

"This is quite an enormous undertaking you've begun, Mr. Roxbury. Do you really think this will work?"

"I have people telling me I'm crazy to attempt this, stating that a venture of this magnitude will never succeed. They tell me it is destined to fail. But how can we not try? I think they are wrong and it will be successful. If it turns out to be an abysmal failure, then I will know I was wrong. And I would have lost a lot of money. However, I can't help but believe that something good will come of all this."

"Has anything like this been done before?" She looked up at him, the expression on her pretty face full of wonder and admiration. Quinton's heart skipped a beat.

"Not that I am aware of."

"What of the children?"

"What about them?"

"Schooling is not compulsory as of yet, although there is talk that it will be eventually," Lisette said. "But I think it should be a requirement of this community that the children living in the houses here, both girls and boys, must attend school every day."

"I agree with you on that. Their education is of the utmost importance. Ignorance only perpetuates poverty. We'll see to it that schooling is a mandatory part of living in the community."

"What shall you call it? This community?"

"I have no idea."

She smiled, slanting a look up at him. "How about Roxbury Park?"

"I would never seek to be so vain as to name it after myself," he said, laughing. "And what if it should be a dismal failure? Then my name will be associated with it forever!"

Lisette laughed lightly with him. "Yes, I see your point."

He loved the sound of her laughter, so sweet and clear. What was it about her that drew him to her as if he had no will of his own? Wishing he could sweep her up in his arms and kiss her, he said only, "I'm sure the committee can come up with a suitable enough name."

As the two of them continued walking along the site, suddenly her boot caught on a large tree root and she stumbled, pitching forward. Quinton reached out to catch her from falling to the ground. His arms quickly wrapped around her small frame, and he pulled her close to him to steady her.

"Are you all right?" He held her in his firm grip, feeling the pounding of her heart next to his chest. She felt so good in his arms, so right. Her body pressed against the length of him, her seductive shape a painful reminder of what he should not want. A slow banked heat began to burn between them. Lisette looked up at him and he saw undisguised desire flash in her pretty green eyes. He felt it, too, wanting to press his lips to hers and take her mouth in a sweet kiss. It would be so easy. The curve of her full lips, slightly parted, enticed him with the memory of their exquisite taste. He could just lean down and kiss her. He was so close . . . However, he steeled himself not to. They stood like that for some minutes, suspended in a dangerous limbo of longing.

"Yes, I'm all right," she finally murmured as she pulled back from him, breaking their little reverie. "Thank you for catching me. I must take more care where I am walking."

He released her with great reluctance, and she took a step or two away from him.

"I suppose we should be getting back," he suggested, suddenly feeling the cold wind more sharply than he had before she had been in his arms.

"Yes." She nodded. "I suppose we should."

Although he longed to, this time he did not take her hand as they walked silently back to his carriage. He felt oddly bereft without her small hand in his, but he knew that not touching her was the wiser course of action even though it went against every instinct of his being. With a sigh of resolve, Quinton directed the coachman to take them to Devon House, and then he helped Lisette into the carriage and took his seat across from her.

"Thank you for bringing me here today," she said as the carriage began to move forward.

"I was happy to show it to you." It was the truth. He'd gained much pleasure from looking at the land through her eyes. Lisette seemed as much a part of the project as any of the financial contributors. "When we have the time to do so properly, I would like to show you the detailed designs for the houses. Your opinion would mean a great deal to me."

"I would love to see the designs! I've never seen the architectural plans for a house before or any other building for that matter."

"I think you would find them qui—"

The carriage jolted to a sudden stop, flinging an unsuspecting Lisette forward with a little squeal of surprise.

Seated across from her, Quinton reached out and barely managed to catch her before she landed on the floor of the carriage in a tangle of skirts. While helping her return to the seat, the carriage lurched into motion once again, causing him to lose his balance and fall upon her. She sprawled back on her seat sideways and their bodies angled together on the seat in such a way that he was on top of her in the most intimate of positions.

Quinton reminded himself to have a talk with his coachman later, but was not sure whether to upbraid him for his poor driving or thank him. Landing atop Lisette Hamilton seemed to be a continuing test of his principles and willpower. It was also heavenly.

Neither of them moved. Nor uttered a single sound. In fact, they barely breathed at all. Their gazes were drawn to each other and they could not look away. The swaying of the carriage rocked them back and forth in a hypnotizing motion. Time hung suspended between them once again. Temptation and desire warred with the consequences and the consciences within their beings.

But this time, Quinton felt his resolve slipping away . . . He was so close. The wild beating of her heart pounded in his ears as he watched the rapid rise and fall of her chest under her velvet cloak. The allure of her lips, the force of her own longing reflected in her sultry eyes, and the feel of her warm body beneath his were more than a man could bear. Within the privacy of the carriage, Quinton could easily kiss Lisette to his heart's content with no one there to see. No one would ever know. Every inch of his being cried out for her. Wanted her. Needed her. Longed to possess her.

Looking into her deep green eyes, now heavy-lidded with desire, he knew she felt the same way. Which did nothing to cool his ardor.

Logic told him to remove himself with all haste and put

a respectable distance between them, all while begging Lisette's forgiveness. But at that moment logic and good sense had no place in his mind. Or in his body.

On the edge of a steep precipice, he let loose an anguished growl before he took her mouth in a ravenous kiss. Lisette kissed him back just as hungrily, her arms reaching up around his neck, pulling him to her. The satisfied little sigh that escaped her parted lips before he touched them excited him beyond measure. He could not get enough of her luscious mouth. In an instant they were locked in a passionate embrace. Heat flared between them as their mouths and tongues devoured each other. Their kisses increased in intensity, consuming them, fueled by a forbidden desire and the need to take what they could while they could.

In spite of the heavy cloaks and gloves they both wore, he pulled her tightly against him, settling himself quite firmly between her legs. She sighed, most unmistakably, with pleasure and it almost undid him. Breaking their kiss, he reached his hands around and pulled his gloves off, and with greater haste removed his coat, flinging it to the floor. His eyes on her, he lifted her hands and gently began to remove her gloves. One by one he slowly released her fingers from their leather coverings. The feel of her silken hands, warm and soft, intertwining with his, took his breath away. He undid the clasp of her cloak, opening the front. He lowered his head and captured her mouth in another kiss.

So lovely was she, that he could drown in her scent and softness without a moment's hesitation. Then his hand slid down with deliberate intent to cover her breast. Even through the layers of clothing he could imagine the feel of her, and he squeezed her with unbridled need. Her back arched at his rough caress, and her fingers splayed in the hair at the back of his neck.

God, how he desired her! Never had he wanted any woman the way he wanted Lisette Hamilton. There was something about her that drew him to her. His desire to remove her cumbersome clothing, to feel her naked skin against his own and to possess her body completely and thoroughly, threatened to overwhelm him.

"Lisette, Lisette," he murmured, kissing her soft cheeks, the curve of her neck.

With a trembling hand, he raised up the skirts of her gown bit by bit, caressing the length of her stocking-clad thigh. Again, Lisette sighed at his intimate touch, melting into him, arching against him. She clung to him, her mouth pressed hungrily against his. Her bare hands wound around his neck, weaving through his hair. Her response thrilled him. She did not protest his advances, and in fact seemed to welcome them. Rock hard with need for her, he realized he could take her right then and there in his carriage.

That terrified him.

Alarm bells rang in his head. This was far too dangerous. The consequences were monumental.

Uttering a strangled cry, he broke away from their embrace, and an anguished sob tore from her throat. He maneuvered to a sitting position and pulled her up so she was cradled in his lap, then he wrapped his arms around her. She rested her head against his chest, and he stroked her back as they both regained their normal breathing.

Christ. How did she do this to him? How had it come to him almost taking her in a moving carriage? He should be ashamed of himself.

"Lisette," he whispered low in her ear. And a pretty, delicate ear it was, too.

"What are we doing?" she asked softly.

There was a wealth of emotion in her question, and his heart longed to give her the answer that his head would not allow him to give. He said simply, "I wish I knew."

"We promised this was not going to happen again."

"Yes we did."

"I've never . . ." Her voice was as soft as rose petals. "I've never been kissed like that before."

A thrill of pride and possessiveness welled within him at her sweet confession. He did not want to think of anyone kissing Lisette the way he just had. Ever. He also had to wonder what was wrong with old Henry that he *hadn't* kissed his beautiful fiancée that way after so many years together.

Then it struck him. Quinton had never even kissed his *own* fiancée that way. Lady Emmeline did not inspire within him the desire to kiss her. He doubted that she ever would.

But Lisette did.

And he held her in his arms most lovingly. If Lisette were his fiancée, he would have married her already because he wouldn't have been able to wait any longer with only her kisses to sustain him.

He lowered his head and kissed her again, his mouth covering hers in a swift and sure motion. She clung to him, her lips hot on his. Before drowning within her completely once again, he pulled back.

"You mean he has never kissed you like that?" he asked, intent on knowing that he was the only one who had elicited such passion in her. He knew it, but he wanted to hear her say it.

With a slow movement she shook her head. "Never."

He asked low, "Do you like when I kiss you that way?"

She met his steady gaze without blinking, without wavering. "Yes."

The passionate look in her eyes almost undid him then and there. If he had her in his bed right now and not a carriage, he would make love to her for days and days on end. His thoughts bordered on the torturous. He had to stop.

"Oh, what are we doing?" she asked again in a distraught whisper.

What the hell *were* they doing? He was not sure what she wanted him to say. Did she expect him to declare his love for her? Did she want him to renounce his engagement to Emmeline and marry her instead? He expected that was what a woman wanted after kissing a man in such a way. To be married. Lisette was not a girl to be trifled with, and he knew that, in spite of his careless handling of her just now. She was worthy of more than he could offer, for he could not marry her.

She wanted an answer. She deserved a decent answer and he had none to give.

"Do you have feelings for me?" Lisette bit her lip in nervousness.

"Yes."

The answer sprang from his mouth before he could consider his options because he simply could not lie to her. He had feelings for Lisette that he didn't even know existed before this. Feelings that left him shaking with desire for wanting her. Feelings that woke him in the middle of the night and occupied his mind all during the day. She was all he thought about, dreamed about. Hell yes, he had feelings for her. He was consumed by his feelings for her. She was in his carriage right now because he could not control his feelings for her.

Quinton pressed a gentle kiss on the silky curve of her cheek. "Do you have feelings for me, Lisette?"

Again, the honesty in her green eyes, cloaked in the shadows of the carriage, astonished him. She did not flinch away, did not look ashamed. "I couldn't allow you to kiss me like this if I didn't."

He knew that. And that was what had troubled him. Lisette was not a light skirt. She hadn't even kissed her fiancé properly after all those years, and Quinton had no right to be kissing her now. Because they were both promised to others, the two of them had entered very, very dangerous territory.

But then again hadn't they entered it over a week ago in Brighton? Hadn't they rushed headfirst into it when they had kissed so passionately on the beach?

"Oh, my Lisette." He sighed her name, pressing kisses into her hair. He continued to hold her in his arms, her head resting against his chest, breathing in the sweet scent of her, marveling at the softness and perfection of her body next to his.

Night fell and he could barely make out the delicate features of her face in the dimness. Neither said another word until they reached her home, and the carriage finally came to a stop.

Before he released her, Quinton kissed her cheek again, afraid that kissing her on the lips would only ignite another passionate embrace that would be too painful to end. He was loath to let her go. He whispered her name in her ear once again.

"Don't follow me out," she murmured thickly. "Just go."

She squeezed his hand tightly before she removed herself from his lap, and the sudden loss of her warmth chilled him. She gathered her gloves and things together, straightening her skirts and neatening her appearance as best she could. He, too, donned his coat, gloves, and hat. In spite of her protests, he leapt from the carriage and helped her down. It was the least he could do, and it gave him a few more seconds with her. He held her a moment longer than he should, wanting to keep her with him.

"Thank you for taking me home," she said. "I had a lovely afternoon."

"I did, too. And you are most welcome."

"Good night, Mr. Roxbury."

"Good night, Miss Hamilton."

After one last longing glance at him, Lisette hurried up the steps and into the house. He stood there for a moment, watching where she had just been a moment before. He wanted nothing more than to drive off with her in his carriage and keep her with him forever.

If only it were that simple.

20

See the Blazing Yule Before Us

"Where have you been?" Paulette demanded as Lisette walked through the front door of Devon House. Paulette's hands were on her hips in indignation, the scowl on her face indicating her annoyance. "We've been worried sick about you."

"I'm sorry. I lost track of time," Lisette mumbled, wondering if her disheveled appearance revealed what she had been doing in Quinton Roxbury's carriage. Luckily her hood covered her tousled hair. She still trembled from his kisses and all they had said to each other.

It was such a dreadful mess.

If she could just get to her room and have some time to collect herself before facing her sisters, it would be better. Maybe she would declare a headache and stay in her room. Yes, that might be best. She truly did not have the energy for Paulette's questions. And Juliette. Juliette's keen eyes would be sure to see the torment in Lisette's expression.

"Mother's here. She arrived hours ago," Paulette continued. "We've been waiting for you all afternoon. Why you would be out on such a night in this terrible weather, I've no idea—Lisette? What is the matter?"

"Nothing. Nothing at all," Lisette said without stopping. "I have a terrible headache." She hurried up the staircase and fled to her bedroom.

Her mother! Good heavens! The last person she needed to confront right now was her mother. The woman who had practically thrown her at Quinton Roxbury's feet! This untenable situation was entirely her mother's fault! If she had not suggested they walk on the beach, she and Quinton would not have kissed. If she had not invited him to supper, they would not have continued talking and getting to know one another. If her mother had not angered her, she would not have stormed out that day in Brighton and run into Quinton at the curio shop and Quinton's friends would not have seen them almost kissing and would not have told Emmeline Tarleton.

And she would not have gotten in his carriage this evening.

Would she?

Once in the relative haven of privacy in her bedroom, Lisette flung off her cape, leaving it in a careless heap on the floor. She hurried to the cheval glass mirror in the corner near her cherrywood dressing table. Taking stock of her reflection, she thanked heaven above that her sisters had not seen her. Her hair had come loose from its pins and her auburn locks hung past her shoulders. Her lips were swollen and her cheeks still red. There was a bit of tenderness on her cheeks from rubbing against Quinton's stubble.

She looked like a well-kissed woman.

Although Paulette and Yvette would not suspect anything, as married women Colette and Juliette certainly would. And perhaps even her mother.

She ran a hand through her long hair, removing the last of the pins. The taste of Quinton Roxbury remained on her lips, and she could smell his scent on her. She breathed deeply and sighed, wishing she were still in his arms.

Staring at herself, she wondered what it was about her that attracted Quinton Roxbury. Or attracted Henry Brooks for that matter. What was it that aroused the passion in one man yet not in another? What kept Henry from kissing her all these years, and what prompted Quinton, in a matter of days, to kiss her within an inch of her life? Was it the way she looked? Was it the way she acted? Why had she allowed Quinton Roxbury, a man she barely knew, to take such liberties with her person when she had never allowed Henry Brooks any? Quinton had had his hands on her breasts. He had been lifting her skirt before he stopped.

And she had not wanted him to stop. She had forgotten she was in a carriage. She had not cared that she was promised to another man. She had disregarded everything important in her life except his kisses . . . The soft, breathy kisses he placed along her neck that made her shiver. The warm, sweet kisses that made her heart flip over in her chest. The deep, ravenous kisses with swirling tongues that made her toes curl and made her long for more.

And God help her, she wanted more. She had wanted to remove her cloak, her gloves, her gown, everything. She longed to feel his heated skin naked and pressed tightly against hers. She ached for him to touch her in intimate ways too scandalous to give name to.

Trembling, she turned from the mirror and flung herself on her four-poster bed.

Oh, she knew what happened between a man and a woman. There had been a thick medical text in the bookshop that explained the act in great detail. *A Complete Study of the Human Anatomy and All Its Functions,* by Doctor T. Everett, had been hidden behind a shelf in the back room, and she had secretly read it when her father and her sisters were not around.

Knowing what she knew and knowing it should only be done between a husband and a wife had not stopped her from wanting to do such things with Quinton in his carriage earlier that evening!

The truth of her feelings shocked her to the core.

She had never thought about doing anything of the sort with Henry, the man she was supposed to marry. She knew she would have to eventually, of course, but she had not given the matter much attention at all. Now she could only imagine doing such things with Quinton, yet Henry was the man she *should* be thinking about doing those intimate acts with. Not a man engaged to another woman!

What was it about Quinton Roxbury that elicited such passion in her? Whereas with Henry she felt none of those feelings, even when she tried.

She lay there on her back for a long time. Thinking. Wondering. Deciding.

Slowly she removed herself from the bed and retrieved her reticule, which lay discarded on the floor beside her cloak. Reaching inside, she found the note from Henry. She had been nervous and angry when she read it earlier on the street with Quinton near her. Note in hand, she returned to lie upon her bed and read it more carefully this time.

Lisette,

> *A matter of great urgency has arisen with an important client and I must travel to Portsmouth with all due haste to attend to things personally. I regret to inform you that I cannot meet you this afternoon as planned. I know you understand that you have my deepest apologies. I shall return within a day or two.*

> > *Yours,*
> > *Henry Brooks*

Lisette stared at the words from her fiancé, the man who was supposed to love her. There was not a word of affection within the lines. The note was efficient and businesslike, as Henry always was. One would never guess from reading it that they were meeting to have her engagement ring fitted properly. Or that they were close in any way. He could have been her solicitor and nothing more.

She had been so mortified in front of Quinton Roxbury to learn that Henry was not meeting her after all. And was ashamed by the enormous sense of relief that had consumed her at the same time. Quinton had wanted to meet him, but she had not wanted Henry to know about Quinton.

A knock on her bedroom door caused her to sit up. "Come in."

"Good evening, *ma petite*!" her mother said, entering her room. Paulette trailed behind her. As Genevieve leaned on her gold-handled cane, which she used more for dramatic flair than out of actual necessity, she made her way across the room and sat on the end of the bed. "*Que qu'il se passe, ma fille?* What is the matter? Why have you not been to see me yet? What is it? Are you not feeling well?"

Lisette wondered at the highly unusual turn of events. Normally she was the one who comforted her mother when her mother felt unwell. "I'm fine, Mother. Just a touch of a headache."

"I see." Her mother eyed her with matter-of-fact precision. "Very well. *Très bien, ma chérie.* We shall leave you to recover then and we shall have something to eat sent up to you." She rose and went to the door. "Come, Paulette," she instructed. "Let us permit your sister to rest. Besides, I wish to spend more time with my beautiful granddaughter. *J'ai de si belles filles. Et maintenant une merveilleuse petite fille.*"

"I shall join you in just a moment, *Maman*."

Lisette groaned inwardly as her mother left and Paulette came in, closing the door behind her.

"What is wrong?" her younger sister inquired.

"I have a headache. You just heard me tell Mother."

"No." She shook her head. "I want to know what is really wrong."

Lisette sighed in weariness. "There is nothing wrong."

"Weren't you supposed to meet Henry Brooks this afternoon to fix your engagement ring?"

"Yes."

"I don't see you wearing it. What happened?"

"He had to travel to Portsmouth unexpectedly. We shall have to try again another time," Lisette explained calmly.

"That's rather odd."

"I don't see why you would think so. Henry works quite hard and is very dedicated to his practice." Unfortunately, he worked to the exclusion of all else. Lisette used to find that quality becoming. Now she had second thoughts.

"What is odd is that I thought I saw Mr. Roxbury bring you home in his carriage."

"He did," Lisette admitted with reluctance, knowing she still looked as if she had been thoroughly kissed.

Narrowing her eyes, Paulette gave her a suspicious look. "How did he come to escort you home?"

"We ran into each other near the jewelry shop. It was very cold so he offered to drive me home in his carriage."

"Is that all?" she insinuated. "Nothing else happened?"

Lisette hated that Paulette had correctly assumed that something had occurred that afternoon, but she was not about to admit anything. She rose from the bed, her heart pounding. "Don't you have anything better to do than spend your time looking out windows and listening to conversations that don't concern you?"

Her sister turned up her pert little nose. "Fine. I hope you feel better. And I hope you don't do anything to jeopardize your engagement to Henry." With that, Paulette left the room.

Trembling, Lisette sat back down upon her bed. Something had to be done. She simply could not go on like this any longer.

21

The Hopes and Fears
of All the Years

Monday, December 15, 1873

Tom's day was not going well. The one purse he'd
managed to pinch was empty! Not a shilling to be had. The
foolish gent he'd spotted must have gambled all his money
away, for he had certainly looked prosperous enough in his
finely cut cloth coat and silk top hat.

Tom had been hanging around Victoria Station for days,
but it hadn't been as good a place to pinch as he'd hoped.
People seemed to be warier of their surroundings when
they traveled and he'd managed to pinch only one other
wallet. And there was not much in it to brag of. In fact,
Victoria Station had been rather disappointing all around.
Just like his whole day. He was tired and hungry.

And he was cold. Colder than Tom ever remembered
being before. The wind seemed to cut right through his
thin body. Pulling his threadbare jacket more tightly
around him, he trudged back home, knowing it was time
he would be leaving the shoemaker's and his mother would
be expecting him about now. She still had not found any

permanent work, but had been doing some piecework at home. It did not bring in half the money she'd earned at the dress shop, and he watched as she grew more and more despondent about their living situation.

Old Mrs. Framingham, learning that Madame La Fleur had let his mother go, had been harping on them about their weekly rent, threatening to cast them out if they were so much as a day late paying her. As bad as their little garret room was, Tom and his mother were still better off than most and had no wish to be forced from their lodgings to a poorer location. Old Framingham, for all her grumbling, at least kept the building in decent shape and they had access to some relatively clean water, which was not the case for some other buildings in the area. No, they had no desire to leave their tiny attic home, unless it was to move to a much-improved residence.

Which, of course, was Tom's plan all along.

He still had his stolen money savings, which they could use if things became desperate, and they would quite shortly. He was in a quandary about how to use the savings without arousing his mother's suspicions as to how he had come by all that money. She was bound to ask questions, and he was quite certain that she would not like his answers. No sir. Tom still had those three pounds, although they weren't hidden safely under the floorboard anymore. Since his mother was home all day, he lived in mortal fear that somehow she would accidentally find them.

As he walked the lane, Tom passed a women's millinery shop and eyed a pair of dainty white lace gloves in the window. Lace gloves like that wouldn't keep his mother's hands very warm, he knew, with all those little holes in them, but they were pretty and she would like them. He stood looking at them, wishing he could buy them for his mother as a Christmas present. She deserved nice things, pretty things like lace gloves that wouldn't even keep her hands warm. How wonderful it would be to surprise her with such a gift, wrapped in a box with a big ribbon for her to open on Christmas morning next week!

He sighed, pressing his face against the cold glass of the shop window.

"Go on now, you filthy little urchin! Get away from here!" The owner of the shop came out and shooed him away. She was a tall, thin woman with a pinched face and a pair of wire spectacles perched on the end of her long nose. "You've got no business being here! Now get!"

His chest tightening, Tom glared at her, but moved on. He hated when people dismissed him, as if he didn't matter. Who was she to tell him to go away? He did have business being there if he wanted to buy something in that shop, like those lacy gloves! And someday he would march right in there and buy those fancy gloves! Yes sir. He wasn't always going to be living in Saint Giles like the rest of them. Tom was going to move up in the world. He was already smarter than everyone he knew.

Besides, that miserable old shopkeeper didn't know that Tom had the money to buy those gloves and more with him right now! In a small leather bag tied with string, hanging around his neck, were the three pounds. He figured it was the safest place until he could figure out what to do with them.

The wind blew around him. He shoved his hands in his pockets and kicked at the rubble in the street. He made his way toward the dingy alley where he lived. Dodging with ease between the many wagons and carts that rumbled along the crowded thoroughfare, his eyes scanned the ground. He wished he did have that keen eye for finding coins in the street, like his mother believed, because he sure would like to find a shilling or two now.

"Well, look who it is! Little Tom Tom!"

Tom froze and his eyes darted around at the sound of his

name being called. This was not good. Three large boys
stood against the side of the building, their mean gazes
alight with the prospect of a little fun. Tom recognized
them, and even knew their names. They lived a few buildings away from Framingham's and were always causing
mischief in the neighborhood, stealing anything that
wasn't nailed down, upsetting vendor carts, tormenting the
little kids, kicking dogs, and generally making themselves
despised by everyone. Tom's little heart began to pound
with heavy, rapid beats, thundering against his chest. He
had met up with these boys a few times before and he
knew without a doubt he was in deep trouble.

"Where are ya going?" Fred Humphries, the shortest
one, called.

"The better question is where has he been?" The tallest
boy, Jerry Gray, had a hawkish nose and dark beady eyes.
He looked even taller than he was because he wore someone's cast-off and badly battered top hat that was more
ash-gray than black. At almost fourteen, Jerry was the
oldest of the terrible trio. He stared hard at Tom, his eyes
glittering.

The three boys had always scared Tom, and he had made
it his priority to steer clear of them on a regular basis. Unfortunately for him, today he had walked right into their
path, much to their delight.

Tall Jerry continued, "Yeah, that's what I want to know.
Where has the little pisser been? What's he been up to?
And what has he got for us?"

The middle boy, Eddie Poole, pushed himself from the
wall and took a few steps toward Tom. He shoved at Tom's
chest, knocking him to the ground. "Where have ya been?"

Tom glared at them as he picked himself up and brushed
himself off. "Around."

"It's been a while since we've seen Little Tom Tom,"

Jerry said in a taunting voice. "I think we should check his pockets and see what he's got for us."

Tom stepped back, but hadn't realized that Fred had gone around behind him. The three older boys now surrounded him. For the first time that day he was glad his pockets were empty. Tom had been caught by them a few times before, and it had galled him something awful to have them swipe his pickings for the day. This time, however, he could only pray they wouldn't notice the little sack of treasure around his neck.

One day he would love to clobber them all, but he wasn't fool enough to take on three decidedly bigger boys. He wanted to call them the vilest names and curse words he knew, yet Tom knew when shouting off his mouth would only cause more trouble than it was worth. He kept his mouth shut tight.

Fred gave him a hard shove from behind. "Come on, Tom Tom. What have you got for us?"

Tom stumbled forward headfirst into Edwin's hard chest, his tattered tweed cap falling to the ground. Edwin pushed him back into Fred, amid their taunting laughter. Tom finally managed to stop himself, bracing his legs on the ground firmly between the two large boys.

"I don't have anything!" he shouted at them. He shoved his hands in his trouser pockets and turned them inside out to prove his claim. He sent a little prayer to heaven that the simpletons believed him.

Jerry gave a mock frown. "Aww, gee, ain't that too sad. Tom Tom don't have nothing to give us." His face turned mean and he ordered, "Check his jacket!"

"I told you I don't have anything!" Tom yelled once again, feeling frantic.

"I told you I don't have anything!" Edwin mimicked in a falsetto voice. Then he shoved Tom face-first to the ground.

"Well then, you are going to owe us double the next time we see ya, Tom Tom," Jerry explained, a twisted smile on his hawklike face. "You haven't given us a gift in some time now."

With his face pressed in the dirt, Tom lay still on the ground hoping the trio of halfwits would leave him in peace. How he hated these boys! He knew he was smarter than all three of them combined and that they would spend their whole lives living in these slums. But not Tom. No sir. He wasn't like these lads one bit.

Edwin began to kick at Tom's legs, with hard, vicious blows from the tips of his filthy boots. Tom spit the dirt out of his mouth and rolled over in a quick motion so he could see where the blows were coming from. Caught unaware by Tom's unexpected movement, Edwin tripped over Tom's legs, fell forward, and landed on top of his chest. The force of the larger boy crashing hard onto Tom's chest knocked the wind right out of him. For a long moment Tom couldn't see, let alone breathe. When he finally tried to gasp for a breath of air, Edwin had leapt off him, but not before the sharp-eyed boy had noticed the heavy bag around Tom's neck. Edwin yanked it as hard as he could. The string around Tom's neck tightened, pulling him up to a sitting position and cutting the tender skin on his neck, before it snapped, setting the bag free.

"Well, well. What do we have here?" Jerry snatched the bag away from Edwin with a gleeful smile.

"Give it back!" Tom cried, struggling to stand on his feet.

"Looks like Little Tom Tom has been holding out on us . . ." Jerry dangled the bag out of Tom's reach, taunting him.

Tom watched in helpless fascination as his whole life savings, his dreams for a house for his mother, were carelessly tossed from one boy to another while they kept the bag away from him. When Jerry next got his hands on the bag, he held on to it.

"Let's see what we got in here, boys!" Jerry yelled.

Tom lunged forward to grab the bag from Jerry, but the other two boys clamped down on his arms and held him back. Fury the likes of which he had never experienced roared through Tom's small body and he shook with rage. How dare these idiots take his hard-earned money! Struggling frantically with Edwin and Freddie, he spit angrily at them.

Watching Tom with amusement, Jerry slowly untied the string, loosening the folds of the worn leather bag that had once belonged to Tom's father. He was about to pour the contents of the bag into his dirty palm, but then he suddenly stopped. His mouth fell open in awe.

"Jaysus!"

Tom continued to fight to free himself from the hold of Freddie and Edwin, who were loosening their grip as they stared with curiosity at Jerry.

"It's a bleedin' fortune in here!" Jerry declared, his beady eyes as wide as they could be. "Where the hell did you get all this?"

With a sudden burst of strength, Tom wrenched free of the two boys, yelling, "Give it back!" as he dove for the bag again.

Jerry saw him coming and swung his fist with a sickening crack into Tom's face, sending the smaller boy to the ground once again. Sprawled on his back, seeing stars and wincing at the pain in his jaw, Tom knew immediately that losing all that money hurt much worse than being punched in the face.

Whooping with glee, the three boys took off running, leaving Tom forgotten in the dirty alley.

He gingerly rose from the grime, rubbing his chin. He should cry from the pain in his face, but he'd be damned if he'd let those three morons make him cry like a baby. No sir. He retrieved his fallen cap and placed it on his head, still blinking back the stinging tears behind his eyes. He was more angry anyway. Angry at the boys for stealing his savings. Angry at himself for being so stupid as to carry the money around with him in the first place. It would have been safer at home, even if his mother had found it. She'd have been mad, but at least he still would have had the money.

Now it was gone. He had nothing. No savings. No house for him and his mother.

Now he would worry about things just as much as his mother did.

Wiping at his nose with the back of his hands, Tom straightened his shirt and jacket against the biting wind and brushed as much of the dirt off him as he could. It was time to head home, as if he'd just come from the shoe-maker's.

When he finally made it up to their cramped little garret room, she was waiting for him. Mama sat at the little table, wearing her same worn-out blue wool dress, with a gray shawl wrapped around her shoulders for warmth. There was some sewing on the table in front of her, and two tallow candles burned in a dish, giving off a dim light. It was difficult for her to sew well with such little light, but they could barely afford to burn the candles.

In the flickering light, he could see that she had a decidedly serious and worried expression on her thin face.

"Where have you been, Tom?" she asked quietly, not moving.

His heart pounding, he stood before her, but he could not meet her eyes. He took off his tattered cap and held it in his hands. "Coming home from Rutledge's."

"No, you haven't."

His heart dropped to his feet and he hung his head,

twisting his cap in his hands. More afraid now than he was with the gang boys, he began, "Mama . . ." and then stopped. He did not know what to say. She knew.

"I went to see you at Mr. Rutledge's this afternoon." Her voice was cold. "That man laughed at me and told me that you haven't worked for him in months. He said that you ran off one day after stealing three pairs of boots from him. He said I owed him money to replace those boots."

Tom's head snapped up and he cried in outrage. "I never took anything from him!" That fat blighter was accusing him of wrongdoing? Tom's face grew red.

"He said you did."

"He's a big old liar. I didn't take anything from him. I never would do such a thing. Besides, he would have come after me if I'd stolen his stinkin' boots."

She stared at him hard, weighing his words. "Don't lie to me, Thomas. I can't bear it."

"I didn't steal from him. Mama, I swear I didn't." He stood unmoving, dreading what was coming next. "I couldn't work for him anymore. He beat me, he . . . he . . ."

She paused, considering his explanation and eyeing him carefully. "Well, I believe you did not steal from Mr. Rutledge. But you have been lying to me . . ."

"Yes." He nodded, his chest tightening. The sting of tears burned behind his eyes for the second time that night. "I'm . . . I'm sorry. I couldn't work for him, though. I just couldn't."

She sighed heavily, her eyes full of a terrible sadness. "What have you been doing all this time I thought you were working for Mr. Rutledge? Where have you been getting the money?"

Tom wiped a hot tear from his eye with the back of his hand. Stupid tears.

Her voice grew frightfully low and tinged with a sense

of dread. "Please tell me you have not joined one of the street gangs."

"No, Mama, I swear to you that I haven't," he pleaded with a desperate need for her to believe him. He was nothing like those boys. Nothing. "I've done everything you told me. I've stayed away from those lads just like you said."

Anna Alcott rose from the chair and came to him. She lifted his chin with her fingers, forcing him to face her, to look her in the eyes. She paused, and concern suddenly edged her voice. "What happened to your face?"

"Nothing."

She ran her fingers gently over the blossoming purple bruise on his jaw. "Tom?"

"Nothing. I'm fine."

Noticing the cut around his neck, she demanded, "What's this?"

Tom shook his head, but said not a word. He couldn't. If he spoke, he would surely cry.

She stared hard at him. "Thomas, I want the truth now. Where have you been getting the money from all this time?"

Tom began to cry. He couldn't prevent it from happening no matter how hard he tried. This was worse than the gang boys hitting him. Big fat tears rolled down his cheeks and slid under his swollen chin. His shame was so great he wished he could disappear into thin air. He had never wanted his mother to find out that he had sunk so low. He didn't want her to know that he was a common thief. "I'm sorry."

He saw her worried expression change as hurt and disappointment filled her eyes.

Her voice shook as she spoke the dreaded words aloud. "You've been stealing then?"

A gut-wrenching sob tore from his chest and the tears continued to spill forth and he couldn't stop them. "I'm sorry. I didn't mean to. I didn't know what else to do. I only wanted to buy us a house. I just didn't want you to be sad anymore, Mama. I'm very sorry."

"Oh, Tom! My sweet little boy." She wrapped her arms around him, pulling him close. "What have we come to?"

He wept into her chest, great wracking sobs. Mama held him tight, her hands smoothing his hair. She should have yelled at him. She should have screamed at him for what he'd done. She should beat him soundly for stealing, for that was the least of what he deserved. Yet her kind words hurt more than a beating. His mother should hate him for letting her down in such a shameful way.

But no, she still loved him. And for that he cried his heart out.

"You must not steal anymore, Tom," she whispered gently as she continued to hold him and his sobs subsided. "You must not steal ever again. Do you hear me?"

He mumbled into her chest that he heard her, shame flooding him. No, he never would steal again. No sir. That was it for him.

"Do you know what would happen if they caught you, Tom? Do you?" Her voice became more agitated, more desperate. "The constables would take you away from me. Is that what you want?"

"No!" he cried. "No!" He was sorry he stole but he was even more regretful of the fact that he had disappointed her. His mother had raised him to be a better boy than that. He thought of his sack of money that had hidden under the floorboard for months. Shame flooded him anew. How could he tell her that not only was he a thief, but he was a good one who had amassed three pounds? He'd rather die than see that hurt look on her face ever again.

She finally released him from her fierce hug. Again she lifted his sore chin to stare in his eyes. "We're all we have left in the world. It's you and me, Tom. And I promise you that we will get by without stealing to survive. I will take care of you. I won't let anything bad happen to you."

He sniffled and wiped his nose. "I won't let anything happen to you either."

"Then you cannot lie to me anymore," she admonished softly.

"I know. I won't." The bag of stolen money weighed heavily on his conscience. "I promise. I promise." He hugged her tightly. "There's . . . There's something else I have to tell you."

She stiffened, as if preparing for the worst. "What is it?"

"I saved most of the money I stole."

She stared at him, uncomprehending.

Tom continued, hoping for the best. "I did. I saved the money I stole because I wanted to buy a house for us. I had almost three pounds."

His mother didn't cry. She didn't yell at him either. She did something he had hoped for all along.

Mama smiled.

"Where is it?" she asked breathlessly, her eyes alight with wonder and something that looked like hope.

"I lost it." He whispered so low he barely heard his own voice. "The gang lads just took it from me on my way home tonight."

His mother cried then. She gathered him in her arms and they cried together.

22

Did Nothing
Take in Scorn

Tuesday, December 16, 1873

At Hamilton's Book Shoppe the next afternoon, an edgy
Lisette finished tutoring one of their delivery boys and two
of the young girls, Lizzie Parker and Victoria Browning,
who worked in the shop. Lisette gave them reading lessons
in the rooms above the shop. Since her family had moved
to Devon House when Colette married Lucien, they had
redesigned their private apartment upstairs into a schoolroom of sorts. From time to time when they were busy at
the shop, they still had meals upstairs as well.

"You all did an excellent job today," Lisette said. "Please
read as much as you can from the history text by the next
time we meet, and I shall see you back here the day after
tomorrow?"

"Yes, thank you, Miss Hamilton." The older of the girls,
Lizzie Parker, adjusted her little cap and grinned. She
and her younger brother, Daniel, had been working at the
shop for only a month or so but had demonstrated remarkable progress.

Lisette watched as the three made their way down the stairs. She stood and began putting away the books and papers she had used for that day's lesson, feeling happy that her pupils had accomplished so much. She hoped that one day the Parker family would be able to live in one of the new homes that Quinton Roxbury was designing. She had hoped to talk to him about it at some point.

In the meantime she had tried to keep Quinton from entering her thoughts, but it seemed the harder she tried not to think of him, the more often he found his way into her mind. She really did need to forget about him, though. Nothing good could come of their being together. Especially after the other night in his carriage. That was proof enough of the dangers of any kind of encounter between them.

Descending the stairs to the shop, she had just reached the bottom step when she ran into Paulette.

"Lisette?" Paulette asked, a puzzled expression on her little face. Wearing a green and black plaid gown with her blond hair pinned neatly upon her head, Paulette looked every inch the efficient shopkeeper.

"Yes?"

"There is a lady here to see you. I offered her my assistance, but she insists on seeing you specifically. She said you helped her with Christmas cards a few days ago and that you know what she wants."

"Oh, yes of course," Lisette murmured but her heart was in her mouth. There would be only one lady she knew of who would insist on seeing her.

Paulette asked, "Do you know her?"

"If it is who I think it is, I believe so, yes." Lisette dared a glance into the main area of the bookshop and held her breath. The tall form of Lady Emmeline Tarleton stood wrapped in a gold embroidered cloak trimmed with black fur. "She is Mr. Roxbury's fiancée."

"The gentleman who dined with us the other evening? The friend of Lucien's? The one who took you home last night?" Paulette showered her with questions.

"Yes."

"Why does she wish to see you, I wonder?"

"I have an idea," Lisette answered a little breathlessly. The woman did seem intent upon seeking her out, this being her second visit to the bookshop. "But I doubt she's interested in buying books."

Paulette watched with growing concern as Lisette smoothed her navy plaid gown with velvet piping and squared her shoulders. She walked as graciously as she could toward the woman waiting for her.

"Good afternoon, Lady Emmeline," Lisette said. "How may I help you today?"

The expression on Lady Emmeline's heart-shaped face changed from one of expectancy to one of surprise. "You know who I am?"

"Yes." Lisette gave her a nod, but did not smile. "And you know who I am."

"Then I guess you can safely assume that I did not come here to purchase Christmas cards," Emmeline said with succinct tightness and pressed her thin lips together.

Lisette's pulse quickened in fear, and the air fairly crackled with tension between them. This woman had every right to be angry with her. Lisette had kissed her fiancé on more than one occasion. But did Lady Emmeline know that?

Lisette asked in the coolest voice she could manage, "Why did you come here?"

With an imperious toss of her head, Emmeline cast her a scathing look. "I came to have a few words with you in private concerning a matter of a highly personal nature of which I believe you are very well aware, Miss Hamilton."

A flood of dizziness swept over Lisette, and her stomach

tied itself into a painful knot. Oh, this was simply dreadful! What in heaven's name would she say to this woman? Should she admit that she had kissed Quinton and apologize profusely? Should she deny everything? With the blood rushing to her head, Lisette nodded once again and murmured her assent. "Very well, then. Please come with me."

Lisette turned and made her way back to the staircase with Lady Emmeline following behind her. Paulette's worried expression did not calm her as she passed by.

"Lady Emmeline and I need a moment of privacy," she said to her sister. "Will you excuse us?"

Paulette nodded. "Yes, of course." She continued to observe them with concern as they climbed the stairs.

Once she and Lady Emmeline were in the rooms above the shop, Lisette closed the door. The last thing she needed was for Paulette or anyone else to overhear their conversation, whatever it might entail. They stood facing each other.

"Would you care to sit down, Lady Emmeline?" Lisette offered, making an attempt at civility.

"I would prefer not to," she said, her eyes scanning the small room in disdain. "This is not a social call."

Fine. "What is it then?" Lisette asked more sharply than she'd intended, her nerves getting the better of her.

"This is most uncomfortable but it needs to be addressed. I believe you know my fiancé, Mr. Quinton Roxbury, do you not?" Lady Emmeline questioned, her expression accusatory.

Lisette opted for admitting as close to the truth as she could. The truth was always best. She swallowed first. "Yes. He is a business associate of my brother-in-law, the Earl of Waverly. Mr. Roxbury was a guest at our home and dined with us a few nights ago."

"But that is not all, is it?"

"What do you mean?" Lisette countered, her stomach

flipping. She willed herself not to fidget and prayed her cheeks were not scarlet.

Emmeline inspected her with a critical eye. "You saw him in Brighton two weeks ago, did you not?"

Again, Lisette could not lie. "Yes, as a matter of fact. We met by chance while shopping one afternoon."

"I find that rather difficult to believe."

"I am sorry about that."

"You are aware that Quinton and I are to be married in less than three weeks?"

"Yes, he told me," Lisette said, wishing she were a thousand miles away.

"I have very good reason to believe that you and *my* fiancé are more than mere acquaintances," Emmeline said.

"That is ridiculous."

"You were seen walking with him on Saturday. It seems you entered his carriage as well."

Lisette recalled the busy London shoppers and cringed. Anyone could have seen them outside the jewelry shop. At the time it was all quite innocent. "We met accidentally on the street. My fiancé was detained and the weather was terrible. Mr. Roxbury kindly drove me home." That part was the absolute truth. It was what happened *inside* the carriage that she did not dare mention.

"Your fiancé?" Emmeline huffed in disbelief.

"Yes."

"Well, Miss Hamilton, I think you need to be spending a little more time with your own fiancé and a little less time with mine," Emmeline declared, anger rising in her voice. "And I have come here to warn you that you should stay away from my fiancé."

"I had no plans to do otherwise."

Emmeline continued as if Lisette had not spoken. "Mark my words, he will be my husband."

"I've no doubt of that." Lisette said quietly, a feeling of

nausea washing over her. How could Quinton even consider marrying a woman such as this? There was something terribly cold about Lady Emmeline Tarleton.

"What do you think? You can't possibly believe that he's going to end our engagement and marry you? Do you?" Lady Emmeline laughed in derision, her lips curled into a snarl. "Think about this before you throw yourself at Quinton again. You could never be the kind of wife that he needs, a wife that would be an asset to him. Look at you! A little bookshop girl! A nobody from an insignificant, low-class family. I know all about you and your grasping sisters. You give yourself airs because your eldest sister got lucky and married an earl. But I know about your wild sister who ran off to New York. You and your sisters working in the shop! Yes, I know all about your incompetent mother, your buffoon of an uncle, and your wastrel of a cousin. You Hamiltons. What a lot! You and your pathetic family would only be a liability to Quinton's political career."

Lisette flinched at her words, almost knocked off her feet by the venom of Lady Emmeline's caustic tirade. What was more scalding was that everything she said was tinged in truth, and that stung more than the biting tone in which Quinton's fiancée uttered them. Lisette remained speechless at the onslaught.

"What do you know about society?" Emmeline continued to berate her in a scathing manner. "How would you make political connections for him? Who would ever want to be seated beside the likes of you at a dinner table? You are not even capable of hosting a party, are you? You'd make a laughable hostess. No, Quinton could never marry someone as low and common as you. The best you could hope for is to be his mistress." Again she let loose a mocking laugh. "So whatever designs you have upon him, I assure you, you can just forget about them because you will never have him. Because Quinton desires something more in life that you will never, ever be able to give him, in spite of your pretty face. Let me remind you of something, Little Miss Shopkeeper, my father is the Duke of Wentworth and I have been raised to this life. I can offer Quinton access to the best of everything. With me, he can climb higher than he ever imagined. With you and your family, he would go nowhere but down. With you—"

"Get out."

Lisette could hardly believe the rude words flew from her mouth, but she could take no more of Emmeline's vitriol. Even though she probably more than deserved this tongue-lashing, for she *had* kissed Quinton on more than one occasion, she did not need to listen to the disparaging remarks about her own family. She repeated her order. "Get out of our shop and never set foot in here again."

Stunned to be spoken to in such a disrespectful tone, Lady Emmeline had the nerve to look affronted. "It will be my pleasure to leave this place." She flounced her gold cloak and turned to the staircase. Then she swung back around and threatened, "Don't forget what I said or you will be very, very sorry," before making her exit.

"Believe me, I shan't," Lisette whispered to herself. She watched the figure of Lady Emmeline Tarleton descend the stairs, but she remained rooted to the spot.

Once she was alone, the trembling set in and she blinked back her tears. She stumbled into what was her former bedroom and sat on the edge of the bed. Grabbing an embroidered pillow, she held it tightly against her waist and rocked back and forth while she took deep breaths.

She had no one to blame but herself for this appalling and humiliating situation. Lady Emmeline had every right to be angry and suspicious of her. What Lisette had done with Quinton was so very, very wrong.

Yet it hurt dreadfully to have Emmeline fling the truth at her.

Lisette knew she could never be with Quinton. Even though she had allowed herself to imagine such a thing for the slightest second, it wounded her to know that even if he did want her, she and her family *would* be nothing but a hindrance to him. Lady Emmeline was correct in her assessment of that. What did Lisette know of politics? Of society? What did she know of being the kind of wife Quinton needed to succeed?

Marrying Henry Brooks and being the wife of a solicitor were all that she was suited for.

Hot tears trickled down her cheeks and a sob escaped her. She had been content with her lot before. What had suddenly changed? What had caused her to long for something more? The answer terrified her.

Quinton Roxbury.

"Are you all right?" Paulette stood at the doorway of the bedroom, her earnest face drawn into a frown of concern.

Lisette wiped at her tears with the back of her hand. Leave it to Paulette to be where she shouldn't be. "You were listening, weren't you?"

Her sister nodded guiltily. "I was worried about you because that woman did not seem very nice. But I only heard the end clearly when she raised her voice."

"Did she say anything to you as she left?" Lisette asked, still trying to quell her tears.

"No, but she almost knocked me down as she passed me on the stairs. Then I watched her march right out of the store." Paulette came and sat beside Lisette on the bed. "*Are* you trying to steal her fiancé?"

Lisette sobbed, "No!" She honestly didn't know what she was doing with Quinton, except that she felt so happy in his presence. And never had she felt more miserable.

Paulette put her arm around Lisette's shoulder. "What is going on then?"

"I don't know." Lisette shook her head.

"Has something happened between you and Mr. Roxbury?"

Lisette admitted with great reluctance, "I suppose something has."

"Lisette!" Horrified, Paulette gasped, pulling her arm away from Lisette's shoulder. "You are engaged to be married! You have given a promise. You cannot break a promise like that!"

"I know all that." She did not need her little sister lecturing her on the rules of engagement. There was nothing that Lisette didn't know about her current situation. A situation she never imagined herself to be involved in.

"Does Mr. Roxbury wish to marry you instead of Lady Emmeline?"

"No." Tears threatened again.

"Then you need to stay away from Mr. Roxbury," Paulette insisted with righteous indignation. "That's all there is to it. You are going to cause an outrageous scandal if you don't. You may have caused one already since Lady Emmeline was here."

"Yes, I know." Lisette nodded wearily. Her sister was right, but still she felt dreadful.

Something had to be done, and there was only one thing to do.

23

God Rest Ye Merry Gentlemen

"Let it go for tonight, would you, Quinton?" John Roxbury, the Earl of Kingston, muttered to his brother later that evening. "I'm tired of hearing about your bloody houses already."

Quinton rolled his eyes at his brother's obvious lack of interest in his goodwill endeavors.

"Aren't you tired of hearing about it, Eddington?" John asked his friend as they reclined in the large study of John's home, enjoying some after-dinner drinks.

Lord Jeffrey Eddington shook his head. "No. I'm actually interested in what Quinton has to say. I think I may invest in such a worthwhile undertaking. There are far worse things I could spend my money on."

"God help me!" John Roxbury groaned in misery and sank deeper into his leather chair, cupping his brandy for comfort. He was shorter than his brother and perhaps a bit wider, but he had the same fair coloring and magnetic smile. But he was not smiling now. "I'm stuck with you two saints for the evening. I was hoping we could play some cards and have a bit of fun and all you boys want to do is save the city's wretched poor."

Jeffrey Eddington and John Roxbury had been friends for years, and because of that, Quinton had become acquainted with him as well. Quinton liked Eddington and had been eager to include him in his housing efforts, especially when he learned about his connection to Lord Waverly.

"Just because Louisa is out of town doesn't mean you can't do something good," Quinton quipped dryly.

"Your brother can only have fun when his wife is away." Eddington gave a good-natured laugh. "So we should do what he likes this evening. I shall get the cards."

"It's easy for you to be magnanimous, Eddington. You do what you wish every night of the week!" John lamented. "And with a different woman each night!"

"Guilty." Eddington held up his hands in mock helplessness. "But in my defense, the Earl of Babey has more of a reputation with the ladies than I do."

"Oh yes, he's rumored to be quite the cocksman. Even more so than you, Eddington. It must be nice not to be shackled to the same woman for the rest of your life," John mused, downing his brandy.

"There are some benefits to being an illegitimate son," Jeffrey quipped. "There's no burden of passing on the family name, so there's no pressure to marry."

"Even so, you have a line of beauties willing to be your wife anyway!"

"You didn't marry too shabbily, Kingston," Jeffrey reminded him. He spoke the truth, for Lady Kingston was a lovely woman.

John sighed, happy in his feigned misery. "Yes, but who knew she would turn into such a harridan? She never allows me to do anything fun."

Quinton chuckled. "Poor John."

"My wife has left me to my own devices while she is visiting her cousin; therefore, I am free to do what I like in the meantime," John defended his position, taking another swig of his fine brandy. "And I would like to enjoy this evening, which does not include listening to you two rattle on about helping all the unfortunate wretches in the city! Louisa returns home tomorrow, so come on, gents!"

"You make it seem as though your wife controls you, instead of the other way around, as it should be," Quinton said to deliberately irritate John.

It was far too tempting to taunt his older brother a bit. It was retribution for all the abuse he took over the years as the youngest in his family, for Quinton's three older brothers had teased him without mercy. He also knew his sister-in-law Louisa was strong-willed and kept his wildish brother on the straight and narrow, as well she should.

"She does control me," John admitted with a resigned groan. He shook his head sadly in defeat.

Eddington commented with a laugh. "That is because Louisa is no fool."

"Just you wait, Quinton," John foretold ominously. "You'll be a married man in a few weeks and you'll see how it is."

"I shall not let my wife control me," Quinton stated. He referred to Emmeline, of course. But as the wedding loomed closer, he found it more difficult to imagine her as his wife. More and more he found himself not thinking of Emmeline Tarleton when he said the word *wife*. It was Lisette Hamilton whom he pictured at his side. He had not slept at all for thinking of her.

Their passionate encounter in his carriage the other night still weighed heavily on his mind. It was torturous.

Eddington scoffed, "We'll be the judge of that after you're married to Lady Emmeline!"

"That reminds me," John began, suddenly sitting up straight. "There is something I've been meaning to talk to you about, Quinton."

"What is it?" Quinton asked, poised to take a sip of his brandy.

"Louisa told me she heard a rumor about you and another woman."

Quinton froze before the glass touched his lips. He had not expected to hear this.

"Now the conversation is finally getting interesting," Eddington remarked with a bit of a lopsided grin. "It's not about Quinton and Lady Trahern, is it? That's old news."

For a moment Quinton wondered if Eddington referred to his recent split with Olivia, but he was more worried about what his sister-in-law had heard.

"No." John's expression was one of confusion, his eyes on Quinton. "Louisa wanted me to check with you. It seems her cousin, Penelope Eaton, told her that she saw you kissing a young lady in a shop in Brighton last week and that same young woman was seen on the street with you yesterday and you both got into your carriage together." He paused for emphasis before adding, "Alone."

Quinton gave a careless shrug. "What of it?"

"Well, is it true?" his brother inquired impatiently.

"Some of it," Quinton admitted with heavy reluctance.

"Come on, Roxbury," Eddington coaxed a bit gleefully. "Give it up."

"What?"

"*Were* you kissing her?" Eddington wanted to know.

Quinton hesitated. "Not in the shop."

"Ho, ho! But you were kissing her at some point then!" John cried in wicked delight and astonishment. "You are in deep trouble, little brother. What are you going to do if Emmeline should hear about this?"

"She already has." He took a big swallow of his brandy, relishing the heated burn in his throat.

"Emmeline knows?" Eddington exclaimed incredulously. "And you are still alive? She hasn't had her father kill you yet?"

"No." He shook his head. "Emmeline and I have discussed the baseless rumor, and I have assured her there is nothing for her to worry about." Quinton only hoped that was the truth.

"Is there anything to worry about?" His brother eyed him carefully, the concern evident on his round face.

"No." Quinton had moved way beyond worry as of last night. He was now in a state of complete agony over his current situation with Lisette Hamilton.

"Well," John sighed. "This is a most unusual development."

"Who is the girl?" Eddington asked with a mischievous gleam in his eyes. "Do we know her?"

"Oh, you might know her, Jeffrey!" John interjected with his typical obliviousness to Quinton's desire to drop the subject. "Louisa told me it was one of those Hamilton sisters. You know, the pretty sisters of Lord Waverly's wife. I can't remember which name she said, but Penelope Eaton saw Quinton with her. You're quite close with that family, aren't you, Jeffrey?"

Quinton groaned. He did not wish for Lisette's name to be bandied about in such a manner. No touch of scandal should mar her beautiful name. It made what was between them seem rather sordid, when it was nothing like that at all. He had only the highest regard for Lisette. His feelings for her were . . . What *were* his feelings for her? Intense. Powerful. All-consuming.

Thunderstruck by this news, Jeffrey Eddington stared at Quinton in utter disbelief. "You are involved with one of the Hamilton sisters?" he cried. "That's impossible!"

Quinton said nothing in his own defense. Once again he swallowed some brandy, now desperately needing the heated burn in his throat.

Clearly disturbed by something, Eddington stood up, eyeing Quinton with what could only be deemed as intense scrutiny and not a little distrust. Jeffrey's usual relaxed state and jovial demeanor disappeared entirely, replaced with a dark, foreboding expression.

Eddington began thinking out loud, "Well, it's obviously not Colette with her about to have a baby any day now. And Juliette's been out of the country. They are both happily married and therefore completely out of the question. Little Yvette is still nothing but a child. Lisette's engaged to be married, so that only leaves Paulette. But Paulette is not the type to—wait!" He stopped and narrowed his ice blue eyes, glaring at Quinton. "Did you say you were in Brighton last week with this woman?"

Quinton gave a brief nod of his head. This evening was not going well at all.

"Jesus!" Jeffrey cried in abject disgust. "You are having a dalliance with *Lisette* Hamilton?"

Quinton buried his face in his hands. There was no getting around it now. He had no one to blame but himself for this god-awful mess.

"Oh, Lord, not Lisette!" Jeffrey continued his rant and on his face was an expression of utter revulsion. "She is the sweetest of all of them. She would never do anything to harm anyone. She couldn't possibly be involved with you! Why, she's been devoted to Henry Brooks for as long as I've known her. I swear, Roxbury, if you have involved that lovely girl in anything illicit or have compromised her in any way, I will flat-out kill you."

Raising his head, Quinton noted the threatening look in Eddington's eyes.

"And if I don't kill you first, you can be sure that Lucien Sinclair will."

Quinton began, "It's not what you think—"

"It's not what I think?" Jeffrey yelled in outrage. "It better not be what I'm thinking, I'll tell you that! If I had my gun with me, I'd shoot you right now."

"Take it easy there, Eddington," John said, watching the heated exchange with wide, nervous eyes. "No one is going to kill anyone here tonight or any other night."

"Those Hamilton girls are like sisters to me, and I would protect them with my life if need be," Jeffrey went on, his ire increasing with his every word. "I don't know what's going on with you and Lisette, Roxbury, but I swear to you—"

"Yes, I know, I know. You will kill me." Quinton stood up and faced him, putting his hand up to stop Eddington's tirade. "And quite honestly, if I did hurt her, I would gladly let you kill me. But I swear to you, I would never intentionally hurt Lisette Hamilton."

"The road to hell is paved with good intentions, Roxbury." Eddington's voice was edgy and cold. "This is not a game! This is her life we're talking about. You are to be married in a matter of weeks, and if Lisette's name is dragged through the mud over this, she will most definitely be hurt, whether you intended her to be or not!"

"I didn't want her name brought into this!" Quinton yelled back. "I wasn't even the one who mentioned her name tonight!"

"But your brother just did!" Eddington pointed out with savage thoroughness. "Your sister-in-law did! God only knows who else knows about this! Obviously Lisette's name has already been linked with yours and I don't like it!" Jeffrey took a step toward him.

"I don't like it any more than you do!" Quinton bellowed back, growing angry at Eddington's accusations and threatening tone. Who was he to be so possessive of

Lisette Hamilton anyway? What right did Eddington have to rebuke him in such a manner? "I would rather die than hurt Lisette."

Jeffrey, giving Quinton a slight shove to the chest, shouted, "Then what in the hell are you doing dallying with a girl like her in the first place?"

"Because I'm in love with her, damn it!"

Stunned to silence at his own words, Quinton slowly sank back down into his chair, his anger deflated. Jeffrey Eddington took a step backward, and his brother John stared at him in complete shock. The room became eerily quiet. No one moved for a minute or two.

"What did you just say?" Eddington's voice was low, just above a cold whisper.

Quinton muttered, "You heard me."

"I need another drink," John declared, heading to the sideboard and bringing back the entire decanter of brandy. He refilled all of their glasses, before taking his seat once again. "I think you had better tell us what is going on, Quinton." He cast a worried glance at Jeffrey. "Before Eddington's head explodes over there."

Jeffrey still hadn't moved. He simply stood there staring at Quinton in complete astonishment. "Yes, do tell us."

"Neither of us expected any of this to happen," Quinton confessed, his voice weary. He rubbed the back of his neck with his hand. "It was a series of coincidental meetings that led us to be together. We met quite accidentally two weeks ago and again while we were in Brighton. It kills me to think her reputation could be tarnished in any way because of me."

"Well, we know how you feel, but what about Lisette?" Eddington asked. "Does she have feelings for you?"

"I don't know." Quinton paused, recalling her sweet words that night in his carriage. There was a look in her green eyes that told him all he needed to know. "Yes," he admitted with some reluctance. "I think she might."

"Jesus," Jeffrey muttered, shaking his head. He sat down in his chair, a grim expression on his face. "What are you going to do?"

"You can't call off the wedding to Emmeline now!" John cried out in dismay.

"You honestly think I don't know that?" Quinton said quietly. "You don't think I've lain awake every night since I met Lisette wondering what in the hell I'm going to do? You don't think I haven't tried to stay away from her or that I haven't tried to talk myself out of loving her? Knowing she is promised to another man? Or that I'm betrothed to another woman? I don't love Emmeline and I never have, but how in God's name do I cancel a wedding to the only daughter of the Duke of Wentworth?"

"You can't," John stated with matter-of-fact calmness. "The scandal would destroy everything."

His brother was right. The scandal would destroy everything Quinton wanted.

And everything he loved.

24

Brought Tidings of the Same

Wednesday, December 17, 1873

"Lisette! Such a surprise to see you, my dear!" Henry exclaimed, looking up from his cluttered desk when Lisette entered his small and cramped office, his name inscribed on a neat sign that hung on the main door.

The busy young clerk out front had let her in with a look of curiosity. She had been to Henry's law office only a few times before, but she had waited impatiently for him to come back from his business trip and could wait no longer.

"What brings you here today?" Henry asked, looking back down and shuffling papers with the ledger spread out before him.

She stood in front of him, nervous but determined. "I was hoping I could have a minute or two to talk to you, Henry."

He avoided her gaze, intent on the papers before him. "Now? I've only just returned from Portsmouth and have stacks of mail and papers to attend to. Perhaps we could talk tomorrow when I am sure to be less busy?"

She stared at the man she was supposed to marry. His sandy-colored beard was neatly trimmed and hair immaculately combed. He had a kind face, honest and open, which was now distracted, his brows furrowed. His head was bent over a thick ledger, his expression intent.

Lisette began, "I haven't seen you since our engagement party last week, and I really would like to talk to you about something important—"

"You are upset about the business with the ring, aren't you?" he interrupted, glancing up briefly from his ledger. "Yes, I know I disappointed you, and I am very sorry about the other day, but the matter could not be helped. We shall go first thing tomorrow morning to the jeweler, I promise."

"I don't wish to go to the jeweler tomorrow morning. Henry, I—"

"Then we shall go tomorrow afternoon." He picked up his pen and began to write in the ledger, while still talking to her. "You deserve to have a ring that fits you properly. I am sorry I made you wait so long before I gave you—"

"Henry!" she exclaimed impatiently, causing him to look up at her in astonishment. "I am not here to discuss our engagement ring. I am here to tell you that . . ."

Lisette paused, now that she'd finally captured his attention and he was staring at her. She slowly sank down into the chair across from his oak desk. She had not wanted to discuss this at his place of business, but he had left her no choice. If she waited any longer, she would be telling him on Christmas. And that was something she did not wish to do.

"You are here to tell me what?" he encouraged her gently, setting down the ink pen and papers he had been holding. "You can tell me anything, you know, although this is really not the best time, my dear."

"Yes, I realize that, but . . ." There would never be

a good time to tell him what she had to say. Lisette swallowed and squeezed her hands together to stop them from shaking. What she had to tell him he would not want to hear. She wanted to throw up. "Henry, I wish to tell you that . . ."

"What is it, Lisette?" He seemed to be a bit irritated with her now.

"Well, I . . . we . . . It's about our engagement."

His sandy eyebrows rose in surprise. "What about it?"

"That is . . . I . . . I wish to break our engagement." There. She had finally said it out loud. To Henry. Her hands stopped trembling immediately, and she felt an enormous sense of relief.

Henry stared at her uncomprehendingly. "You what? I'm afraid I don't understand."

Dear God in heaven. He was going to make her repeat it. She took a deep breath before beginning again, feeling a little stronger this time. "Henry, I am so very sorry, but after giving the matter a great deal of thought and consideration, I think it might be best if we don't marry after all."

He sat back in his chair, stunned by her words. "You cannot mean that!"

Lisette said very low, "I do mean it."

He cleared his throat. "I must say this comes as quite a shock to me, Lisette."

"I know it is, believe me, and I am truly very sorry for that."

"Why?" he mumbled, his expression one of confusion. His gray eyes filled with hurt. "Why now? After all these years together?"

"As I said, after thinking about it a great deal, I just don't think a marriage will work between us. This is not some decision I made on a whim. This has been a very difficult conclusion to come to, Henry, because I do care about you."

She did care about Henry. But she was finding that she cared about Quinton Roxbury more than she ought to. Lisette did not know how Quinton Roxbury felt about her or what his intentions were toward her. But she knew how she felt about *him* and how Quinton made her feel when she was with him. When she was with him, she rode a wave of emotions that left her breathless. When she was with Quinton, she felt alive in every cell of her body. And she knew without a doubt she could never marry Henry Brooks when she harbored such intense feelings for another man. How could she ever be a good wife when she desired someone other than her husband? Henry was a kind and decent man and he deserved much better than that from her.

"What wouldn't work? What has changed in the last week?" He seemed almost frantic. For the first time since she'd walked into his office, she felt as if she had captured his full attention at last. "What has happened to you, Lisette?"

"Henry, I've changed. Somehow something within me has changed. Perhaps I've grown up a little," she whispered, hoping he would not press her for details. She had no wish to explain what had happened between her and Quinton the last few weeks. "I've discussed it with my family, and I have decided to have a Season after all."

He laughed in derision and rolled his eyes. "That is the most ridiculous thing I've ever heard! You have no need of a Season. We are getting married in June. You cannot be serious about this, Lisette!"

"I am quite serious, Henry." She met his eyes directly, without flinching. He blinked.

"Why?" he asked again, full of confusion.

"I don't know that I can explain it all to you adequately."

"Perhaps you simply need more time to adjust to the idea of marriage."

Her smile was a bit rueful. "Even you have to admit that we have had more than ample time to become acquainted with each other and know if we would suit. We've had more time together than most, Henry."

"I don't see what has prompted this sudden change in you, Lisette," he muttered, growing angry. He suddenly rose to his feet. "I have always treated you well. I have given you no cause to end our engagement."

"Nor have you given me cause to wish to be your wife," she said quietly.

The more she had thought about it, the more she had realized it was the truth. Had he simply taken it for granted that she would marry him from the start and therefore made no effort to woo her with romantic gestures? Whenever they had discussed their future together, it was in the most practical terms. There had been no talk of love. No kisses. The most romantic overture he ever expressed was giving her an engagement ring last week and that didn't even fit her. Besides, by then it was already too late.

She had already met Mr. Roxbury.

Perhaps she was making a foolish decision in breaking her engagement to Henry, but in her heart she knew she could do nothing else. She simply could not marry him feeling the way she did about Quinton Roxbury.

Henry slowly sank back into the chair, his face perplexed. "What do you mean by that?"

"You have not behaved in any way to inspire love, Henry."

"Love? You know I love you!" he cried in outraged protest, his face growing red. "Of course I love you! I've loved you for years!"

"You have never told me."

"I shouldn't have to tell you!" he objected. "I wouldn't have asked you to marry me if I didn't love you."

"Do you really love me, Henry? In all these years, you have never given me more than a chaste kiss—"

"Because I respect you! I cherish and adore you!" he interrupted. "I've treated you with the utmost care and consideration as a true gentleman should!" He suddenly paused and rose to his feet again, looking at her most suspiciously. He pressed his hands wide against the edge of the desk and leaned across to her. "You've been kissing someone else, haven't you?"

Lisette remained silent, her eyes downcast. She desperately wished that she could deny the truth, but she could not lie to him.

"Who is he?" he ground out through clenched teeth, his gray eyes flashing.

"Does it matter?" Lisette had never seen Henry angry before, and she did not like that she was the cause of such anger. In fact, she was surprised to see such strong emotion in him in the first place.

He stood straight again and crossed his arms across his chest. He began to accuse her as a solicitor. "It has to be someone you met in Brighton. You kissed me that night you returned. You kissed me like a—" He stopped himself and paused, nodding his head. "I thought you behaved strangely the night of our party, but I believed you were just excited and nervous about our wedding. I should have known better, but I never suspected you of something like this, Lisette." He shook his head in disgust. "It's so unlike you."

If the floor would open up and swallow her whole, Lisette would gladly have gone. Never had she felt so humiliated.

"Who is he?" Henry demanded to know.

"Please don't do this," she begged in a whisper.

"Don't you think I have the right to know who my fiancée is leaving me for?"

"I am not leaving you for anyone. It's not what you think, Henry."

"It's not what I think?" he said, his words dripping with sarcasm. "Did my fiancée just come to my office to end our engagement after three years? Did she just tell me that I don't love her enough to kiss her passionately? That she no longer wishes to be my wife? Did she just reveal that she has been kissing another man? Don't tell me it's not what I think! I know very well what is going on here, Lisette."

The silence between them was deafening. The comfort and ease they once shared in each other's company had disappeared in an instant. There was nothing more to do. Lisette stood on trembling legs.

"I am sorry, Henry. I do not know what else to say." Removing a small package from her reticule, she placed it on his desk. "I had embroidered your initials on some linen handkerchiefs as a Christmas gift, but now . . ." Her voice failed her and she turned toward the door.

"Lisette, please."

She faced him with a heavy heart.

His sad gray eyes pleaded with her. "Will you at least give it . . . give us . . . more time?"

Lisette sighed. "Henry, I have never lied to you and I cannot lie to you now. I have a great affection for you, but I no longer believe a marriage between us will work. And I do not think that more time will change my mind on this point."

"I think you are wrong and you are acting foolish," he added. "I think we would have a successful and happy marriage and I have always thought so. It saddens me that you no longer agree with me. However, I will wait for you just the same."

"Good-bye, Henry," she said in a soft voice.

"I won't say good-bye, Lisette."

She slowly shook her head before turning back to the door. As she exited the building, an enormous sense of relief washed over her. As sad as she was for Henry and the end of their plans together, she knew without a doubt that she had made the right decision. Ever since her trip to Brighton, she had struggled with her desire for Quinton and her guilt over kissing him. She could not have married Henry in all honesty while harboring secret feelings for Quinton Roxbury. Her conscience would not allow it.

Perhaps she would never meet another man who made her feel the way Quinton did, but she would not settle for less. She finally understood what her mother and sisters had been trying to tell her. She would not settle.

Quinton Roxbury. She now needed to erase him from her mind. And her heart. For she could never have him.

The Devon House carriage waited for her, but Lisette had no wish to ride. She needed to walk, needed to feel the bracing, cold air on her face. Dismissing the Devon House coachman, she would walk to the bookshop on her own.

With her boots clicking on the cobblestones, she pulled her hood over her head and walked along the busy London streets, dodging the crowds of people hurrying about. The sights and sounds of the city surrounded her. Ringing bells and horses' hooves, vendors calling out their wares, selling baked potatoes, meat pies, roasted chestnuts, and ginger beer from their barrows. Street urchins ran about the wagons, hoping to find something to eat, their dirty faces drawn thin with hunger.

Lisette watched them and wondered where they lived, but knew it was more than likely they called the slums their home. One small boy caught her eye, sitting on top of a large barrel alongside a building. A tattered cap covered his head, but distinctive red strands escaped the bottom. His round, freckled little face looked almost cherubic, and he couldn't have been more than eight years old. For an instant his big blue eyes met hers and she was shocked by the depth of pain she saw within them for a child so young.

There was something familiar about him. As if she had seen him before. A mixture of innocence and world-weary wisdom was hidden within his young face and pulled at her heartstrings. Without thinking, she reached her gloved hand out to him. He shook his head, but did not look away from her.

She motioned for him to wait a moment.

Lisette walked to one of the vendors, but could still feel the intense eyes of the boy upon her. She purchased a few baked potatoes and some warm bread. Turning around, she walked toward the little lad. She offered the food to him. His eyes widened but he did not hesitate. He snatched the potatoes and bread from her hands before she realized he had even hopped down from his perch on the barrel.

"Thank you, miss," he said hurriedly as he made a move to run from her.

"Wait!" Lisette called out to him. "Please don't go yet!"

The little boy paused, turning around, and watched her carefully.

She reached into her reticule and grabbed the last of the shillings she had with her. Again she held her hand out to him. He approached her and moved to take the money, but she pulled her hand away before he could take the coins. "What is your name?"

He gazed at her with wariness, surprised and impressed at how quickly she moved her hand away. Judging that she meant him no harm, he answered her. "Tom."

She moved her hand closer, tempting him with the money. "Tom what?"

"Tom Alcott." He cocked his head to the side and smiled at her. "Who're you?"

His smile almost knocked her over, so bright and charming was it. She grinned helplessly back at him. He was interested enough to ask her name. That was progress. She gave him two shillings, which he pocketed immediately.

She said, "I'm Miss Lisette Hamilton. How old are you?"

"Ten."

Ten? Heavens, he was so small for ten! She had guessed him to be only about eight years old. She gave him a coin for sharing his age, but she wanted to know more.

While offering yet another shilling, she asked, "Where do you live, Tom?"

"Saint Giles." He pocketed the money she had given him, while struggling to hold the bread and potatoes.

Lisette had guessed that was where he lived. It was the poorest neighborhood in the city. Hating to think of this boy living there, she held out another shilling for him. "Who takes care of you?"

"Myself." He grabbed the money but looked anxious to be on his way, as if he was afraid she would take back what she had given him.

"I see." Her heart broke to think of this sweet boy all alone in the world. She held out one more shilling to him. "If you like, I can help you a little. Come by Hamilton's Book Shoppe, just off Bond Street, and ask for me anytime. I can give you some work, and some food, and maybe even teach you to read."

"Why?" His wide eyes looked at her with wonder.

"Because I want to and I think you need a little help." She smiled at him. "Remember, it's Hamilton's Book Shoppe."

"Thanks, miss." He grabbed the coin from her hand in a quick motion and fled down the alley, disappearing as if he had not been there at all.

Lisette stood there on the corner, trembling with an emotion she could not name. She had never done that before, connected with a child like that. She had seen hundreds of children just like him over the years, dirty and miserable and needing help. Yet there was something about that little red-haired boy that touched her heart and she had the strongest urge to help him in any way she could. She wondered if Tom Alcott would come to the shop as she'd asked but held little hope that he would. More than likely he would vanish into the impoverished underworld of the city and she would never see him again.

The thought saddened her.

No longer feeling the cold December chill, she continued along the crowded street, her mind a whirlwind of thoughts and ideas, most of them concerning Quinton Roxbury and his plans for helping people like little Tom Alcott. She wanted to be a part of that, wanted to help make a difference in their lives. She decided she would accept Quinton's offer to be on the housing selection committee. It would be good to be associated with something important and vital, to belong to something bigger than herself.

That was what fascinated her about Quinton Roxbury. He imagined the future and took steps to make it happen. Ignoring the skeptics and naysayers, he moved forward against overwhelming odds to help others. He wanted to improve the world around him. The extraordinary qualities that he possessed drew her to him. Standing with him at the building site the other day, her hand in his, had filled her with happiness.

"Lisette Annabelle Hamilton!" a strong male voice called out, distracting her from her thoughts.

Looking up, Lisette grinned at the handsome sight of Lord Jeffrey Eddington striding toward her. Wearing a long black coat and a tall top hat, he appeared most dashing. He had a way about him that always made her feel lighter just being in his presence. She was never more grateful to see anyone in her life. Smiling up at him, she cried, "Jeffrey! Hello!"

"Now this is a wonderful surprise to see you, for I was just thinking of you," he said, taking her arm in his and falling into step with her. They continued walking together. "I was just on my way to visit your wayward sister. Colette sent a note around to me that Juliette has arrived back home. And with a daughter, no less!"

"Oh yes!" Lisette exclaimed in excitement. "Wait until you see her, Jeffrey. She is simply beautiful!"

"I've no doubt of that," he said with a knowing grin. "Now what are you about today, miss? Christmas shopping?"

"No, I'm on my way to the bookshop."

He appeared puzzled. "Coming from this direction?"

"I was just leaving Henry's office," she offered in explanation. She glanced hesitantly at Jeffrey's face and saw concern in his eyes. Before she could stop herself, she blurted out, "I've just broken off my engagement with him."

In a swift movement he turned her around and they began walking in the opposite direction before she could even utter a protest.

"Then you are not going to the bookshop," he declared with complete authority.

"Why?" she managed to ask, hurrying to keep up with his quick pace. "Jeffrey, where are we going?"

"You are coming with me."

"But why?" she gasped, confused by this sudden change of events.

"Because I said so."

As Jeffrey continued to march her forward along the busy city thoroughfare, Lisette was at a complete loss as to where he intended to take her. Or why.

25

Hail the New,
Ye Lads and Lasses

Friday, December 19, 1873

Lisette stared at her reflection in the cheval glass mirror and smiled nervously, quite pleased with how she looked. Her hair! Oh, they had spent hours curling her long auburn tresses with a hot iron, and the elegant effect was astonishing. She appeared sophisticated and more elegant. The stylish and low-cut bustle gown of emerald silk and velvet edged with black embroidered lace brought out the green in her eyes and was the most daring and fashionable dress she had ever worn. It made her feel powerful. And Lisette needed to feel powerful tonight.

She had told Henry that she was going to participate in the Season this spring and she meant it. In the meantime she would make her first foray into society this winter.

Looking at her reflection, if she didn't know any better, she would think she attended balls every day as a matter of course. Going to the Duke of Rathmore's Christmas Ball gave her a shiver of trepidation, but she was determined to make the best of it. To prove to herself that she could do it.

All she had heard from anyone was what a fool she had been to pass up the social opportunity of a lifetime by forgoing a traditional Season two years ago. Well, that was about to change now.

After her interesting and quite informative little talk with Lord Jeffrey Eddington two days ago, she was ready to transform her life a little and he agreed to escort her to his father's annual Christmas Ball. There was a good chance that Quinton Roxbury and Lady Emmeline Tarleton would be attending the ball as well, but she tried not to think about that. Tonight, she was going to step out of her shell for the first time.

"Are you ready?" Juliette asked, walking into her bedroom. Her sister looked stunning in a gown of scarlet silk, her raven hair arranged in cascading curls down her back.

Lisette nodded hurriedly. "Yes. I'm quite ready."

"You do know that I wouldn't do this for anyone else but you?" Juliette gave her a knowing glance. They all were aware how much Juliette detested attending formal social functions of any kind. "As long as this is what you truly want."

"It is."

Lisette's mother and sisters had been very surprised when she told them of her sudden break with Henry Brooks, but they had been more than understanding and supportive of her. She had expected a chorus of "I told you so's," but oddly enough they refrained from that type of remark. They merely hugged her and told her that everything would be fine. Although Colette and Paulette had an idea of her feelings toward Quinton Roxbury, they had both kept their opinions on the matter to themselves and for that Lisette was most grateful.

Just then Colette, Yvette, and Paulette entered her bedroom, as well as her mother.

"The gentlemen are waiting for you downstairs," Colette announced. "And they both look most dashing."

Genevieve, thrilled that Lisette had decided to venture forth into a Season, smiled with pleasure. "*Tu es ravissante!* You look lovely, Lisette. *Magnifique!* You, too, Juliette. *J'ai de si belles filles.*"

"Oh, your gowns both look so gorgeous! The colors complement your skin tones perfectly," Yvette gushed, the longing in her voice quite clear. "I wish I could go to the ball with you."

Paulette rolled her eyes in condescension. "You always wish you could go with them."

"Because I think it would be such fun, especially a Christmas Ball! Don't you ever wish to go to a ball, Paulette?" Yvette swung herself onto Lisette's bed, her hand wrapped around one of the four tall posts.

"I have more important things to do than worry about balls and dresses," Paulette murmured with unfailing superiority. Her glance fell on Lisette and Juliette. "But you both do look very pretty."

"I almost wish I could go with you, too, but thank you for going in my place," Colette added, her hand on her belly. She appeared weary again. "You shall have a wonderful time tonight, in any case."

"Are you nervous, Lisette?" Paulette asked.

Lisette nodded with a weak smile. "Yes, a little bit."

"Well, you don't look it. Just go and enjoy yourself. Who knows whom you'll meet tonight?" Yvette suggested. Her eternal optimism and love of all things social and romantic were evident in her yearning expression. Yvette could not wait until she was old enough to make her debut, and she no doubt would enjoy it thoroughly. "They say everyone who is anyone attends the Duke of Rathmore's parties."

Which was just what made Lisette so nervous. Ever

since Lady Emmeline Tarleton had verbally attacked her in the bookshop, something inside Lisette had snapped and she didn't feel the same. Lady Emmeline's snide words and disparaging assessment of Lisette and her sisters had angered her more than she realized.

Lisette wanted to prove to herself that she could carry herself in high social circles in spite of her middle-class bookshop background. She knew that class meant very little when weighed against the worth of a person's character, but most people did not see each other that way. They judged a person by social class alone, as Lady Emmeline Tarleton did. The Hamiltons were a fine family and her grandfather had been a lord. The La Brecques on her mother's side in France had come from an illustrious family background as well. It had been her father, Thomas Hamilton's obsession with books that had entered the family into trade.

As her sisters had, Lisette had grown up extremely well read and educated by her father to believe that people should be judged only on the merits of their character, not by where they hailed from. She had never believed she was a less deserving or less worthy person than anyone else, and Lady Emmeline's comments had lit a fire within her. How dare the woman say she was not good enough to be the wife of someone like Quinton Roxbury, simply because her father sold books? How dare she say that no one would care to socialize with the likes of a shopkeeper's daughter?

Lisette had not told her sisters about her encounter with Lady Emmeline, nor had she divulged to them the specifics of her break with Henry. She was certain they harbored their own suspicions of her sudden desire to participate in a Season after all. But she had told Jeffrey Eddington everything that afternoon he met her on the street. He had taken her to his town house, where he had given her a good talking to about Quinton Roxbury. Surprised by how much Jeffrey knew about their situation, she had hung on his every word. When she explained to Jeffrey about her reasoning behind wishing to enter into society, he had more than willingly agreed to help her.

Juliette announced hurriedly, "We should go now. I'm sure my husband is pacing the floor like a caged tiger about now. Harrison hates to be kept waiting."

Within minutes Lisette was seated beside her brother-in-law, Lucien Sinclair, in the elegant Devon House carriage with Captain Harrison Fleming and Juliette on their way to the Duke of Rathmore's town house. The duke was hosting some of the most powerful and influential people in the country. And Lisette Hamilton would be among them.

"Lisette, I hope you behave better than your sister did at her first ball," Lucien said teasingly while they were still in the carriage.

"I haven't the faintest idea what you're referring to," Juliette responded with mock innocence. "I behaved like a perfect lady that night, so please don't listen to a word he says, Harrison."

"Knowing you, Juliette, I can't imagine that you ever behaved like a perfect lady." Captain Fleming chuckled and placed a kiss on his wife's cheek. "But that is part of who you are."

Lisette was growing to like Juliette's American husband. Tall, with tawny hair and gray eyes, he was handsome and good-hearted. And he had managed to capture the elusive Juliette, so that alone made him special.

Lucien continued to tease Juliette about the night he had first met her. "I seem to recall you ignoring the guidance of your uncle, dancing with the most inappropriate men, and flirting outrageously all evening."

Juliette's light laughter filled the carriage. "You were so

disapproving, Lucien. You had a permanent scowl on your face every time I saw you that night."

"Because I could not believe a young lady such as yourself would stick your tongue out at Lord Eddington."

"That sounds exactly like something Juliette would do," Lisette remarked in amusement. She had only heard Colette's version of her sister's first foray into society. Lucien's side was much more interesting.

"Jeffrey deserved it," Juliette pointed out. "He was so impertinent."

"Jeffrey is always impertinent. But I can assure you, Lucien," Lisette added, "that I intend to behave myself this evening. I shall comport myself with the utmost decorum."

"But you should try to have a little fun, too, Lisette," Juliette suggested, with a mischievous glint in her eyes. "I, however, won't make any such assurances about my behavior this evening."

"Hold on to your hat, Harrison," Lucien warned, feigning alarm at Juliette's declaration. "I think we're in for it tonight."

Lisette beamed in contentment, her anxiety about the party forgotten in the warm companionship of the carriage ride. She was lucky to have such a family. Not only did she have four sisters who loved her, but she now had two brothers-in-law who loved her as well. She merely mentioned that she wanted to have a Season and they had all dropped everything in order to escort her to her first ball. These two men, and their dear friend Jeffrey, were so good to her. Her two older sisters had managed to find incredible husbands who loved them and their family as well. Lisette could only hope to be so lucky.

The image of Quinton Roxbury entered her mind, and it occurred to her that he would fit in easily with these men. A deep longing filled her heart.

Oh, how she needed to stop thinking about him! She had not seen Quinton since the evening in his carriage, when they admitted they had feelings for each other. Obviously nothing good could come of those feelings. Yet by meeting Quinton Roxbury, she learned she did not truly love Henry Brooks. Maybe it was fate that had suddenly brought Quinton into her life, however briefly, in order to save her from making a dreadful mistake by marrying a man she did not love?

Was that all it was?

At times that was how it seemed to her, and that thought filled her with sadness.

There was a crush of carriages arriving at the duke's town house, and it took them almost an hour before they could get from the carriage into the house. When they finally managed to make their way through the crowd of guests, Lord Jeffrey Eddington came to greet them, with his usual charming smile. He looked handsome in his formal evening clothes, his black hair slicked back.

"Welcome!" Then he added dryly, "Nice of you to stop by for my father's little party."

One could only laugh at Jeffrey's humorous assessment of the extravagant event. The Duke of Rathmore had spared no expense for his lavish Christmas Ball as hundreds of guests filled the ornate town house. Decorated with evergreen garlands, pine wreaths, and boughs of holly leaves tied with red and gold silk ribbons, the rooms sparkled with a myriad of beeswax candles and gaslights. An enormous Christmas tree stood majestically in the center of the hallway and reached almost to the top of the twenty-foot ceiling, impressing even the most jaded of socialites. Decorated with more candles and German glass ornaments in lovely colors, the tree glistened with cranberry garlands and red silk ribbons.

Liveried servants scurried about, serving punch and champagne, and an endless variety of foods were displayed on elaborately arranged tables. An orchestra played "The First Noel" while carolers sang with angelic voices. The older guests were occupied partaking of the refreshments and greeting old friends while the younger ones were busy flirting and waiting for the waltzing to begin.

"You haven't lived until you've been to one of Rathmore's Christmas parties," Lucien said to the others. "I've attended them for as long as I can remember and they are not to be missed."

The three men had been good friends for many years. Lucien and Jeffrey had known each other since childhood, and it was through their business association with Captain Fleming that they eventually became good friends with Harrison, too.

Jeffrey took her hand in his. "Lisette, you look even more beautiful than you usually do."

"Thank you." For the first time in her life, Lisette actually felt beautiful. Well, at least she did not feel like her usual self. And no wonder! She had spent practically the entire day in preparation for this evening, with her lady's maid and her sisters fussing over her for hours, but the effect had certainly been worth it.

"What about me, Jeffrey?" Juliette asked with an arched brow.

"You look like a presentable married lady, Mrs. Fleming. A most charming wife and mother."

Juliette stuck her tongue out at him and Jeffrey erupted in laughter.

"You haven't changed a bit, Juliette!" he exclaimed, embracing her. "Come with me, everyone." He then ushered them into the ballroom and toward the receiving line. They were each announced as they entered and they followed Jeffrey to the head of the line to meet his father.

The Duke of Rathmore, surrounded by a large group of people, was an older version of Jeffrey, Lisette thought, struck by the similarities between the two men. The duke's hair was gray, while Jeffrey's was black, and they were both certainly handsome men, but it was the spark in their eyes that was so striking. There was no doubt that these men were father and son.

Lisette had heard the story that Jeffrey was illegitimate, but he had been claimed by his father (for who could doubt it, given their remarkable resemblance?) and given a title. Jeffrey was raised knowing he was not the heir to his father's dukedom, but had been treated as his son in all other ways. Of course, Lisette had always wondered about Jeffrey's mother. It was common knowledge that she had been a beautiful dancer, but who was she? And where was she now? Lisette had never had the courage to broach the subject with him. The Duke of Rathmore's long-suffering wife, who had turned a blind eye to her husband's numerous affairs and had quite graciously accepted Jeffrey into her home, had died some years ago, but the duke had not remarried. The talk going around was that his latest mistress was an Italian opera singer.

Lisette had to admit that she trembled a little at meeting this infamous man.

The handsome Duke of Rathmore turned his attention to Jeffrey as they approached.

"Father, I would like to present some very good friends of mine," Jeffrey began. "You know Lucien, of course. His wife, Colette, is unable to join us tonight."

Lucien shook hands with the duke, whom he had known since he was a child.

Jeffrey continued with the introductions. "You remember my friend Captain Harrison Fleming, from New York. This is Harrison's wife, Mrs. Juliette Fleming, who also happens to be Lucien's sister-in-law."

"At last I am able to meet the infamous Juliette Hamilton, whom my son has been telling me about for so long," the duke said, his merry eyes twinkling.

"I'm afraid I've been in America for the last two years, Your Grace." Juliette replied engagingly. "I would have come to meet you much sooner had I known you were more handsome than your son." Not at all intimidated by the duke's wealth and importance, Juliette flirted expertly with him and the older man was charmed with her, as most men were upon meeting her.

The duke laughed with her. "Well, I'm delighted that you made it back in time for my Christmas party this year. It's always a privilege to have a beautiful woman as one's guest. And, Captain Fleming, you are a most fortunate man to have such a wife."

Harrison laughed. "So I have been told."

Jeffrey continued the introductions. "And, Father, this is yet another of Lucien's sisters-in-law, Miss Lisette Hamilton."

After he shook hands with Harrison, the duke's keen eyes fell upon Lisette. "Miss Hamilton, it is my pleasure to meet you."

"Good evening, Your Grace. Thank you for inviting me."

"My dear, you are most welcome. The party will not lack for lovely ladies this evening, that is certain." The duke turned to his son. "Another beautiful Hamilton sister? I hope you are planning on marrying this one, since you let the first two slip away, Jeffrey."

"I think Miss Hamilton has her sights set for someone far more deserving of her affections than I, Father," Jeffrey said with his usual self-deprecating good humor.

The duke smiled broadly at Lisette. "Well, Miss Hamilton, my son may be right at that, but I have a feeling that he's still a fool not to try for you. Now, my dear, come with me. I need someone lovely and charming by my side while

I greet my guests, and I think you will do quite nicely." He extended his arm to her.

With no choice but to politely accept his invitation, Lisette swallowed her fear. After all, this was the main reason she had come out this evening in the first place, to see and be seen. With a bright smile, she placed her hand on the duke's arm.

"I would be honored, Your Grace."

With the amused eyes of the others upon her, Lisette allowed the Duke of Rathmore to lead her among the distinguished guests at his party. She spent the next hour being introduced to every significant peer of the realm as well as all the political players in the government. When she found herself discussing education reform with the prime minister, William Gladstone, Lisette felt a bit faint. But she surprised herself, too. She possessed more self-assurance than she had thought.

As she moved through the crowd with the duke, Lisette noted with great satisfaction that no one turned up their nose at her. Not one person looked askance or questioned what a shopkeeper's daughter was doing at such a high-society event as the Duke of Rathmore's Christmas Ball in the first place. Not a single gentleman looked bored or seemed uninterested in anything she had to say. Everyone was polite and charming to her, inquiring about her with something akin to fascination.

Perhaps it was merely because she was with the duke himself, and who would dare disapprove of her in his presence? But Lisette had to attribute some of her social accomplishment to herself. People genuinely seemed to like her and enjoy her company. Lady Emmeline's spiteful words faded away to nothingness.

When the dancing began, Lucien came to claim her for a waltz and for that she was most grateful.

The duke relinquished her graciously. "I must thank

you, my dear Miss Hamilton, for being such a lovely companion this evening."

"Oh, thank you, Your Grace. I have had a most wonderful time meeting everyone."

"You are quite welcome, but you can thank me by saving a dance for me later on." He gave her a wink.

She laughed, promising him a waltz, and she moved to the ballroom with her brother-in-law.

To the strains of one of the Strauss waltzes—she never could remember the names of them—Lisette realized she was thoroughly enjoying herself. Attending a major social function was not as arduous a task as she had first anticipated.

"I'm happy to see that beautiful smile, Lisette," Lucien said to her. "Everyone is talking about you. It means you are quite a success."

"I am?" A thrill of pride welled within her.

"Yes. You are the belle of the ball, unquestionably. I've been bombarded by so many questions about my pretty, and unattached, sister-in-law all evening that I am exhausted with answering them all. You have made quite an impression."

"Have I truly?" Her jaw dropped in astonishment and shock that anyone would ask about her.

It always surprised her when people even remembered her name. Lisette was simply another one of the Hamilton sisters, the quiet one with auburn hair. She didn't think that she stood out in any special way. She was not businesslike, determined, and independent like Colette. She wasn't wild and reckless as Juliette had been. She was not at all smart and bookish like Paulette, and was not charming and girlish like Yvette. She was not the smartest nor the wittiest nor the prettiest among them. Her sisters all stood out in their own way, while Lisette was just Lisette—unassuming and quiet, in the background, doing nothing in particular of any note. At least that was how she saw herself. So to have made an impression upon people she did not even know left her quite speechless.

"Yes, you've made an impression," Lucien continued to tell her. "And more than a few very eligible gentlemen have expressed an interest in meeting you. Shall I introduce you?"

"Oh, I don't know!" Nervous laughter bubbled within her. "I don't know if I'm quite ready for that just yet, Lucien."

"Well, let me know when you are and I will arrange something."

"Thank you."

Lucien gave her a knowing look. "I seem to recall an interesting conversation with you over breakfast recently. You asked me questions about Quinton Roxbury." He paused. "And from what I have gathered from Colette, it seems to me that it is not a coincidence that you have broken your engagement to Henry, is it?"

"No. It's not," she answered softly, looking into Lucien's warm green eyes.

"If you need my help in any way, I am here for you, Lisette."

"Thank you, Lucien." She really did appreciate her brother-in-law's concern and felt a bit overwhelmed by his care of her.

As the waltz ended, Lord Jeffrey Eddington stepped in for the next dance. "My turn."

With a dramatic bow, Lucien stepped aside and handed her over to his friend. "I shall see you both later."

Lisette smiled as Jeffrey spun her around.

"I have something to tell you," he whispered low when they were alone on the dance floor.

"What is it?"

"Quinton Roxbury is here. With Lady Emmeline."

Lisette was lucky that Jeffrey caught her before she landed on the floor when she tripped over her own feet. Oh, that was not what she wanted to hear! Her heart somersaulted in her chest. The two of them were there in the ballroom with her. Of course she had known there was a very good chance that Quinton and his fiancée would be in attendance that evening and had been prepared to face them both, but now the reality of the situation sent her into a bit of a panic.

"Take it easy there, girl."

"Where is he?" She could barely breathe at the thought of him in the same room.

"Calm down. You look like a cornered deer." Jeffrey attempted to pacify her. "I only told you because I thought you would want to know, not to terrify you. Don't look over there and make it obvious, but he is standing with Lord and Lady Dandridge, over by the arched doorway near the Christmas tree."

"Oh, God in heaven. Do you think he knows I'm here?"

"Believe me, he knows you are here. Every man in this room knows you are here."

On the afternoon two days ago when she had met Jeffrey on the street, Lisette had confided in him what had happened between her and Quinton Roxbury. Well, almost everything. There were some things a lady simply didn't share. But all in all Jeffrey had known surprisingly more about her circumstances than she had expected and had proven most supportive, giving her some sage advice on how to handle the situation. He admitted that he heard that her name had been linked with Roxbury's, but he did not think it was widely known. Thank heaven. He had applauded her for ending her engagement to Henry Brooks when she did, especially in light of her feelings for Quinton, and had agreed to assist her socially. Jeffrey had been so sweet and had a way about him that made her feel very comfortable confiding in him. He really had become the brother she never had.

"How can you be sure?" She forced herself not to turn her head and look in Quinton's direction. The urge to see him was so very tempting. And the impulse to see what he was like while he was with Emmeline both fascinated and repulsed her.

"He's been watching you for at least the last twenty minutes that I can attest to."

"Really?" she whispered frantically, her heart tripping. "What do I do now?"

"My darling girl, you do nothing." His encouraging smile comforted her. "You continue on as you have and enjoy the ball. Especially dancing with me. Do you know how many women are eyeing you with undisguised envy right now?" His eyes gleamed merrily.

"Jeffrey, be serious."

"I am completely serious, Lisette." He managed to remove the smile from his handsome face to prove it to her. "There is nothing for you to do but continue on as if they were not here."

"If you say so."

"I do."

After the waltz ended, they slowly walked from the dance floor. His advice was reasonable, but what she wanted was for someone to tell her to run and hide. It was not Quinton she feared seeing so much as confronting his fiancée and her terrible condescension. Lady Emmeline's visit to the bookshop had shaken Lisette's self-confidence more than she liked to admit. And that bothered her. She turned to Jeffrey.

"Take me to see them."

"What?" Jeffrey asked in confusion.

"I would like you to take me over to extend my regards to Mr. Roxbury and Lady Emmeline." Determined to make the evening a test of her strength, she wanted to face what she dreaded the most. Besides, if there were rumors about her and Quinton floating around, she wanted to put them to rest. Being seen greeting Quinton and his fiancée would be sure to extinguish any malicious gossip.

"You're serious?" He gave her a look of admiration.

"Quite." She offered a weak little smile. "But let's hurry before I lose my nerve."

"It would be my pleasure, Miss Hamilton." He extended his arm to her, beaming with pride. "Shall we go then?"

26

Fast Away the Old Year Passes

On Lord Eddington's arm, Lisette glided over to where Quinton and Emmeline were standing together. Emmeline looked tall and regal in a rich amethyst gown, her brunette hair swept fashionably atop her face. The couple they had been speaking with had just left them to go to the refreshment tables, so they were now standing alone. Quinton and Emmeline did not stand close to each other. In fact, there was a distinct coldness between them, Lisette noticed with some satisfaction. One would never guess that they were to be married two weeks from tomorrow.

Emmeline's dark eyes widened with surprise and something akin to dismay as she saw them approach, but Quinton smiled broadly.

Lisette gripped Jeffrey's arm tighter and her mouth went dry.

"Good evening, Lady Emmeline. Roxbury," Jeffrey said with his usual effortless charm. "I believe you are both already acquainted with Miss Hamilton."

"Yes. Good evening, Lord Eddington. Miss Hamilton," Emmeline murmured hurriedly, her body stiffening.

Quinton remained quiet, but nodded his head at her in acknowledgment. An amused smile played at the corners of his mouth, as if he knew exactly why Lisette had come over to them.

"It's so nice to see you again, Lady Emmeline," Lisette said, forcing her voice to remain low and calm. "Your gown is quite a lovely shade of violet."

"Thank you." Emmeline grudgingly offered her thanks at Lisette's compliment, as she placed her hand possessively on Quinton's arm and inched closer to him.

Taking a deep breath, Lisette mustered a bright smile at Quinton. He looked devastatingly handsome that evening, almost taking her breath away. "Are you enjoying the ball, Mr. Roxbury?"

"Yes, very much." Quinton gave her a knowing look that Lisette felt down to the tips of her toes. He seemed pleased that she had come over to greet him. "And how are you this evening, Miss Hamilton?"

"Very well, thank you."

"Lady Emmeline, I understand that you've visited Hamilton's Book Shoppe this week," Jeffrey said pointedly.

Lisette caught her breath at Jeffrey's boldness. The awkward tension between the four of them was palpable, and taunting Emmeline about their encounter in the bookshop was too much. Perhaps it was wrong of Lisette to greet them as she had. She should not have come over. It was obvious that Emmeline was as ill at ease as Lisette was. Quinton, on the other hand, did not seem upset in the least by Lisette's presence.

"Yes," Emmeline snapped, her mouth forming a thin, tight line at Jeffrey's reference to the bookshop.

Surprised, Quinton looked toward his fiancée. "I did not know you visited the bookshop, Emmeline."

"Well, I did." Lady Emmeline did not elaborate.

Enjoying Emmeline's obvious discomfort a little too much, Jeffrey turned his attention to Quinton. "Have you ever visited the Hamiltons' bookshop, Roxbury?"

"No, I can't say that I have, but I would like to someday. I've heard such wonderful things about it," Quinton responded, very much at ease given the situation.

"Their shop is most impressive and I suggest you visit when you can, Roxbury. However, I believe my father claimed the next dance with Miss Hamilton, so I must deliver her to him. If you will excuse us." Jeffrey finally decided to put Emmeline out of her misery. "Please continue to enjoy the party."

Lisette pasted a bright smile on her face and made a point to say to both of them, "Congratulations on your upcoming wedding."

Once again, Emmeline managed a brittle thank-you between gritted teeth, before Jeffrey escorted Lisette away.

"Oh, that was simply horrid!" Lisette exclaimed when they were out of earshot. She still held on to Jeffrey's arm for support. "And you were terrible!" she scolded him affectionately.

He merely shrugged. "Lady Emmeline deserved a little of that after the nasty things she said to you. But I'm proud of you, Lisette. You handled yourself quite admirably back there. And that was a nice touch, congratulating them on the wedding."

"I could not have faced them without you by my side." But she had done it. She had conversed with them both, and anyone was sure to have noted that they spoke amicably together as if nothing were amiss. "Thank you, Jeffrey. For everything."

He favored her with one of his infamous smiles. "You are more than welcome."

"There she is!" The Duke of Rathmore came to claim his waltz with Lisette and Jeffrey left her in his father's care.

"Well, Miss Hamilton, you are creating quite a buzz this evening. Everyone is asking me about you," the handsome duke told her with a wink as he led her to the dance floor.

"That's funny, Your Grace," she retorted with a warm smile. "Everyone's been asking me about you!"

The duke's deep laughter caused a few heads to turn in their direction.

After their dance, the duke handed her over to the young gentleman who was listed next on her dance card. She danced the galop, an extremely fast dance, with Lord Eads, a pleasant dark-haired gentleman, followed by dancing the quadrille with a good-looking gentleman by the name of Frank Crow. Both men were sweet and charming enough, but neither was anyone who made her heart flutter the way it did when she was with Quinton. When the quadrille came to an end, she thanked the handsome Mr. Crow and then she looked about for Jeffrey and Lucien. Or Juliette and Harrison.

Leaving the ballroom, she searched for her family, not wishing to be alone in case she ran into Quinton or Emmeline again. She had lost sight of them during the first quadrille and had no idea where they had gone. She thought she recognized Juliette's scarlet dress and moved toward the figure near the buffet tables, but realized upon closer inspection that it was not her sister after all. She continued to press through the thick crowd, acknowledging the faces she had recently been introduced to but could not place their names, and consequently nodded in greeting with a smile.

Seeing a small, red velvet settee along the wall in the main room near the Christmas tree that was blessedly unoccupied, she rested her dance-weary feet and wondered where Juliette and the others were. She was ready to go home, having had her fill of high society for one evening.

"Ah, at last I see you are finally alone, Miss Hamilton."

She glanced up in surprise, her pulse increasing. Quinton stood before her. "Mr. Roxbury!"

"I did not expect to see you here this evening. Yet here you are." He grinned appreciatively at her. "Looking more beautiful than ever and the belle of the ball at that."

Pleased that he had noticed her popularity, she smiled. "Thank you, but I am sure you exaggerate."

She had never seen Quinton dressed in formal attire before, and the effect was quite impressive. He looked handsomer than she could have imagined in his finely tailored black suit. His golden blond hair was combed back stylishly, and his clean-shaven face only emphasized his handsomeness and the chiseled line of his jaw. It almost hurt to look at him, so badly did she long to reach out and touch him.

"I am not exaggerating, but your unassuming nature is part of what makes you so irresistibly charming, Miss Hamilton."

Secretly thrilled by his comment yet knowing she should not be, she scanned the area in nervous apprehension, afraid Lady Emmeline would see the two of them together. Above all, she wished to avoid a confrontation or a scene of any kind with her. Being well liked and popular was one thing, but being a party to a scandal was something else entirely.

Noting Lisette's anxiety, Quinton informed her, "She left already."

"She did?" Surprised by this bit of news, she relaxed slightly.

"It seems Lady Emmeline was overwhelmed by the

sudden onset of a severe headache and her parents took her home not long ago."

Feeling a twinge of guilt, Lisette asked hesitantly, "Would that sudden headache have anything to do with me?"

Quinton shrugged his shoulders. "Perhaps."

"She came to see me at the bookshop again a few days ago."

"I gathered that from Eddington's comment earlier." His expression grew concerned. "Emmeline did not mention her visit to me. I hope it was not unpleasant."

"It was not what one would describe as a friendly visit."

The look on his face changed from one of concern to one of displeasure. "I am very sorry about that."

"It seems I was seen entering your carriage last weekend and she was not pleased to hear about that." She cast him a shy glance. "People are talking about us, Mr. Roxbury."

"I am even more regretful about that outcome than you could imagine, Miss Hamilton." The earnestness in his voice touched her.

"Lady Emmeline warned me to stay away from you and told me that as a mere shopkeeper's daughter I wasn't good enough for you anyway." What had prompted her to repeat Lady Emmeline's snide remarks to him? She had certainly not intended to, but it was quite interesting to see the reaction on his face. He was more than a little disturbed by the report of his fiancée's behavior. He was horrified.

"She said that?" His voice grew angry and the look on his face hardened. "Emmeline had no right to say such things to you."

"Didn't she?" Guilt had riddled Lisette's conscience since she met Lady Emmeline because Lisette knew that her own actions were not blameless.

Quinton eyed her levelly without a hint of indecision.

"No, she did not. She had no right at all to insult you. Everything she has heard is based solely on circumstantial gossip. She knows nothing. If she should insult anyone, it should be me, not you. Since she cannot, and most likely will not apologize to you, I will apologize for what she said."

"Thank you." Lisette appreciated his defense of her, but deep down she believed Lady Emmeline was justified in her accusations. "However, people do talk and will continue to talk. You must not be seen with me as you are now. It will only cause more gossip and speculation before your wedding. Even now people are watching us."

"I am now well aware of the consequences of being seen with you, Miss Hamilton."

At that point, she expected him to take his leave of her. Yet he still stood there. He did not move away as he should. He did not bid her good night and walk away.

Defying all the conventional rules of behavior, Quinton whispered low, "Could we please talk for a moment together privately somewhere?"

"I think you know that is not possible, Mr. Roxbury." Lisette rose to stand on her feet, however wobbly. If he would not leave, then she would. She took one step away from him, but his next words stopped her in her tracks.

"I could not help but notice that Henry Brooks is not in attendance with you this evening."

Quinton did not know! But of course! How would he know that she had broken her engagement to Henry? She had not seen him since she had done so. They had not spoken privately together until now. It surprised her that Jeffrey had not mentioned it to him at some point in the evening. However, she felt that telling Quinton the truth at this moment would only prompt him to do or say something that could cause even more speculation about them.

It would be wiser, and the safer course of action, to allow him to believe she was still betrothed.

Lisette turned to face him. "Mr. Brooks had a previous commitment this evening and was unable to attend."

His eyes flickered with interest. "I see."

They stood staring at each other, the silence thick with unspoken words.

Finally Lisette recalled that she wanted to ask him something. "Actually, Mr. Roxbury, there is something I wish to discuss with you."

He seemed intrigued by her statement. "Please go on."

"About the housing selection committee . . . I would like to be a part of that. In fact, I already have a particular family in mind for one of your new houses. One of the girls in the shop, Lizzie Parker, and her younger brother, Daniel. They are a deserving family who is struggling. They live in a dreadful neighborhood since their parents passed away and are being cared for by an aunt. They would benefit immensely by moving into one of your homes. I would vouch for their character personally."

"Then they can have the first house."

"That's it?" she asked incredulously, shocked by the ease of his agreement. "Just like that?"

"Yes." Quinton grinned with satisfaction. "I trust your judgment, Miss Hamilton. If you feel they would be a good fit, then I agree with you."

"Oh, Mr. Roxbury, you are too kind. That is wonderful of you!"

"No," he said with intensity, stepping closer to her. "You are wonderful."

Again the wild impulse to go to him, to move into his warm embrace, threatened to overwhelm her. Her heart pounded with the need to reach out and touch him, to feel her body pressed against his, to feel his mouth on hers.

And she knew instinctively that he felt the same way. They stared into each other's eyes as her breathing became more rapid. She wanted him to kiss her and she wished they were alone somewhere, not at a Christmas ball surrounded by hundreds of guests.

"Lisette, there you are!" Juliette approached them, with Harrison at her side.

Startled by the interruption, both Lisette and Quinton stepped back from each other. Lisette mentally shook herself for acting so foolish. What was it about Quinton Roxbury that made her act scandalously?

"We've been looking for you." Juliette cast her assessing gaze pointedly over Quinton.

Lisette had no choice but to make the introductions. "I'd like to introduce you both to Mr. Quinton Roxbury. Mr. Roxbury, this is my sister, Mrs. Juliette Fleming. And her husband, Captain Harrison Fleming. They are visiting from New York for Christmas." Lisette watched the expression on Quinton's face and knew exactly what he was thinking.

"Yet another Hamilton sister . . . By God, but you all look alike!" He held out his hand to Juliette. "It is a pleasure to meet you, Mrs. Fleming."

"Mr. Roxbury." Taking his hand, Juliette smiled warmly at him. "I've heard so much about you."

He seemed pleased by that comment. "Have you?"

"Yes." Juliette looked him up and down. "Most of it true, I'd say."

"I'm not sure how to take that, Mrs. Fleming." Quinton suppressed a laugh.

"You may take it however you wish."

Harrison Fleming shook hands with Quinton. "I'm afraid my wife can be a little impertinent."

Quinton laughed. "So I see."

Lucien and Jeffrey came to join them then and Lisette relaxed a little more. Nobody would suspect anything untoward between her and Quinton with such a large group of people surrounding them.

While the gentlemen began to talk, Juliette whispered to Lisette, "I can see why you ended your engagement to Henry."

Her cheeks growing warm, Lisette hushed her sister. "Mr. Roxbury and I were simply discussing his new houses."

Juliette smirked. "That explains why it looked as if he were about to kiss you."

"Juliette!" Mortified by her sister's quick assessment of what had been going on, Lisette felt her cheeks burn.

"Not that I blame you in the least," Juliette continued to murmur in her ear. "Mr. Roxbury is a good-looking man. My God, just look at them standing there." She inclined her head to the male group beside them. "They all are gorgeous."

Lisette had to admit that the striking dark-haired looks of Lucien Sinclair and Jeffrey Eddington and the golden blond manes of Harrison Fleming and Quinton Roxbury were stunning. They each stood over six feet tall and carried themselves with an inbred self-assurance. Seeing all four men standing together made quite an impressive display of handsome masculinity. It almost took one's breath away.

Secretly Lisette thought Quinton the handsomest of the lot.

"Good evening, everyone!"

An elegant and petite woman, with pale blond hair and dressed in a gown of silver shot with ice blue, joined their little group.

"Lady Trahern," Jeffrey murmured smoothly, taking her hand in his. "It is a pleasure to see you again."

"It is always a pleasure to see you, Lord Eddington," she said merrily. "And how could I possibly stay away from such a gorgeous group of gentlemen? Honestly, it is a crying shame that all you boys aren't standing under the mistletoe!"

As the laughter at Lady Trahern's remark subsided and the introductions went around, Quinton found himself watching the lovely Olivia Trahern greet the lovelier Lisette Hamilton and his heart pounded in his chest while the two of them spoke quietly to each other.

He had been observing Lisette all evening, and indeed she had never looked more alluring. The emerald gown brought out the green in her eyes and showed off her curvaceous figure to perfection. She had been on the Duke of Rathmore's arm for a good portion of the night, talking and laughing graciously with everyone she met. He'd seen the reactions of the young gentlemen who'd danced with her and knew that they were smitten with the beautiful Lisette. As was he.

All night Quinton had listened patiently to Emmeline and her mother prattle on about which of the Duke of Rathmore's guests at the ball would be attending their wedding in two weeks and which ones wouldn't. He had given proper responses, accepted the congratulations on his upcoming nuptials from everyone he encountered, and had danced an obligatory dance with his fiancée, but through it all, he could not keep his eyes off Lisette Hamilton.

When Lisette and Lord Eddington had come over to greet them earlier, he was secretly thrilled that Lisette had made the effort to speak to him. The ridiculously awkward situation had not fazed him in the least. And it should have. He knew very well that Lisette's presence had upset Emmeline. But he didn't care. All he cared about was seeing Lisette.

As soon as Emmeline stated her wish to return home because of a headache, he knew it was simply because Lisette Hamilton was at the ball. Relieved to finally be free of his fiancée's company, Quinton had immediately sought out Lisette, even though he knew it was a dangerous thing to do. Being seen with her alone would cause even more gossip. Yet he could not resist the temptation to talk to her, to be near her. Even standing next to Lisette, as he did now, was a constant test of his resistance to temptation. And he was failing.

"I think your father has outdone even himself with this year's ball," Olivia Trahern went on, flirting with Jeffrey. "You'll have much to do to match him yourself one day, Lord Eddington."

"I wouldn't dare compete with the likes of my father," Jeffrey quipped.

"Wouldn't you though?" Olivia mused, her meaning more than hosting parties.

Quinton watched the little scene with quiet amusement, wondering idly if Eddington would take Olivia up on her rather irresistible offer. It also surprised him to realize that he did not care in the least if Eddington did.

Too soon Juliette Fleming turned to her sister and her husband. "Well, it's getting rather late and I think it may be time we took our leave."

Lisette agreed rather quickly, "Yes, I suppose we should."

As the good-byes started, Quinton took Lisette's hand in his. "As always, it has been wonderful to see you, Miss Hamilton." He squeezed her hand, wishing he could speak to her in private. Yet what good would that do? Prolong the inevitable?

"Thank you. It was lovely to see you as well. Good night, Mr. Roxbury," Lisette whispered, her emerald eyes looking up at him with undisguised longing.

Quinton watched her walk away with the others, as Lord Eddington escorted them to the entrance hall.

Lady Olivia Trahern sidled up next to him, her cool eyes watching his expression carefully. "She's the one, isn't she?" she whispered in his ear.

"Yes." Quinton could not deny it as he stared at the retreating figure of Lisette Hamilton.

"I knew it. I noticed you couldn't take your eyes off of her." Olivia paused and added, "Nor she you, for that matter."

He said nothing.

"She's very beautiful."

Quinton nodded wordlessly. Lisette Hamilton was more than beautiful. She was everything good, everything precious, everything he wanted, all in one person. The thought astonished him.

"Oh, my poor Quinton. You are terribly in love with her, aren't you?"

He sighed. "Olivia, please . . ."

She gave him an easy smile and said merely, "If you plan on doing something about it, you had better hurry. You're running out of time, my darling."

It was the nineteenth of December. He had two weeks until his wedding day on the third of January. And only a little over two weeks had passed since he had met Lisette on December first. In that short amount of time, the woman had turned his life upside down. Now he needed to figure out what to do about it.

"Yes, I suppose I am running out of time." Turning to Olivia, Quinton gave her a careless wink. "Shouldn't you be hunting down Lord Babey?"

Her deep throaty laugh surrounded them. "Oh, he's hunting me down, I assure you. I'm just giving him a good chase. Men do so enjoy that."

"That they do."

"Tick tock," Olivia said, flashing him a knowing smile before sashaying off toward the ballroom, intent on her own quest.

Quinton wondered if somehow he had already made his decision when he ended his affair with Olivia two weeks ago. With a heavy sigh, he decided it was time he took his leave of the ball as well.

27

While I Tell of
Yuletide Treasure

Monday, December 22, 1873

"What in blazes are you saying?" the Duke of Wentworth bellowed. His round face was mottled with outrage, and his bloated fingers were clenched in fury.

Remaining calm, Quinton was more than ready to face his wrath. Without question, it was well deserved. He spoke quietly, "You know quite well what I am saying, Your Grace. And yes, I understand all too well the ramifications and the serious nature of the situation." Hadn't he wrestled with this decision for days?

"Then you must be out of your bleeding mind!" The duke paced back and forth in front of the mantel, not knowing what to do with his raging temper. "Christmas is in three days, the wedding in less than ten days. This will break Emmeline's heart!"

"Yes. Perhaps it will." Quinton paused, his voice calm in stark contrast with the duke's. "However, wouldn't it be better for her to face the truth now rather than later, when it is too late to do anything about it?"

The duke's eyes narrowed in suspicion. "There is another woman then?"

"Yes."

"Jesus Christ, Quinton!" The duke ran his chubby fingers through his graying hair. "If that is all it is, can't you just set your tart up in a little house somewhere? I don't give a damn if you keep a paramour! No one would care. Emmeline wouldn't even have to know about her. You cannot cancel this wedding, which is the social event of the year, less than two weeks before the ceremony all over some little strumpet!"

Quinton used every ounce of self-control not to punch the man. Lisette did not deserve to be called names. "She is not a strumpet. I intend to marry her. If she'll have me."

The duke scoffed at him, scorn etched in his face. "You're giving up all of this and you're not even sure of the girl?"

"Yes." He did not even wish to contemplate what he would do if Lisette insisted on marrying Henry Brooks. All he knew was that he had made a life-altering decision. And he felt to his core that it was the right decision.

After seeing Lisette at the Duke of Rathmore's Christmas Ball, he realized just how much he was in love with her. Upon wrestling with his conscience for two days, it was suddenly crystal clear what he had to do. He had come directly to the Duke of Wentworth first to break the news. Lady Emmeline's father deserved to be told foremost, since he was the one who had offered up the terms of this deal in the first place. He still had yet to face Lady Emmeline himself.

"You realize everything you will be losing? Everything you will be giving up?"

Quinton nodded. He had weighed all his options carefully and knew the potential losses were great. However, none was greater than losing Lisette Hamilton. He wanted her as his wife. He wanted to spend his life with her by his side. Her wedding was not until June, so he had plenty of time to convince her otherwise. And he had no doubt that he would.

The Duke of Wentworth puffed out his barrel chest. "I warn you, I fully intend to rescind all my financial backing for your housing endeavor."

"Your Grace, I wouldn't expect anything less from you." Quinton had known this would be a consequence, and he had been busy thinking up alternate ways of funding his housing project. He had already contacted a few potential donors to replace his losses.

The duke continued his threats. "And I will not support your bid for Parliament when that time comes."

"I understand that as well. That is your choice to make."

Frustrated that his threats were not working, the duke ran his fingers through his hair again. His gray tresses now stood out in crazy angles, giving him the appearance of a wild man. "Is there nothing I can do to stop you from doing this ludicrous thing, which I know you will come to regret one day?"

"No."

The duke's eyes glittered with coldness. "You are determined then?"

"Yes." Quinton was more determined than he'd ever been in his life. "I should like to speak with your daughter now."

The older man shook his head in disgust. "You are an idiot, Quinton Roxbury. A great ass. I never took you for the foolish type, but I guess I was mistaken." He paused and gave him a murderous stare. "You know I can ruin you?"

Quinton studied the duke with a resolved calmness. "Yes, and there is nothing I can do to prevent you from doing such a thing if you wish to. However, I do not believe you will."

"You think not?" the duke ground out between clenched teeth. "You throw over my only daughter, my precious girl, for another woman less than two weeks before her wedding and you think I will not avenge her honor in some way?"

Again, Quinton stayed unshakably calm at the duke's threats. His voice remained controlled as he reasoned with the older man. "I think you are more honorable than you realize, Your Grace. Ruining me would only add fire to the scandal and cause Emmeline further embarrassment. And think of this . . . Would you rather I married your daughter, knowing full well I love another, and make Emmeline miserable for the rest of her life? Don't you think your daughter is deserving of a husband who will love and cherish her properly?"

The duke remained oddly silent. Quinton's point had hit its mark.

"As your only daughter, your precious girl, don't you wish for Emmeline to be loved? To be happy?" Quinton used the duke's own words against him. "I cannot make her happy. I should never have agreed to your offer to marry her in the first place. I am convinced that a union between us would be nothing short of disastrous."

The Duke of Wentworth continued to stare at the floor.

"Your Grace?" Quinton asked. "Do you see my point?"

The Duke of Wentworth dismissed Quinton with a wave of his hand and turned away to face the mantel. Quinton surmised that the duke had agreed with him.

Leaving the duke's private study, he now had a more daunting task ahead of him. When he reached the salon, he paused outside the door. He took a deep breath before entering. The duchess and her daughter were both seated expectantly.

Quinton began, "Lady Wentworth, your husband wishes for you to join him in his study so that I might have a moment or two of privacy with Lady Emmeline."

Her expression growing more worried, Emmeline's mother murmured in agreement and hurried out of the room, casting a nervous glance at them before she left.

Quinton stood still, waiting, dreading what he had to say to the young woman seated before him.

"Please sit down, Quinton," Emmeline instructed, her voice sweeter than usual.

He moved to sit on the footstool before her. He took her hand in his. Surprised by the coldness of her skin, he gave her hand a light squeeze. "I'm afraid you will be very hurt and disappointed by what I am about to say, Emmeline, and you must believe it was never my intention to hurt you."

She blinked rapidly and her thin lips trembled. "I have a feeling I already know what you're going to say, but please go on."

"I've just spoken to your father and explained the situation to him." God, but this was awful. Better to get it over with quickly. "I am very sorry, but I wish to call off our wedding, Emmeline."

She pulled her hand from his as if she were burned and rose to her feet. "I knew it." She moved away from him, her ruby silk skirts swishing behind her. "Everyone who is anyone in society is coming to our wedding, do you realize that? I shall be ruined. Publicly humiliated."

"Canceling our wedding does not necessarily mean public humiliation." He stood and followed her.

"It does when your fiancé is leaving you for another woman."

He stilled at her words. "Emmeline."

She spun around to face him, her expression accusatory. "You cannot deny it, can you?"

"No." There was nothing more to say.

Her angular shoulders hunched. "So it's true? You'd rather be with that insignificant little shop girl than with the daughter of a duke? I admit that she's pretty, but really, Quinton, must you stoop so low?"

He ignored her aspersions on Lisette, although his chest tightened. "Would you rather marry me knowing I love her instead?"

She flinched and he knew his remark had hit home. He felt her pain and wished somehow that he were not the cause of it.

"I never meant for this to happen, Emmeline. I met her quite by accident only a few weeks ago. I cannot even begin to explain how all of this came about, but I am deeply sorry for hurting you."

"So Penelope Eaton was right? She did see you kissing Lisette Hamilton in Brighton, didn't she?"

Every time Quinton thought about that day, he did not regret talking to Lisette. He did not regret almost kissing her in public. He did not even regret being seen by the Eaton sisters. But what he regretted, what he wished more than anything, was that he had not let Lisette run from the curio shop alone. He should have gone after her. "No, Penelope Eaton is mistaken. Miss Hamilton and I were not kissing. However, we were having a rather intense conversation about our . . . situation."

"But you have kissed her?"

There was no point in hiding the truth from Emmeline now. "Yes."

"What about the day I spoke to you about her? Did you lie to me that day?"

"I was lying to myself that day, denying I had feelings for her and insisting on going through with our wedding. I had no wish to hurt you, Emmeline. I never did."

There was a long pause. She moved to seat herself on

the sofa and a heavy sigh escaped her. "But how do we explain this? What do we say to everyone?" Her voice quavered a bit, her lips continuing to tremble.

"What do you wish to say to them?"

"I would rather not say anything and have our wedding as planned, that is what I wish." With a petulant flounce, she threw herself against the back of the sofa.

"I know, and for that I apologize again. You can tell people whatever you think best. You can call me a cad. You can say whatever you want about me, Emmeline. But perhaps it might be best if we give them the reason closest to the truth?"

She scoffed in derision, "What? That you're in love with someone else? A shop girl? Oh, yes, Quinton, that would make everything all better."

Again he ignored her sarcasm and tried to speak calmly. "No. We can say that we have discovered that we do not suit and have parted as the dearest of friends."

"Are we friends?" she asked ruefully.

"I'd like to think so," he began. "We do not have to give them anything to gossip about. If we end it quietly, without any drama, and send out a notice from the both of us, canceling the wedding, and go about our lives as normal, what can anyone say? Let's not give them a scandal, Emmeline."

She stared at him with a helpless expression, her brown eyes filled with sadness and disappointment, like a child being denied a long-promised treat. "You never loved me at all, did you, Quinton?"

He moved to sit beside her, placing a hand on her shoulder. This was not an easy conversation, but he supposed she deserved an honest answer from him. "I agreed to marry you because your father made me an attractive offer. It was time I married and you were an excellent choice."

"That's the sorriest thing I ever heard." Tears welled in

her eyes and he steeled himself for hysterics, but she surprised him by controlling herself.

"I agree with you. I should never have accepted your father's offer when I didn't really know you. But to be fair, Emmeline, you didn't know me either," Quinton said as softly as he could. "I was like something pretty you saw in a shop window that you wanted your father to purchase for you. And he did. You don't really care about anything that I do, not my designs, not my houses. You don't care about me."

Emmeline flinched at his words. She grew silent.

"What are you thinking?" he asked at last.

"I think you may be right," she admitted very softly. Looking at him with her dark eyes, she continued, "I think I knew all along that you didn't love me, although it was nice to believe that you did. But you never acted lover-like or sentimental, or brought me little tokens. You never wrote love notes to me or even tried to kiss me. You never led me to believe that you loved me, I'll admit that to you. We hardly even saw each other."

It was true. He could not deny it. His courtship of Emmeline lacked any emotion or warmth because he had felt nothing for her. She was just the means to an end. Marriage was merely a business transaction as far as he had been concerned. But all his preconceived thoughts about marriage changed when he met Lisette Hamilton.

"I kept hoping that things would be different after we got married," she added.

"I don't think they would have."

She sighed. "You are most likely right even though it doesn't make me feel any better at the moment."

"I never should have agreed to marry you in the first place. It was unfair to you, Emmeline. You deserve to marry a man who loves you with his whole heart. I know that man is out there somewhere for you. Although I'm sure it does not feel like it right now, someday you will be very glad that you did not marry me."

After a long silence she said softly, "It's my birthday."

"Excuse me?"

Emmeline tilted her head and stared at him in reproach. "Our wedding date is also my birthday."

"It is?" How had Quinton not known that? Somehow this news made him feel even worse.

"The fact that you don't know my birthday . . ." She shook her head. "Perhaps we can turn the wedding reception into a birthday party for me instead." She let out a rueful little laugh.

"I cannot apologize profusely enough for this mess, Emmeline. And I admire you for accepting the situation with such good grace." He rose to his feet in a motion to take his leave.

"What choice do I have now? Making a scene would not improve matters, would it?" She glanced up helplessly at him with her big brown eyes.

"Thank you for being so understanding." He leaned down and kissed her lightly on the cheek. "Good-bye, Emmeline."

"Good-bye, Quinton."

He was just reaching the door when her voice stopped him.

"Quinton?"

He turned to her. "Yes?"

"Isn't Lisette Hamilton still engaged?"

"Yes, she is." Yes, there was that obstacle to overcome yet. Henry Brooks now stood between him and the woman he loved.

"I thought so."

Quinton couldn't be sure, but he thought he saw a satisfied smirk on Emmeline's face as he left.

28

'Tis the Season

Wednesday, December 24, 1873

Hamilton's Book Shoppe overflowed with customers all day long, and Lisette had been on her feet helping shoppers select Christmas gifts since the store opened. People bought a good deal of stationery and dozens of children's books, and she had sold more Christmas cards than she could count. As the last of the customers paid for their purchases, Lisette glanced at the clock. She would close the shop and lock up at seven o'clock. Only ten more minutes to go. It seemed like an eternity.

Lisette usually did not mind working in the store and at times quite enjoyed it, but she did not like the responsibility of being in charge of the shop alone. Usually Colette or Paulette was there with her, but with Colette heavy with child and Paulette suffering from a terrible cold and in bed with a fever, it was left to Lisette to mind the store, for Juliette was as useless as was Yvette with shop matters. Lisette had help, of course, from Lizzie Parker and Victoria Browning, two of the young ladies they had hired, but all the decision making and locking up of the store fell to Lisette. It was all her responsibility.

When the large grandfather clock struck seven, she could barely contain herself from ushering the last of the customers out the front door, which was bedecked with a cheery Christmas wreath. When they were finally gone, Lisette immediately flipped the OPEN sign to read CLOSED.

"We're done!" she cried in triumph.

"Merry Christmas," Lizzie said wearily. "I'm glad they've all gone."

"Why don't you two girls head home now?" Lisette offered. "I'll lock up after you've gone." It was Christmas Eve after all, and they wanted to be home with their families. As did Lisette.

"Oh, Miss Hamilton, that would be wonderful!" Victoria declared. The two women couldn't get their coats and hats on fast enough.

After many warm Christmas wishes, the girls finally took their leave and Lisette was alone. Wearily, she began to close the books and straighten up the counter when she heard a light tapping on the door.

Last-minute shoppers. Could they not read the CLOSED sign? With a heavy sigh, she opened the door.

In the cold December night, a light snow was beginning to fall. A small boy with a grubby freckled little face shivered before her, his tattered cap pulled down low. Shoving his hands in the pockets of his threadbare jacket, he looked up at her with hopeful, searching eyes. Lisette would have known him anywhere.

"Tom Alcott!" she cried in delight. It was the little boy she'd met on the street last week.

"You remember me?" He was incredulous.

"Of course I remember you." She gave him her warmest smile.

"Yeah?" Relief flickered in the world-weary blue depths of his eyes. Eyes that were far too old for such a young boy.

"Yes. Now why don't you come inside with me and warm up a bit? We can talk, too."

He hesitated an instant, glancing left and right, as if making sure no one was following him on this frosty December night, and then bolted past her into the shop, almost knocking Lisette off her feet. She closed the door against the cold and snow and gave her attention to the little street urchin she had just let into their store.

His round ruddy face was chilled, and he kept his hands stuffed in the pockets of his jacket. She ushered him toward the large potbellied stove that warmed the store.

He said hesitantly, "I came by a few days ago, but there were too many people in here. I didn't see you."

"I'm sorry that I missed seeing you, but I'm so glad you came back."

"This is your shop?"

"It's my family's shop, yes. We sell books and things here. Do you like books, Tom?"

He gave a careless shrug. "Don't know. Can't read." Approaching the heat emanating from the stove, he held his hands out to the warmth.

"Would you like to learn how to read? I could teach you."

"I've not the kind of smarts for readin'," he confessed in shame.

"Why, of course you do!" she protested. "Everybody does."

He rolled his eyes in abject disbelief, giving a little snort of scorn.

"If you are smart enough to speak, you are smart enough to read," Lisette explained in a soft voice. Her instinct told her that this boy was bright enough to learn anything he put his mind to. "And I've heard you speak, Tom, so I know that you know words. Reading is simply words printed on paper. You just need to practice."

He gazed around the shop, taking in what she said, weighing his options. It was almost as if she could see the wheels in his little head turning. "I don't know."

"I've taught lots of boys like you to read." That fact was true enough. Each of their delivery boys, once having mastered reading and writing, had moved on to better-paying positions, which was as it should be. One of their former delivery boys now worked as a clerk for Henry Brooks. It all depended on how quickly they learned and how much effort the boys put into their education. They had better futures because of their ability to read and were better able to help their families survive. Lisette planned to help some of them move into Quinton's houses when they were built.

"People read all these books?" he asked in wonder.

"Yes. Most people like to read."

"You mean they read for fun?"

"Sometimes, yes. Other times we read to learn more."

Tom walked to one of the shelves full of history books and ran his fingers along the spines of a few books. He turned back to face her. "I thought you'd give me a job here, like you said that day on the street."

"My sisters and I can give you a job here, delivering books to customers, running errands for us, and helping to sweep up and things like that. But since this is a bookshop, you have to learn to read in order to work here. We can pay you fair wages for your work, but part of your work is to learn how to read and write."

He stared at her as if she had suddenly sprouted another head. "You aren't foolin' me?"

She asked calmly, "Why would I want to fool you?"

He tilted his head to the side and studied her hard. "What's your name again anyhow?"

"I'm Lisette Hamilton." She moved to the side counter, where they had laid out a lovely display of holiday refreshments for their customers. She took a handful of gingerbread cookies that she had brought from Devon House that morning and held them out to the boy.

He stepped closer to her, eyeing the sweets hungrily.

"You can have them," she encouraged with a smile. "It's all right. I wish I had more to give you. We had a lot of customers today."

He took the cookies from her. "Thank you, miss," he managed to mutter before shoving them in his mouth and devouring them as quickly as he could.

Well, at least he knew his manners and remembered to say thank you. Lisette smiled and poured him some tea, which had grown rather cool, but it was all she had to offer him on such short notice. She wondered if she should run upstairs and make him something proper to eat in the kitchen.

"Have you had supper yet this evening?"

Still gobbling the cookies, he nodded. She did not quite believe him, but had no wish to insult his pride by insisting. She handed him the cup of tepid tea and he swallowed it in a series of hurried gulps.

"Who takes care of you, Tom?" she asked. "Have you any family?"

"Just my ma." He wiped his mouth with the back of his dirty hand and held out the empty cup. "Thank you, miss."

"You are welcome." She took the cup from him and placed it back on the counter. "Where is your father?"

"He died." A shadow crossed his small features. "When I was five."

"Oh, I'm so sorry, Tom," she said. "I understand how you feel because my father died, just a few years ago."

He shuffled his feet. "My little sister died, too. Last Christmas."

"Oh, Tom." The obvious heartbreak on his sweet face caused her eyes to well with tears. "That must have been terrible for you."

His little chin went up and he squared his thin shoulders. "But I'm all right now, though."

"Yes, I can see that," she agreed. Watching him put up a brave front, Lisette felt an aching in her heart for this child and wanted nothing more than to help him.

"Now it's only me and my mother left."

"You must be a great comfort to her. Does she work?"

"Madame La Fleur let her go and she can't find work. I'm the man of the house now. So I need to earn money."

"And that's why you wish to work here?"

"It's nice here." He nodded his little head, adding softly, "You're nice."

"Thank you." She smiled. "You're nice, too." She pulled a high stool around to the front of the counter and motioned for him to sit there. Moving another stool beside it, she quickly retrieved a small copybook from behind the counter. She sat next to him and opened the copybook.

"In order to read, you have to know your letters," she explained. "Do you know your letters?"

"Some of them. Just the first couple of ones. My ma tried to teach me, but she's not so good at reading either." He paused. "I know my numbers, though."

"Good! That's wonderful, because numbers are very important, too. How about we first start with your name?" With her neat hand, Lisette printed "Tom Alcott" on the first page of the copybook. "Now this is your book, with your name on it."

"That's my name?" His eyes moved from the page of the book to her face and back to the book. And back to her face. He smiled in wonder.

The boy had the most amazing smile. He could light the room with the warmth of his smile.

"Are you an angel?" he asked, his voice filled with awe.

"No." Lisette laughed lightly. "No, I'm just a lady who wishes to help. If you come back after Christmas, I will have some work for you to do and we'll have a little reading lesson together. And I will give you a few shillings to start. Will you come?"

Reverently he ran a dirty finger over the letters and nodded. "It really says my name right there? Tom Alcott?"

"Yes. Maybe next time we can learn Thomas Alcott," she suggested.

"Thomas Francis Alcott sounds more grand."

"Most definitely." She smiled, but bit her lip to keep from laughing at his endearing self-importance. "I have a fondness for the name 'Thomas.' It was my father's name."

"I like knowing that." Another grin spread across his face. "Can I keep the book?"

"Yes, absolutely, Thomas Francis Alcott. It's yours."

"My ma will like this," he said softly. "And now I can earn a wage and learn my letters. She's been wanting me to learn to read for my whole life."

"Your mother sounds like a very smart woman, Tom. Why don't you bring her here with you when you come, too? I would like to meet her."

"Why?" His eyes narrowed, full of suspicion.

"Because it would be nice to meet her. I like you, so I would think that I would like your mother. Perhaps we could find a position for her at the bookshop, too, if she wishes."

"I'll bring her," Tom agreed immediately. "I think she'd

like very much that I was working here for you, and if she could work here, too, I'd think we were both in heaven."

Hesitantly Tom picked up the pencil and with a shaky hand copied his name with great care and concentration. When he finished, he glanced up at her with his face full of questionable and hopeful pride. It was a fair first attempt and Lisette was pleased by his promise.

"Why, Tom, that's wonderful!"

"I'm smarter than most boys," he said, beaming with satisfaction. "You won't regret hiring me, miss."

Lisette, a lump forming in her throat, could barely get the words out. "I don't think I will ever regret hiring you, Tom Alcott."

A heavy knock on the shop door caused them both to glance up, startled by the intrusion. Quick as a wink, Tom slipped off the stool and raced to the door. He opened it a crack and peered out. Lisette watched him, impressed that he was so quick to work.

"It's some fancy gent. Isn't the store closed now?" he called back to her. "Should I let him in?"

Touched by his protective nature, she looked on in amusement. "Ask who it is first."

"Who is it?" he barked. Then, "I work for Miss Hamilton."

Lisette could hear a male voice outside but couldn't distinguish what was being said. Thrilled by her progress with Tom, she smiled. She liked the boy. It was apparent that he had a good heart and an eager willingness to learn and better himself.

"He says he's Mr. Roxbury."

Her heart flipped over in her chest and she almost fell off the stool. Good heavens! What was Quinton doing at the shop? "You . . . you can let him in, Tom."

"By the look on your face, I should send him away."

But the shrewd little Tom went against his better judgment and opened the door wide, the bells above jingling, and Quinton Roxbury stepped inside amid a swirl of snow. He wore a long black coat and a tall black hat, with a plaid wool scarf wrapped around his neck. Even scattered with snowflakes and his cheeks reddened from the cold, Quinton still looked stunningly handsome.

"Merry Christmas," he said. His warm blue eyes searched hers.

"Mr. Roxbury, this is quite a surprise."

"I stopped by Devon House and your family told me I would find you here." He paused and looked at Tom. "I see you have some company."

So this was not simply a random shopping excursion for him. He had deliberately sought her out at home and then came to see her at the shop. That thought caused a knot to form low in her belly and a little quiver to race through her body.

"Yes, let me introduce you," Lisette began. "This is Thomas Francis Alcott and he just agreed to work for me here at the store and I'm going to give him reading lessons. Tom, this is Mr. Quinton Roxbury."

"We've met," Tom muttered, his suspicious glance falling on Quinton.

"It's an honor to meet you, Master Alcott." Quinton gave a quick bow and held his hand out to the boy.

Tom's eyes grew round at the grandness of the older man's gesture. There was no patronizing quality, no condescension whatsoever in Quinton's greeting. The child regarded him for a moment before slowly accepting his overture of a handshake. Imitating the mannerisms with incredible precision, he, too, bowed and then said, "'Tis an honor to meet you, too, sir."

A little swell of affection flooded Lisette at how quickly Quinton won over the boy. She had not observed Quinton with children before and seeing this filled her with happiness.

"Well, Tom, I see you have the good sense to take Miss Hamilton's lessons. It's important for a boy to learn his letters. It makes him a better man. A boy with an education can become anything he puts his mind to. I can see good things in you. A grand future." Quinton spoke to Tom as an equal, his expression warm. Lisette loved how Quinton immediately understood the situation and saw in Tom all the potential that she saw.

The boy fairly burst with pride, so much did he want to believe the words being said to him. "Thank you. Yes sir. I'm bringin' my ma here after Christmas to meet Miss Hamilton and start work here at the shop."

"Again, you show fine judgment, so don't neglect your lessons for frivolous pursuits or you shall be letting down Miss Hamilton," Quinton warned.

"No sir. I won't forget." Tom turned to Lisette. "I won't let you down, I promise." He shuffled his feet. "I should be gettin' home to my ma now. I don't like to leave her alone for long. And it's Christmas Eve."

Quinton reached into his pocket and took out a coin. Handing Tom a guinea, he said with great seriousness, "You show great promise, Tom. This is because you did such a good job protecting Miss Hamilton this evening."

The boy's eyes grew round at the sight of that much money. His small hand shook as he reached to take it. He spoke in an awed whisper. "I can get a special Christmas dinner with this. Thank you very much, sir."

"You are welcome."

Lisette reminded him to take his copybook and practice writing his name before he returned. He nodded in obedience, holding the book reverently in his hands. On an impulse, Lisette hurried to the stationery cabinet and took out the last of the gilt-edged Christmas cards. It was a simple but lovely one, embossed with a garland of flowers and elegant calligraphy. She handed it to Tom.

"Why don't you give this card to your mother, as a little Christmas gift? You can write your name in it for her."

"I can have it?" He looked at the pretty card with awe. "I've always wanted to give my ma something fancy like this, something that she didn't even need. Thank you!" The boy flung his arms around Lisette's waist in a brief but fierce hug. "Thank you."

"Merry Christmas, Tom," she said, filled with joy at his brimming happiness.

His sweet face lit up from his smile. "Merry Christmas, miss." He turned to Quinton. "And Merry Christmas to you, too, sir!" Tom Alcott fled from the shop almost as quickly as he'd come, the bells above the shop door jingling.

Feeling self-conscious now that they were alone together in the deserted shop, Lisette wiped at the tears that threatened to overwhelm her.

"That was a beautiful thing you just did," Quinton said softly, his warm gaze steady on her.

"It was nothing," she whispered. "I gave him a little card, a token. I had no idea it would make him so happy." She couldn't help the one tear that ran down her cheek. It had taken so little to make that sweet boy smile.

"Well, it was a lot more than that to him. He is quite a little character, isn't he?" he asked, removing his tall top hat, woolen scarf, and leather gloves and placing them on the counter. Slowly he unfastened the buttons of his coat.

Gaining control of her emotions, Lisette eyed his movements carefully, surmising he had no intention of leaving anytime soon.

"Yes, he is a character. I met him last week on the street and he seemed a good boy, one in need of help. There was something in his eyes that compelled me to speak to him

that day. I invited him to come here, but I wasn't sure if
he would."

"But you are happy now that he did come to you."

"I am so happy that he came." She could not help
smiling.

"And you are thinking you would like Tom Alcott and
his mother to have one of my houses when they are complete, aren't you?'

"Yes, I was, as a matter of fact." She was pleased that
he seemed to have read her thoughts so easily.

"They shall be one of the first on my list."

Her heart swelled. "Oh, Quinton, thank you! That would
be wonderful."

He took a step toward her, and paused. "That is the first
time you ever called me by my name."

"Is it?" She had not realized. In her thoughts she always
referred to him as Quinton.

"I like the sound of my name on your lips."

Her heart was pounding an erratic rhythm, and it felt a
hundred times too large for her chest. "Mr. Roxbury, you
should not say such things to me."

"I know I should not."

"But you do it regardless?"

"It seems I am quite powerless to do what I should when
I am in your presence."

She slanted a look up at him. "Why have you come here
tonight?"

"I wanted to wish you a Merry Christmas." He retrieved
a small package from the pocket of his coat. He held it out
to her with an expectant smile.

He brought her a present? He should not be gifting her
in any way. Immobile, she stood staring at his hand, on
which rested a small box tied with a bright red ribbon.

"Please take it," he encouraged her.

With a trembling hand she reached for the box. "Oh, but I have no gift for you. I did not think that—"

"I do not give gifts with the expectation that I get one in return. I give gifts because it brings me pleasure to do so. And this brings me great pleasure." He removed his coat in a fluid gesture. "Please open it, Lisette."

Her name sounded like velvet when he said it, and she shivered at the softness of his voice. Their eyes met and held. She took a deep breath and looked back at the small package. With trembling fingers, she untied the ribbon and opened the box.

"Oh, Quinton!" she cried in pure delight.

It was the silver locket she had seen in the curio shop that day in Brighton, the one with four panels in which she could place photos of each of her sisters and inscribed with an elegant script *L*. She had loved it the moment she saw it, but with all that had happened that afternoon, she had completely forgotten about the locket. He must have bought it for her that day. Touched beyond words that Quinton would think to give her something so special, she blinked back the tears welling in her eyes once again.

"It was not my intention to make you cry." He stepped closer to her.

"Thank you so much." Half laughing at her sentimental foolishness, she sniffled and drew a steadying breath. "I seem to be a watering pot this evening. Forgive me. It was so thoughtful of you to remember that I wanted the locket. I didn't expect . . ." She grew quiet.

"What is it?"

"Nothing." She shook her head. "I really shouldn't accept this from you. It's not appropriate."

"I don't give a damn if it is appropriate or it isn't. I want you to have that necklace because it makes you happy."

She gently touched the locket with her fingers. It would

be fun having photographs taken of her sisters to place inside.

"Here," he said, reaching for the locket. "Let me help you put it on."

Before she could protest, he had clasped the chain around her neck, the silver locket resting on her chest. He stepped back to admire it.

"It looks beautiful on you," he announced. "But then anything would look beautiful on you."

Her heart flipped over at his words. Oh, but this was absolute torture. Lisette gave him a hard look, attempting to cool the situation. "Thank you, Mr. Roxbury, but you are engaged to be married and should not be bringing me gifts."

"I am not engaged any longer."

She gasped, covering her mouth with her hand. The bookshop spun around her. Slowly, her hand slid down from her face to cover her throat. "Since when?"

"The night before last. There shall be a notice in the paper after Christmas."

"Oh, Quinton, I am so sorry!" Lisette was quite stunned by this news. "What happened? If I in any way caused problems between you and Lady Emmeline, I would never forgive myself. Did someone say something about seeing us together at the Duke of Rathmore's ball? I hope I had nothing to do with it."

"You had everything to do with it."

Lisette's mouth dropped open in surprise at his words. Had Emmeline called off the wedding? Would there be a dreadful scandal? Was she named as the cause? A wave of nausea flooded her. She couldn't speak and just looked at him.

Quinton stared back at her, his blue eyes intense. "Lisette, you are the reason I cannot marry Lady Emmeline."

"What are you saying?"

"I spoke with the Duke of Wentworth and Lady Emmeline and explained that I was in love with someone else and could not in good conscience marry Emmeline."

The look Quinton gave her caused goose bumps to rise on her arms. Reeling from both revelations, she did not know which one was more shocking, that he broke his engagement or his reference to being in love with her. Her mouth went dry. "You did what?"

"I am no longer betrothed to Emmeline Tarleton."

"You're not?" she squeaked, feeling like an idiot. Her chest tightened.

"No. I am not."

"Oh."

A smile tugged at the corners of his mouth. "Is that all you can say?"

"Won't the scandal ruin your building career and your political hopes?"

He shook his head. "I don't believe there will be a scandal. When I broached the subject, Emmeline agreed with me that we did not truly suit. There will be talk, of course, but our goal is to avoid an outright scandal. We have parted as friends."

"She wasn't angry about it? Angry with you?"

"Oh no, she was quite angry with me to be sure. And hurt, too. But when she calmed down a bit, she saw the logic and reasoning behind my motives. We have barely seen each other in the last six months. I think she was more in love with having a wedding than with being married or even in love with me for that matter. Eventually she and her father will see the wisdom in this outcome, even if they can't right now."

"Oh." She could not get her head around the news. Quinton was no longer engaged to be married!

"Her father had calmed down by the end as well. I will lose his political support and his financial backing for the houses, but I will find other donors. I am no longer worried about that aspect."

"Oh, Quinton." She twisted her hands together. "I'm so sorry."

"Sorry you saved me from an extremely unhappy marriage?"

"But I did nothing. I did not do any—"

"You did everything and nothing at all. You were simply you." He paused and placed his hand under her chin, tilting her face up to his. "Lisette, you made me fall in love with you."

"You're . . . You are in love with me?" The very words made her feel hot and shaky inside. A wave of dizziness washed over her. She blinked.

"Madly in love with you." His voice was like velvet.

"Oh, I see." Coherent words, clever responses all eluded her.

"But now I have another dilemma."

"Which is?" Her heart pounded wildly.

"I am in love with you. But you, Lisette, you are still engaged to Henry Brooks."

"Oh, but I am not!" she cried out in surprise.

Now it was Quinton's turned to be stunned. He dropped his hand from her face and his eyes widened. "You're not?"

She shook her head, a faint smile beginning to spread across her face.

"Since when?" he questioned.

"A week ago. I broke off with him."

"You did?" He was incredulous but enormously pleased.

"Yes." She nodded happily, a wild thrill of elation racing through every nerve in her body. He was no longer engaged and neither was she. They were both free.

"Why did no one tell me? How did I not hear?"

"I don't know."

He thought for a moment. "You had broken off with him before the Christmas Ball at the Duke of Rathmore's?"

"Yes."

"Why didn't you tell me that night?"

"You were still engaged, remember?"

"Yes . . ." His eyes narrowed on her. "Why did you break off with Henry?"

"Because I could not in good conscience marry him." She hesitated for a fraction of a second. Her eyes meeting his, she saw everything she'd ever wanted in Quinton Roxbury, and her heart flipped over in her chest. "Because I am in love with you."

"Ah, Lisette." Quinton pulled her to him in a sudden movement.

For the first time, she moved into the warm circle of his arms with a completely clear conscience. They had not intended for any of this to happen. They had only bumped into each other one day and their lives were never to be the same. Lisette breathed in his scent and sighed, drawing comfort from the strength that encircled her.

"You have turned my world upside down and I am glad of it." He placed a sweet, soft kiss on her lips. He then cupped her chin in his palm once again, tilting her face up to look in her eyes. "I want to marry you, Lisette Hamilton. I want to make a life with you by my side."

Nothing would make her happier than spending the rest of her life with this man. She would do anything for him. He had come into her life out of nowhere, and with him he brought a vividness, a vibrancy, and a purpose to her life that had been lacking. He inspired her and filled her with emotions she had only dreamed of and read about. With him she felt more herself than she had ever felt with Henry Brooks.

"I want you, too, Quinton."

"If you want me even half as much as I want you, you'll make me the happiest man in the world." His mouth covered hers in a searing and possessive kiss, leaving no doubt how he felt about her.

This kiss made her shiver in anticipation. Hot and hungry, their mouths joined, and Lisette responded with complete abandon. Her arms moved around his neck, and he pulled her closer. Her mouth parted and his tongue met with hers. Desire flickered through her, fast and furious.

There were no restrictions on them anymore. He was free. He was hers. A thrill of happiness surged within her and she wanted to give herself to him.

29

That Glorious Song of Old

Alone in the bookshop on Christmas Eve with snow falling outside, Lisette kissed Quinton Roxbury with absolute indulgence and without an ounce of guilt. Never had she felt such joy mingled with unrestrained passion. His hands moved around her, stroking her back while stoking the fire that smoldered within her. She wanted him desperately. Wanted to feel him. All of him.

Lisette pulled away from his kiss. "Wait." She could barely catch her breath, could barely find the wherewithal to speak.

Disappointment shadowed his face. "Yes, of course, if you—"

"No." She shook her head, her body trembling. "Let's go upstairs."

"Upstairs?" His brows drew together in confusion.

"Follow me," Lisette whispered.

She took his hand in hers and led him to the staircase at the back of the shop. Opening the door, she continued up the steps to the rooms above where her family had lived for so many years. The space had been refurnished and repurposed, but two bedrooms still remained. They lit the lamps, and he followed her into one of the bedchambers, with a large bed in the center. The air chilled them and Quinton quickly and expertly started a fire in the fireplace. The room was still cold, but the promise of coming warmth comforted them.

Lisette shivered but only because she was cold. She should be nervous, but she wasn't. Not a bit. It surprised her, this lack of nervousness, yet thrilled her at the same time. What she was about to do was scandalous. But she was going to do it anyway. Placing a lit candle on the bedside table, she turned to face Quinton. His blond hair glistened like gold in the firelight, and the lines of his face seemed more striking, more masculine in the shadows. The look of intense desire in his expression captivated her. This was not like the night in his carriage. This night was something else entirely.

Again, Quinton drew her to him, holding her against his warm body. Her arms wrapped around his neck, reveling in the solidness of him, soaking up his being. She loved the feel of him.

"You are sure you want to do this?" he asked, his voice low and husky with longing.

Her breath caught in her chest. "Yes. More than anything."

His mouth slanted over hers in response, igniting the yearning fire within her once again. She surrendered to it, letting herself become a part of him. Nothing about their meeting or falling in love had been proper or traditional. They both had belonged to others. Now they belonged only to each other. So why should this be any different? Why should she wait until they were married?

She had waited her whole life to feel this way, to feel loved and wanted.

And now she wanted Quinton.

With deft fingers, he began to remove the pins that held her hair so neatly in place. Her thick, auburn tresses fell softly around her shoulders, hanging nearly to her waist. She shook her head. His fingers splayed through her hair, loosening it even more.

"God, I've wanted to do that since the day I met you," he whispered, breathing in the clean, lavender scent of her hair.

He grinned as he carefully removed the locket that he had just given her. He placed it on the nightstand. Then he undid the hooks of her plaid gown, slowly, carefully. He eased the fabric down around her. She stepped out of the gown with his assistance and some rueful smiles at the cumbersomeness of her attire. Lisette stood before him in only her corset and chemise. Together they untied the laces of her corset, releasing the tightness that bound her body. Left in nothing but her chemise, she waited, trembling in anticipation.

Without words, Quinton removed his jacket and shirt. She reached out to touch him, fascinated by the broad planes of his bare, muscled chest. The warmth of his skin felt wonderful, and she wished she could curl into him and absorb his heat. As if reading her thoughts, he scooped her up in his arms and carried her to the bed, laying her against the cool counterpane and covering her body with his own. His warmth penetrated her, seeped within her very being.

Her mouth sought his with a feverish, hungry need. He kissed her, as she wanted him to. His tongue, hot and slick, intertwined with hers, causing potent desire to unfurl deep and low within her. Mesmerized by the masculine feel of his body, she ran her fingers along the taut muscles of his back, sensing the innate strength that lay beneath. A man's body, so large and broad, layered with firm muscles and unexpected softness and warmth, fascinated her. His strong arms held her while his lips moved over her skin, burning a path down her throat, sending shivers of delight to the tips of her toes.

With surprising skill, Quinton helped her out of her chemise, leaving her chest bare to him. He lowered his head, placing delicate kisses over her breasts, his heated tongue laving her nipples. Lisette thought she would faint from the wonder of it all.

In a bed with this man, she could barely takc it all in. As if all of her dreams were suddenly coming true, she melted into him, arching her body against him. The hard evidence of his arousal thrilled her, and frightened her a little, too. She held her breath in anticipation of the next delight he had in store for her, her hands braced against his bare shoulders.

The heat of the fire began to take the chill out of the air. Lost in the feel of each other, they had already begun to make their own heat. A heat that seemed as if it would consume them both.

"Quinton," she whispered on a frantic breath.

"I love when you say my name."

So of course, Lisette whispered it again and again.

He rained kisses on her face, her cheeks, her neck. His mouth returned to her breasts, sucking her nipples. Her body trembling with need, she cried out with pleasure as longing surged within her. Breaking from her, he removed his trousers and underclothes. Casting a quick glance below, she gasped at the sight of him. With a hesitant hand she reached out to touch him, amazed at the silky warmth of his male body. He groaned low and pulled her toward him once again. Naked body against naked body, they fell back into the pillows, their mouths meeting in a fervent kiss.

She opened to him and held her breath. He entered in a swift and sure motion. She gasped at the intrusion. He stilled and murmured her name. Their eyes met in the darkness. Unable to speak, she leaned forward to kiss him, to let him know she wanted him, and then he continued to move within her. Arching her back to meet him, Lisette gave in to the new sensations that swept over her body.

He grew more urgent in his movements, and she matched him stroke for stroke. She held on to him, clinging to his broad shoulders, never imagining that two people could be this close. Her breathing became shallower as she followed his movements and began to move her hips against him, wanting something she was unaware even existed. Soon she was consumed by a wave of bliss that enveloped her entire being, sending her spinning into a spiral of pleasure that left her faint and dizzy. He called her name as he shuddered at his own release, burying his face in her neck.

Completely spent, they lay in each other's arms, warm even though the fire had died to glowing embers. In the glow of candlelight, they wrapped themselves in blankets and held each other tightly. Lisette languished in the aftermath of sensations that left her body as weak as a little kitten. Never had she done anything that had felt so right than being in Quinton Roxbury's naked embrace. More comfortable with this type of intimacy than she had a right to be, she smiled to herself.

"Where are we anyway?" he asked in the flickering darkness.

"In my old bedroom."

"Seriously?"

"Mmm-hmm." She snuggled against him, her naked

legs intertwined with his, her head resting on his broad chest. "I grew up in this room."

"Why, Miss Hamilton," he scolded her with mock indignation, "you are quite the scandal. Inviting a man into your bedroom. *Tsk-tsk*."

Giggling, she kissed him with reckless abandon. Yes, she was scandalous. And for once in her life, she didn't care at all that she was.

"I'm glad you did invite me up here." He kissed her mouth, his hand gently caressing her back, stroking her long hair.

"Me, too."

"This is not how I expected this evening to end when I came to the shop."

"What did you expect?" she asked.

"I simply wanted to wish you a Merry Christmas and give you the locket. And of course, tell you that I was no longer engaged to be married. I hoped you would be happy to hear that."

Lisette had a grin from ear to ear. "I was very happy to hear that."

"Yes, but I didn't know that you had broken your engagement. Henry has been a part of your life for so long and you've only known me for a few weeks. I wasn't sure what you wanted."

His voice was so honest and his uncertainty touched her deeply. He always seemed so self-assured that it was almost impossible to imagine Quinton nervous about seeing her. Lisette rose and rested her head on her arm. "What I wanted was you, Quinton."

He kissed her lips, caressing her face with his fingers. "Good God, I love you, Lisette."

"And I love you."

"I knew it would be like this with you."

"Like what?" she questioned, placing a kiss on his chest.

"Perfect."

"Really?" she asked, filled with female pride at pleasing him. "I had no idea what I was doing."

"Trust me." He patted her derriere. "You did just fine."

She slid her naked body over his, covering him. "Like this?"

"Yes. Like that. See? You're a natural." His mouth sought hers in a passionate kiss.

An unstoppable heat, swift and strong, grew between them. Liquid currents of desire coursed through Lisette's veins as her tongue swept into his mouth. She didn't think it was possible to feel this aroused again, to want him so desperately so soon after they had just had each other. But she did want him and she let him know it by her kisses, which became more ardent. She soon found herself astride him. Thrilled by this change of position and the power it afforded her, she began to move with undulating waves of her hips, causing Quinton to moan with delight.

With a sudden turn, he shifted his weight over her, his muscular body now covering hers. He thrust deep within her and once again they lost themselves in each other. This time was different, though. Lisette knew what to expect and could anticipate what she wanted and move her body to get it. Clinging to him, she cried out as that incredible burst of blissfulness washed over her. A few moments later, he growled her name as he found his own pleasure.

Afterward they lay in each other's arms, just holding each other.

"If this is an example of married life," Lisette said, still breathing heavily, "I am going to be a very contented wife."

"I plan on making sure that you are," Quinton promised with a wicked gleam in his eyes. "Every single night."

"Then you had better marry me very soon, Mr. Roxbury."

"That was my thought exactly, Miss Hamilton." He

kissed her cheek. "There will be talk about us, you know. No matter how I tried to smooth things over with Lady Emmeline and her father. Are you prepared to face that with me?"

"With you, yes." She nodded, quite sure she could weather any storm to be with Quinton. "Are you?"

"Absolutely. The gossip will die down eventually, as it always does. I will postpone any political overtures for a bit longer, though, and wait until the time is right. As long as you are with me, Lisette, nothing else really matters."

"I love you, Quinton."

"And I love you."

Lisette rested her head on his chest, listening to the sound of his heartbeat, wondering how she had come to love this man so much. Never had she been a part of anything so completely lovely.

Quinton whispered, "As much as I wish I could hold you like this all night long, I should probably take you home now, Lisette. It's very late. Your family must be worried about you."

"Oh, my heavens!" Lisette bolted upright to a sitting position. "I forgot it was Christmas Eve!"

"Come then," Quinton said, ever practical. "Let's get you home."

"It's almost midnight," she worried. "What shall I say to everyone when they ask where I've been all night?"

"We'll think of something."

With great reluctance they rose from the warm bed and began to dress hurriedly in the cold of the room, amid playful laughter together. Quinton helped her with the buttons on her dress, but he seemed to unbutton them more than fasten them. It was a wonder they ever finished dressing, the way that they kept stopping to kiss each other. Then he clasped the locket around her neck once again. Lisette was just straightening up the bedclothes when they heard a heavy knock on the bedroom door. They both froze and stared at each other with wide eyes.

"Who would be knocking on your bedroom door at this hour?" he whispered low.

"I don't know!" she whispered back frantically, still standing by the bed, afraid to move. She could not imagine who it could be!

Whoever it was knocked again, louder this time.

"Who is it?" Quinton called out, moving closer to the door.

"Roxbury?" the voice on the other side called back. "It's me, Eddington. Lisette's in there with you?"

"It's Jeffrey?" Lisette cried out in confusion, mortified to be caught in such a compromising position, since it was quite obvious what she and Quinton had been doing in that room all evening.

Quinton flung the bedroom door open. "What the hell are you doing here?"

Lord Jeffrey Eddington stood in his hat and coat with his arms folded across his chest, a scowl on his face. "I could ask you the same question, but instead I'll wish you a Merry Christmas and you can thank me later for not killing you right now."

Lisette rushed to Quinton's side. He wrapped his arm around her shoulder protectively, pulling her close against him. Grateful, she leaned into him for support.

"What is it, Jeffrey?" she asked, her heart pounding. Something had to be dreadfully wrong for him to seek her out this way.

"Colette's having the baby, and I've been sent to find you"—he raised an eyebrow at Quinton—"and bring you home."

"The baby!" Lisette exclaimed with excitement.

Still sporting a disapproving expression, Jeffrey continued, "The door was unlocked and the lights were still on downstairs in the shop and I . . . assumed you were up here."

"I'm marrying her," Quinton said for Jeffrey's benefit.

Jeffrey gave him a pointed look. "You had better be."

"He is," Lisette assured him with a shy smile. "We are."

"Congratulations. Now hurry up." Jeffrey ordered. "I'll meet you both downstairs, where we can think up some reasonable excuse to tell her family as to what Lisette has been doing all night because I don't think the truth will be appropriate right now." He moved to leave them but then suddenly paused and turned back. "And Lisette, you might want to fix your hair. That's a dead giveaway." He gave her a quick wink before he exited the room.

Alone again, Lisette sank into Quinton's arms. "Oh, my God, I have never been so embarrassed in my entire life."

"It's all right, it's all right." Quinton kissed her, smoothing her hair with his hand. "Eddington won't say anything about it. He's a gentleman."

"Yes, but he . . . he *knows*!" She buried her face in his chest.

Quinton shrugged matter-of-factly and kissed her again. "There's nothing we can do about that now, my sweet."

"And I can't believe I forgot to lock the store!" she cried in self-reproach. "Heavens! Anyone could have walked in here!"

"You were a little distracted. It's all my fault."

"No. It's mine."

"That's the least of our worries, Lisette. We're lucky it was only Eddington who found us together. Now come on, let's get you ready to go home."

As Lisette stood in front of the mirror, she swept her thick hair atop her head, fastening it in place with the pins that Quinton had removed earlier with such tenderness. "Will you come home with me?" she asked him.

His golden brows drew together. "Do you think that's such a good idea?"

"Why not?" She placed the last of the pins in her hair.

He gave her a wry look. "Well, for one, Eddington wants to kill me, your sister is having a baby, your family knew I was coming to see you here tonight, and I can only imagine that everyone will think the worst of us."

Lisette moved to him, placing her hands on his chest. "Then I need you with me more than ever."

He wrapped his strong arms around her and said, "In that case, I will most certainly go with you."

30

On Christmas Day in the Morning

Thursday, December 25, 1873

When Quinton, Lisette, and Jeffrey arrived at Devon House after midnight, they were met at the door by Granger, whose face was as white as a sheet. The usually staid butler was beside himself with stress and worry.

Lisette patted the elderly man's arm in comfort. "Lady Waverly will be just fine, Granger."

"I know, Miss Lisette, but I can't help but worry at times like this. The waiting is the worst," he muttered, helping brush the snow off them. He took their coats and began ushering them toward the drawing room.

"Is the doctor here yet?" she asked him.

"The doctor is upstairs now and Lord Waverly is with her, too," Granger explained. "Cook made some hot buttered rum and there's plenty to eat if you want. Cook has been keeping herself occupied making tarts. The whole household is still up."

"Thank you, Granger." Lisette smiled at him.

The three of them made their way to join the rest of the family.

Inside the drawing room, which hosted a tall Christmas tree by the front window, Quinton was faced with Lisette's entire family. Her mother, whom he had not seen since Brighton, was seated beside the fire. Her two younger sisters were there, as well as Harrison Fleming, whom he'd met at Rathmore's ball. Fleming held his baby daughter in his arms, wrapped in a blanket. Lucien's parents, Lord and Lady Stancliff, were also there, eagerly awaiting the birth of their second grandchild.

"Well, we were wondering what happened to you!" Mrs. Hamilton said as they stood in the doorway of the parlor. "*Merci*, Lord Eddington, for bringing my daughter home."

"I'm sorry I'm so late," Lisette began to explain hurriedly. "There was much to do at the shop for it was quite busy all day. Then Mr. Roxbury and I met the most interesting little boy, Tom Alcott. He's so sweet and bright and I'm teaching him how to read. Somehow we lost track of time and with the snow . . ." Her voice trailed off as she made a helpless little gesture with her hand.

"I apologize for keeping Miss Hamilton out so long," Quinton added. He left it at that, figuring the less said, the better.

"*Monsieur* Roxbury, it is a pleasure to see you again! I see you found my daughter." Genevieve Hamilton greeted him with a warm and knowing smile. "*Joyeux Noël.* It is a special evening, is it not?"

"It is good to see you, too, Mrs. Hamilton," Quinton said, feeling slightly out of place. They had no idea just how special an evening it had been for Lisette and him. "And yes, it is a very special evening. Merry Christmas, everyone."

Lady Stancliff, an elegant woman with dark hair who clearly resembled Lucien, welcomed him as well. "And a

Merry Christmas to you, Mr. Roxbury. Please come in and join us."

"Lisette, isn't it exciting?" Yvette said breathlessly, rising from her seat. "Colette's baby will be born on Christmas!"

Paulette Hamilton, looking rather pale, was wrapped in a thick blanket and reclining on the large sofa. "Hello, Mr. Roxbury," she whispered in a nasal tone.

"You must excuse Paulette," Lisette explained to him. "She's not feeling well."

"Well, it's Christmas Eve, and I'm not going to spend it alone in my room upstairs, even if I do have a cold," Paulette said with a sniffle. "How was everything at the shop tonight?"

"It was very, very busy and I think I hired another errand boy. And I have the most wonderful idea about helping him and his mother, Paulette, but I shall tell you all about him later," Lisette answered. "Is Juliette upstairs with Colette?"

"Yes," Yvette informed her eagerly. "Colette made Mother leave right off."

Genevieve Hamilton threw her hands up in the air in a helpless gesture. "Apparently I make my own daughter nervous. *Est-ce que tu as déjà entendu parler d'une chose aussi ridicule?* Have you ever heard anything so ridiculous? *Je suis sa mère.* I am her mother. Imagine such a thing!"

Lady Stancliff calmed her. "Don't worry, Genevieve. You know how difficult having a baby is. Colette doesn't mean to slight you. I'm surprised she hasn't thrown Lucien out yet."

"I'm surprised Lucien hasn't thrown Juliette out!" Paulette added with a laugh from her perch on the sofa.

Quinton smiled at the Hamilton family dynamics, which

were not that different from how his own siblings acted when they were all together. He felt right at home.

Lisette turned to him, her deep green eyes looking at him with love. "I want to go up to her. Will you be all right? Will you wait until I return?"

"Yes, of course. Go be with your sister." The impulse to kiss her was so strong that Quinton had to restrain himself. He wanted to hug her to him, to touch her cheek, or even squeeze her hand. After everything they had just shared together earlier that evening, he merely wanted to be close to her. Yet he could do none of those things with her family's eyes upon them.

"Thank you." With a brief smile, Lisette fled from the drawing room. Quinton turned to find a number of curious eyes on him.

Yvette Hamilton, wearing a festive red and black plaid gown and her long blond hair arranged on her head with red ribbons, walked over to him and Jeffrey. With a great sense of elegance, the sixteen-year-old took them each by the arm and guided them into the room. "Now you two fine gentlemen, come join us and have a seat. We just finished decorating the Christmas tree. Doesn't it look lovely?"

The large pine stood before the tall front window, decorated with handmade paper angels, pretty silver and gold Dresdens, small cornucopias filled with sweet candies, and lit with tiny white candles.

"You did a splendid job decorating it, sweet girl," Eddington said to her. "It's even better than last year."

Thrilled with his compliment, Yvette smiled and then led Quinton to a comfortable chair near Harrison Fleming and brought Eddington to the card table.

"Now, Jeffrey, you shall play cards with me, for no one

else wants to." Yvette sat across from him and began to expertly shuffle the deck.

"How can I turn down such a charming offer?" Eddington answered gallantly, seating himself across from her.

Quinton wondered how long he should stay at Devon House. He also wondered why no one had questioned his presence there, aside from Mrs. Hamilton's veiled reference to seeing him again. He supposed they were distracted with excitement of the baby's arrival, but still . . . He wanted to let them know that he and Lisette were to be married. All that had happened between them that evening was still racing around his mind. Lisette was now his and he wanted to shout it from the rooftops. *Lisette was his.*

"When shall we exchange presents?" Yvette questioned the room as she fanned her cards in her hands.

"I suppose we should wait until the baby is born," Lady Stancliff proposed, while handing a cup of tea to her husband. "It somehow seems wrong for us all to be down here opening gifts, while Colette is upstairs otherwise occupied."

Lord Stancliff, a rather frail-looking figure, added in his gruff voice, "We should wait for Colette."

"I vote we wait until the baby comes," Harrison Fleming chimed in from his seat next to Quinton. Still holding his sleeping daughter in his arms, Harrison turned to Quinton and confided, "I've learned you have to add your two cents in whenever you can with this family, or you get outvoted."

Quinton laughed, realizing he would very soon be a part of this family, too. And that made him exceptionally happy.

"Fine. I suppose we should wait then," Yvette grudgingly agreed. However, her blue eyes sparkled at another prospect. "Did you bring a special present for me, Jeffrey?"

He winked at her. "How could I forget a present for you, Yvette?"

Quinton watched the exchange between them with amusement, thinking how charming Lisette's sisters were. He had already grown to like her family and felt very comfortable with them. He suddenly realized what he had to do.

"Mrs. Hamilton?" Quinton addressed Lisette's mother.

"*Oui, Monsieur* Roxbury?" Genevieve turned to him with questioning eyes.

"I think there is something you should know." Quinton rose to his feet. "Something you all should know."

All eyes turned to him and the room grew quiet with expectancy. Eddington folded his arms across his chest.

Quinton cleared his throat, suddenly feeling nervous. "Earlier this evening, I asked Lisette to marry me."

The room remained silent.

"Excuse me," Paulette finally piped up from the sofa. "But aren't you already engaged to Lady Emmeline Tarleton?"

"I was," Quinton explained a bit sheepishly. "But I ended our engagement a few days ago. I am no longer getting married to Lady Emmeline on January third."

There were a few gasps of astonishment.

"What did Lisette say when you asked her?" Yvette could barely contain her excitement.

"She said yes."

"I knew it!" exclaimed Genevieve in triumph. "*J'avais raison dans cette affaire, n'est-ce pas?* I was right all along about the two of you, *Monsieur* Roxbury. *C'est tellement romantique!* This is wonderful news! *Tu me rends la plus heureuse.* This makes me happier than you know."

"Why did the rest of us not know about this?" Yvette questioned, her brows furrowed in consternation.

"I knew," Jeffrey stated, teasing Yvette with a smug expression.

"So that's why you all came home so late," Paulette added with a knowing look. "You were proposing to her?"

That explained it as well as anything else. Quinton could not risk looking in Eddington's direction. "Yes. We had quite a lot to discuss, what with my wedding being canceled," he managed to say.

"This is wonderful!" Harrison chimed in loudly. "Congratulations, Roxbury!"

Genevieve Hamilton seemed the happiest of all, clapping her hands gleefully. "*C'est si passionnant!* I am so pleased!"

Quinton began to accept congratulations from the others, feeling happier about this quiet betrothal with Lisette than he ever had with his grand engagement with Lady Emmeline.

At that moment, Lisette and Juliette rushed into the drawing room, their faces aglow and their smiles beaming with joy.

"Well?" Paulette encouraged, sitting upright in expectation. "What is it?"

"It's a boy!" Juliette announced in triumph. "He is big, healthy, and beautiful and Colette is doing just fine!"

A chorus of happy exclamations and shouts of congratulations sounded in the room, as everyone stood and hugged and shook hands. Lady Stancliff called for champagne to be brought out as laughter and joyous cries filled the air.

Caught up in the emotional moment, Quinton rushed to Lisette's side. To his delight, she flung her arms around his neck and he wrapped her in his embrace.

"I believe we need champagne to toast an engagement as well," Lady Stancliff declared, pointedly looking in their direction.

Suddenly aware that everyone was looking at the two

of them, Quinton whispered to Lisette, "I told them that I asked you to marry me."

"You did?"

He nodded, as Lisette slowly faced her family, his arms still around her.

"Yes," she confirmed the news shyly. "Quinton and I are to be married."

"You see? *J'avais raison dans cette affaire, n'est-ce pas?* I was right in this matter, was I not, Lisette?" Genevieve Hamilton exclaimed in triumph. "Now . . . Now you look happy and in love because he is the man for you! *Voilà de bien merveilleuses nouvelles.* This is wonderful!"

"Thank you, Mother." Lisette smiled. "You were right all along."

"When will you be married?" Yvette asked, full of excitement that there was still to be a wedding after all.

"We haven't decided yet," Lisette began slowly.

"But very soon," Quinton added with an unabashed grin. He couldn't marry her soon enough. Waiting any length of time would feel too long.

"Well, now you must kiss her, Mr. Roxbury!" Yvette declared with mischievous glee.

Her face turning red, Lisette asked, "Why?"

"Don't you see where you are both standing?" she exclaimed with delight. "You're under the mistletoe!"

Glancing up, he saw the telltale green leaves and white berries tied with a red ribbon hanging over them. Loving his future sister-in-law for pointing this out, Quinton laughed. "Well, if I must . . ."

He lowered his head to capture Lisette's sweet mouth in a gentle kiss. Recalling all that had happened between them earlier that evening, his heart overflowed with love for her. Hardly able to believe everything had worked out so well, he squeezed her hand in his.

Everyone clapped and they were soon handed crystal

glasses full of champagne. Toasts were made to the health of Colette and Lucien's new baby boy and to Lisette and Quinton's surprise engagement.

"Congratulations, Roxbury." Jeffrey Eddington shook Quinton's hand, a wide smile on his face. "Now I won't have to kill you."

"Thank you." Quinton laughed good-naturedly. "I appreciate you looking out for Lisette."

"My pleasure. She's like a sister to me." Jeffrey's expression turned serious. "There's bound to be talk over the cancellation of your wedding, you know. However, if the Duke of Wentworth gives you any trouble, my father will back you publicly. He would do anything to help Lisette. I think he fell a little in love with her the night of the ball."

"Who wouldn't?" Quinton hugged Lisette to him tightly. To Eddington he added, "Thank you."

Jeffrey turned to Lisette and asked, "I don't get the impression you wish to escape this wedding, do I?"

"No," Lisette stated emphatically. "Never. But it is now your turn to get married, Jeffrey."

"Oh, I am far too young to entertain thoughts of marriage yet," Jeffrey quipped dryly. "Besides, where would I find someone as special as you?"

"Can we please, please open presents *now*?" Yvette pleaded with impatience to the room in general. "I've been waiting all night."

Jeffrey called out, "Can someone please let this sweet girl open her Christmas gifts?"

"*Oui*, we can open presents now! Yes! *Joyeux Noël!*" Mrs. Hamilton finally acquiesced to her daughter.

Grabbing Jeffrey's arm, Yvette dragged him to the Christmas tree with her and began to hand out gifts.

Laughing, Quinton still held Lisette's hand in his. "Aren't you going to open any of your presents?"

Lisette shook her head, a satisfied smile on her pretty face. "No."

"Why not?"

Quinton's lovely new fiancée looked up at him, her eyes glistening with love. "I don't want anything else. I have already received the best Christmas present ever. You."

He kissed her, knowing that what had happened that Christmas made him happier than he had ever been. He had gained the woman he loved. "Merry Christmas, Lisette."

31

Sing We Joyous,
All Together

Saturday, December 27, 1873

After Tom came home to Framingham's garret on Christmas Eve, at first his mother didn't believe the tale he told. With some meat pies and a pair of practical warm gloves as a gift for her, he described to her what had happened at the lovely little bookshop. He presented her with the elegant Christmas card that had his name written on it neatly. He showed her the copybook where he was to practice his letters. And he gave her the money.

"They gave you all this? For nothing but the promise of a job after she met you on the street last week?" his mother asked, her usual weary expression replaced by a look of incredulity. "Tom, that doesn't make any sense at all."

"Well, they did." He couldn't believe it either at first. Tom had been nervous walking home that night with the money. But luck had been with him for he did not meet up with Tall Jerry and the other lads. The snow and cold weather must have kept them inside.

"And she wants to teach you to read?"

"Yes, and Miss Hamilton wants to meet you, too. We're to go to the shop together after Christmas. She might have a job for you, Mama."

"What would I do in a bookstore?" she scoffed. Anna Alcott gave her son a hard look. "Tom, did you steal these things from the shop?"

"No!" he protested vociferously.

He would never steal anything from Miss Hamilton. No sir. That lady had been too good to him already, and he would never betray her in that way. And Mr. Roxbury, too. After his promise to his mother, he would never again take anything that didn't belong to him as long as he lived. He would never let either woman down. And that was a promise he made to himself.

"Mama, I swear it. If I was going to steal anything, it wouldn't be a copybook. It would be something much more useful. Miss Hamilton is a very kind lady. Truly. Just come with me and meet her."

"I don't know . . ." His mother hesitated, her eyes on the copybook. Her fingers traced the lines Tom had written to form the letters of his name. Then she glanced at the pretty Christmas card, with the gilt edges and raised letters. A flicker of hope glowed in her gray eyes.

"You'd like her," Tom cajoled, giving her his best smile. "She's very nice. And the shop is a grand place. Miss Hamilton would never say mean things to you like Madame La Fleur did."

Anna Alcott smiled and shook her head in amazement. "It just seems too good to be true, Tom. But if it is true, I think this might be the best Christmas we've ever had."

In the end, Anna's curiosity got the better of her and she did come with Tom to the bookshop two days after Christmas. Bundled up against the cold, mother and son made their way to Hamilton's Book Shoppe, just off Bond Street.

It was early and there were no customers at the bookshop yet, but Lisette waited nervously for Tom to arrive. At least she hoped he would arrive. That little boy had found his way into her heart in a surprisingly short amount of time, and she would be very disappointed if he did not appear. Lisette had come up with an idea to help both Tom and his mother, and she hoped they would be receptive to it. She had told her family everything about him and had Colette's approval to hire him. Paulette was at the shop with her that morning, having recovered enough from her cold to resume her responsibilities, and was looking forward to meeting the boy.

When the bells over the front door jingled to herald their arrival, Lisette looked up from the counter with a welcoming smile.

"Good morning, Tom! I'm so glad to see you again."

The little boy smiled with relief. "Good morning to you, Miss Hamilton. I've come just like you said to. And I brought my mother."

Lisette walked around the counter to greet them. "Hello, Mrs. Alcott. It's a pleasure to meet you. You have a very special little boy."

The woman's eyes grew wide, as if she didn't know how to react to such kindness. "Thank you."

"And I would like both of you to meet my sister, Miss Paulette Hamilton. She's the one who is really in charge here at the shop. But I've told her all about you, Tom, and how bright you are and how we'd like for you to work here."

Tom looked at Paulette, who had stepped forward to meet them. "Another Miss Hamilton?"

"Yes." Paulette grinned at the young boy and his mother. "It's nice to meet you both. Mrs. Alcott, do you read?"

The woman shook her head sadly. "Not very well, I'm afraid."

"Well, we can help you with that," Lisette declared. "If you both would like, I can arrange for lessons."

"Why on earth would you do such a kind thing?" Tom's mother asked.

"I've lived above a bookshop my entire life, Mrs. Alcott, and it pains me to think of people not being able to enjoy books. I see great promise in your son. And I understand how hard it is to balance the desire for an education with the need for wages. My sisters and I can be of assistance in that area," Lisette explained. "I've offered your son a position here, delivering books and messages and helping us around the shop in general. He will receive a fair wage, but he will be expected to attend reading lessons. Tom told me that he would like this arrangement, but I would like to have your approval for him to accept the position."

"Why, why, yes . . ." The woman's gray eyes welled with tears. "You have no idea how happy that would make me to have my son learn to read and write properly."

Tom held his mother's hand tightly. "See, Mama? I told you she was nice."

"He's a very good boy," Anna Alcott said. "He won't cause you any trouble at all. He will work hard."

"I've already recognized that goodness in him," Lisette said, handing the woman a handkerchief.

"Bless you," she said, dabbing at her teary eyes. "I'm so thankful, I don't know if I have enough words."

A knowing look passed between Lisette and her sister, along with a quick nod of approval, before Paulette chimed in. "Mrs. Alcott, my sister and I have another suggestion we would like to propose to you."

Anna Alcott looked at Paulette in awe. "Yes?"

"Our family used to live upstairs, above the shop, but we no longer do so," Paulette explained. "We were thinking it would be nice to have someone stay at the shop full-time. We cannot always be here as much as we would like, and we would feel better if we had someone living in the rooms upstairs. It would ease our minds greatly knowing that someone was always at the shop. Caretakers, so to speak. Someone who would make the refreshments that we serve to our customers and things of that nature. We have been discussing the idea for some time, but agreed that we needed a nice family to take up residence."

Lisette said, "You and your son could live here above the shop in return for helping us. We were wondering if you would be interested in taking the position?"

Swaying a bit, Tom's mother looked as if she might faint, and even Tom's eyes filled with surprise. "I wasn't expecting anything like this," she murmured.

"You mean we wouldn't have to live at old Framingham's anymore?" Tom asked. "We could live right here?"

"Well, that would be up to your mother, Tom," Lisette said. It would be months before Quinton's houses were ready for Tom and his mother to move into, and the idea of little Tom going back to live in the slums of Saint Giles repulsed her. She had been thrilled when this idea had occurred to her. And as soon as she met Tom's mother, she instinctively knew they were a perfect fit. "But I assure you, the rooms upstairs are lovely, and we would pay you a salary, of course."

"Live here? In this lovely neighborhood? Working for you ladies? With my son learning to read?" She looked at both Paulette and Lisette with gratitude. "You'd be changing our lives for the better. How could I refuse such an offer?"

Tom gave a little whoop of joy, his smile brightening the room.

"Thank you both," his mother said, her voice trembling

with emotion. "I don't know that I can ever thank you enough for all this."

"Thank you for helping us," Paulette said kindly. "Now why don't I take you upstairs and show you the rooms to see if they are to your liking?"

Mrs. Alcott smiled. "I'm sure they are more than suitable for us."

The bells above the door jingled as Quinton Roxbury entered the bookshop, looking like a golden prince. A thrill of delight raced through Lisette at the sight of him.

"Well, Tom, I see you made the wise decision to come back," he said.

The boy beamed at Quinton. "Yes, sir."

After Lisette introduced her fiancé to Mrs. Alcott, Paulette took Tom and his mother upstairs to see the rooms.

"So they have accepted the position?" Quinton asked when they were alone, taking Lisette's warm hand in his.

"Yes." Lisette nodded in satisfaction. "She's a very nice woman and this will be a good change for both of them. Tom is so happy."

"Not as happy as I am." Quinton leaned down and kissed her lips, and Lisette's heart skipped a beat. "I cannot wait to marry you, Miss Hamilton."

They had decided to wed quietly in a small ceremony with just their family around them next month, followed by a wedding trip abroad.

"And I cannot wait to be your wife, Mr. Roxbury."

Quinton said, "I believe this has been the best Christmas I've ever had."

Filled with happiness, Lisette kissed her fiancé back. "I couldn't agree with you more."

Dear Readers,

I hope you enjoyed reading It Happened One Christmas *as much as I loved writing this story! Christmas is my favorite time of year, so setting Lisette and Quinton's romance in December seemed to make their story even more romantic.*

Now, if you are interested in learning what happens with the two youngest Hamilton sisters, I've included part of the first chapter of my next book—which, of course, is about the fourth sister. When self-assured, strong-minded, and practical Paulette Hamilton meets a handsome widower with a dark and dangerous past, will she throw caution to the wind and follow her heart? You'll have to read the book to find out, but here's a little preview in the meantime. Enjoy!

Thanks for reading!
Kaitlin O'Riley
www.KaitlinORiley.com

London
August 1875

The bells above the entrance of Hamilton's Book Shoppe jingled as the front door opened and the drizzling summer rain drifted in momentarily. It had been a slow afternoon with little business and Paulette Hamilton looked up in eager anticipation at the customer who had ventured out on such a dreary August day. A tall gentleman stepped into the shop, holding an umbrella in one hand and clutching the hand of a reluctant little girl in the other.

"Welcome to Hamilton's!" Paulette greeted the customers with an animated smile. New customers always made her happy.

As the gentleman folded his wet umbrella, Paulette took note of him. He was older, tall and rather broad. Beneath his elegant black hat, strands of chocolate-colored hair were visible. He was handsome enough, she supposed in a dark, brooding sort of way, but she had never favored that look. Paulette usually found herself drawn to golden, fair-haired heroes. At least she did in the books that she read.

Using her best shopkeeper's voice, she asked, "How may I help you this afternoon?"

"My little daughter here would like a new book," he explained, indicating the child hiding with shyness behind him.

The rich, melodic timbre of his words, laced with the notes of a vaguely familiar accent, filled the air around her. Unable to resist the magnetic attraction of his voice, Paulette suddenly eyed him with keen interest as he looked toward the little girl.

The man possessed an aquiline nose, a strong jaw, and a lean face with dark eyebrows. He was clean-shaven, but she could easily imagine a thin black mustache upon him, giving him the look of a wicked pirate. He seemed tense, almost as if he held his feelings tightly in check, but the slightest upset could set him loose in a fury. His full mouth was set in a grim line. In fact, he had a look about his face that conveyed the distinct impression that he had not smiled in a long, long while.

Something about the man unsettled her and the dark intensity about him brought to mind the words "sinister" or "dangerous."

A little shiver raced through her.

Feeling slightly nervous in his presence and somewhat relieved knowing that her assistant was close at hand in the back room, Paulette silently reprimanded herself for being so foolish as to think of herself in any kind of danger. She had never felt this way about a customer before. Why on earth would she think that this man would cause her any harm? Perhaps she had been reading one too many gothic romance novels lately!

Her attention was drawn to the little girl, who still attempted to hide behind the man's dark trousers. The child could not have been more than four years old, with a sweet chubby face framed by golden curls mostly covered under a wide-brimmed bonnet.

Paulette knew exactly what the little girl wanted. Hamilton's carried the best children's books in the city and because of that she had dealt with all manner of children in the shop before, from the most well behaved to the most spoiled, so she was no stranger to bashful children either. This sweet-looking girl would be easy to please.

"Well, you are quite a lucky young lady for your father to give you such a special treat," Paulette began, favoring the girl with a warm grin. "We have some lovely fairy-tale books with the most beautiful pictures in them. Would you like me to show them to you?"

Peeking out from behind her father's leg, the little girl nodded in agreement. She did not make a sound, but her cherubic face lit with excitement.

"Thank you," the gentleman said, seeming a bit relieved by Paulette's suggestion.

"Why don't you both come with me to the children's section of the shop?" she suggested brightly.

They followed her to the rear of the store, where she and Colette had designed an inviting space for their smallest customers. They'd had shelves built at a lower height and miniature-sized tables and chairs to better fit little bodies. A brightly colored area rug covered the wooden floor, lending warmth to the section of books on display. Paulette immediately located their most popular selling book, a gorgeously illustrated volume of fairy tales. She placed the book on the table and motioned for the child to join her while she sat herself on one of the tiny chairs as well.

"I think you might like this one."

The little girl glanced up hesitantly at her father, seeking his permission. He patted her head in encouragement. "It's all right."

She moved slowly forward, taking hesitant steps to the table where Paulette waited for her. When she reached the small table, the girl stopped and stared at Paulette in expectation.

"Do you have a favorite story?" Paulette questioned.

The girl shook her head, her expression extraordinarily serious for one so young.

"Do you like the story of *Sleeping Beauty*?"

The child gave the slightest nod of assent.

"That story has always been a favorite of mine." Opening the thick volume, Paulette turned to the page that had an elaborate and richly drawn illustration of a grand castle tower covered with an overgrown tangle of thorn-laden vines and a profusion of red roses. The little girl's eyes widened and a small gasp of awe escaped her.

Paulette asked, "Isn't this picture lovely?"

Again, the girl merely nodded. She had not uttered one word since entering the shop.

"I'm Miss Hamilton," Paulette said, hoping to coax a response from her. "What is your name?"

The child blinked at her and shrugged her tiny shoulders.

"What is your name?" she repeated.

The little girl still did not respond. Paulette had never seen such a withdrawn child! Did she not speak at all? Paulette was usually able to cajole bashful children into an easy conversation by this point. But not this girl. From what she sensed, it was not merely shyness that kept the girl from speaking. Was there something wrong with her? Was she a mute? Paulette's natural curiosity peaked and she wished to ask the gentleman about it, but it was certainly not her place to ask such intimate questions of a stranger.

The girl's father finally answered for her. "Her name is Mara."

Aware that the man's eyes had been focused on her

during the entire exchange with his daughter, Paulette glanced up at him.

They held each other's gaze for longer than two strangers normally would. His deep green eyes were fringed with thick dark lashes that were startlingly long for a man. A tingling sensation raced through her and in that instant, Paulette was almost knocked off the tiny chair upon which she sat.

He was not as old as she had first thought him to be and that surprised her. Although she guessed he was not yet thirty, an aged weariness had settled in his eyes. Struck by the sadness she saw within the emerald depths, she recognized that a profound heartache dwelled within this man. What had happened to him? Paulette was at a complete loss to explain the sudden surge of intense feelings that rushed through her as he looked back at her.

Somehow he seemed less forbidding than he had a moment ago.

"And your name, sir?" she managed to ask, suddenly needing to know.

"Forgive me, Miss Hamilton," he acknowledged her with a slight bow, removing his hat. "I am Declan Reeves."

Of course. The accent. Now she recognized it. He must be from Ireland. She wondered what he was doing in London. Paulette forced her gaze away from his mysteriously sad eyes and turned her attention back to the child. His child.

"Mara is such a pretty name," she murmured to the little girl. Paulette was more than aware that the man's eyes were still on her. She could feel the intensity of his gaze. Her hand moved to smooth her own blond hair.

Again the child did not say a word, just looked at Paulette with somber green eyes that now seemed remarkably like her father's. Mara reached out a hand and slowly began turning the pages in the book of fairy tales, mesmerized by the colorful pictures.

"She was named after her mother." His voice, smooth and melodic, spilled around her, sending a shiver of a different kind through Paulette.

The mother. Of course there would be a mother, this man's wife.

Paulette rose from the tiny chair, brushing her navy skirts with her hands in a nervous gesture. "I think Mara likes the fairy-tale book." She returned to being the efficient bookseller. "Is there anything else I can get for you today, Mr. Reeves?"

She found herself staring into his emerald eyes again and Declan Reeves answered her question with a desperate look of longing that caused her heart to constrict in her chest. He seemed to be asking her for something, anything, and she wanted desperately to give it to him but she was not even sure what it was. She held her breath.

Why did this man unsettle her so?

Shaking herself from her overactive imagination, for surely she could only have imagined what had just passed between them, she straightened her shoulders. Paulette then blurted out the first thing that came to mind. "Does your daughter not speak?"

Paulette immediately regretted her impolite question. Why couldn't she keep her mouth closed? Her sisters were always telling her to mind her own business. She really tried to, but for the most part Paulette could not help herself and always said what she thought. And yes, once in a while she overheard conversations she shouldn't, but that was not her fault. She was simply very aware of what was going on around her.

Still it was rude of her. Feeling remorseful, she was about to apologize to him for her bad manners.

"No, she doesn't talk anymore." He shook his head,

sadness emanating from him. "She hasn't spoken a single word since her mother passed away."

"Oh, I see," Paulette murmured. His daughter had been struck dumb with grief at losing her mother. How tragic! That poor little girl, losing her mother so young! And he had lost his wife.

Heart pounding, she eyed Declan Reeves anew as it suddenly dawned on her.

He was not a married man.

About the Author

Acclaimed author Kaitlin O'Riley first fell in love with historical romance novels when she was just fourteen years old, and shortly thereafter she began writing her own stories in spiral notebooks. Fortunately for her, none of those early efforts survive today. She is still an avid reader and can often be found curled up on a sofa with a book in her hands. Her debut novel was *Secrets of a Duchess*, which *Romantic Times* declared, "added freshness to the genre." This was followed by *One Sinful Night* and the popular Hamilton Sisters series, about five sisters living in Victorian England, which includes the titles *When His Kiss Is Wicked*, *Desire in His Eyes*, and *It Happened One Christmas*. A starred review from *Publishers Weekly* said O'Riley's writing was set "well apart from the usual romance fare." Her first foray into paranormal romance was a dreamy vampire novella released in *Yours for Eternity*, with authors Hannah Howell and Alexandra Ivy. Her second novella, "A Summer Love Affair," is part of the anthology *Invitation to Sin*, with authors Sally MacKenzie, Vanessa Kelly, and Jo Beverley. Kaitlin grew up in New Jersey, but now she lives in sunny Southern California, where she is busy writing her next book. She loves hearing from readers, so please visit her at www.KaitlinORiley.com.

GREAT BOOKS, GREAT SAVINGS!

When You Visit Our Website:
www.kensingtonbooks.com
You Can Save Money Off The Retail Price
Of Any Book You Purchase!

- All Your Favorite Kensington Authors
- New Releases & Timeless Classics
- Overnight Shipping Available
- eBooks Available For Many Titles
- All Major Credit Cards Accepted

Visit Us Today To Start Saving!
www.kensingtonbooks.com

All Orders Are Subject To Availability.
Shipping and Handling Charges Apply.
Offers and Prices Subject To Change Without Notice.